The World According To Two-Fingers

The Only Safe Place to Live is on an Indian Reservation

Steve C. Schneider, JD

TABLE OF CONTENTS

The mystique surrounding being "Indian" is enticing, but the reality, more often than not, is a life on a reservation devoid of any glamour or mystique. Two-Fingers learned firsthand that reservation life is synonymous with incarceration. He spent most of his life fighting all forms of institutionalized control. He appreciated the traits and attributes of his proud, noble, and free ancestors. Two-Fingers incorporated those virtues into his everyday life, and paid a heavy price for doing so. Yet, he gladly paid that price. The story of his life is one of redemption, sacrifice, and honor. Two-Fingers strongly believed that America is the last bastion of freedom and that if that freedom is lost, America will become one large reservation stretching from sea to shining sea. Welcome to the reservation.

"Government dependency is evil; it saps character and strength by encouraging self-loathing and weakness. On the reservation, we eventually recognized this and developed programs where people work and take pride in their work. We took responsibility for our actions and escaped the traps of dependency and control. We found power in the opportunities of today. Indians had their land stolen, treaties broken; they were massacred, scalped, put into slavery, and placed on reservations where they were left to die. But the worst thing the government did to us was make us dependent on them.

Two-Fingers

Since we have become a nation of disclaimers, here is one for you:

This is a work of fiction; names, characters, places, and incidents are products of my imagination, and any resemblance to actual events, or persons living or dead, is entirely coincidental. And if that's not good enough for you, sue me."

One more thing: I use actual Blackfeet last names in my story, and they are as common on the reservation as Smith and Jones are in white society. However, any connection between the names and the events portrayed is purely coincidental. Trust me, nobody wants to take credit or blame for what is about to unfold.

"When searching for truth, you will never find it until you are honest with yourself."

Two-Fingers

This work, as well as my life, is dedicated to my beautiful, loving, and caring wife, Rosa.

In the Olden Days

Blackfeet Indians reigned supreme over the Northern Plains for centuries. They were referred to as the "Lords of the Plains." They were the strongest, meanest, and most feared tribe in a land filled with strong and fierce Indian tribes. Their traditional enemies feared them more than the grizzly bear, mountain lion, flash floods, or lightning. They were the baddest of the bad. In short, the Blackfeet were warriors and masters of their destiny long before there was a United States of America.

Their name, Blackfeet, originates from the distinctive black color of their moccasins, moccasins that turned black from dancing in the ashes of campfires. They are not naturally "black-footed."

At one time, the Blackfeet domain included parts of what are now, Montana, North Dakota, Minnesota, Alberta, Saskatchewan, Manitoba, and Ontario. It stretched from the Great Lakes all the way west to the Rocky Mountains.

The Blackfeet were nomadic meat-eaters who traveled great distances in search of game. They thrived on bison, deer, and elk meat. Before they had guns and horses, the Blackfeet hunted on foot with bows and arrows. They would chase large herds of bison off cliffs to their deaths, so many that it would take days to skin them and prepare the meat for the long winters. They ate berries and vegetable roots and would only eat fish as a last resort.

The Blackfeet Nation is made up of three large, distinct bands: the Northern Piegan, the Blood, and the Southern Piegan. During the summer, the Blackfeet from these bands lived together in large tribal camps. It was during this time that they hunted the large herds of bison and engaged in traditional dances and other ceremonial endeavors.

Competition was fierce among the bands to see who was the fastest, bravest, and smartest. Contests of manhood were held to determine who would lead and who would follow. Leaders were chosen based on what they could do for the community, and any leader who didn't deliver on community needs was swiftly replaced and banished from the tribe. The leader, the Chief, was always chosen from the strongest, not the weakest.

When the bands gathered in the summer, they formed distinct camps separated by a stream or other natural boundary. When the Southern Piegan, Blood, and Northern Piegan joined for ceremonial purposes, each band camped in a circle. In late fall or early winter, they went their separate ways and foraged for food in traditional hunting areas. Generally, they separated into small bands of 10 to 20 lodges, and each band had its own Chief.

Religion played an important role in their lives. The religious aspect of life for the Blackfeet centered on medicine bundles, which were individually owned and originated in encounters with supernatural spirits. These encounters came about through dreams or visions, often sought in a vision quest. A young Blackfeet brave, with the help of a medicine man, would go to a lonely, distant place away from the tribe and fast until he had a vision.

Bundles were symbols of their religious beliefs. Symbolism is important in all religions, and the Blackfeet drew strength from the different rituals they performed, just as modern religions draw strength from their symbols and rituals.

The Blackfeet believed in circles "what goes around, comes around," so to speak. The harmony of spirit and the continuity of the universe were their primary concerns. They didn't believe one person owned land at the expense of others. Rather, land was to be used by everyone and taken care of by everybody. Wealth came in the form of great deeds accomplished, not in how many possessions a person owned. Their lives were centered on community needs, not individual needs.

Around 1622, the French began moving deep into the Great Lakes region. Shortly after that, the Blackfeet began migrating westward, eventually settling in what is now northern Montana and southern Alberta.

For years, the Blackfeet tried to avoid contact with white settlers. In fact, they didn't trade with them until 1831. In 1837, a smallpox epidemic broke out and killed more than 6,000 Blackfeet, over two-thirds of their population.

In 1855, even though the Blackfeet were never conquered in battle, they agreed to a peace treaty that guaranteed them a large portion of their traditional land. Less than five years later, that treaty was broken when white settlers encroached on their territory.

In 1865, fighting broke out between white settlers and the Blackfeet. In 1874, without consulting the Blackfeet, Congress arbitrarily and unilaterally moved their reservation boundaries north to the Birch Creek-Marias River line. This resulted in the loss of the Blackfeet's best land, land that was sacred and holy, filled with trees, lakes, streams, game, and a variety of natural resources.

Even with the loss of their best land, the Blackfeet were able to live without federal assistance. That changed during the Starvation Winter of 1883-1884, when the bison herds disappeared, and more than 600 Blackfeet starved to death. After that, the tribe became dependent on government rations. In 1896, desperate for food, the Blackfeet sold the land that is now Glacier National Park for one million five hundred thousand dollars.

The Blackfeet have struggled to survive for years. Throughout the 1900s, they endured several federal policy changes, policies created by people outside the reservation who didn't truly understand the Blackfeet or their needs. To survive, the Blackfeet had to assimilate into white culture and forget about their own.

Historically, the Blackfeet were a once-proud people. They may still have pride, but it is now masked behind the harsh realities of reservation life, a life filled with drug and alcohol abuse, abject poverty, and domestic violence.

The once-mighty and feared Blackfeet, the Southern Piegan, now scratch out a living on windswept, barren reservation land with fixed boundaries. Over the years, their reservation has been reduced in size to a mere 1.5 million acres, land nobody else wanted. The reservation lies in north-central Montana; its boundaries run east to Cut Bank Creek, west to Glacier National Park, north to Alberta, and south to the Birch Creek-Marias-River line.

The tribal headquarters of the reservation is in the town of Browning. Browning lies in the shadow of the Rocky Mountains, which the Blackfeet call, "The Backbone of the World." Browning, Montana, the place of broken dreams and unhappy endings.

Chapter 1
My Family Moved Me to the Reservation

When I was young, virtually everything I came in contact with appeared to be larger than it is today. Age clarified size and shape for me. My earliest perceptions linger and have shaped how I view things like size. Size does matter, especially when you are young. First impressions matter too.

Here are my first impressions of Browning, Montana, the headquarters of the Blackfeet Reservation. As the saying goes, "It certainly isn't the end of the world, but you can see it from there." Well, that's Browning in a nutshell. It was, and still is, a hard town; visually and emotionally hard. It's a hardness honed from years of neglect and self-loathing. I guess that's what happens when you are isolated on a strip of land you would rather not be on and loathe yourself for not mustering up the strength to leave or improve it.

On my first trip to the center of the city, I fixated on the size and shape of a very large, fake teepee painted bright red, white, and blue that dominated the center of town. The structure was a Standard Oil gas station made of stucco, plastered and painted red, white, and blue. It stood there, in the center of Browning, like a beacon, a symbol, of man's inhumanity to man. It was a gas station owned by individuals who did not live on the reservation. Corporate interests took precedence over cultural integrity. To add insult to injury, the gas company's marketing geniuses, adorned this large stucco plastered teepee with fake totem poles strategically placed at the very top to lend an air of authenticity to something that would never look or be authentic. At the time, very few citizens recognized the subliminal effects, that's why it's called subliminal. It wasn't until many years later that the citizens realized it was just one more structure desecrating the land of the once mighty Blackfeet. It was a symbol of modernization. Modernization, and its consequences had stripped them of their freedom and self-sufficiency, and it took far too long for the tribe to realize that. Time has developed my sense of exploitation. But, at the time, I too thought it was rather cool looking. Hats off to the geniuses in marketing.

The stucco teepee was as phony as the government's desire to help the Blackfeet adjust to modern society, a society foreign to them, an unnatural consequence of treaties. Corporate influence remains a tool of assimilation and is extremely effective at controlling the behavior of those it seeks to control. In that regard, corporations are far more subtle than the numerous government agencies that dominate the reservation. Government, and buildings that house its agents, exist as focal points of power from which they exert control over the citizenry.

In retrospect, my initial impressions haven't really changed much over the years; I have. Browning remains a hard town, hard to live in and hard to leave if you are a Blackfeet Indian. Hardness: rocks and boulders of various sizes rose from the ground everywhere I looked. Hardness surrounded me.

There were a few paved streets back then, but most roads were either gravel or dirt. In the spring, the roads became mud puddles, and in the summer, after the mud dried, clouds of dust and dirt filled the air, narrowly missing their intended goal of blocking out the sun.

The first winter I spent there was a real eye-opener and a sign of things to come. The snow got so deep that entire neighborhoods were buried and hidden from view. Snow tunnels were dug from the streets to the doorsteps of the stranded, and those tunnels remained until spring. I learned early on that the Blackfeet were constantly digging themselves out from underneath something.

A positive consequence of all the snow and blizzards that descended on Browning was the cancellation of school. Hardness:

Browning is one of the coldest towns in America. Violently cold winters and unbearably hot summers. The wind seldom stops blowing, that's one reason why there isn't a tree in Browning. There are lawns, but not as many as you would think. As a consequence, lawn service companies do not exist in Browning. However, the big game in town remains the snow removal companies. After five years of being paid to dig out the citizenry, a person could move to Tahiti and live a carefree life.

The few lawns that did exist back then were those found at Government Square. It remains a large, square section of land, manicured to the specifications of those in charge. In the center of the square is a large field of mowed grass. They actually mow the grass and bale it, that's how big the lawn is. That tradition continues to this day.

Around the perimeter of the square is where you find federal employees' housing. The houses are set out in perfect rows, well-kept, and with lawns. It's temporary housing provided to federal employees who are serving their time until they can figure out a way to get transferred off the reservation.

Government Square has always been the place where the local Bureau of Indian Affairs (BIA) offices are. Behind the BIA complex is the local jail, tribally owned and operated. Not far from the jail is a large warehouse where the commodities are stored. Every Saturday morning, commodities are distributed to all enrolled members of the Blackfeet tribe. You have to be an enrolled member to receive commodities, health care, and tribal-related payments. The government requires a certain percentage of Blackfeet blood to be coursing through the veins of the enrolled. If that threshold is not met, hunger becomes a stark reality. If you are enrolled, life is tolerable. The government provides the necessities of life to the enrolled Blackfeet, but it comes at a heavy price. Assimilation, dependency, and hopelessness are too high a price to pay without any return on investment.

Saturday mornings are highly anticipated. Cars, trucks, and pickups line the street leading to the warehouse where hungry families wait patiently to receive their allotment of powdered milk, pinto beans, canned chopped meat, bread, and commodity cheese. The commodity cheese comes in five pound packages and is considered a delicacy, and therefore highly sought after. The cheese is so popular that winos sell their allotment for cash to buy Muscatel wine, and they never have to haggle over price. Wine and cheese are a big deal on the reservation. Well, the wine is; the cheese is an after-thought once the wine kicks in.

Government Square is conspicuously separated from Browning by a very large, steel-grated cattle guard that you have to cross if you choose to enter. Perhaps a futile attempt at keeping the Blackfeet out so the white people can live their lives separately, unattached and unburdened by the hardships they perpetuate. A major flaw in their scheme to remain aloof and detached from the local citizenry is the fact that they have to send their children to Browning public schools. That's too bad, it is integration at its finest.

Catholicism remains the dominant religion on the reservation; all good Blackfeet are Catholics. The Catholic Church, being the largest denomination on the reservation, has a large, two-story rock building with a separate rectory for the nuns and priests. It sits in the center of Browning not far from Main Street and a very large, red, white, and blue stucco gas station designed to look like a teepee. There is a small Mormon church on the reservation near Moccasin Flats, but it's sparsely attended. The Mormons have always been unsuccessful in their recruiting efforts, and the majority of the Blackfeet remain Catholic. Over the years, the Blackfeet have been asked to give up their ancestral religious beliefs and assimilate into white society, and they have largely done so. The Blackfeet are always being asked to give up something.

Like most towns, Main Street is where the majority of businesses are located. Those businesses relied heavily on the summer tourist trade, and since Browning is close to Glacier National Park, business was good back in the day. Tourists stopped to get gas, spend the night, eat, and take a few pictures in front of the fake teepee. That place always drew large crowds of picture takers because everybody wanted their picture taken in front of a very large red, white, and blue stucco building designed to look like a teepee, everybody. It cast a spell on residents and visitors alike.

Going to Glacier National Park has always been a big deal. Before leaving town on the road that takes you there are two really nice museums: the Museum of the Plains Indians and Bob Scriver's Museum. Bob was a local celebrity who once appeared on the show "What's My Line?" He became nationally known for his bronze sculptures, and his museum was always a major tourist attraction. Bob's place no longer exists, but the Museum of the Plains Indians continues on and serves as one of the last bastions of Blackfeet culture. It's one of the few holdouts in an ever-changing world. Across the street from the Museum of the Plains Indians sits the Junction Drive-In. It's not like I'm trying to promote the Junction, but they still put out a nice cheeseburger and onion rings.

The neighborhoods surrounding the businesses were made up of a variety of housing types. Keep in mind, this was and is the reservation, and zoning laws hold no sway over the Blackfeet. Trailer houses were scattered among the brick and mortar residences and yards were filled with broken-down cars and half-dressed children, acts of defiance against a system that had long since betrayed them. Regardless of the situation, defiance is the one emotion the Blackfeet find compelling.

Packs of wild dogs ran loose, and that tradition continues to be a mainstay of life in Browning. I firmly believe that's the reason Browning has never been invaded, wild dogs keep the place safe. There used to be a lot of wild cats running around until someone opened a Chinese food restaurant. The tourists really seemed to like that place.

The alleys continue to be home to the winos who seek shelter from their inner storms and a safe place to drink. The few paved streets were bumpy and rough regardless of the time of year, and the ditches were filled with empty whiskey bottles, wine bottles, beer bottles, beer cans, and pop bottles. This never changed, even in the best of times. Garbage still tumbles down the streets before becoming permanently attached to the barbed wire fences. Like I said, Browning is a hard place, and it remains one step behind the rest of society, close, yet so far away. We never had handicap parking back then, plenty of handicaps, just no handicap parking. That's changed over the years, and we now have an abundance of blue stickers with the wheelchair design hanging from rear view mirrors next to dreamcatchers.

Over time, my opinion of Browning changed from that of an awestruck young white kid living on the reservation to an awestruck old white man who has learned to embrace the essence of a culture seemingly lost, buried under the minutiae of progress. Still, hope of a free life remains clouded by the reality of boundaries and the mind-numbing, soul-destroying unearthly fixation on trinkets.

This isn't a warning about Browning, honest. Not that you shouldn't be warned. Hell, I wish I had been warned, for all the good it would've done me. Wouldn't you want to be warned if you were getting too close to quicksand or about to walk off a cliff? Browning has grown on me, but it's still a place where you can fall and never be seen again.

Browning, is the place my father and my mother consciously decided to settle their family after moving west from Cherry Hill, New Jersey. To my knowledge, no one put a gun to their heads and forced them onto the reservation. Unlike the Blackfeet, they moved there of their own accord. My older brother, Stan, and I, given our limited options, reluctantly went with them. I am their youngest son, and my name is Tony Church, and I, along with my entire family, am white. White as the driven snow. White like white on rice. Even though we claim to be a color-blind society, I think you should know that. In my capacity as a white guy and the best friend of Two-Fingers, I will serve as the narrator, the storyteller, if you will, of the life of the greatest Blackfeet Indian leader in modern history. Two-Fingers wasn't born into that position; he earned it the hard way through sacrifice and the relentless pursuit of basic fairness.

We met early on in our lives, and ever since that initial meeting, our careers and experiences have intersected and melded together. His story needs to be told and analyzed for future generations, and I have taken on that task because I want his failures and successes documented honestly and forthrightly. I will judiciously expose his warts as well as his virtues, as only those closest to him can.

Occasionally, less so with the passage of time, I am asked how a semi-bright white individual ended up on an Indian reservation. That's easy: I was forced by my father, Robert "Bud" Church and my mother, Ruby Fitzgerald Church to live there. It wasn't like I was physically kidnapped and taken to an undisclosed location by a group of criminals. No, their deception was far more devious, they told my brother and me that sacrifice is what families do. Of course, I was never given much say in any family matter, so the notion of sacrifice fell at the feet of the powerless. My older brother, Stan, sacrificed too until he finally broke free. But he still ended up going to the reservation to finish his senior year of high school. Stan was older than me by almost four years, and that's a big gap when you're an impressionable fourteen-year-old who looked up to him as an example of hope and sanity.

Anyway, as the story goes, Dad went off to live out west at an early age, and he ended up loving it. He rodeoed and worked on a ranch in

Wyoming before joining the army at the outset of World War II. While on the rodeo circuit, he met and became best friends with a cowboy by the name of Charles "Charley" Owen. Charley is from Cut Bank, Montana, a town not far from Browning. He happened to be the only child of the widower Bob Owens, the owner of a massive ranch where the largest oil deposit in all of Montana is located.

When World War II broke out, Dad joined the Army, and Charley joined the Marines. Dad ended up getting badly wounded while serving in Italy. Charley made it back from the Pacific without any physical wounds, but Dad always said nobody is unscathed by war, and that was true for him and Charley.

While recuperating stateside in New York, Dad met Mom. Mom worked as a nurse's aide and cared for many returning soldiers who were wounded and maimed overseas. She fell in love with Dad almost immediately. Evidently, she admired his strength and courage. There was also an element of mystery to Dad that appealed to her. Dad noticed how caring and loving my mother was, and he vowed to win her over. Mom was very beautiful and extremely popular with the wounded men, but she only had eyes for Dad, and when he proposed, she let him think it was his idea.

Mom always said her happiest years were after the war when she and Dad married, settled down, and started a life together. She said she loved the three men in her life, regardless of the many sacrifices she made on our behalf. She loved living in Cherry Hill, New Jersey, it was her home. Ironically, as it turned out, it was Dad's hometown too. Dad, on the other hand, never loved Cherry Hill as much as Mom did. He could never get adjusted to "big city life," as he referred to it. Cherry Hill isn't a big place, but Dad yearned for more freedom and the wide open spaces out west. Once you see the beauty of Wyoming, it's hard to readjust to paved parking lots and congestion, I suppose.

Over the years, Dad tried to make the best of it, and he ended up buying his parents' bar and running it as well as he could. But he was unhappy, and before long, he was spending more time on the customer side of the bar than on the working side. His war injuries took a long time to heal, and the alcohol he consumed helped with the pain.

When Dad's parents died in a horrific car accident, he sold the bar, and convinced my mom that Cut Bank, Montana, was the place for us, a new start, a new beginning. Mom, against her better judgment, supported her husband's decision. When the decision was made to move, I was finishing the eighth grade, and Stan was finishing his junior year in high school. Stan and I pleaded with our parents not to move. Dad insisted it would be fun and a great adventure, it would make men of us. He was certain that we needed to get out to the wild open spaces of Montana, and he didn't listen to any of us.

So, on June 26, 1967, we loaded all of our worldly possessions into and onto our '57 Chevy four-door sedan and started off to Montana. Dad drove the entire 2,622 miles in three days. He only stopped when it was absolutely necessary, which meant only when he needed gas or groceries. Peeing turned out to be a luxury; the man had a bladder the size of Ohio, and he thought everybody else did, too. There was no denying him, Dad was on a mission.

Mom made bologna sandwiches in the front seat, and Stan and I suppressed our urges to pee as mile after lonesome mile passed us by. The really weird thing was that we all slept in the car during the trip west, no fancy motels for us. In the back seat, Stan and I slept crunched up in knots with our cheeks pressed against the windows. Stan was a big dude, and when he stretched out, he took up the majority of the back seat; I was constantly fighting for space. Dad's tactics paid off. After a thousand miles of continuous driving, we were too worn out and exhausted to continue the fight.

With each passing mile, Dad grew stronger and stronger while the rest of us grew weaker. I don't think the old man slept more than six hours the whole trip. I vividly remember the day we finally reached the city limits of Cut Bank, Montana. There was this big, green sign with black lettering that simply said, "Welcome to Cut Bank, the Oil Capital of Montana, population 3,367." I was never so happy to see a sign in my life. I normally didn't get excited over a sign, but it made me happy, not because we were in Cut Bank, but because I finally got to pee.

As soon as Dad stopped to get gas at a Texaco station, Mom, Stan, and I sprinted to the restrooms. It's little things like that that make life worth living. When I finished peeing, I walked around the station to stretch my legs, and as I walked by the gas pump, I overheard Dad asking the attendant for directions to the Owen Ranch.

"Owen spread? Can't miss it. Continue down the road you're on for about a mile, and you'll come to a big oil refinery; they own it," the attendant said, pointing in the direction of the refinery. "Now, to get to their home place, take the first left after the refinery and stay on that road for about five miles. That's all their land. At the end of the road, you'll see their place, can't miss it." He said all this while cleaning smashed, dead grasshoppers off of the windshield. It was really nice hearing another person's voice.

After paying for the gas and getting everybody loaded back into the car, Dad followed the directions perfectly, and before long we were on the road leading to the Owen Ranch. I was amazed at how many oil wells there were, hundreds of them pumping methodically on a warm summer day. Herds of Black Angus cattle leisurely grazed between the derricks and dozens of horses ran across the wide open prairie that stretched as far as the eye could see.

We drove on and on until we reached a large, black cast iron ornamental sign with the words, "Owen Ranch" cut into it; it dominated the skyline. Within minutes, we were parked in the front yard looking up at a huge, white colonial-style mansion. The place was massive. Large columns reached skyward, and the porch wrapped around the entire structure with white handrails that seemed to run on forever. Like I mentioned earlier, when I was young, everything seemed bigger. It was one of those great houses your parents didn't have to tell you to behave in, you instinctively knew not to start roughhousing in a place like that.

I remember stretching the kinks out as I stared at the house and the huge red barn that stood nearby. Without warning, a big cowboy came running out of the barn toward us. I had never seen Charley before, but I figured this had to be him. As it turned out, Charley was in the barn tending to one of his prize Black Angus bulls when we arrived. He shook my dad's hand for what seemed like five minutes before he introduced himself to Stan and me. After the introductions were made, Charley led us up the steps of his mansion, opened the door, and let us in. He was a very gracious host, humble, unassuming with cow shit on his boots.

When he opened the front door, I couldn't help but whistle. The place looked like a set from a movie. The floor was made of marble, and there was a spiral staircase that ran from the foyer to the second floor. It looked like the staircase in "Gone with the Wind." I remember standing there gawking when Charley's dad, Bob, and Charley's wife Juanita came bursting in. They were arguing about something and didn't spend much time chit chatting. Soon, they both stormed off in opposite directions, leaving the rest of us standing in the foyer looking at each other.

I will never forget the first time I saw that ranch or the first time I saw Juanita. Let's just say, to a teenage boy, she was more impressive than the house. When she was mad, her coal black eyes seemed to burn right through whatever she stared at. They melted away any resistance she encountered. Whoever was on the receiving end of her beautiful, glaring eyes would eventually succumb to whatever demands she made.

Over the course of our several-week stay, I got to know Juanita pretty well. She had an old, green Army jeep that she took me riding in, and we explored the ranch and talked. She talked to me a lot, and I stared at her a lot, occasionally nodding my head like I knew what she was talking about. She really wasn't that much older than me, maybe ten years or so. However, she was twenty years younger than Charley and was reminded of that daily by her father-in-law, Bob. She said Bob told her she was a gold digger who only married Charley for his money. I never figured out why she told me all this personal stuff, maybe it was because I listened and kept quiet. It was the first time any adult women, other than my mom and my grandmothers, ever really talked to me. We enjoyed each other's company. She took me horseback riding and fishing. She was probably the most beautiful woman I had ever seen up to that point in my life, and I continued staring at her; she seemingly never noticed, and she was always talking.

As it turned out, her mother and father lived and worked on the ranch and had for years. Her parents, Helen and Ivan Bear Medicine, were both full blooded Blackfeet. Juanita was born on the ranch in the cabin that Ivan and Helen lived in. They had another child, a boy named Phillip, who died in a car wreck a year before she left the ranch and moved to Los Angeles. She said I reminded her of her brother, and she took a liking to me. After moving to California, she found work as an extra in Hollywood because they were always in search of authentic-looking Indians for all the westerns. She was authentic, all right. So authentic that, as a Blackfeet woman living in a strange land, she wanted to return to her roots, have children, and live a quiet life. She was authentic, Hollywood was phony. So, she left Los Angeles and returned to the ranch a full grown woman with dreams and aspirations of a better life. It wasn't long after her return when Charley proposed, and they had been married about three years by the time we showed up.

After spending a week on the ranch looking at her and all the other scenery, I no longer missed New Jersey. Stan seemed to adjust to his new surroundings, too. I remember him borrowing the Chevy every night, driving into Cut Bank then returning in the wee hours of the morning; nobody said a word to him about that.

It wasn't long before Dad found us an apartment to rent in Cut Bank. Charley wanted Dad to stay on and work at the ranch. Stan and I both thought that was a great idea, but Dad had other plans; he wanted to own and operate a gas station, it was his dream, he said. He liked working on cars, and he figured he could make a good living at the right location.

So, we settled into life in Cut Bank, and I started the ninth grade while Stan started his senior year at Cut Bank High. Stan was a very good athlete, he was the star of the football team and very popular. Before long, Dad found his gas station. It turned out to be a Chevron station that was open twenty-four hours a day, a real moneymaker, so he said. There was only one hitch; it was located 35 miles northwest of Cut Bank on the Blackfeet Indian Reservation in Browning, Montana.

I vividly remember Mom and Dad having arguments over that decision. Dad always seemed to win all the arguments. He had a way of wearing you down.

"Bud, did you say… an Indian reservation?" I remember my mom asking with a look of horror on her face.

"That's right, sweetheart, and it's a great bargain. The current owners are really motivated to sell," Dad laid it on thick.

"I would be too, Bud. We can't raise our boys on an Indian reservation. What are the schools like? Stan is at the age where he's looking at girls all the time. Do you want him to marry an Indian girl?

And what about Tony? He's our baby. There is no way we are moving our children onto an Indian reservation, no way."

For a brief, shining moment, I thought Mom was finally going to win an argument. It was at that moment I realized Mom had been kidnapped, too.

That was early November of 1967. By December, we had taken up residency in Browning, Montana, the headquarters of the Blackfeet Indian Reservation. Our Chevron station had an attached three bedroom living area and a four-unit motel. It didn't take us long to settle in; we all pitched in and worked hard at our new business, and business was good. The only businesses that did better were the liquor stores and the funeral homes.

Chapter 2
My First Day of Lessons

I remember the date and everything else about my first day of school in Browning, it was January 5, 1968. I couldn't have started at the beginning of the school year, oh no, I had to start mid-year and be the new guy in class. Browning High School wasn't far from home, so I decided to walk on that fateful first day. Of course, my mother would have none of that and insisted on driving me. I could tell she was nervous; her youngest son was headed off into the vast unknown. I'm sure she was worried and wanted to protect me, but there are certain things a parent can't save you from, and one of those things is your first day at a new school. That was the real reason I was determined to walk. The last thing I wanted was my mother to drop me off and have the Blackfeet students tease me about it. No way, I stood my ground, and I finally won the argument. Mom always had a hard time winning arguments.

I walked the half mile to school without anything catastrophic happening. I remember it was bone-chillingly cold and windy, so I walked as fast as I could in a vain attempt to keep warm. I arrived at school in one piece and was standing at the front door when, all of a sudden, six or seven hard packed snowballs came cascading down on me. Luckily, I wasn't too badly hurt. The natives were obviously a little restless, and I learned three valuable lessons from that experience: the Blackfeet have very strong arms, excellent aim, and they show up when you least expect them.

I'm still not sure why Mr. Howard Blackstone, the principal, was standing in the front lobby waiting to greet me. It must have been unusual to see a white student. "Are you okay? Don't pay any attention to them, that's just a display of Indian lovin," Mr. Blackstone said with a big, shit eating grin stretched across his round, plump face. "Follow me, I'll show you to your room." He turned and walked down the hall with me following close behind. "Your ninth-grade teacher is Miss Ash, and she is very nice, a recent graduate of Montana State University down in Bozeman."

Miss Ash, as it turned out, was a beautiful young white woman. Looking at her took some of the sting out of my recent injuries, some. "Tony, you will be sitting up here in the front row," Miss Ash said as she pointed to a small desk not far from hers. I remember sitting down at my assigned wooden desk and being immediately drawn to the intricate carvings etched onto the surface. As I examined it closely, I was amazed to see an entire crime scene portrayed in perfect detail. Upon further review, I suddenly realized that the "crime scene" was actually a group of men and women engaging in what appeared to be sex. More lessons learned: the Blackfeet are artistic and very imaginative.

Miss Ash was going over a few things with me when, all of a sudden, the bell rang, the classroom door swung open, and in rushed a mob of laughing, noisy Blackfeet. After everyone had settled into their seats, I stood up and began walking to the coat room to hang up my coat. I was about halfway there when I tripped. I fell hard and bounced across the floor. After I stopped bouncing, I jumped up and took a swing at the boy who had tripped me. Unfortunately, I missed, and the other boy didn't. He punched me on the chin, and down I went for the second time in less than 30 seconds. I remember lying in the middle of the room, staring up at a mob of laughing, jeering Indians before Miss Ash helped me to my feet. She asked me what happened, and I told her I slipped on some snow. I hate lying, I really do.

Later that morning, I felt a light tap on my shoulder, and as I slowly turned around, I saw a pretty Blackfeet Indian girl sitting directly behind me. I quickly found out she wasn't flirting; she was passing me a note from the guy who had tripped me. I cautiously opened it and read the following words very slowly and carefully: "White Guy, I will see you down behind Vic's Grocery after school." It was signed, Ronnie Joe Stabs-in-the-Back.

I found out later that Ronnie Joe was the class bully in a room full of class bullies. Evidently, it was his second attempt at passing the ninth grade, and he was proud of that. He liked being the biggest kid in class, it helped his confidence. After I read the note, I crumbled it up and glanced at the author. Ronnie, all puffed up and feeling good about himself stared back at me with a cold, stoic look on his face. I wasn't absolutely certain, but I figured we weren't going to the grocery store to buy candy.

For the rest of that day, I found it very hard to concentrate. I stared at the clock to the point of distraction. When the bell finally rang, signaling the end of the school day, everybody jumped up and ran to get their coats. Everybody except me, I sat at my desk and stared at the clock.

It wasn't long before I stood up and retrieved my coat. Miss Ash had been cleaning the blackboard, and when she set the eraser down, I asked her, "Miss Ash, where is Vic's Grocery?" She smiled and gave me directions. As it turned out, Vic's Grocery was the designated battlefield, and she seemed to know a lot about it. It was as close to the school as you could get without being on school property. I remember her sitting me down and giving me some of the best advice I have ever been given. She said she understood I was probably scared, but I had to go. If I ran away, I would be running for the rest of my time on the reservation. The worst thing I could do was run, she said. She explained, in no uncertain terms, that the Blackfeet hate cowards. On the other hand, they reward bravery, and if I ran, they would never let me stop running. Instinctively, I knew she was right. I was scared, but I knew I had to go, I had to. So I thanked her and quickly made my way to Vic's.

As I approached the alley behind Vic's, I became increasingly aware of the roaring crowd. It seemed like the entire school was there. Kids of all ages lined both sides of the alley yelling, jeering, and pointing at me. I had watched the movie "Spartacus" when I was younger, and I got the same gut-wrenching feeling the gladiators must have felt when they were being thrown to the lions. At least I imagined their guts wrenched, because mine sure did.

In the middle of the crowd stood Ronnie Joe Stabs-in-the-Back, acting and looking tough. As I approached, he slowly began to remove his coat. After taking off my coat, the same girl who had passed me the note in class came up and volunteered to hold it. That act of kindness seemed to piss him off. He yelled, "I'm going to give you a bloody stick in the mud, White Guy!" I correctly figured it was fight time.

Ronnie Joe quickly closed the gap between us and threw a right hand that caught me square on the jaw, and down I went for the third time that day. To my surprise, I wasn't badly hurt, I credit the adrenaline that pumped through me like water through a garden hose.

Ronnie Joe rushed me once I stood up, and once again, I found myself lying on the ground. He stood over me and proceeded to put the boots to me with the intensity reserved for the truly insane. His heavy, pointed cowboy boots were having the desired effect when he suddenly slipped and fell. I rolled away and jumped to my feet as quickly as possible. When he started to get up, I swung as hard as I could and hit him squarely on the top of his head. Man, did that hurt! I thought I had broken my hand. Another lesson: the Blackfeet are hard-headed. The blow must have done some serious damage because Ronnie Joe continued to lie on his back withering in pain.

That was when one of his fellow tribesmen copped a sneaker on me. In Blackfeet terminology, copping a sneaker means you get hit by some chickenshit when you aren't looking.

Surprisingly, I wasn't knocked to the ground, and because I didn't fall, I was able to spin around and face my new attacker. We were engaged in hand-to-hand combat before we both tumbled to the ground, rolling around, cussing and swinging at each other like our lives depended on it.

Evidently, Ronnie Joe had recuperated enough to stand up because he started to put the boots to me once again. I covered my head the best I could and peeked up at Ronnie Joe, just in time to see him suddenly and viciously flattened by a tackle that would've made Jim Thorpe proud. The speed and force of the impact sent him flying through the air. He may have kept flying if he hadn't slammed into the hard, unforgiving back wall of Vic's Grocery. He seemed to stick to the bricks for an inordinately long period of time before gravity took hold and he slowly slid to the ground. He was finished for the day.

I got to my feet when the guy I had been fighting let go. He and I, along with the entire crowd, stood in silence and stared at the guy who knocked Ronnie Joe flat. The crowd nodded their heads in approval. Then the tackler announced, "It's time to go home now. We can beat up the white guy again tomorrow. I'll bring the popcorn." The crowd laughed and slowly began to disperse. The cute little Blackfeet girl who held my coat dropped it at my feet and said, "You aren't much of a fighter but you sure can roll." She giggled as she walked away.

I asked the tackler, "Who is that girl?"

"Her name is Vicki Eagle Feathers, and I think she likes you."

"Really, what makes you say that?"

"She gave back your coat."

That was the time I met Two-Fingers and we have been friends ever since. Turns out he hated Ronnie Joe because he was a first rate asshole who always picked on people he thought he could bully. Two-Fingers said he was okay with me getting my ass kicked as long as it was a fair fight, but when the other guy jumped in, he decided to help. I was thankful he did, not too many people risk helping a complete stranger. He has always made light of helping me, but it was, and still is, a big deal to me.

We spent a few minutes talking as the crowd thinned out. After a while, we formally introduced ourselves to each other. He told me everybody called him Two-Fingers, but his real name was Donny R. Schwartz. He had missed school that day because he had to help his dad with a few chores at their house. As it turned out, we were approximately the same age and in the same class.

As we stood there talking, I noticed his left hand for the first time. To be honest, it startled the hell out of me, and I've told him that every time the subject comes up, which is seldom. His hand consisted of a long index finger and a curved thumb. It was mangled and distorted; technically, it was one finger and a thumb, but I wasn't about to point that out to him.

He must have noticed me staring because he raised his hand over his head and announced, "I was born this way. My mom says I was so eager to get into the world I didn't hang around long enough for her to finish her job. I tell her she starved me when I was an infant, and I ended up gnawing the other three fingers off to survive."

That made me laugh

"Well, at least you kept your sense of humor," was the best response I could come up with.

"On the reservation, that's about all they let you keep," Two-Fingers said as he turned and walked down the alley.

"Hey, wait a second, I'll walk with you."

"Okay, White Guy, but you need to hurry, I have things to do."

We walked a short distance in silence before I asked, "Why did you call me White Guy instead of Tony?"

"Everybody, sooner or later, has a nickname on the reservation. You, whether you like it or not, are the White Guy." Actually, that sounded pretty good to me. I always wanted a nickname, and now I had one. Trust me, over the years, I've been called a lot worse.

"Would you like to come to my place?" I asked.

"Do you have any Kool-Aid?"

"Yeah, and a pop machine filled with pop. My dad bought the Chevron station."

"I know," Two-Fingers said. "On the reservation, everybody knows everything about everyone else's business. You can't fart on the reservation without everybody knowing how it smells." That made me laugh, too.

I found myself sneaking peeks at this strange-looking person. Two-Fingers was my size, but he acted bigger somehow. He walked with an air of confidence, as if he were normal, normal physically.

As we approached our Chevron station, I asked, "Do you have any brothers or sisters?"

"I have two older sisters," he said matter-of-factly. "I have an older brother named Stan."

Two-Fingers nodded and kept walking.

Dad was pumping gas when we arrived at the station. He looked up from what he was doing, and I remember him meekly waving at us before we entered the front door of our station. After we each grabbed a pop, we walked into the kitchen where Mom was frosting a cake.

"Hello, Tony, how was your first day at school?" Mom asked, with a look of relief on her face.

"It was okay. At least nobody died."

I introduced Two-Fingers to my mother, and he politely shook her hand and smiled.

Mom said, "It's nice to meet you, Donny." I noticed Mom staring at Two-Fingers' left hand before she asked, "Oh my, what happened to your poor hand?"

"Well, when I was a baby, my parents left me at home with my two older sisters. They were watching Captain Kangaroo on TV when a wolf broke into our teepee and chewed off my fingers."

Two-Fingers said all that with a straight face. Over the course of our lifelong friendship, I have never known Two-Fingers to give the same answer twice when he's asked, "What happened to your hand?" Over the years, I've come to realize he uses these stories as a defense mechanism.

Lesson: Fiction is less painful than fact, especially on the reservation.

My mom looked heartbroken and only occasionally glanced at his hand after he responded.

"You'd better sit down and have some German chocolate cake; I just took it out of the oven." Mom served up two large helpings, and we devoured the cake like we hadn't eaten in a week.

After a second serving, Two-Fingers said, "Mrs. Church, that was almost as good as my mom's fry bread."

"Thank you, Donny. I'll send some home with you. Make sure you keep it away from any wild wolves you might run into on your way home!"

Well, there you have it. That was the day we met and some of the early lessons I learned.

Looking back, I am reminded of Two-Fingers' strength and his determination to stand up for the little guy, me. He faced down all the

Blackfeet in the circle that day and protected me. He risked a lot and gained little. Over the years, he has risked a lot defending what he believes to be right, and he has a clear vision of what is right and what is wrong.

Most people do, I suppose; the difference is he always sticks his neck out to defend what he believes, and that virtue has rubbed off on me. He came by it naturally; I had to have it pounded into my head more than once.

For example, we never looked at each other as white or Indian, race was never an issue with him or me. Other people get caught up in that type of thing, but we never did. I always thought he was weird-looking, but my opinion of him never had anything to do with his color.

Over time, Two-Fingers and I came to the conclusion that people are essentially good, but governments are filled with far too many bad people who make policies centered on race because they want to separate and polarize people for their own political gain. It took me longer than Two-Fingers to come to that conclusion, but I eventually did. Unified, independent people are harder to control.

Chapter 3
Death and Death Defying

I have never forgotten a blizzard. The harshness is easily recalled, and I certainly haven't forgotten my first one. For me, some things are hard to forget, and blizzards are one of them. It was the night after my first day of school when a massive blizzard swept across the northern Rockies of Montana and dumped two feet of snow on us in less than eight hours. After it stopped snowing, the temperature dropped to ten degrees below zero, and a strong, cold wind piled the snow high over the roads, making driving virtually impossible.

I found out firsthand that Montana has cold, harsh winters, and that Browning is the coldest place in the state. As I said earlier, Browning doesn't have a tree in the entire town; the wind and cold see to that. Changes in weather occur rapidly on the reservation, and when it gets really bad, school is usually canceled.

That's what happened the next morning. Then, around 11 a.m., a chinook wind miraculously appeared and the temperature began to rise dramatically, I have learned to love chinook winds.

At 11:10 a.m., Two-Fingers showed up at our gas station. I was inside stocking our Pepsi cooler with pop when he slid through the doors and said, "White Guy, let's go sledding." Two-Fingers never really asked questions back then. Instead, he made pronouncements. He figured everybody was looking for a good time, and it began when he showed up. He was right about that.

So, I stopped what I was doing, grabbed my coat, gloves, scarf, ear muffs, and was frantically looking for the electric hand warmers I had gotten for Christmas when Two-Fingers, with a real demeaning look on his face, said, "Pussy." He stretched out his arms as if to say, I have no gloves, no scarf, no ear muffs, and my coat isn't even zipped up. I slowly put down my gloves, scarf, and ear muffs and followed him out the door into a winter wonderland.

"Where we going?" I asked.

"There's a hill about a half mile west of town that's great for sledding. Get on my toboggan, and I'll give you a ride."

I saw no reason to argue, so I happily jumped on the toboggan. Two-Fingers gave it a mighty tug, and soon we were cruising down the icy highway. He pulled hard as we climbed a small hill. When we reached the top, he jumped on the toboggan and we rode it down the other side until it stopped. That maneuver was repeated over and over until we reached the sledding area known as "Racine Hill."

Evidently, Old Man Racine liked seeing his hill filled with sledders. He kept a fire going in a fifty gallon oil barrel and warmed himself as he watched the sledders fly down the hill. The hill is very steep, and at its base is a small lake about three hundred yards wide and long. On that day, it was a solid sheet of thick ice.

We trudged through waist deep snow until we reached the top of the hill. We were breathing hard and panting like whipped pups. I remember standing there desperately trying to catch my breath, all the while thinking what a beautiful day it was. The sky was a deep royal blue filled with puffy white clouds that hung over the Rocky Mountains close enough to touch. It took a while before I finally got enough oxygen to my brain and realized that wasn't going to happen.

I eventually turned my attention to the activity below and was amazed to see groups of sledders bouncing off a small snow drift and launching skyward before landing on the icy surface of the lake at breakneck speeds. Once the sleds hit the ice, they seemed to shift into a higher gear as they raced out of control into a large snowbank on the far side of the lake. Bodies flew in all directions, and much to my surprise, all the passengers lived. In fact, they laughed hysterically and started back up the hill for another run.

After watching all the activity for a quite a while, I noticed Two-Fingers sitting patiently on the toboggan with a get your ass on the toboggan look on his face. I figured it was a good day to die, so I jumped on behind him before we tucked our legs inside the toboggan and started down the hill hell bent for leather. About a quarter of the way down, a couple of not-too-smart braves tried to jump on the toboggan and ended up crashing into each other.

We flew down the hill and soon found ourselves approaching the biggest snow drift on the hill. As we reached Mach-one speed, we hit the drift and went airborne. Higher and higher we went as we flew on. No kidding, I looked down and birds were flying below us. I looked over my left shoulder and saw Old Man Racine slowly rising from his seat with a look of terror on his face. Well, it was either terror or delight; at that altitude, I wasn't sure.

It seemed like a lifetime before we landed, and when we did, we hit hard, real hard. The toboggan made a loud cracking sound, and instead of going straight, it began to spin in circles. I held onto Two-Fingers with all my strength before noticing we were no longer sitting on the toboggan. Instead, we were bouncing along the hard, icy surface of the lake, headed toward a group of sledders who were desperately trying to get out of our way. Too late, we slammed into them, and they went down like pins at a bowling alley.

Two-Fingers, shaken but not rattled, jumped up and said, "That was a strike."

Two-Fingers has always had a way of defusing a situation, either with his fist or with his tongue. Over the years, I grew to appreciate that, but never more than at that moment.

"You're crazy, Two-Fingers! You could've killed us!" screamed Buzzy Still Smoking as he brushed himself off.

"What's with you?" yelled Chubby Skunk Cap. "Don't you know riding with a white guy is hazardous to your health!"

"Crack you, Chubby!" Two-Fingers replied.

"Bone you, Two-Fingers." Was the best Chubby could come up with.

Seconds later, a sled full of Blackfeet slammed into Chubby and Buzzy and took them out at the knees. The Blackfeet Health Center was very busy that day.

We were gathering up the splintered wood that was once Two-Fingers' toboggan when Old Man Racine suddenly appeared and said, "Donny R., you sure know how to make friends. Who is this pale-looking bird with you?"

"His name is Tony Church, and his parents own the Chevron station in town."

"I'm heading into town if you want a ride." Old Man Racine continued staring at me.

"Okay, but I want to pay you. How about some firewood?" Two-Fingers asked as he pointed toward the shattered remains of the toboggan.

Old Man Racine nodded his head and said, "Okay-noc-kee," before raising his hand in an arching motion and staring off into the clear, blue sky. Old Man Racine always had a way with words. It was a mixture of broken English and a native language that was rapidly disappearing.

Old Man Racine dropped us off and quickly left without saying a word. He only waved his hand in another arching motion and left us standing in front of Two-Fingers' place and disappeared into the sunset. Two-Fingers' parents owned an apartment house and a curio shop in the center of town on Main Street back then. The place wasn't much of a money maker, but it did provide plenty of work. Over the years, I became very close to his family and sometimes it was too close for comfort.

Having said that, I met his family that day, and my life, for better or worse, was changed forever. Two-Fingers' father, Maximillian "Max" Schwartz, was a tall, dark, and handsome man who inherited the best traits from his German-American father and Blackfeet mother. Max is a half breed on a reservation that is quickly becoming a place of diminished bloodlines. He was raised on a ranch not far from town. Max was never comfortable in the white world, and, prior to marrying his wife, Pam, he wasn't that comfortable on the reservation either. He has adjusted pretty well and is no longer the loner he once was.

Two-Fingers' mother, Pam Spotted Eagle Schwartz, is a beautiful woman with high cheekbones and piercing dark eyes. She is a full-blooded Blackfeet woman who traces her lineage back to the great Blackfeet Chief Two Guns White Calf. At one time, she was the most educated Blackfeet on the reservation. She went to high school at an Indian boarding school in South Dakota, and after graduating, attended Carlisle College in Pennsylvania, where she graduated with honors. As it turned out, Pam spent a lot of time in the white world learning their values at the expense of her own. She set aside her traditional beliefs and tried to raise her children to be good little apples, red on the outside and white on the inside.

Max and Pam have three children: Donny R. is the youngest, Cindy Ann is the oldest, and Paula is the middle child.

Cindy Ann was breathtakingly beautiful. She was in her senior year at Browning High School and was a cheerleader who was extremely athletic in a very, feminine way. She was blessed with the very best features of her parents. She was mild-mannered and laughed easily. If all the boys in town weren't already in love with her, they hadn't met her yet.

Paula was a sophomore at that time and very pretty in her own right. Actually, she was the prettiest tomboy I had ever seen. If we ever needed someone on our side in a fight, we called on Paula. She and Two-Fingers are extremely close, but she still doesn't allow him to pull any crap on her, and he respects her for that. She has always been very protective of her "little" brother.

The family was seated in their living room when Two-Fingers and I entered their large, tastefully decorated apartment. Introductions were made, and I instantly felt welcome. Their greetings were warm, genuine, and inviting. I could tell right away they were good people.

"Donny R., how was your sledding adventure?" Max asked with a Camel cigarette dangling from his lips.

"Great, Pop, except Tony broke the toboggan."

"He what? How did he do that?" Pam asked.

"Let's just say he was a little careless on the hill, you know, new kid in town and all. I'll help him pay for it by doing some extra chores around here. Tony will pitch in, too."

I stood in silence, not wanting to get in the way of Two-Fingers' story. I figured he knew how to handle these types of things; he seemed to have had a lot of practice.

"You sure he's the one that broke it, Donny R.?" Paula asked with a skeptical tone of voice.

"He already feels bad about it, Paula. Let's not make him feel any worse, okay?" Two-Fingers said.

"Yeah, right, Donny R. What's for dinner?" Paula asked, successfully changing the subject.

Later, after dinner, I asked Two-Fingers why he blamed me for the broken toboggan.

"Simple. Now you and I have an excuse to hang out together. We can do a few chores here and there and have a lot of fun in between."

Later that night, on my walk home, I tried to figure out why we needed an excuse to hang out together. Must have been a color-barrier thing. An Indian kid didn't want to look bad, especially in front of his parents, if the friendship didn't work out. I haven't given it much thought over the years, but Two-Fingers may have been feeling the heat from his Blackfeet buddies and maybe his family, too for befriending a white guy. Who knows? The subject never came up again, and the fact that he is a Blackfeet Indian and I am a white guy was never an issue for us. We were colorblind before color blindness was cool.

There was a lot of serious limping going on at school the next day, so Two-Fingers and I kept low and moved fast until school ended. After school, we decided to do some "hooking." Well, actually, Two-Fingers decided we would do some "hooking."

In the winter, hooking is a popular and dangerous pastime on the reservation. The idea is to grab onto a moving vehicle and let it pull you on an icy street, the icier, the better. Icy, paved streets work the best; gravel roads are hazardous to your health. Hit some gravel and you'll end up on your ass.

Two-Fingers had perfected a one-handed grab-and-pull method because he had little choice in the matter. Being new to the game, I was less proficient. However, after an hour of hooking, I finally got the hang of it and was getting down-right cocky.

A little before dark, a group of underage drivers in a Volkswagen Bug stopped at a stop sign near us, As the Bug began to pull away, we ran over and grabbed onto its thin, flimsy rear bumper. The driver spotted us immediately and quickly downshifted before gunning the engine. This caused the lightweight Bug to begin spinning in circles.

Two-Fingers eventually let go and was thrown into a half-frozen snowdrift alongside the road. I wish I had done the same thing, but I resisted the temptation and immediately regretted that decision. Instead, I hung on for dear life until my feet slipped out from underneath me, and down I went, directly in the path of the out-of-control Bug.

I tried desperately to escape getting run over by rolling on the ground, but I couldn't avoid the impact. The Bug ended up running over my right arm with its right front tire. Luckily, most of the weight is in the rear of Volkswagen Bugs, and I avoided any long-lasting physical injuries. When the Bug sped away, Two-Fingers ran over to help me up as I sat in the middle of the road inspecting the damage. "Wow, that was wild," was the best the glib, fast talking Two-Fingers could come up with as he brushed snow and gravel off my back and shoulders.

I remember standing in the middle of the street, flexing the muscles in my right arm, thankful and amazed that it still worked. I didn't have any broken bones, but I did have a strong desire to get off the hard, icy street and go home. So, after a few moments of silence and introspection, I turned and started walking that way. I hadn't walked far when I turned around and watched Two-Fingers disappear into the night. I remember thinking that if I lived through the weekend, it would be a miracle. My odds seemed pretty good since it was Friday night.

In addition to working at our station and doing chores around the house, my father thought it would be a great idea for me to get a paper route, you know, to build character and improve my survival skills. It seems he had one when he was a kid, and he liked the idea of keeping me as busy as possible. So, Dad worked out a deal where I would deliver a paper from Cut Bank called the Western Breeze. I only had to deliver it on Saturdays and Tuesdays because it was only printed twice a week. The Blackfeet liked it because it had the showtimes for movies in Cut Bank and good coverage of the local sports teams.

My route consisted of all the local businesses and a few select older people, mostly widows. Glasses of something good to drink, cookies, and fry bread were a few of the perks. After initially rejecting the idea, I found that I really enjoyed delivering the paper because of the great exercise and because I ended up meeting virtually everybody in town in a very short period of time. Plus, I made about $10.00 a week, and back then, that was pretty good money. I would walk to the post office to pick up my bundle of papers, and on the way there, I would occasionally swing by Two-Fingers' house and talk him into going with me. If he was finished with his chores, he would go. If not, I would deliver the papers by myself.

It was the Saturday morning after I had been run over by the Bug, and as usual, it was cold and windy in Browning. Two-Fingers and I were merrily selling papers and talking about what we were going to do that night when loud barking caught our attention. It wasn't really barking; it was more like blood-curdling howls and lots of whimpering.

As we turned and walked down the alley behind the movie theater, I noticed a pack of dogs surrounding a large Saint Bernard. Two dogs were lying face down in the snow with blood pouring out of their bodies so fast that there was no way they were going to survive. Dark red blood glistened in the white, windswept snow.

"That is Old McGraw. He's the meanest, toughest dog in town. He killed my dog two years ago. He's a psychotic killer. He's been known to fight packs of dogs without getting a scratch, watch him," Two-Fingers said.

Watch him? Hell, I couldn't keep my eyes off him. I remember standing there as he savagely attacked his victims with mesmerizing speed and accuracy. He took on the entire pack and threw them to the ground before going for their throats; he showed absolutely no mercy. The dogs attacked from different angles, and Old McGraw outmaneuvered them each and every time. Finally, the last surviving dog limped off whimpering, its tail securely tucked between its legs. I counted five dogs lying in the blood-soaked snow, dead or dying. The entire area looked like a large cherry snow cone, minus the cone.

"Someday, I'm going to kill that dog," Two-Fingers said.

"Why doesn't somebody do something about him?" I asked.

"Because he belongs to the mayor, and the mayor says we can't afford a dog catcher, and Old McGraw provides a valuable public service.

That may be true to some extent. Only problem is, Old McGraw kills the good and the bad."

"Does he attack humans?" I asked.

"Not that I know of. Nobody goes around the vicious bastard to find out. Let this be a lesson for you, White Guy, avoid him at all costs."

After we finished delivering the papers, we decided to count the money. We should have been more aware of our surroundings because we soon found ourselves encircled by a group of Blackfeet boys. At the head of the group was Kenny Stabs-in-the-Back, Ronnie Joe's older brother. Ronnie Joe was there too, along with two of their cousins, Babe and Smiley Black Weasel.

"What are you doing with all my money?" Kenny asked.

"Gee, what a coincidence I just saw Old McGraw, and I was wondering what's Kenny up to today." Two-Fingers was talking and that was a good sign.

"What's that supposed to mean?" Kenny asked. He was big and fast; he just wasn't too quick.

"You know, you and McGraw are always picking on things smaller than yourselves. Don't you ever get tired of that, Kenny?"

"No, now hand over that money or I'm going to bust you up." Kenny said as his gang began to close the circle.

Just then, a pickup came to a screeching halt, and out jumped Paula. Kenny and his gang scattered. It turned out Paula had dog-slapped Kenny on a number of occasions.

"Sister Girl, how about a ride home?" Two-Fingers asked.

"Sure, jump in the back," Paula said as she stared in Kenny's direction.

On the way to Two-Fingers' place, as we huddled under a cold tarp trying not to freeze to death, we continued our discussion about what we were going to do that night. Not too many options on a Saturday night in the big city, then or now. Actually, there was only one real option that was legal for minors: we were going to the movies.

Back then, Browning had one theater, and you knew it was a theater because the sign out front said so. The owner, Mr. Boswell, was one of the few wealthy men in town and he got rich by not spending any of his profits on furniture or decorations. It was strictly a no-frills operation, lacking in customer service like most monopolies. There wasn't a customary lobby, no place to buy candy, pop, popcorn, sunflower seeds, or anything like that. Those purchases were made at one of the two drugstores nearby. Pop and sunflower seeds were the snacks of choice for the younger crowd, and hard liquor was the preference of a surprisingly large number of the theater going public. Fueled by alcohol, things tended to get a little rowdy halfway through a film, no matter how good it was. If it was really bad, bottles of varying sizes and shapes were routinely thrown around the place.

The first five rows at the front of the theater consisted of hardwood benches where the youngest kids were supposed to sit. The rows of seats behind the benches were actual seats with backs, but no cushions, the cushions had been destroyed years before and never replaced. Going to the bathroom was an adventure that added little enjoyment to the theatrical experience; fist-shaped holes in the doors and walls made the lack of privacy a foregone conclusion. Each bathroom, the Braves and the Squaws, housed a single toilet, no paper of any kind, just a toilet. As a special treat, they were equipped with sinks that leaked rusty, alkaline-laced water onto rotted out-floors that trembled under the weight of even the smallest adventure seeker. Consequently, the theater going crowd generally used other facilities before going to the movies or held their piss in a legs-crossed act of defiance. I truly believe that's why the Blackfeet had an abnormally high rate of kidney failure, it was the theater's fault. My kidney issues are unrelated to the theater, just saying.

That night, the assembled crowd was large and enthusiastic. It was a John Wayne movie, and John Wayne was always a big draw. He was always able to kill all the Indians, but unlike other westerns, he made you feel good about it. Besides, they were different tribes getting killed off, never the Blackfeet. The Sioux, Crow, Apache, the Comanches, and a bunch of other tribes got killed, but never the Blackfeet.

Two-Fingers and I were up near the front of the ticket line, and the two-bit admission price was burning a hole in our pockets. When it was finally our turn to pay, Two-Fingers pulled out four-bits and said, "Two for the balcony and keep the change."

"You're a real funny guy, aren't you, Donny R.? Keep cracking wise, and you'll be going to the end of the line." Mr. Boswell said as he reluctantly handed over two tickets. Mr. Boswell was like most of the other white merchants in town, with no sense of humor and an air of superiority that did not serve him well. Two-Fingers snapped off a nice salute, turned, and marched into the darkened theater. I followed close behind.

We slowly made our way down to the front of the theater as our eyes adjusted to the darkness. Two-Fingers continued to lead the way, walking confidently as he surveyed the scene. He held his head high and pranced down the aisle like he owned the place. He checked out some girls who were smiling and checking him out. Suddenly, after a brief moment of deliberation, he made his move. He made room for himself next to a girl named Veronica Comes-At-Night. Next to her sat Vicki Eagle Feathers.

"Move over, cousin, and make room for this poor white guy I found wandering around the bathroom looking for toilet paper."

The girls giggled and quickly made room for us. There the four of us sat, Two-Fingers next to the wall, Veronica next to him, Vicki next to Veronica, and me in the aisle seat. It was all very cozy and not at all what I expected.

When the lights dimmed, a Woody Woodpecker cartoon came on, and it proved to be very popular. Catcalls and laughter erupted when someone in the back of the theater yelled, "Woody's got a wooden pecker like Old Man Boswell!"

"You ought to know!" another patron yelled as the theater going crowd broke into hysterics.

I remember glancing over at Two-Fingers, who had his arm draped over Veronica's shoulder and a smile on his face. Two-Fingers glanced back at me and nodded his head toward Vicki. I wasn't sure what he wanted me to do, so I sat there like a bump on a log. Vicki noticed Two-Fingers' gesture and whispered in my ear, "He wants you to put your arm around me."

I briefly hesitated before raising my left arm and slowly placing it on Vicki's shoulders. I kept my eyes glued to the screen because I wasn't brave enough to look at her. Vicki slowly moved my way before snuggling up real close. At first I thought she was cold. I wasn't sure how that was possible because I was sweating bullets. Bullets, arrows, John Wayne, and Vicki in the same night, if I could have taken a piss, it would've been the perfect evening.

After the movie, Two-Fingers and I went outside and found a place to relieve ourselves; no way in hell were we going to use the theater's toilet. Besides, there was a really long line, surprisingly long. We walked to the alley behind the theater, found an unoccupied spot, and quickly took care of business. To successfully piss on a cold, windy Montana night takes a degree of practice that I could ill afford, I had to go bad. So I learned the hard way: never piss out in the open because the wind is unforgiving. I'll tell you the truth, I shook a lot of piss off my boots while growing up in Browning.

As we were finishing, the siren attached to the water tower screeched its obnoxious warning, the ten o'clock curfew was in effect, and all minors had to get off the streets.

Of course, the young Blackfeet made a game out of avoiding arrest. They dodged in front of tribal police cars and then sprinted off to where they couldn't be easily followed. This usually went on for hours until the police gave up. Besides, they were usually kept busy with barroom brawls, car wrecks, domestic violence calls, and any number of unlawful and dangerous acts. On the weekends, the jail and the hospital were always "Standing Room Only."

On the reservation, school was the one place where there was a semblance of order. To keep it that way, discipline was meted out with a vengeance, with absolutely no consideration given to any potential psychological damage. Punishment was swift and harsh, with no appeals. There was a kind of beauty to it as long as you weren't the person on the receiving end. However, it really wasn't the teachers I worried about; I worried about the students. I generally put in my time and never went out of my way to cause problems and Two-Fingers tried to do the same. My routine was pretty simple: get to class, hang up my coat, take my seat, and don't speak unless spoken to. It seemed to have worked; I'm still alive, and I only have a small amount of psychological damage, extremely minuscule.

That first winter was hard and seemed to never end, but eventually it did. In late April of that year, the sun shone brightly through a break in the clouds, and it was actually nice and warm for a brief moment. Two-Fingers and I had cabin fever and were overdue for an adventure. We decided it was time to play hooky from school and hitchhike up to East Glacier. It was a great day for a road trip. East Glacier is thirteen miles west of Browning and is the east entrance to Glacier National Park. We decided to check it out before all the tourists showed up.

As we walked past the Junction Drive-In, we were oblivious to traffic; walking just felt good. We walked along the highway toward East Glacier, throwing rocks at beer bottles, wine bottles, whiskey bottles, anything made of glass. Occasionally, we found a gopher to throw at, but mainly it was glass. Before I realized it, we had walked all the way out to Old Man Racine's place. The ice on the lake was as hard and thick as ever, or so I thought.

We made a game out of racing along the edge of the lake and sliding on the soles of our shoes. Once again, I was oblivious to everything around me and didn't realize I had drifted a long way from the shoreline. Suddenly, Two-Fingers yelled at me and, as I stopped to listen, the ice began to crack slightly beneath my feet before suddenly giving way. Down I went into the murky, freezing water. As I began to sink, I was overwhelmed by a feeling of helplessness. I desperately tried to pull myself out of the death trap, but the ice kept breaking away each time I reached the surface. That was when I began to panic big time.

After thrashing around for what seemed like an eternity, I finally managed to resurface and find ice I hoped was strong enough to hold me, all the while freezing and gasping for air. I gathered the last of my strength and tried one more time to escape the hell I'd fallen into. I was almost out of the water when the ice gave way again, and down I went once more. I kept thinking it was too nice of a day to die. I was running out of energy, but somehow found the strength to keep searching for solid ice. My hands were numb, and my teeth chattered uncontrollably. I soon found myself sinking deep into the lake for a third time and looking up at the clear, blue sky.

Exhausted and scared, I somehow mustered enough courage and strength to fight my way out of the mess I'd created. I pushed the pain aside and began to swim toward the hole in the ice. As I reached the surface, I saw Two-Fingers' Levi jacket floating above me. I was able to grab it and pull myself up, and when my head cleared the water, I belched up icy cold water and what appeared to be a small minnow. There, lying flat on the ice, was Two-Fingers, carefully and slowly pulling me out of the hole. I continued belching and puking up lake water while trying to catch my breath. I held on to the arm of his jacket for dear life, and he dragged me away from the hole and onto solid ice.

Once I was safe, I rolled over and lay on my back like a beached whale gasping for air as my teeth continued chattering. I had lost all feeling in my hands and legs, but I was alive. Two-Fingers had crawled out on thin ice and saved my life while risking his own. After I caught my breath, he helped me to my feet, and we slowly made our way to Old Man Racine's fire barrel and made a fire. Actually, Two-Fingers made the fire; I sat on a big log and choked up muddy lake water. The fire was nice and toasty, and I soon began to get feeling back in my body. Two-Fingers kept throwing wood in the barrel, and the flames kept getting higher and higher while ashes floated into the air before falling on my wet clothes, sizzling as they disappeared.

To my knowledge, Two-Fingers never mentioned this incident to anyone. He was never one to brag about things like saving my life. We both knew he had, and that was enough for him. To this day, I don't know too many people willing to save another person's life when it puts their own life in danger. Maybe my family would, but they've never been put to the test. Two-Fingers was tested, and he didn't hesitate. I'd like to think I'm that courageous, but I'm not sure. Hopefully, I'll never be tested, and if I am, I hope I'm as brave as Two-Fingers. Our friendship was enriched that day; bonds were strengthened, and from that day forward, Two-Fingers and I became virtually inseparable.

It was several weeks after my near drowning that school was adjourned for summer break. There were no celebrations on the reservation when school was dismissed, no trips to the ice cream parlor, and no sleepovers. Just a bunch of kids trying to get home safely without getting run over by a drunk driver or a speeding tourist.

I remember my brother Stan was especially glad to get out of school. He had graduated and was looking forward to summer and getting on with life. I really hadn't seen much of Stan during his senior year; he was too busy fighting his own battles. Big and powerful, Stan never took any crap from anybody. He was a good athlete who found pleasure in playing sports with and against the Blackfeet. The Blackfeet are very good athletes, very good. Over the years, I've concluded there must be a secret ingredient in all that fry bread they eat because they can run all day long. On the reservation, people were always running to or from something.

Later that summer, Stan had a date with Two-Fingers' sister Paula, and he was very excited about that. I remember Stan picking her up at the Schwartz's place in our '57 Chevy. He was all cleaned up and smelling ripe, the pungent scent of Old Spice hung in the air as he walked up the steps leading to their apartment building. His greasy, slicked-back hair glistened as he knocked on the front door. Two-Fingers was sitting out on the porch with me when he suddenly yelled out,

"Don't try anything with my sister, Stan, or I'll kick your ass." Stan briefly glanced at Two-Fingers and said, "Yeah, I'll keep that in mind."

"You better," Two-Fingers said in a not-too-subtle tone. Stan looked over at me, and all I could do was shrug my shoulders and grin. Two-Fingers always had to have the last word.

While Stan was inside picking up Paula, Two-Fingers and I sat outside and surveyed the scene. There was a lot going on in Browning that night. I swear I heard hearts breaking.

Stan was in the Schwartz's place for what seemed to be a long time. Finally, he and Paula made their escape and, as Stan held the car door open for her, she glanced up at Two-Fingers and smiled. I remember staring at her with my mouth open; it was the first time I had seen Paula wearing a dress, and her nylon stockings seemed to run on forever. Her perfume was intoxicating and banished the Old Spice smell to the hell it deserved. Her jet-black hair was pulled back, accentuating her high cheekbones, and the only makeup she wore was a touch of red lipstick that glistened in the setting sunlight. Stan stood patiently by the passenger door waiting for her, and as she sat down, I was able to briefly glimpse the top of her nylon stockings before falling off the porch and chipping my tooth.

As Stan and Paula prepared to drive off, Two-Fingers yelled, "Don't forget what I told you, Stan."

"Okay, little man, I won't forget." Stan smiled and then gave us both the finger. The '57 Chevy took off in a cloud of dust with Fats Domino blaring on the radio, "Blue Monday, oh how I love Blue Monday..."

"Little man? Who the hell is he calling little man?" Two-Fingers asked as he stood up and shook his fist in an act of defiance.

"Hey, he's gone. You don't have to get the last word in with me." I said as I haltingly climbed back up the steps to my perch.

Not long after their exit, Cindy Ann came running out the front door and past us when her boyfriend, Stogie Man, pulled up to the curb and honked his horn. Stogie Man was the captain of the basketball team, and he got his nickname because he had smoked Camel cigarettes since he was ten years old, hence the name. He was a great basketball player, but by the fourth quarter, he always seemed to run out of gas. That issue hadn't stopped Montana State University from offering him a full-ride scholarship to play basketball on the condition that he quit smoking. Everybody was keeping their fingers crossed.

Stogie Man and Cindy Ann were planning on getting married before they left for college. Of course, Stogie Man, being the big man on campus, didn't bother opening the door for Cindy Ann. He was too busy styling his greasy crew cut. Yeah, he was that guy.

Chapter 4
The Descent Begins

At the risk of overstating the obvious, alcoholism is a very bad thing. Alcoholics, no matter where they are, are on their very own reservations; heartache and despair are their boundaries. Being an alcoholic on the reservation is very, very bad but at least there's a lot of company. Eventually, the path is lonely no matter who goes along for the ride. Two-Fingers and I witnessed this firsthand, and as teenagers, we were constantly surrounded by drinking, it was as common as breathing. We both started young, and it took us a long time to shake the habit, too long. Alcohol devastates lives, and after years of drinking, it takes tremendous willpower to quit. To quit, you have to find the power within yourself; nobody can do it for you. There are a lot of good people struggling to get sober. Drinking was a fun thing to do when we were young, but as we grew older, it became a full-time, tedious job.

Two-Fingers and I were always able to get an adult to buy us booze. His sister's friends bought us booze most of the time, if they weren't around, we could always find a wino to get us whatever we wanted. It cost a little more money to have the winos buy it, but that never bothered us. We liked to drink and raise hell, it was our favorite pastime. You can warn somebody about the evil effects of alcohol, but that advice, like most advice, usually falls on deaf ears. People have to learn the hard way. But if you have fallen and are able to find the strength to get up, it opens the world to a whole new reality. Sobriety is a wonderful thing.

Two-Fingers and I turned out to be good, upstanding citizens, but when we were kids, we were wild. I want you to know that because I'm not going to sugarcoat our youth. Well, I am a little bit, because even

I can't adequately describe life on an Indian reservation. Everyone is shaped by their life experience, and they either turn out good or they turn out bad. Two-Fingers and I turned out pretty good, and I'm not really sure why. Of course, "pretty good" is relative.

Two-Fingers' parents' apartment building sat directly across the street from the Business Man's Club. Now, the Business Man's Club was probably the swankiest bar in town back then, but it still didn't have any windows, plenty of booze, just no windows. Anyway, Two-Fingers and I were sitting on the front steps of the apartment building later that summer, bored out of our minds, watching the traffic pass by. So, we decided to get some whiskey and have our own party. We quickly found a wino and got a fifth of Seagrams whiskey. We ended up drinking it all that night and partying until the wee hours of the morning.

I only mention this because the very next day was Friday, July 29, 1968, and the first day of the North American Indian Days Powwow celebration held annually in Browning. The celebration goes on non-stop for ten days and tribes from all over Canada and the United States descend upon Browning to join the festivities. Each year, the celebration kicks off with a big parade, and Indians of all ages participate. Indian regalia, unlike anything I had ever seen, was on display virtually everywhere. I remember watching for the first time as beautifully decorated horses pranced up and down Main Street, ridden by visiting and local riders in full headdress and buckskin clothing. Convertibles with their tops down displayed the lovely Indian girls who were vying for "Miss North American Indian Princess." Indian Days continues to be the Blackfeet's favorite time of year, and ironically, mine too.

Two-Fingers and I were at our usual resting place on his front porch, taking it all in. We were nursing monster hangovers, and I wasn't sure if I was going to survive. I had already thrown up twice, and Two-Fingers looked a little green around the gills. Of course, he didn't admit he was feeling poorly, not his style.

As the floats streamed by, tourists standing on the side of the road took pictures and clapped their hands like trained seals. The sun was high in the sky, and it was downright hot, painfully hot. While we sat there trying not to melt, we noticed Kenny and Ronnie Joe Stabs-in-the-Back walking down the street with their cousins, Babe and Smiley Black Weasel. They were all dressed up in their best Levi jeans and cowboy shirts; their boots were shined, their hair slicked back, and they reeked of Old Spice. They stopped on the sidewalk in front of us and watched as the parade passed by.

Before long, the float carrying the reigning "Miss North America Indian Princess," Miss Cindy Ann Schwartz, pulled into view, and that's when Kenny yelled out, "They have to get rid of her because she's no longer a maiden."

"Stogie Man saw to that!" Ronnie Joe yelled out.

"Yeah, shit, I hear they got to get married." Babe Black Weasel screamed.

"I'd marry her too if she let me have some of that." Smiley Black Weasel yelled.

After listening to all the crap he was going to, Two-Fingers stood up and slowly walked over to their fence and motioned for the gang to come closer, and they did so gladly. By that time, Two-Fingers was no longer green; he had turned a bright red, and he had this strange, faraway look in his eyes. Kenny began to roll up the sleeves of his cowboy shirt. Ronnie Joe was glaring at me, and the Black Weasel boys were lined up between the Stabs-in-the-Backs, all leaning over the fence.

Two-Fingers, seemingly filled with rage, began to vomit. He blew huge chunks of puke all over them, stream after stream of vile, greenish-yellow vomit gushed from his mouth and splattered their fancy clothes and boots. Their hair was no longer slicked back; instead, it hung down below their eyes as the slimy bile dripped off them before gathering on the sidewalk, where it formed a septic pool. At that point, I was no longer able to control myself, so I joined the attack, and the remaining fluid in my body spilled out over my lips and onto Ronnie Joe. Soon, a large crowd of tourists gathered and started taking pictures. Kenny and his gang were desperately trying to climb over the fence, but they were unable to gain the necessary footing, the sidewalk was slicker than they were.

I still remember the look of hatred in their eyes. They seemed to be in a trance fueled by that hatred. They suddenly quit trying to get over the fence when they became aware of the crowd, it had grown in size and was very loud and pushy. The gang couldn't stand the vomit, but they hated the laughter even more. So, they gave up and sulked off. I remember thinking that the next time we met them, all hell was going to break loose.

Later that day, after we had finished our chores, Two-Fingers and I went to the fairgrounds to scope out the scene and watch the festivities. The fairground was filled with hundreds of teepees. Tents were plentiful too, but the primary lodging was teepees. Tall, majestic teepees stood in an act of defiance against modernization and the death of their freedom, true freedom. It was a good day to be Indian.

A number of Two-Fingers' relatives were busy setting up their teepees, so there were plenty of places to stay. Even if there were no blood relatives with teepees or tents, during Indian Days, all Indians are "related." Finding a place to sleep or something to eat is never an issue. In addition to that, there were concession stands selling Indian tacos, ice cones, corn dogs, hot dogs, hamburgers, bison burgers, and cotton candy. Plus, each campsite had something cooking over an open fire pit. No carnival rides were allowed, nothing mechanical.

Indian Days are all about the traditions of the past, which include a lot of dancing, stick games, and singing, several days of being Indian.

I ate my first Indian taco at that celebration and haven't turned back since. Indian tacos are made of fry bread and pinto beans, cheap, easy to make, and very tasty. The key is the bread dough, which is deep-fried in grease. Then pinto beans are strategically placed over the fry bread, thereby finishing the creation of Indian tacos. Commodity beans, of course; the reservation was never short of commodities, and when you subsist on commodities you have to be creative in planning your menu. Indian tacos are a result of that creativity. Two-Fingers and I gorged ourselves on Indian tacos and pop, we needed to replace all the fluids we had spewed on the gang. After we ate, we walked around the encampment, taking in all the sights and sounds.

In the cool of the evening, we ran into two pretty blondes about our age who turned out to be sisters. We literally ran into them. We were looking around and not paying close attention to where we were going when we nearly knocked them over. They too were drinking pop, and it spilled all over their blouses. We apologized and offered to buy them more pop, and to my surprise, they said okay. They both stared at Two-Fingers and looked away after discovering his left hand. They introduced themselves and told us how exciting it was to be at a real-life, authentic Indian celebration. Their names were Samantha and Lisa, and after some small talk, they asked us if we would show them around, and we quickly agreed.

As darkness approached, the encampment took on a solemn, peaceful mood after the frenzy of activity earlier in the day. Serenity was, and is, an unusual thing to find on the reservation, but that night was very serene. Campfires filled with dried wood roared to life, and the flames had a mesmerizing effect on us. Watching flames in a campfire is truly serene and relaxing. We watched as children darted in and out of the many hiding places, playing cowboys and Indians, and the Indians were having a very good night; no additional lands lost and very few casualties.

Large canvas tents were filled with blackjack players, mostly old women with a tight grip on the cards and an even tighter grip on their money. Men were playing stick games at a frantic pace. The "bones" were hidden, and wagers were placed on who had the "bones." Piles of money lay at their feet, and soon the gambling took on a serious and ominous tone. Who had the "bones"? Stick games, poker, blackjack, you name it, they bet on it. The Blackfeet love to gamble, and we took it all in as we walked.

As I reflect back on that night, I now realize how important Indian celebrations like these are to the Blackfeet. For a very brief time, they are once again free from government control. They share their innermost beliefs during these celebrations. In modern vernacular, they let it all hang out. They were happy to display parts of their culture, and the tourists were enamored with their storytelling and hospitality. Young and old, rich and poor, white and red, all mingled together and shared time without concern for their station in life. The essence of these celebrations was absorbed into the very souls of those willing to embrace the beauty of it all; worries were swept away, and the rejuvenation of the spirit took center stage for a brief, shining moment. The Blackfeet were the stars that night. I have often thought, was this the way it was before the white man? Was life this beautiful in the days before the credit card and the house payment? Was life ever going to be this good again? Freedom, once highly sought after, has become an elusive commodity. Commodities, handouts from the rich to the poor to help ease their conscience, were received by the downtrodden and never appreciated because they were not earned.

Reservation life is a misery because of a lack of self-worth. White society's idea of achievement and the Indian way of looking at things are at opposite ends of the spectrum. Human frustration is directly related to the chasing of trinkets. Hell, even the Indians on Long Island gave up their land and souls for twenty-six dollars' worth of trinkets, why not? Humanity is giving up a lot more for a lot less. We are losing individual freedoms daily, and very few people seem to care. Anyway, I became a lot more "Indian" that night.

Teepee crawling on the reservation is the Blackfeet's version of musical chairs, without the chairs. The Blackfeet are not certain when teepee crawling first took hold in their culture, but they are glad it did. Something about a teepee causes the Blackfeet to get horny, no wonder they are always camping. The key to teepee crawling is knowing whose teepee you're crawling into. Pick the wrong teepee, and you can get your ass whipped, or shot. Always try to find a willing, unattached person and hope like hell you don't get trampled. Sex on the reservation is more of an adventure than one might think.

"Have you girls ever been inside a real warrior's teepee?" Two-Fingers asked as he pulled back the flap of his parents' teepee.

"Yeah, this will be our third one this month," Samantha said as she lowered her head and entered.

Lisa giggled and followed her.

"Nice to see you white girls have a good sense of humor," Two-Fingers replied.

"Who says I'm kidding?" Samantha said before leaning forward and kissing Two-Fingers on the lips.

Two-Fingers seemed momentarily caught off guard but quickly figured it out. Samantha was breathing hard, and I was concerned she might have emphysema. One of my grandmothers had died from it, just saying. Lisa turned her eyes away and quickly stepped outside. I followed her out when Two-Fingers asked, "Hey, White Guy, why don't you get yourself a corn dog?"

"Samantha has always been boy crazy," Lisa said as we walked to the nearest corn dog stand.

As we stood there enjoying our corn dogs and pop, Kenny and Ronnie Joe Stabs-in-the-Back suddenly appeared with their groupie cousins, Babe and Smiley Black Weasel.

"Hey, White Guy, what are you doing with my girlfriend?" Ronnie Joe yelled at the top of his lungs.

To this day, I'm not sure why Ronnie Joe was always yelling. I do know this: when you add a pretty girl into an already volatile situation, bad things tend to happen. Dip shits who think they're tough are always trying to impress females. They always try to make themselves look good in their eyes, when the truth is, girls think they're even bigger dip shits for always fighting and carrying on.

Ronnie Joe walked over to Lisa and took a bite out of her corn dog. Lisa stared at him for a brief moment before she threw her pop at him and kicked him in the knee. Ronnie Joe retaliated by hitting me square in the chest, right above my heart. I was temporarily winded and fell to the ground in agony. Kenny, Babe, and Smiley quickly stepped in and took turns kicking me in the head with their puke-stained boots, and nobody stepped in to break up the "fight."

As it turned out, Lisa had run off to find Two-Fingers when I was attacked. I was on the ground in a state of semi-consciousness, and I vaguely remember Two-Fingers showing up with a rock in his hand before he jumped into the fight and started using it. He hit Kenny squarely in the eye; Kenny shrieked in pain and fell to the ground next to me, covering his face as blood poured from his wound. Two-Fingers turned on Ronnie Joe and threw the rock at him with enough force to tear a hole in his cheekbone, and blood flew everywhere. Ronnie Joe, Babe, and Smiley turned and ran away, leaving Kenny and a pool of blood behind.

I vaguely remember Two-Fingers leaning over me, but I couldn't make out what he was saying. I wasn't hearing very well because blood was flowing into my left ear, and I certainly wasn't comprehending much. He helped me to my feet, and it was excruciatingly painful to stand. But stand I did, wobbling on shaky legs and looking for help before a couple of tribal policemen finally appeared and pranced through the assembled crowd like liberators.

"What the hell is going on here? Fighting over weenies?" Smiley Heavy Runner asked. Smiley was known as the smart-ass of smart-asses on the reservation; nobody ever called him that to his face because he was always armed and dangerous. Corn Dog Man wasn't compelled to step in and stop the attack, but he was all too eager to tell the cops about it. The tribal policemen showed a surprisingly profound lack of interest in details. I suspect they were more concerned with getting things straightened out as soon as possible so they could make a triumphant return to the stick games.

They took their time assisting Kenny, who lay curled up on the ground in a fetal position with his hands still covering his face. Even in my diminished state, I could tell Kenny was bleeding like a stuck hog and appeared to be blacking out. Officer Heavy Runner forcibly removed his hands from his face and seemed startled by what he saw. Kenny's left eye was gouged out of the socket and was hanging precariously against his cheek The crowd let out a loud gasp as they pushed their way forward for a better look.

Officer Heavy Runner seemed to realize that the situation required serious action and asked, "Who did this?" Two-Fingers continued to hold onto me so I wouldn't fall as he tried to explain what he knew. The other officer, Sassy Mad Plume, took a closer look at me and decided it was time to send for an ambulance.

Officer Mad Plume used his radio to call the Blackfeet Health Center, and soon an ambulance arrived.

"That was quick." Officer Mad Plume said to the driver as he stepped out of the ambulance.

"Yeah, I was parked over by the rodeo grounds waiting for customers," the driver said as he pulled out a couple of stretchers.

Without any further fanfare, they loaded Kenny and me onto stretchers and put us in the back of the ambulance together. Before the rear doors closed, Two-Fingers jumped in and rode with me all the way to Cut Bank. Before we left town, Kenny was dropped off at the Blackfeet Health Center, no whites allowed.

Chapter 5
Boarding School Trauma

After spending two weeks in the white man's hospital in Cut Bank, I was finally released. They treated me for several injuries, but the most serious and lasting was the injury to my left ear. I've lost hearing in that ear, but I figure that's not too bad considering Kenny Stabs-in-the-Back lost his left eye and still walks around with a stained, ill-fitting black eyepatch he seemingly never washes.

The drive back home from the hospital with Mom, Dad, and Stan made me yearn for a couple more days of hospital food. They were really quiet at first, eerily quiet. Mom was upset with the old man, and she eventually started to unload on him; she wouldn't let it go. Quiet turned into noisy real fast. Stan told me he had been in three separate fights with relatives of the gang and wanted more. When I asked about Two-Fingers, I was told he had been sent off to an Indian boarding school in South Dakota. When I asked why, Mom said she spoke to Pam about it, and Pam thought it was the safest place for her son. Evidently, the Stabs-in-the-Backs sought revenge for the loss of their son's eye. Pam thought it was best to have him someplace safe until things cooled down. As I mentioned earlier, Pam was educated at an Indian boarding school, and she thought Two-Fingers could use some guidance and discipline. She told my mom the two of us had been pretty wild that summer and the change would do us both good.

I'm not sure what hurt the most: the pain in my ear, the hearing I lost, or my best friend leaving town for who knew how long. For the first time since all this happened, after all the pain I suffered, I found myself on the verge of tears. Years later, when we finally met up again, Two-Fingers told me all about leaving town and what he thought of his boarding school experience.

As it turned out, crying was the last thing on Two-Fingers' mind while he traveled on the Great Northern train from Browning to Pierre, South Dakota. He was angry, confused, and disillusioned. Being uprooted from his friends and family was the worst punishment imaginable. He heard his parents' explanation and knew they meant well, yet his anger was unrelenting. He was headed to a strange town, a strange school, and his melancholy grew with each passing mile. Still, tears were the last thing on his mind.

The Pierre Boarding School was one of over a hundred boarding schools established for Indian children since 1905. Initially, boarding schools were viewed as important instruments used by the federal government to assimilate young Indian boys and girls into white society. The intent was to throw away Indian culture, values, and identities and replace them with non-Indian beliefs. The power structure wanted to make sure it was no longer a good day to be Indian.

Pam, along with many of her generation and the generations dating back to the turn of the century, was assimilated in this manner, uprooted from friends and family and sent off to an Indian boarding school where they were taught the white way of doing things by white teachers, disciplined by white teachers, and denied their birthright by white teachers. They spent the school year at the boarding schools and returned home for the summer. Back home, they lived in the Indian world for three months and then shipped back to the boarding schools. On the train trips back and forth, the Indian side passed the white side, and they wondered why they were confused about who the hell they were.

In the late 1960s, sociologists and other learned professionals began to understand that this was a very harmful practice, and attempts were made to encourage Indians to be more aware and respectful of their heritage and culture. Too late, generations of Indians were lost to this problem, and only a few survived without any lasting emotional damage. Pam was one of the lucky ones. Two-Fingers survived it too, but he never thought luck had much to do with it.

To my knowledge, I was the only person he truly confided in about his experience there. In fact, he talked to me so much about his time away that somewhere along the line, I began to think I went with him. The letters he wrote were filled with what he thought of boarding schools. From what he could tell, boarding schools were a lot like prisons, some better than others, but all bad. Boarding schools in the 1960s were little more than detention centers for the troubled and the troubling. Two-Fingers was neither, but he was the only one at school who seemed to know that.

According to Two-Fingers, the vicious and overbearing headmaster at the Pierre Boarding School was a white guy named John Wiseman. He had been in that position for 28 years by the time Two-Fingers showed up. Evidently, he reminded all the Indians of this every day, hoping they would succumb to his power and kiss his ring. According to Two-Fingers, Wiseman never got emotional over the plight of the "inmates." He remained aloof and isolated from their emotional needs. He believed in the old teaching methods for Indians, who he felt needed to forgo their culture and enter the white world at all costs. He provided them with the essentials of life, food, shelter, clothing, and a large dose of discipline for good measure. All new students reported directly to Mr. Wiseman upon arrival.

Two-Fingers said he sat in the waiting area outside of Mr. Wiseman's office fidgeting with his shirt collar while trying to remain cool, or so he said. He softly whistled while he waited, and was about to get up and use the bathroom when the office door suddenly opened and out walked Mr. Wiseman. It had to be him, Two-Fingers thought. Nobody else could've been that arrogant. Mr. Wiseman immediately walked up to Two-Fingers and asked why he was whistling. Two-Fingers shrugged and didn't say a word.

"There will be no whistling at the Pierre Boarding School." Mr. Wiseman said as he led him into the office. He closed the door behind them and quickly launched into an interrogation.

"What's your name?"

"My name is Donny R. Schwartz," Two-Fingers replied.

"Are you German?" Mr. Wiseman asked.

"Blackfeet."

Two-Fingers told me Mr. Wiseman was standing so close, he could smell his breath. "We do not get a lot of Blackfeet here. We get a lot of Sioux, Crow, Arapaho, and Northern Cheyenne, not too many Blackfeet." Then he noticed Two-Fingers' deformed left hand. "What happened to your hand?"

"I was trimming my fingernails and I got carried away."

According to Two-Fingers, Mr. Wiseman's face turned a bright crimson red, and he didn't speak for a minute or two. When he finally spoke, he said, "Is that so? Well, Donny..."

"My friends call me Two-Fingers." He took a chance at interrupting the headmaster.

"I see. Well, Donny, as I was saying, you and I will get along fine as long as you study hard and follow the rules. I am firm, but I believe I am fair. You have been assigned to Building E-5, where you will find a bed and a place to clean up. You may go now, and remember what I said about following the rules, and we will get along fine."

Two-Fingers said they had a list of rules longer than his arm. Initially, Two-Fingers tried to be a good little apple and follow them to the letter, but that didn't last long.

Two-Fingers rarely spoke of the mistreatment he received at boarding school, and he never wrote to me about it. I learned about it at a time when he was reliving his past in order to shape a better future. When he spoke, he talked about a large paddle used for whipping. It had large holes punched into the wood for added effect, and a large steel ruler with a sharp edge, used indiscriminately on anyone who spoke out or disobeyed. Both of those instruments of pain were used on him. But, unlike the other victims, he was never beaten with the ruler flat against the skin. He was beaten with the sharp edge of the ruler on his deformed left hand. The large whipping paddles with holes cut into them were used on his ass with such force that they broke off at the handle several times, and Two-Fingers was forced to make replacements in his wood shop class.

To say he was picked on is an understatement. True to his character, Two-Fingers found himself in constant trouble because he hated the way his Indian classmates were treated, and he routinely voiced his displeasure. He never capitulated to the terror that was his life, and he maintained his honor and his self-reliance to the very end. I've always suspected he never told me the full story of the abuse he endured. Some things need to be hidden away in a very dark place for as long as possible. Sunlight isn't always the best disinfectant.

He suffered through the abuse without complaint and, in an act of defiance aimed at his parents, he didn't return home to visit during the summer months. Those months were spent working for a local veterinarian who came to the boarding school one day looking for an Indian boy he could help. Two-Fingers was chosen when the veterinarian noticed his damaged left hand. He ended up spending a lot of time working with animals and with the veterinarian himself. The veterinarian and his wife were very kind to him, and Two-Fingers reciprocated that kindness. They didn't have children of their own, and they spoiled Two-Fingers rotten. They inadvertently helped him heal from the abuse he suffered, and he repaid them by filling a void in their lives.

For my part, after Two-Fingers left Browning for boarding school, life became even more surreal for me, if that was possible. Physically, aside from occasional headaches and difficulty hearing, I was fine. I kept busy with my paper route, worked at our gas station, and mostly kept to myself. That routine briefly changed when I attended Stogie Man and Cindy Ann's wedding. I remember it being very well attended, and the reception at the American Legion Hall was a lot of fun.

Browning bars are a lot like its theater, no frills and even less toilet paper. The American Legion Hall was selected to host the reception because it had a big dance floor and plenty of seating. The other bars in town, the War Bonnet, Paradise Bar, Oasis Bar, Aubert's, Napi's, and the Business Man's Club, were all rejected because of their limited seating capacity. Even so, none of the bars in town could have passed a fire department seating capacity inspection. Then again, nobody went to the bars for fire; they went to put their fires out.

For years, Browning and the other towns on the reservation were "dry." No alcohol was allowed because the authorities firmly believed that Indians had a unique blood configuration that caused them to have a drinking problem, and white society was going to help them by not allowing the lawful sale of alcohol anywhere on the reservation. That decision worked about as well on the reservation as Prohibition worked in white society. Bootleggers sprang up virtually everywhere, and car wrecks caused by "runs" to towns off the reservation occurred daily. Deaths mounted at an astounding pace until the powers that be decided to allow alcohol sales on the reservation. That didn't stop the carnage; it isolated it to the reservation. Bootleggers were still plentiful, and they attracted the after-hours crowd.

The American Legion was one of the first bars built on the reservation after alcohol sales were permitted. The idea behind that decision was based on a desire to provide a place for all veterans of war and their families to come and socialize. Well, everybody is "related" on the reservation, so the doors were virtually wide open from day one. The Blackfeet have a long and distinguished record of serving admirably in foreign wars, as do most American Indian tribes. However, there are more Blackfeet casualties at the Legion on a weekend than there were in all of World War II. Anyway, Stan and Paula kept me in beer, and I had a very good time. Someone even rode a horse onto the dance floor before being thrown out after the horse crapped all over the place. Everyone agreed that was a shitty thing to do, but the Blackfeet never let a little horse shit get in the way of a good time.

Chapter 6
One Leaves and One Returns

Subtle changes had taken place on the reservation during the time Two-Fingers was gone. The war in Vietnam picked up steam, and a number of Blackfeet were drafted, with more being drafted monthly. There were no college deferrals for the Blackfeet and certainly no preferential treatment. Few Blackfeet went away to school because they didn't do well when they attended college. Usually, they got homesick and returned home before one semester was completed. That's how it had been for years. Some of the best basketball players in Montana are Blackfeet. Certainly, the best long-distance runners are Blackfeet. Yet, even when they went away to college on full-ride scholarships, they never stayed gone. Evidently, college life didn't provide the necessary support system for the Blackfeet. There's a certain beauty in loving your friends and family so much that you can't stand being away from them for an extended period of time. Or, perhaps the pressures of white society were more than they could handle. Prejudice and racism are dreadful emotions that cause damage to the people displaying them and to those on the receiving end. No good comes from either.

Being drafted, now that was a whole different matter. If a Blackfeet man was drafted, he would leave home and serve his country. No running off to Canada, even though it was only a few miles away and there were plenty of Canadian relatives up there. No draft dodgers on the reservation, that was an act of cowardice that would not be tolerated. The Blackfeet were still warriors; that virtue hadn't been pounded out of them.

During September of 1968, the green Army bus from Helena arrived way too often in Browning to pick up the draftees.

Unfortunately, on one of those days, it arrived to pick up an unexpected passenger, my brother Stan. Stan planned to catch a ride down to Helena and enlist.

"What the hell do you mean you want to enlist?" Dad was physically shaking when he asked Stan that question.

"It's what I want to do," Stan replied.

The three of us were standing inside the gas station drinking coffee. Stan had already confided his intentions to me the night of the wedding, and I had hoped he would change his mind. That didn't happen. Once he made up his mind to do something, nobody was going to change his way of thinking, nobody.

"Son, war is a terrible thing, and make no mistake, we are at war. Young kids are getting maimed and killed over in Vietnam, and the whole thing is senseless," Dad said, shaking his head.

Old soldiers appreciate the gravity of war and know there is no glamour in it.

"I need to get away from here, Pop. I need to do something with my life, and I don't want to go to college. I've made up my mind," Stan said as he looked Dad squarely in the eyes.

"What about Paula? What does she think about all this?" Dad asked.

"She really doesn't understand it either, Pop. I thought you, of all people, would understand," Stan said as he gazed down at his boots.

"Son, war is total bullshit. Trust me on this," Dad said. He was losing the battle, and he knew it.

"Have you told your mother?"

"Not yet. I thought we would tell her together," Stan said.

"Your mother has been through so much since we moved here.

This will break her heart," Dad said quietly.

"You are both going to have to understand this is something I have to do. I'll be fine. I probably won't even go to Vietnam," Stan said.

After Mom was told what Stan planned to do, she went to her bedroom, locked the door, and cried for most of the night. We could hear her through the thin walls of our living quarters. Stan couldn't take much of it, so he went downtown. I went to pump gas and sell candy, and Dad went to the tire shop and got piss-limber.

The next morning, Mom wore a brave face as she prepared Stan's breakfast and a sack lunch for the long trip to Helena.

"You make sure you write me as often as you can, Stan," Mom said as she served him ham and eggs.

I was seated next to him, and she didn't seem to notice me. I figured my breakfast could wait, so I sat there sipping coffee. Dad got up from the table and hurried out to the tire shop.

The green Army bus was already parked in the lot of the Bureau of Indian Affairs (BIA) complex when we drove up. Stan said his goodbyes and quickly boarded the bus, grabbing a window seat before waving bravely to Mom, Dad, and me. Soon, the last of the passengers were seated, and the trip to Helena began. The bus pulled away slowly with hazard lights flashing before picking up speed as it drove toward Main Street. We followed closely behind in the '57 Chevy.

The bus slowed down as it passed over the cattle guards that separate the Government Square from the rest of town. When it did, it created a heavy clunking sound that interrupted the silence of the solemn moment.

As the bus traveled down Main Street, the winos sitting on window ledges in the shade of the buildings slowly rose and offered weak salutes to the passengers before returning to their bottles of wine, which they held to their chests in brown paper sacks. The bus gained speed after turning onto the main road to Helena and quickly disappeared from view. The draftees and volunteers left for their physicals, and if they passed, they would be shipped off to boot camp. Stan had no trouble passing the physical.

I was lonely after Stan and Two-Fingers left, and a lot of the joy in my life left with them. I spent more time working at the station than I had before. I worked every weekend and after school, pumping gas when I wasn't delivering my papers. Business was still pretty good back then. Our four-unit motel was always full regardless of the time of year. It's funny how some of the prominent, married male citizens always needed a room for the weekend. I would rent them a room, and when I looked out the window to see who they were with, it was never their wives. I kept their secrets, and the old guys trusted me and appreciated my silence. I learned early on the importance of keeping secrets. What the old guys didn't know was that I kept their wives' secrets too.

School was fine. After the incident where I was jumped and had my ear damaged, the Blackfeet backed off and left me alone. In fact, they had shunned the Stabs-in-the-Backs and the Black Weasels. They viewed what they did to me as an act of cowardice, and only their closest relatives would have anything to do with them. Don't get me wrong, I had friends and did things, but it wasn't the same.

Stan and Two-Fingers wrote sparingly, and I was just as bad. Every time I sat down to write, I would start feeling lonesome, so before long I quit altogether. Staring out the windows of the station as the months passed gave me time to reflect on how much my life had changed since we moved to the reservation. I did a lot of reflecting on slow, snowy nights.

Sweeping changes had taken place all across the United States in the late sixties and early seventies, and they weren't subtle changes. The war in Vietnam escalated, the anti-war movement took center stage, and President Lyndon B. Johnson decided not to seek reelection. Richard Nixon was elected on the promise that he would bring an honorable end to the war. Social unrest bordering on anarchy became the order of the day, everybody seemed to be marching and protesting something. The pace of change quickened on the reservation during this time, too. It's still uncertain to me whether these changes were a by-product of the broader national upheaval or the result of internal, reservation-specific pressures. Whatever the reason, dramatic social changes intensified both on and off the reservation.

I do know this much: the younger Blackfeet began challenging the status quo, and Blackfeet veterans returning from Vietnam were, in large part, the catalyst for that change. They had seen firsthand the insanity of war, and they were deeply affected by it. Far too many of their fellow Blackfeet were shipped home in body bags, and the reservation cemeteries began to fill at an alarming rate. The returning warriors understood that war was sometimes necessary, but 'Nam was an unnecessary war. Many Blackfeet, some who had never been more than a hundred miles from the reservation, sought change too. They became increasingly aware of the deprivation that existed on the reservation and wanted a better life. They sought change. They wanted to run their own affairs without the help of the white man, and the local white business owners began to feel the pressure. Blackfeet tribal members started operating businesses, which had a negative economic impact on white business owners, and my family suffered with them.

The Blackfeet turned away from white-owned businesses and began doing business exclusively with other Blackfeet, slowly forcing white businessmen out. They were replaced with inexperienced Blackfeet businessmen, which caused an even greater economic backlash on the reservation because that generation of Blackfeet businessmen was not particularly skilled at running their own operations; they lacked experience and know-how. Credit was extended to friends and relatives, and in most cases, it was never repaid.

Grants and loans from the federal government were needed to prop up these ailing businesses, and the economic situation worsened with each passing day. Government funding helped perpetuate the demise of the capitalistic system and created a socialist, "Don't worry about failing because we'll bail you out," attitude that inevitably led to ruin. Thankfully, the tourist trade kept us in business because tourists stopped at well-kept stations, and our Chevron station was very well maintained. Other white-owned businesses were not as fortunate.

During the two-year period Two-Fingers was gone, I too experienced changes in both my physical appearance and my mental state. I grew to six feet tall and about one hundred eighty pounds. The extra weight was a direct result of all the fry bread I was given when I delivered my papers. I wouldn't say I was handsome or anything, but I did get my fair share of attention from the girls at school. I had all my teeth, and everything worked except my left ear. However, I was no longer the carefree kid I had been before Two-Fingers and Stan left. I hardened myself to the inevitability of the situation I was in, a situation I had little or no control over. Deprivation of spirit and soul surrounded me, and I steeled myself against it and matured. Perception of life is different for all of us. Look for the good in things, and your chances of finding it are greatly enhanced. Accept the realities of unavoidable hardships and address the issues they create head-on. Maturity has a way of sneaking up on you.

Two-Fingers, as it turned out, grew and matured a lot, too. I could tell from the letters he wrote me. His last letters were more serious and contemplative than the earlier ones. In them, he told me he had withstood the onslaught of change that was forced upon him and had prospered from it. Doesn't that sound like maturity?

According to him, he was very popular with the other students. Even the staff and Mr. Wiseman eventually backed off the smart-ass Blackfeet Indian from Browning, Montana. Two-Fingers loved working for the veterinarian and had second thoughts about leaving South Dakota and returning to Browning for his senior year of high school, but he put those thoughts behind him and came home. It took him far too long to get over his feelings of betrayal and abandonment. Once he decided to return home, he acted quickly, and so did his parents. They wired him fifty dollars for train fare and incidentals. Two-Fingers was eager to get home, but the allure of one last poker game got the better of him, and he ended up losing all but seven dollars. He had no choice but to hitchhike home.

According to Two-Fingers, the veterinarian and his wife insisted on giving him a ride to the I-90 on-ramp not far from the boarding school. He said he had second thoughts about leaving them, so once they arrived at the on-ramp, he quickly said goodbye and walked away without looking back. It was hard to leave, but there was no sense getting mushy about it.

Most of his worldly possessions were stuffed into a big, worn-out suitcase that he half-dragged down the freeway while cars passed him by. He said he sat on that suitcase a lot that first day and was sitting on it when a shiny new 1970 Chevy El Camino raced past him. The driver suddenly slammed on his brakes, stopped, and then backed up to where Two-Fingers was sitting. He initially hesitated when he was offered a ride because, as desperate as he was for one, he wasn't sure he wanted to ride with the redneck, crew-cut-looking dude driving the El Camino. That hesitation faded quickly when he looked around and didn't see another car in sight. When he first told me this story, I figured the redneck probably had second thoughts about offering the ride once he got an up-close look at Two-Fingers. His hair was shoulder-length, and he looked very much like an Indian.

Once they agreed on the traveling arrangements the driver opened the lid covering the back of the El Camino, and Two-Fingers squeezed his suitcase into the only space available. He noticed the El Camino was packed full of stuff; he was barely able to get his suitcase to fit. They drove a long way in complete silence, only glancing at each other occasionally. It was Two-Fingers who broke the ice, and after introductions, the driver, whose name was Bob Richardson, began talking incessantly. Evidently, he was traveling from the Indianapolis 500 and headed to Mount Rushmore for a little sightseeing. From there, he was going home to Davenport, Washington, where he planned to run for mayor.

He had been a lieutenant in the Army who was in charge of unloading the planes at a military base in North Carolina that brought our dead boys back from 'Nam, and after a couple of years of that bullshit, he resigned his commission. He had been a true-blue, righteous military man, a West Point graduate, who became disillusioned by the war and all the carnage he witnessed on a daily basis. The men working under him were always getting stoned on the weed they confiscated from shipments containing the dead bodies, and he always resisted the temptation until one day he took them up on their offer. It changed his way of thinking, and he resigned shortly thereafter.

Two-Fingers decided to take him up on his offer to smoke weed and did so willingly. Soon, he was as high as a kite and talking incessantly too. He told me later on that he was so stoned he thought he had temporarily lost sight in one eye. They continued smoking and exchanging snappy banter all the way to Mount Rushmore, where, after parking in the lot below the visitor center and taking one more hit off Bob's pipe they stumbled out of the El Camino. As they exited, a large cloud of smoke escaped and temporarily blocked out the sun.

Two-Fingers and Bob were standing at the observation deck when Bob decided he wanted to climb up the mountain and get inside Teddy Roosevelt's nose. Of course, the park rangers frowned on such things, so they politely asked Two-Fingers and Bob to vacate the premises. When he was young, Two-Fingers had a way of embellishing things. Only as he aged did he subject all of us to his serious side. His humor eventually gave way to a solemnity reserved for the serious-minded. Age has a way of doing that.

Somewhere along the line, Bob decided to take Two-Fingers to Browning even though it was considerably out of his way. So he drove through the night as Two-Fingers slept. Two-Fingers said he woke up fully rested, he had never slept that soundly in his life. After waking, it took him a while to focus and realize they were in Browning. Bob was driving past our station when Two-Fingers asked him to let him out. Bob pulled off the highway about twenty feet from the station before getting out and stretching.

Two-Fingers said he dug into his pockets and pulled out his last seven dollars, asking Bob if he could buy some of his weed. He said Bob laughed and walked around to the back of the El Camino, opened its cover, and let him look inside one of seven large ice cream canisters stuffed full of opium-soaked pot. Neither one of them had anything to put the pot in, so Two-Fingers told Bob to stay where he was while he went to find something.

Two-Fingers ran to our station, where I was finishing my graveyard shift. He burst through the front door in a panic, and without saying hello, kiss my ass, or anything else, demanded a milk carton. Without a word, I walked into our living quarters, grabbed a half-gallon container of milk, and brought it back to him. He promptly stepped outside, emptied it, and ran off. As I watched him, I couldn't help thinking he had lost his mind.

He returned carrying his suitcase and the milk carton. He dropped his suitcase on the ground next to me, but he held onto the milk carton with both hands, as if it were gold, resting it gently against his chest. All he said was, "I'll tell you all about it later. Let's go."

That was when the old man came out of our living quarters to relieve me. When he saw Two-Fingers standing there with the milk carton pressed against his chest, all he said was, "Would you like some cereal to go along with that?" The three of us stood there talking for a few seconds before Two-Fingers insisted he needed to get going, all the while shielding the milk carton from Dad because it smelled like skunk piss.

The two of us left the scene of the crime and soon found ourselves walking in the general direction of the high school. We were wandering around aimlessly when he asked if I knew where Cindy Ann and Stogie Man were living. I knew exactly where so we immediately started walking in that direction.

By the time Two-Fingers returned home, Stogie Man and Cindy Ann had been living back in Browning for over a year. They had gone off to Bozeman and were excited about Stogie Man playing basketball for the Bobcats of Montana State. He had a full ride and a perfect jump shot. That lasted until the first week of practice, when Stogie Man blew out his left knee. After two surgeries and endless hours of rehabilitation, all he had to show for his athletic prowess was a pronounced limp and a severe drinking problem. He quit school, moved back to Browning, and moved his family into a low rent-house up on Moccasin Flats, where he spent most of his time drinking and reliving his high school glory days.

On our walk to Moccasin Flats, we caught up on what we'd been doing since we last saw each other. He was amazed by all the new duplexes and other types of housing scattered about. During his absence, the federal government had built a number of low-rent houses in Browning. The Blackfeet called these new houses "Easter egg" houses because, like Easter egg dye, they only came in six colors: bright pink, red, blue, purple, green, and yellow. The colors were painted in that order until every house was eventually painted. Cindy Ann and Stogie Man lived in one of those "Easter egg" houses.

When we arrived at their front door, we were greeted by Stogie Man, who yelled, "The things you see when you don't have a gun!" He opened the screen door, which didn't have a screen, and gave Two-Fingers a big hug. He merely looked at me and nodded his head as dispassionately as humanly possible.

Cindy Ann was in the kitchen cooking breakfast when she discovered who was at the front door. She turned to look at Two-Fingers, wiped her hands on her apron, and seemed confused by what she was seeing. Then, in a flash, she ran over, grabbed Two-Fingers, and held him tight before she began crying and squeezing him even harder. She was sobbing, shaking, and cursing simultaneously. Two-Fingers softly stroked her hair before saying, "Sister Girl, Sister Girl, you have to quit squeezing so hard, or my belly button is going to pop out."

Luckily, Two-Fingers had left the milk container on the porch with his suitcase, or it would have been flattened like a pancake.

Cindy Ann finally let him go before yelling in earnest, "Why didn't you let us know when you were coming home?" she asked.

"Didn't you get my smoke signal? Two-Fingers asked while smiling.

"Geez, you're pissy. I'm glad you haven't changed, Cindy Ann said before laughing. Have you seen Mom and Dad yet? Paula is going to kick your ass, little brother."

Cindy Ann grabbed him for another bear hug.

"No, I haven't seen Mom and Dad," he said. "I wanted you to get the first crack at me. Where's Paula?"

"She's up in the Park fighting fire. There's been a bad fire up there, and it's so early in the season. Hopefully, she'll be home soon. I hear the fire is almost out."

Cindy Ann made another move toward Two-Fingers, but he wouldn't have anything more to do with her. "Holy shit, Cindy Ann, give me a break. Hug White Guy for a while."

Cindy Ann turned to me and gave me a big hug, and I'll be honest with you, I didn't mind one bit. In fact, when she tried to break away, I hung on.

"Okay, okay, that's enough, White Guy. What are we going to have to do, hose you down?" Two-Fingers asked, and we all started laughing, all of us except Stogie Man, who had made his way to the couch.

Cindy Ann still looked good, even though she had recently given birth to their second child. She and Stogie Man were the proud parents of two girls.

"Where are my nieces? I want to see my nieces," Two-Fingers said.

"They're still asleep. Let me get them up for you."

Cindy Ann walked to the bedroom in the rear of the house and returned holding their new baby. Their firstborn walked next to her mom holding onto her pant leg with her index finger gently pressed against her lips.

When Two-Fingers started acting goofy trying to make them laugh, the baby fell back asleep, and the firstborn started crying hysterically when she noticed his deformed hand. The more he tried to make her laugh, the harder she cried.

"Two-Fingers, quit scaring my little girl, you ugly bastard," Stogie Man yelled from his perch on the couch where he sat watching TV. "When is breakfast?"

After eating, Stogie Man, Cindy Ann, and the two girls drove to the grocery store to pick up provisions and run errands. After they left, Two-Fingers turned on their oven and found a cookie sheet. He retrieved the milk carton from the porch and spread some of its contents onto the cookie sheet before sliding it into the oven. It took less than a minute for the weed to dry, and when it was ready, he carefully placed it into baggies. He repeated that process until the last batch went into the oven.

Two-Fingers searched for papers, finally finding some in Stogie Man's jacket, and began to roll a joint. I watched closely as he rolled.

"Where did you learn to roll like that?"

"From this old cowboy back in South Dakota. He owned a small ranch and was a client of the vet I worked for. He smoked Bull Durham cigarettes like there was no tomorrow, and he could roll one while riding horseback. No shit, he'd open the Bull Durham bag with his teeth, sprinkle some tobacco in the paper, roll it tight, and never spill a drop. I practiced until I was almost as good," Two-Fingers said.

When the joint was ready, Two-Fingers lit a stick match on his pant zipper. He took a big hit before offering it to me. I'd only smoked pot once before, so I hesitated for a few seconds before taking a hit. When I did, I started choking and gagging, but I refused to give up the joint. Two-Fingers shook his head before rolling his own.

We were both stoned out of our minds when we happened to notice the house was on fire. Well, not the whole house, only the oven. Two-Fingers had forgotten to take the last batch of pot out of the oven, and it was smoking up the place.

"Holy shit," he said as he opened the smoke-filled oven. He blew on the weed, which served to reignite it. Finally, he turned off the oven, grabbed a dish towel, removed the cookie sheet, and set it on top of the stove. The contents continued smoking, so he bent down and started inhaling the smoke with his nose. I struggled to my feet and went over to join him. We kept at it until the weed finally burned itself out.

The first time I got stoned was when Stan came home on leave. I'm not even sure I can call it getting stoned. We smoked this stuff he called "Wyoming Yellow," and the only way I felt anything was by holding my breath for about five minutes and falling over and hitting my head on the floor. I'm not even sure I got a buzz, I think I just got dizzy from not breathing. Either way, the "Wyoming Yellow" was nothing compared to what we smoked that day.

After smoking and inhaling, I was so thirsty I could've spit dust. Luckily, Stogie Man had a six-pack of cold Rainier beer in the refrigerator. I helped myself and handed a can to Two-Fingers. We downed our beers in one long, glorious gulp. We finished off the entire six-pack before realizing the house reeked of marijuana. It smelled like three-day-old cat piss. We were absolutely whacked, and we knew we should do something about the smell, but we couldn't seem to get motivated.

After mustering enough strength to do so, we opened the windows and the front door. That was about as far as we got. Two-Fingers rolled several joints and stuffed them into his coat pockets. Then he put the remaining pot in his suitcase and hid the suitcase under Cindy Ann and Stogie Man's bed for safekeeping.

"Let's go," Two-Fingers said as he walked out the front door. I didn't bother asking him where we were going, it never did any good. For better or worse, spontaneity ruled his life back then. As it turned out, we went to see his parents.

Chapter 7
No Longer Defiant

Two-Fingers' reunion with his parents was a joyous event. They embraced, and the remaining anger inside Two-Fingers was seemingly swept away. They hugged, kissed, and shed tears of joy. While that was going on, I sat on their living room couch and feasted on day-old fry bread and pop. It was my first real experience with the munchies. Two-Fingers smiled and told stories, and his parents had a hard time getting a word in edgewise. Some things never change.

When Two-Fingers finally wore down, his parents spoke about things that had happened on the reservation during his absence. Quite frankly, it wasn't very inspirational. It was mostly a litany of tragic events that had taken place in the two years he had been gone. I knew most of the events, but hearing them again helped to clear my head. Tragedy was an unfortunate way of life on the reservation, and that hadn't changed during Two-Fingers' time away.

Pam cooked a big lunch featuring many of Two-Fingers' favorites. "I missed everything about this place, especially your fry bread, Mom," Two-Fingers said as he worked his way through a second helping. We were seated at the kitchen table, talking nonstop about more pleasant things like family and friends, when Two-Fingers asked to borrow the family car.

"You got a driver's license?" Max asked.

"Since when do you need a driver's license to drive on the reservation?" Two-Fingers asked.

"The cops are really cracking down on things lately. There's been a lot of dope running around here, and the drunks and potheads are getting behind the wheel and getting into accidents. It seems like someone is getting killed every day; the highways on the reservation are littered with crosses. Last week, Ivan Redhead's boys were out joyriding and ran into a telephone pole, and they didn't have a driver's license, so they were thrown into jail. I don't think it's a good idea. Get your license, and then you can drive," Max said.

"Fair enough. We are going to hitchhike to East Glacier." Two-Fingers said as he reached for his Levi jacket.

"Be careful. The Stabs-in-the-Backs are still around," Pam said with a trembling voice and a look of concern etched on her face.

We skipped down their front steps, walked across the street, and stood in front of the Business Man's Club, taking in the sights and sounds of Browning. The winos were in their assigned seating, and they all requested a handout.

"Geez, Rubber Joe, how much money are you taking in these days? Are you paying your income taxes?" Two-Fingers asked as he handed Rubber Joe one of my dollars.

"Ah hell, Two-Fingers, you know them bastards would just buy another bomb or something as useless with it," Rubber Joe said.

Before Rubber Joe began his descent into alcoholism, he was a rancher with a pretty good-sized spread north of town. His house caught fire one day and his two small children burned to death. Shortly thereafter, Rubber Joe lost everything to drink and became one of the town's winos. He was called Rubber Joe because he bounced around aimlessly.

"What about your Auntie, Two-Fingers? Don't forget Auntie," Maggie Stink Pits said as she extended her hand.

Maggie wasn't Two-Fingers' aunt. Maggie didn't have any relatives on the reservation, and nobody was quite sure where she came from. Rumors and speculation swirled around the reservation like wildfires when it came to the winos. At that moment, we didn't know her story either. It was rumored that she was very promiscuous when she was a young woman, the Blackfeet say she sold herself professionally. The story floating around was that she used to pull quite a few tricks during the course of a day, and she was never too concerned about her personal hygiene. Evidently, after servicing ten guys one day, number eleven came in and was going at it real hard, his head buried between her ample breasts, when he suddenly yelled out, "Maggie, your pits stink!"

Gossip smells as bad as Maggie's pits. That's the story, but I don't think anybody knew for sure, nobody except Maggie.

Two-Fingers handed her one of my dollars.

"Bless you, my boy," was all Maggie said as she clutched the wrinkled and worn dollar bill.

We were walking away when Two-Fingers suddenly stopped after noticing another wino passed out on the shady side of the Business Man's Club.

"That, my friend, is the Governor," Two-Fingers whispered. "When I was a little kid, I swiped pennies from my old man and gave them to the Governor here. He used to live in the alley behind our place," Two-Fingers said as he pointed across the street to their apartment building. "I used to sneak him food, too. He was a great athlete back in the 1930s. He told me he was selected for the Olympics and knew Jesse Owens personally. He also told me his parents were killed when a train hit the truck they were riding in. He had qualified for the Olympics, but he never went. Back when I was little, he carried around a small case with medals in it."

Two-Fingers said this as he searched the Governor's coat pockets, looking for the case. Just then, the Governor stirred to life and started to slap at Two-Fingers' hand.

"Leave me alone, leave me alone," the Governor said as he struggled to his feet.

He was rummy-eyed, so it took him a while to recognize Two-Fingers, and when he did, he smiled and said, "Oh, it's you, my boy. I thought you were one of those damn winos trying to roll me again. How are you, my boy?" the Governor asked before stepping forward and giving Two-Fingers a hug.

"I'm fine, Gov. How are you doing? Won any races lately?" Two-Fingers asked.

"Not since I ran you into the ground last year," the Governor said proudly.

"I wasn't around last year Gov. You must be thinking of someone else," Two-Fingers said.

"Well, hell, why don't we give it a try right now?" the Governor asked before assuming a sprinter's stance.

"No, no, not today, I need to train a little more before I'm ready for you, Gov."

Two-Fingers said as he gently brushed dust and ants off the Governor's coat. "I'm sorry I disturbed you. I wanted to show my friend your medals. Do you still have them?" Two-Fingers asked.

"Sure, I have some of them, but I have to hide them. The damn winos are always trying to steal them and sell them for Muscatel wine. You know how it is, Donny R.," the Governor said as he opened his shirt to reveal a worn, paper-thin money belt. He looked around suspiciously before slowly removing a tiny black case from its hiding place.

He gently opened the case and gingerly removed one of two medals, then handed it to Two-Fingers. "I won this gold medal for the mile in 1935 down in California. I was running for my old school, Carlisle, back in those days. You know Carlisle, don't you, Donny R.? That's the school Jim Thorpe went to. I never finished school…" The Governor stared off into the distance with a pained look on his face. "A lot of Indian boys went to Carlisle back then, a lot of good runners. All we did all day long was run. Run to town, run to school, run home, and run away from it all. We were always running," The Governor said as he clutched his other medal.

"When did you win that medal?" Two-Fingers asked as he pointed to the medal the Governor held.

"I won this in high school. It's for the 100-yard dash. I won a lot of races that day. It was the first time my parents were able to see me run competitively. I put on quite a show." The Governor smiled broadly as he once again gazed off into space.

Two-Fingers reached over, took the medal from the Governor, and examined it. It was very old, and the engraving on the back was mostly worn off. We both had a hard time making out the inscription. Finally, the sunlight caught it just right, and we were able to make out the words: "1932-1st Place-100-yd dash."

"I used to have a lot of medals, but I've been rolled so many times that these are the only two left," the Governor said before gathering them up and returning them to their hiding place. "Donny R., I sure could use something to eat. Do you have a dollar I can borrow?" the Governor asked as he extended his hand.

"Sure, Gov," Two-Fingers said as he handed him my five-dollar bill. "I owe you this from last year when you ran me into the ground, remember?"

"Hell yes, I remember! I had you by a good quarter of a mile, Donny R.," the Governor said before he slowly turned and walked into the Business Man's Club.

After the Governor left, we looked around and realized we were the only two people left in front of the Business Man's Club.

"Well, brother, I'd buy you a cold one, but it appears you're running out of money. By the way, how are you situated financially?"

"I have twenty dollars left, but at the rate you are handing it out, we'll be broke before we hit the Junction," I said as we turned and started walking in that direction.

During the summer, the Junction Drive-In is the hot spot in Browning. People cruising Main Street went past the Junction at least a dozen times a day. The Junction sat back from the main highway, allowing for plenty of parking in its gravel lot. As I stated earlier, the Junction still serves the best cheeseburgers in town and the coldest pop, but personally, back then, I liked it because the Junction employed the prettiest carhops.

As we leisurely made our way to the Junction, we were stopped by friends, acquaintances, and other well-wishers. People drove past us and yelled things like, "Nice to see you got out of prison in one piece, Two-Fingers!" "Been real quiet around here since you left, Two-Fingers!" "Two-Fingers, where's the money you owe me?" Half the town seemed to ask that question, and I understood why. Two-Fingers smiled and waved at everybody. He really ate it up.

He turned to me and said, "Should leave town more often."

"Yeah, this is really nice, but you would think one of them sumbitches would give us a ride," I said as we continued walking.

It was a busy afternoon at the Junction. The parking lot was full, and the air was heavy with dust from all the traffic driving on and off the loosely graveled lot. Two-Fingers continued to take his bows while making small talk with as many patrons as he could get to listen. As he moved from car to car, I went inside to get something to drink and was happy to see Vicki Eagle Feathers at the counter waiting for an order. Vicki had been working there the previous two summers as a carhop.

"Hey, Tony, I see your friend has finally made it back. Maybe now you'll quit moping around," Vicki said before walking out the door with the order.

"Moping, I haven't been moping," I said as the screen door slammed into my face.

Two-Fingers had finally finished campaigning and was walking toward the screen door of the Junction. When he opened it, Vicki rushed back inside with another order.

"You're certainly welcome, ma'am," Two-Fingers said as he bowed at the waist.

"Welcome? I'll show you who's welcome," Vicki said as she picked up a fly swatter and smacked Two-Fingers on the arm. "You too good to let anybody know you're coming home? Most people don't give a shit, but some people do," she said as she glanced at me.

"I didn't know you missed me, Vicki, or I would've written, honest," Two-Fingers said as he rubbed his arm.

"You wish I missed you, asshole," Vicki said as she rushed out the door with an order.

"That chick is spoon-fed crazy. Well, enough of this welcome-home horse shit. I've secured a ride to East Glacier for us," Two-Fingers said as he reopened the screen door.

"Who with?" I asked as we walked outside.

"Jimmy B has offered, and I have accepted."

It took me a few seconds to fully digest his response, and when I had, I stopped dead in my tracks. There was no way I was getting into a vehicle with Jimmy B. He was the fastest-driving maniac on the reservation, and it was a miracle he was still alive. To make things worse, he had recently purchased a used black 1969 Chevy Super Sport with the money his dearly departed grandmother had left him. It had a 396-cubic inch engine and four on the floor, and the entire car only weighed about ninety pounds. It was light, and the thing literally flew.

"Two-Fingers, listen to me. You've been gone a long time, and you don't fully understand what you are getting us into. Trust me, you do not want Jimmy B driving you anywhere."

"Who said anything about him driving? Get in the back."

Jimmy B was already sitting in the front passenger seat, smoking a joint. "Now remember, Two-Fingers, keep it under a hundred," Jimmy B said as ashes fell down the front of his shirt.

Two-Fingers fired up the Super Sport, put it in first gear, and looked back at me with a shit eating grin on his face and said, "Are you buckled up?"

Before I could say anything, Two-Fingers put the pedal to the metal, and we spun out of the parking lot and onto Highway 2, leaving a cloud of dust that temporarily hid the Junction from view.

Two-Fingers got rubber in second and then third gear as we rapidly came up behind a Volkswagen van from Iowa. Well, I think it was from Iowa, but at the speed we were going, I wasn't certain. Jimmy B waved at the occupants of the Volkswagen as we flew past. Two-Fingers was holding onto the steering wheel with his left hand while reaching for a joint with his right. The telephone poles along the highway passed at an alarming rate as Two-Fingers reached down and pushed in the cigarette lighter. When it popped out, he placed the hot end on the tip of the joint before handing it back to me.

"You need to learn to relax, White Guy. Haven't you seen Steve McQueen in Bullitt?" Two-Fingers said as he lit up a joint for himself.

"Bullitt? What the hell does that mean?" I asked.

Two-Fingers never answered, but he eventually slowed down once the grass took hold.

Actually, we all mellowed out rather quickly on our drive to East

Glacier. We focused on the sights and sounds of the reservation. Partially clothed children played on top of broken-down cars, cars that were left in front yards with the promise of someday being repaired. Packs of dogs ran wild, and off in the distance, a group of youngsters rode horses bareback across the barren, windswept plains.

"God, how I've missed this place," Two-Fingers said before slipping a Jim Croce tape into the eight-track player.

Thirst had reared its ugly head by the time we reached East Glacier. Jimmy B was selected to get us a case of beer at the Glacier Park Bar. Jimmy B was a recent graduate of Browning High and was an eighteen-year-old who didn't look a day under thirty-five, so much for clean living.

"Shit yeah, I'll go in and get us a case of Rainier. Pull up over there," Jimmy B said as he pointed to a space in front of the Glacier Park Bar.

"You got any money, Two-Fingers?" he asked as he hopped out of his Chevy.

"Let me talk to my banker." Two-Fingers turned to me and held out his hand.

I handed over my last twenty dollars and said, "Make sure you get a receipt."

Two-Fingers and I sat patiently waiting for what seemed like an eternity before deciding to go find out what was keeping Jimmy B. After entering the joint, it took a while for my eyes to adjust to the dimly lit, smoky bar. Once I regained my sight, I was surprised to see how busy it was.

It was around three in the afternoon, and standing room only was already at a premium. Jimmy B stood at the counter, frantically waving at the bartender, who was busy getting change for a couple of pool players. We slowly eased our way through the crowd and made a place to stand next to Jimmy B. As I looked around the place, I noticed a few married women from Browning having drinks with men who were definitely not their husbands. There's no place to hide on the reservation. I noticed Two-Fingers staring at two pretty brunettes who were making selections on the jukebox. Things were pretty civilized, but it was early.

"Hey bartender I'm tired of waiting, I need a case of Rainier," Jimmy B said as he slammed my twenty onto the bar.

"Don't you see I'm busy down here? I'll be with you in a minute," the bartender yelled.

Jimmy B reached into a large bowl of unshelled peanuts and grabbed a handful. He popped a couple into his mouth as the two brunettes nudged their way to the bar and said, "You're in our spots." They stared at us with piercing brown eyes and demanded that we move.

Before Two-Fingers and I could say anything, Jimmy B, with his mouth full of peanut shells, tried to talk, but all he managed to do was spit peanut shells all over the girls. Finally, he swallowed hard, and the remaining shells flushed their way down his dry, parched throat.

"Can we buy you a beer?" Jimmy B said in a raspy voice as he reached over to brush the saliva-soaked shells from the girls' blouses.

"Keep your hands off us and get out of our spots!" one of the brunettes yelled just as the bartender arrived on the scene.

"What can I get you, Bud?" the bartender asked as he wiped spit-soaked peanut shells off the bar.

"A case of Rainier," Jimmy B said as the three of us watched the brunettes turn and walk out the door.

"Damn white women, they think their shit doesn't stink," Jimmy B mumbled.

The bartender returned with a case of Rainier in cans. Since the advent of pop tops in 1963, canned beer had gained a large foothold with the alcohol-consuming public on the reservation. Besides staying cooler longer than bottled beer, it was easier to open; trying to open a bottle of beer with a church key while driving is downright dangerous. Pop tops have been credited with saving hundreds of lives on the reservation.

"Five dollars? What the hell do you mean by five dollars? I don't want to buy the place, I only wanted a case of beer, Bud," Jimmy B said before stuffing my change into his shirt pocket. Every Blackfeet with a cold case of beer and change in his pocket will always try to get the last word in.

The day Two-Fingers returned home from boarding school marked Paula's third full week of firefighting. The Blackfeet are always in demand as fire fighters, they are very good at it. The Vietnam War had depleted the supply of able-bodied young Blackfeet men, so women were getting their first real taste of firefighting.

Paula's crew had been called upon to fight a fire in the Quartz Creek area of Glacier National Park, and after battling the blaze for almost three weeks, they had it pretty well contained. Then it started to rain that night and continued well into the next day. That hard, glorious rain fell and put out all remaining signs of the fire. That meant the crews would be going back to Browning for days of celebration, and the Blackfeet crew needed to put out their personal fires.

Word quickly spread that the fire crews were headed back to Browning. All the bar owners were happy when they came to town. Big John Fisher, the owner of the Oasis Bar, gladly extended credit because he knew that once they were paid, he would be cashing a lot of government checks and selling a lot of liquor. If he wasn't repaid in a timely fashion, he charged serious interest to those who dared to be late with their repayment. Over time, the other bars in town started extending credit on such occasions, but Big John was the first to do so, and that meant his bar got the first crack at the firefighters. The Blackfeet never forget a good deed.

Two-Fingers, Jimmy B, and I were coming off a two-day runner when we found out Paula was down at the Oasis celebrating. Two-Fingers was fired up to see her, but Jimmy B and I were both showing serious signs of wear and tear. So, no matter how much guilt-tripping Two-Fingers put on him, Jimmy B declined the invitation to go with us. I went along, but I insisted on getting food. Besides, I needed to check in with my parents and let them know I was still alive, slightly wounded but alive.

After briefly arguing about it, Two-Fingers finally agreed to get something to eat. So, Jimmy B dropped us at our station so we could re-energize with food and a little rest.

Mom and Dad were very glad to see us. I explained to them that we couldn't stay long, I needed some food and a change of clothes. Mom fixed us big breakfasts, and after I drank several cups of coffee, I was able to catch a second wind. My folks seemed to understand, and they made no effort to stop us. So, after eating, Two-Fingers and I walked the half mile to the Oasis. I remember thinking how good it was to walk and, by the time we got there, I was almost sober.

The front door was slightly ajar when Two-Fingers kicked it wide open and yelled, "Anybody in here kill a bison lately?" A hush fell over the crowd as they looked in our direction.

"Nope? That makes two of us," Two-Fingers said as our eyes adjusted to the smoky, dimly lit bar.

I just now realized something, I spent a good portion of my youth adjusting to dimly lit bars and dimwitted bartenders.

"I see you're still a smart-ass, Two-Fingers," Big John said.

"Still a smart-ass, always a smart-ass, and looking for some ass. Now, get me a beer, Big John, and while you're there, get White Guy a half of one," Two-Fingers said with his back to the door.

"How about I bounce your phony ass out of here," Big John said.

Before any blood was spilled, Paula jumped up from her barstool and ran toward Two-Fingers, and for a split second, I thought she was going to haul off and hit him. Instead, she jumped into his waiting arms. Two-Fingers wobbled backward as he tried to maintain his balance, but he tripped, and they both tumbled to the floor.

"Holy shit, Paula, you've got to lay off the fry bread," Two-Fingers said as he held her in his arms on the peanut-shell, beer and vomit-soaked floor.

"You need to eat more, little brother, you're getting weak," Paula said before tugging on his long hair. "What's this all about? You gone hippie on me?"

"Naw, just defying the dress code I've been subjected to. You know the drill, cut all the Indians' hair off, put them in white shirts, Levi's, and boots, and everything will be all right." Two-Fingers helped her up. "I started to let it grow as soon as I got those white folks thinking right."

"What are you crying about, Two-Fingers?" Bitsy Running Rabbit asked as he walked over and handed Paula a Rainier.

"Crying? I'll show you who will be crying," Two-Fingers said as he started to shadowbox around Bitsy.

Just then, Curly Big Springs came up behind Two-Fingers, wrapped his arms around him, and effortlessly lifted him up and gently shook him.

"Say uncle or I'm going to have to hurt you," Curly said as he continued to shake Two-Fingers.

"I always knew you had a thing for me, Curly," Two-Fingers said when Curly let him go.

"It's because you're so pretty, Two-Fingers," Liquid Louie Arrowtop said as he handed him a beer.

Two-Fingers turned his back to Big John and gulped down half the beer before handing it to me. "White Guy and I have been on a little runner and we need to get our juices flowing. Why don't we get some beer and go swimming at Cut Bank Creek?" he asked the crowd.

"What a great idea, I could use a swim. What about you guys?" Paula asked her crewmates.

"Swimming? I don't know about getting wet, but I wouldn't mind seeing you in a swimsuit," Curly said.

Paula replied sweetly, "Who said anything about a swimsuit?"

That was all it took. After hearing that, the entire bar emptied out, leaving Big John alone with his thoughts and a stack of IOUs.

Two-Fingers, Paula, Curly, Liquid Louie, and I jumped into Bitsy's Volkswagen Bug, and before going to Cut Bank Creek, we made a quick stop at Stogie Man and Cindy Ann's so Two-Fingers could retrieve some of his stash. It was a short fifteen-minute drive to Cut Bank Creek, but it seemed longer as I struggled for space with four of us stacked on top of each other in the back seat of the Bug.

"So, my little brother returns home a pothead," Paula said as she sat on Curly's lap and watched Two-Fingers roll joints.

"Don't tell me you never smoked any dope, Sister Girl?" Two-Fingers said in his defense.

"I've tried it, and I don't see the big deal," Paula said.

"Well, the big deal is this," Two-Fingers said as he lit a joint and handed it to her.

Paula took a small, insignificant puff and passed it to Curly who knew exactly what to do with it. The joint quickly made its rounds and ended up back in Paula's hands. After hitting it a second time, she was suddenly less willing to give it up. The other passengers insisted on getting their turn, but Paula steadfastly refused to give up the joint.

"Man, this shit's good."

Those were the last words spoken on our voyage to salvation.

It was around noon when we arrived at Cut Bank Creek. It was a hot June day, and the swimming area was packed with Blackfeet. Swimmers dove off the cliffs into the deep, cold water before quickly returning for another turn. The early arrivals from the fire crew had already established a nice camp in a shaded area next to the creek, where several cases of beer were strategically placed in the water to keep them cold.

Paula haltingly climbed out of the back seat of the Volkswagen and eventually stretched out on a nice grassy area near a large pine tree. We followed her, and soon we were resting comfortably, trying not to doze off.

"Sister Girl, is it time for a nap?"

"Nope, it's time for a swim," Paula said as she stood and stripped off her boots, Levi's, and her green Park Service blouse. Only her bra and panties remained as she stepped into the cold, refreshing water.

"I've created a monster," Two-Fingers said, shaking his head as he handed out beer.

After Paula entered the water, the remaining crew members who weren't already swimming, quickly stripped down to their underwear and jumped in next to her. The additional swimmers caused the water level to rise three feet, and I worried the entire area would flood if Paula took off any more clothes.

Curly retrieved a bar of soap from his backpack before swimming out to Paula. I watched as he slowly rubbed the bar of soap along her shoulders until a nice lather formed. Paula turned toward him as he continued to scrub her down. She reached behind to unclasp her bra, and Curly focused his efforts on her breasts, taking his job way too seriously before Paula swam away.

"That isn't natural," Two-Fingers said as he chugged a beer.

"What's not natural?" I asked.

"Sister Girl getting naked like that."

"I think it's a beautiful and natural thing for her to do. I think your ancestors would be very proud of her. Why don't you fire up a joint so we can appreciate the beauty of it all?"

"Keep your eyes in your head, White Guy," Two-Fingers said as he lit up.

"Hey, if I had a sister who looked like Paula, I'd be proud to show her off."

Two-Fingers said, "Skin you," before we stripped down and joined the party.

Soon, we were swimming and diving off the cliffs as the heat increased, and we found ourselves both hot and thirsty. The cold water had temporarily rejuvenated the crew, and they drank like crazy. Bitsy drove back into town and picked up more beer as the party shifted into overdrive. Someone had built a fire, and the swimmers gathered around it to dry off as the sun began its descent. Two-Fingers walked into the crowd and started passing out joints, which proved to be a very popular move.

"Yeah, I ran into this guy who had recently resigned his commission from the Army. He had all kinds of pot soaking in opium, and he gave me some." Two-Fingers said as he searched for his Levi's to put on.

"My cousin had some shit like this when he came home on his last leave," Curly said as he took another hit.

"Yeah, I know a lot of guys are trying this stuff. I think it's good; it seems to mellow them out a little. Even the Stabs-in-the-Backs have settled down," Liquid Louie said.

A few minutes passed before Big Man Bear Claw chimed in, "When I was in 'Nam, everybody was getting stoned." Big Man was only about 5'8", but he was a tough son of a bitch. After he returned from 'Nam, everybody remarked on how kind and gentle he had become.

"Talk about mellowing, what about Big Man? He used to beat people up for looking at him the wrong way," Brenda "Peaches" Running Wolf said.

Big Man stared blankly into the fire, puffing on a joint before he said, "I don't want to hurt anyone anymore. I saw too much of that shit in 'Nam. The young guys around here are still trying to get tough with me, and I ignore them. What's the point?" Big Man took another hit before passing the joint.

"I always knew I could kick your ass," Two-Fingers said as he started his shadowboxing routine.

"Shut up," was all Paula said before she slapped Two-Fingers along the side of his head.

"Two-Fingers, still has to get the last word in," Big Man said as he passed him the joint. "Keep getting smart, little man, and I'll come out of retirement." Big Man continued staring into the fire.

Two-Fingers was about to say something when Paula reached over and slapped him on top of his head.

"So, Two-Fingers, how did you like boarding school?" Peaches asked.

"Typical white horse shit. Always someone telling you what to do, where to go, and what to think. They tried to make a good little apple out of me, and they almost succeeded until I figured out how to play their game. When I first got down there, I had my share of fights with the other Indians. But shit, I eventually realized we were all in the same boat and needed to stick together. We should've done that four hundred years ago, and there wouldn't be any whites here now."

Two-Fingers looked around the campfire and gave me the finger.

"Shit, don't mind me, tell us how you really feel about it," I said as I reached for a proffered joint.

"You're my brother. Besides, you'll be more Indian than all of us if you don't change your evil ways," Two-Fingers said as the other Blackfeet nodded their heads.

"I saw a lot of stuff in South Dakota. The whites are rich, and all they care about is money, trying to keep up with the Joneses. Indians are poor, the Crow, Sioux, Flathead, Northern Cheyenne, and all the other tribes, we are poor. We live off what the whites give us, and then we piss it away as soon as we get it. Whether we realize it or not, we are dependent on the government, and they give us everything but hope. Greed has screwed them up to the point of no return. Their desire for trinkets is insatiable," Two-Fingers said before gulping down his beer.

I told you he matured.

"I know, a lot of the tribes are getting educated, sending their kids off to college and shit. Some tribes are even starting their own four-year colleges," Curly said.

"Look at the Flathead, right over there on the other side of those mountains, they're building a college to help educate their people," Big Man said as he pointed west in the direction of the Rocky Mountains.

Two-Fingers rolled more joints as darkness fell on our impromptu camp. Additional firewood was gathered and thrown onto the fire, and the beer was consumed at a slower, more methodical pace as the citizens continued to reflect on their circumstances.

"I'm going to college in Missoula," Paula announced. "I decided that the first day of firefighting. It can't be any worse than breathing in smoke all day." The crowd voiced their approval with grunts and hand gestures.

"We can get government grants and all kinds of shit. I say we use their guilt money and beat them at their own game. Politicians have always said how bad they feel for us when it's their policies that have caused all the problems, they want us to depend on them. Their Great Society bullshit will be a failure exactly like their Indian policy is a failure. Before they started their national giveaway welfare programs, they should have spent some time living on a reservation. A blind man could see that type of policy doesn't work. All it does is create a society filled with people with no hope, no dreams, and no motivation."

"I got philosophical on the fire line once I caught my breath. I like working, and I don't want to sit on my ass all day watching my life slip away. We need to get educated on taking care of ourselves."

"Why don't you do that, Paula, and let us know how it works out for you?" Peaches said.

"Hey, I'm no chicken shit, I'll go, and you can stay here and be pregnant and barefoot," Paula said as she stared back at Peaches.

"Don't talk to me like I'm ignorant, Paula. I'm not scared of you. You think you're so damn tough," Peaches said as she stood up and shook her fist.

"Where has all that brotherly love gone?" Two-Fingers asked as he slowly rose to his feet.

"You better hurry up with those joints, the women are ready to go on the warpath," Big Man said as he handed out more beer.

"That's what I'm saying, we are always fighting amongst ourselves over the stupidest things," Two-Fingers said as he lit another joint and passed it to Paula.

"Look who's talking," Paula said as she puffed away.

Chapter 8
Burning at Both Ends

Days later, on July 5, 1970, Paula and her fire crew were called to fight a blaze near the Many Glacier area of Glacier National Park. No official investigation was made, but it was suspected someone had started the fire by shooting off fireworks. How it started was unclear. What was clear, was that it was moving quickly and posed a serious threat to the Park.

The next day, the winds picked up and the fire spread at an alarming rate. The Lodge at Many Glacier burned to the ground in a matter of hours, and the entire area was evacuated as smoke poured out of the Park, casting Browning into virtual darkness. More help was desperately needed, so calls went out for all able-bodied volunteers to help fight the runaway fire. Max, Two-Fingers, and I volunteered and left town immediately in a blue Forest Service bus loaded with Blackfeet of various ages; the young and old went off to fight because the fire was serious and the professional crews needed replacements.

Browning was approximately fifty miles from the fire, but it took us over three hours to get there, it was slow going. Smoke and ashes filled the air, and visibility was terrible. It was so bad that we never reached the Many Glacier area. We were stopped by a park ranger who told our driver to empty the bus and get the hell out of there. The fire was burning so hot it was jumping back and forth across the road ahead of us, and a water truck and two caterpillars had already burned to the ground, leaving behind piles of smoldering steel and ash.

Max took charge of the volunteers, and we marched up the road in single file. I nearly passed out from the intense heat and smoke. Two-Fingers made no mention of the misery, that wasn't his style, no matter how dire the circumstances. When we reached the top of a distant hill, we were greeted by a small group of professional firefighters sitting alongside the road, resting and taking nourishment. Paula was in that group. She was rightly concerned that Max, Two-Fingers, and I were there; we had the equipment to fight a fire, but that was about it. Max had fought fires when he was younger, but he was too old and out of shape to be of any real help. Still, when the call for help came, he insisted on going, and Two-Fingers, and I decided to fight alongside him.

It wasn't long before an old Army jeep rolled to a stop in front of us with Two Shoes Cross Guns at the wheel. Two Shoes was in the unenviable position of being in charge, and the enormity of the task weighed heavily on his dirt-streaked, ashen-gray face. "Max, I'm sure glad you're here. We can use all the help we can get," Two Shoes said as he walked up to Paula, Two-Fingers, Max, and me. "This thing is really getting out of hand. I've called for reinforcements and was told the Governor is releasing some of the National Guard to help out. The problem is, they won't be here for quite a while, so in the meantime, the Forest Service is sending in planes to douse this thing along with some smoke jumpers out of Missoula. They should be getting here soon." Two Shoes leaned back against the jeep and wiped sweat from his face and arms with a tattered, filthy handkerchief.

"What do you want us to do?" Max asked.

"I need you to take your crew over to the north side of Swift Current Lake to clear brush and establish a fire line. I'm going to promote you to line boss and put you in charge of these volunteers." Two Shoes said before taking a long drink from his Forest Service-issued canteen.

"What a damn mess is all I have to say," Two Shoes added before continuing. "We've established a camp down by Lower Swift Current Creek, and I'm pulling Paula's crew out of here and sending them down there to rest up. They've been going at it since their arrival, and they need rest. If you can keep this thing from spreading north, we may have a chance." He spread a map out on top of the hood of the jeep. "Swift Current Lake will stop it from spreading to the south, and if the smoke jumpers and planes do their job and keep it from going any farther west, we should be in pretty good shape. I wish we had more people." Two Shoes said as he folded up the map.

"The problem with your plan, Two Shoes, is you need more people up on that ridge," Paula said, pointing north. "If we can get the northern area contained, then you're right, we'll have a chance. You need to send all of us to get it done." She looked to Max for approval.

"Paula, Two Shoes is right. Your crew is tired, and you all need a break. We can get up there and hold this thing until the National Guard arrives," Max said with as much conviction as he could muster.

"Shit, the National Guard my ass," Paula said before kicking the ground in disgust. "Those boys have never been around a forest fire. They'll get in our way like Donny R. and Tony. Why did you let them come, Dad?" She didn't wait for an answer. "Besides, it could be days before they get here, and we can't wait that long. And your crew won't be enough help, Dad." Paula removed her hard hat and wiped her face with the sleeve of her lime green, Forest Service shirt.

Max and Two Shoes knew she was right. Hell, even Two-Fingers and I knew she was right, and we didn't know much about anything. Two Shoes walked over to talk with Curly, who was the line boss of his crew, and asked his opinion.

"If we don't get this thing contained, it's going to run all the way into Canada. We have no choice but to get everyone involved, and the sooner the better." I remember looking up as a plane flew overhead. "Then we'd better get a move on. If they stop this thing from spreading to the west, it'll have to start going north."

"Okay, double time it up there. I'll try to find out where the hell the reinforcements are and when we can expect them," Two Shoes said before driving away in his jeep.

Curly and Max took charge of their crews, and all of us walked in the direction of the main blaze. As we neared the ridge, the crews spread out and began cutting down trees and brush in an attempt to establish a fire line. Planes to the west of us dumped fire retardant on the flames, and smoke jumpers worked hard to stop it from spreading. All the hard work seemed to be paying off until the wind shifted direction and the fire started heading due north with a vengeance.

"Curly, we need the planes to stop dropping to the west of here and concentrate on the north. Get on the radio and let Two Shoes know what the hell is going on," Max yelled over the roar of the flames. "We need to get these crews away from here. This thing is starting to get too hot. Let's try to reach Kennedy Lake and establish a fire line there. We need to get farther north." Sheer panic took over as we found ourselves surrounded by flames.

Two-Fingers and I had been "fighting" the fire for less than three hours, and we were already worn out. "I can't get him on the radio, Max. I think the heat has melted the insides of this damn thing," Curly said, shaking the radio in a vain attempt to jump-start it.

"Give it to me," Max said before yanking the radio away from Curly. "Shit, this thing is deader than a doornail." Max threw the radio down the hill, and I watched as it immediately burst into flames. "Let's move," Max said. "You two stay close to me."

Max, Curly, Two-Fingers, and I moved as quickly as possible down the fire line gathering up crew members and trying to get them headed north. Max frantically searched for Paula, and when he saw Bitsy he grabbed his arm and asked, "Where the hell is Paula?"

"Last time I saw her, she was going over that ridge," Bitsy said before shaking his arm loose and pointing to an area south of us.

Max, Two-Fingers, and I reached the top of the ridge as quickly as possible, but we didn't see her. The smoke was thick and the heat unbearable. We yelled Paula's name repeatedly and as loudly as we could. No answer, our pleas were drowned out by the roar of the fire.

We kept searching until we finally found Paula. She was desperately struggling to get back up the other side of the ridge. Surrounded by an inferno of burning trees, her situation looked hopeless. Two-Fingers ran toward her, jumped over a fallen, burning tree, and was within twenty feet of Paula when a large pine tree started to fall in her direction. He sprinted down the ridge toward her with speed he never displayed before or since. Max and I followed as quickly as possible but it was Two-Fingers who reached Paula first and it was Two-Fingers who shoved her just as the pine tree crashed to the ground. Paula was momentarily stunned when a burning branch from the pine tree grazed the side of her head. She tumbled to the ground and lay motionless.

Two-Fingers and I were pulling her to safety when a large, burning pine tree fell on Max. He disappeared under the flaming tree, and we struggled mightily trying to get him out from underneath it. Finally, Curly and Bitsy arrived and, with their help, we were able to save Max from certain death. Max lay on the smoldering hot ground unconscious, the whole left side of his body a mangled mess. Two-Fingers and Bitsy lifted Max, and gently placed him over Curly's shoulder. Once secured, Curly slowly walked up the hill and away from any immediate danger.

Paula, with only a little assistance from me, made it to the top of the hill and to her father. Once there, she started screaming hysterically when she realized the severity of Max's injuries. She screamed so loudly the roar of the fire couldn't drown her out. She lay down next to him and wept and Two-Fingers threw his shovel into the raging fire.

Max lost a lot of blood before he finally arrived at the Blackfeet

Health Center in Browning. Even in his weakened state, it took half the emergency room staff to hold him down when he was told his left leg had to be amputated. After being strapped down and heavily sedated, Max was wheeled into the operating room, where his leg was unceremoniously chopped off. Friends and family were shocked when they heard the news, so much for socialized medicine.

That wasn't the last of the bad news that hit the reservation that day. Mom and Dad received a telegram from the War Department informing them that my brother Stan was missing in action. Dad delivered the news to me at the Blackfeet Health Center, and before leaving, he left it to me to tell Paula. Mom was hysterical when she heard the news and had to be heavily sedated, and Dad didn't want to be away from her too long.

Two-Fingers and I, along with the rest of his family, sat quietly in the waiting room while Max was having surgery. They were so deep in thought that I began to feel like nobody knew I was there. Paula finally reached over and held my hands. "We're glad you're here. It means a lot to us." She stood, brushed the hair away from my eyes, and gave me a hug. I stared at her briefly before blurting out, "Paula, we received word that Stan is missing in action."

Without saying anything, she ran out the front door and didn't look back. Two-Fingers, Pam, Cindy Ann, and Stogie Man looked as if they were trying to digest the news. Stogie Man blinked wildly before saying, "What do they mean by missing in action? He's supposed to be getting discharged in a couple of months," he said as he fumbled for a cigarette.

"Let's get out of here," Two-Fingers said as he led me out the front door. After exiting, I noticed business was starting to pick up. Cars and trucks were being unloaded at a rapid pace while new arrivals were taken to the check-in area. It was business as usual on another tragic day on the reservation.

Two-Fingers and I put as much distance as we could between ourselves and the Blackfeet Health Center. Then, out of nowhere, Jimmy B suddenly appeared.

"Hey, numb nuts, what's up?" Jimmy B asked as he brought his Chevy to a complete stop beside us.

"What do you mean? What's up? Where the hell have you been?" Two-Fingers asked before opening the passenger door.

"I've been in Great Falls and just pulled into town. So, what's up?"

"You're not going to believe this shit. Drive, we'll tell you all about it," Two Fingers said as I jumped into the back seat.

After digesting the news, Jimmy B said, "Brothers, that's some bad shit, and it doesn't get any better. Guess who got drafted?" Jimmy B said as he pulled a bottle of Seagrams whiskey from under the front seat.

"Don't tell me, you got drafted?" Two-Fingers let out a whistle and reached for the whiskey.

"You can't go, Jimmy B. You've got to escape to Canada, man. You can't go to 'Nam." I was pleading with him as I reached for the bottle.

"Lots of people are going to Canada these days. Shit, Canada is less than forty miles from here, man. You can stay with some of our northern brothers and sisters, they'll never find you up there. You know what they say: we all look alike," Two-Fingers said as he raised the whiskey bottle to his lips.

"They've never seen you if they think we all look alike. Hell man, you don't look like anyone on this planet. Besides, those cowards aren't Indians, they're not warriors."

"Crack you, Jimmy B," Two Fingers said as he yanked the bottle out of Jimmy B's mouth.

"Bone you, Two-Fingers," Jimmy B said as he gunned the engine.

That sudden acceleration caused Two-Fingers to lose his grip on the Seagrams bottle, and it banged off the windshield. Luckily, the bottle only caused a small crack on the passenger side, and most of the whiskey was saved.

"Screw it," Jimmy B said as he surveyed the damage. "Nothing stays new forever."

"Nothing stays new forever, and nobody lives forever. You start crying about all the bad shit that happens on and off the reservation, and you'll end up crying your life away. My brother is probably dead, and I don't know if I can handle that."

I wasn't thinking clearly. I was overwhelmed with a sense of loss, and they both extended their sympathies before Jimmy B said, "Well, I say we get some beer, drown our sorrows, and get to partying."

We drove on in silence before Jimmy B rolled down his window and tossed the empty Seagrams bottle at a bullet riddled "Do Not Litter" sign.

"When are you going in?" Two-Fingers asked.

"Two weeks, three days, and twelve hours," Jimmy B said, and with that, silence filled the cab as we drove aimlessly into the night.

After several minutes, Two-Fingers broke the silence and said, "Let's go up to Moccasin Flats so I can pick up some of my stash. The whiskey has really messed me up."

As we reentered the city limits of Browning, Too Slim Running Bear nearly ran us off the road in his pickup, going like a bat out of hell. Too Slim was Stogie Man's closest friend and his best man at his wedding. Jimmy B could never resist a challenge, so he took off after him, and in no time, we were right on his tail.

Jimmy B flashed his brights off and on trying to get Too Slim to pull over. He repeatedly honked his horn before Juanita Bear Medicine Owen rose up out of nowhere and gave us the finger. Too Slim grabbed the top of her head and pushed her from view.

"Oh, shit. Did you see who that was?" I asked as we slowed down and watched Too Slim's pickup fade from view.

We stayed out all night, drowning our sorrows and our livers. My tears had dried. By daybreak the next morning, we were running on fumes. Jimmy B drove to our Chevron station for some gas and a handful of Slim Jims.

I had dozed off in the back seat and was startled wide awake when I saw my old man and Charley Owen standing in front of us.

I was filling up Jimmy B's Chevy and washing his windshield when Dad and Charley asked if we had seen Juanita. Evidently, she was having a hard time finding her way back home. I remember feeling very uncomfortable and unsure of what to say when Jimmy B blurted out, "Never seen her. We were out rabbit hunting and never saw her."

 Dad looked at us suspiciously before Two-Fingers said, "I'm sorry about Stan. He's a good man. I hope they find him alive and well, Mr. Church." Jimmy B nodded in agreement.

"I'm sorry about the whole damn thing," Charley said as he turned and walked to his pickup.

"You have to excuse Charley, he's been up all night looking for Juanita. She's been drinking more than usual lately and acting more erratic with each passing day." Dad shook his head before walking to the tire shop.

We drove to the Blackfeet Health Center to check on Max. Two-Fingers was nervous and apprehensive when we entered the waiting room. It was completely empty except for Stogie Man sleeping in one of the chairs.

"Stogie Man, wake up. Where is everybody?" Two-Fingers shook him so hard I thought he was going to break something.

Stogie Man finally woke up, but it took him a while to get his bearings straight. "Your dad came around early this morning, and the women have been in his room ever since." Stogie Man yawned, stretched his legs out, and quickly fell back asleep.

The three of us walked down the corridor leading to the Intensive Care Unit and began looking into rooms, hoping to find Max. After waking up most of the sick and the dying, we finally found Max's room at the very end of the hallway.

Pam, Paula, and Cindy Ann were standing guard over Max, and we received decidedly cold looks when we entered.

"Nice you could show up, Donny R," Paula said.

"Shit, Sis, I'm sorry, but I can't take this," Two-Fingers said as he paced back and forth.

Max lay in bed with tubes and wires running in and out of him. His skin was a deep yellow color, and there was a hollow spot under his comforter where his left leg used to be. He was asleep, but it was a fitful sleep. He tossed and turned as if reliving the horror of his accident.

Pam was by his side, holding his right hand. "My boy, there isn't anything you can do here." She smiled at Donny R. "Why don't you take the girls and go get something to eat?"

Paula and Cindy Ann would have none of it and insisted on staying, so the three of us took the opportunity to get out of there. Before the door closed, I heard Pam say, "Don't be too hard on him. He's never been able to handle these types of things."

That was an understatement. Two-Fingers has always been deeply affected whenever anyone he likes or loves is harassed, hurt, or killed. He always roots for the underdog and has a real problem with unfairness, and he takes those things seriously, more seriously than most. It's difficult to acknowledge sensitivity in a place as insensitive as the reservation because sensitivity is a foreign concept. Yet Two-Fingers is sensitive, sensitive to the plight of others, and confused about why injustices happen. His father's injuries had him questioning a lot of things, and he began searching for answers. The first stop on this quest was the Paradise Bar, where the patrons are always searching for something.

Chapter 9
Paradise Found

The Paradise had just opened, and the place was already filled to capacity. I began to wonder if there was ever an empty seat at any bar on the reservation, and that question remains open to this day. Jimmy B, Two-Fingers, and I made room for ourselves at the bar and ordered a round. The bartender quickly served us without asking questions. The Paradise was notorious for serving anybody and everybody.

There were only three rules at the Paradise: First, to get served, you had to be as tall as the bar, which was four feet high. Second, you had to have money; bullshit walks and money talks. Third, your head must never hit the bar. If your head hit the bar, you were taken out back and laid in the alley until you sobered up. There was so much booze being consumed that day, I concluded the alley would need to be enlarged to hold the overflow.

The Paradise was, and still is, the filthiest bar on the reservation. In fact, it's so ugly and beat up that it makes the other bars on the reservation look like piano bars. Of course, nobody goes there for the scenery or stimulating conversation; they go there to drown their sorrows. For those who have fallen, it's an oasis.

We were working on our third boilermaker when Two-Fingers said, "I'm starting to like this place." I happened to be chasing a shot of whiskey with a beer when he said that, and I ended up spewing the beer across the bar and onto the cracked and poorly taped mirror behind the bartender.

"If that's the case, it's time to go," I said as I slowly wiped the beer from my chin with my shirt sleeve.

"Go where? Where are we going to go? If you go into the Paradise, there isn't any place left to go," Jimmy B said as he ordered another round.

"That's pretty heavy shit there, Jimmy B. I never knew you to be so philosophical," Two-Fingers said as his attention shifted to the front door entrance. "Oh shit, here comes Red Stabs-in-the-Back." Two-Fingers took a long drink of his beer before setting it down on the bar.

Red was Kenny, and Ronnie Joe's uncle, and he was one mean son-of-a-bitch. Mean but not particularly bright, those attributes seemed to run in their family.

"So, Two-Fingers, I heard your dad had a little bad luck," Red said as he stepped up to the bar and stood next to me.

Two-Fingers didn't say a word, he just nodded his head while staring into the taped-up mirror.

"Well, you know, maybe you and he can join the circus and be in one of those freak shows. You could call yourselves, "Two-Fingers and the One-Legged Gimp," Red said smiling as he continued staring at Two-Fingers.

Two-Fingers slowly turned to look directly at Red before saying, "I have a better idea. Why don't you, my dad, and I start a band? We can call it, "Two-Fingers, One Leg and No Brain."

That's when things got weird.

Red made a move toward Two-Fingers, and when he did, I turned and hit him square in the Adam's apple. He immediately dropped to his knees before rolling over onto his back on the whiskey and beer-soaked floor. He lay there holding his throat with both hands while choking up blood. He made a real mess of the place, and I didn't think that was possible, you've got to put some effort into messing up the Paradise.

He mumbled something inaudible before I kicked him square in the nuts. Then I stood over him and yelled, "What did you say? I can't hear you. What did you say?" He slowly rolled onto his side and curled up into a fetal position.

Nobody in the bar moved, and it suddenly became deathly quiet. Two-Fingers and Jimmy B stood with their backs to the bar, ready for any action that might come their way. We looked around to see if the other patrons were going to join the fight, but nobody seemed to give a shit, least of all the bartender.

"Well now, uh, White Guy, what do you say we get out of here?" Two-Fingers asked as he waved his hand in front of my eyes. Evidently, I was in a trance-like state. That's what happens when bottled-up rage comes to the surface. Hate and boilermakers will make a weak man strong, strong until he sobers up.

Jimmy B ordered and paid for a case of Rainier. I vaguely remember us easing our way out the front door and getting into Jimmy B's Chevy. Before we drove off, he spun out of the parking lot and narrowly missed hitting a tourist taking pictures of the very large red, white, and blue stucco gas station with fake totem poles shaped like a teepee. I think the guy was Asian, but I'm not sure. My blood was pumping pretty good. I'm not sure why I'm mentioning this, but I think it's important to know the nationality of everybody you nearly run over, right?

After leaving the Paradise, we drove around the reservation for hours, drinking beer and checking our rearview mirrors.

"Never seen a guy drop like that, went to his knees faster than a five-dollar hooker," Jimmy B said for the umpteenth time.

Fights on the reservation rarely last more than a few minutes, but the retelling of them lasts a lifetime, especially if you think you've won. Of course, on the reservation you never really know who has "won" because fights last for years. The time between the fighting is an intermission. I know guys on the reservation who have been fighting each other for over twenty years. Every time they see each other, the fight is back on.

"It looks like Too Slim is having a party," Two-Fingers said as we drove by his house.

Too Slim lived in an "Easter egg" house on Moccasin Flats, not far from Stogie Man and Cindy Ann's place. Too Slim was always throwing a party, so the announcement didn't come as much of a surprise.

There were eight cars strategically parked in what appeared to be his front yard when Jimmy B drove his Chevy onto the grassless yard and made it nine. We stumbled out of the Chevy and walked directly into Too Slim's house, nobody locks their doors on the reservation.

It was around five p.m., and the party was well underway. In the living room, a sixteen gallon keg was tapped, and the beer was flowing liberally, and some of the beer actually made it into cups.

"Oki, oki, good party but no whiskey," Two-Fingers said as we made our grand entrance.

Over in the corner, sitting on the couch, were Stogie Man and Juanita Owen, engaged in what appeared to be a meaningful conversation. Two-Fingers walked directly over to them and asked, "So, who is taking care of my nieces tonight?"

Stogie Man staggered to his feet and said, "None of your business, that's who."

Just then, Too Slim rushed in from the kitchen and stood between them. "If you want to stay here, you'll keep your mouth shut," he said.

Two-Fingers looked past both of them and stared at Juanita. "One word and we get after it right here."

Too Slim laid a hand on Two-Fingers' shoulder. That's when I intervened and sat down next to Juanita.

"How are you doing tonight, Mrs. Owen? We ran into your husband this morning, and he asked if we had seen you last night. We told him we hadn't, but I could've sworn we saw you in Too Slim's pickup truck. Charley seemed awfully worried." I glanced at Too Slim, and he had turned as white as I am. "Listen, why don't you guys have some beer and relax." Too Slim said before taking his hand off Two-Fingers' shoulder and quickly disappearing into the kitchen.

"Relax? We are relaxed. You guys are the ones who need to relax. White Guy and I have been out making the streets safe for the women and children while you guys have been hiding out up here. Jimmy B, how about a beer?" Two-Fingers said as he walked to the keg.

"You're sitting in my seat, White Guy," Stogie Man said staring down at me.

"Why don't you run downtown and get us some whiskey, Stogie Man?" Juanita asked, handing him a wrinkled one-hundred dollar bill. "Tony will keep your spot warm, won't you, Tony?" She patted my leg.

"If this spot gets any warmer, the whole place is going to burn down," I said as Stogie Man made his way out the front door.

Juanita laughed and moved a little closer to me. "You turned out to be a handsome white boy." Before I could reply, she asked, "You don't like me much do you, Tony?"

"I like you fine. But since you asked, you're married to my father's best friend, remember?"

She ran her fingers through my hair.

"Remember?"

"How the hell can I forget? If you're married to an Owen, you're not allowed to forget."

"Well, I'm forgetting him and his whole damn family. Besides, I can't give him a baby, so what difference does it make?" Juanita asked as she lit a cigarette.

Two-Fingers walked over and handed me a cup of beer. "Sister, can I bum a smoke from you?"

"You can have the whole pack if I don't have to look at your ugly face the rest of the night," Juanita said as she handed him her newly opened pack of Marlboros.

"Hey, I leave, and White Guy leaves with me," Two-Fingers said as he continued to fill his Levi jacket pockets with cigarettes.

"What, you two joined at the hip? I can give him something you can only dream about," Juanita said as she inspected the empty cigarette pack Two-Fingers returned to her.

His eyes widened as he glanced at me, and we both began to get a better understanding of the possibilities the opportunity presented.

"Well, now, is that Peaches Running Wolf I see out there in the kitchen? If you two will excuse me, I have to run along," Two-Fingers said as he removed himself from our space.

"He's always the gentleman, that one. Let's dance," Juanita said as she stood and extended her hand to me.

I stood up and took her hand when someone turned up the radio. Soon, the place was hopping, and Juanita and I found ourselves slow dancing on a crowded, makeshift dance floor.

That was when Juanita whispered into my ear, "I think I'll stay sober tonight."

I wasn't sure what to think of that. In fact, I wasn't thinking about much once Juanita climbed into my arms. The only thing I knew with absolute certainty was I had a hard-on a cat couldn't scratch.

Stogie Man came back with a half rack of Jack Daniels, and the party soon shifted into overdrive. Cars full of people arrived, and the valet service went to hell. Too Slim's front yard began to look like a large used-car lot filled with cars with their doors left wide open.

Juanita and I were standing in the middle of the living room, swaying to the music, when she took my hand and led me down the hallway. The crowd stopped to watch us go into the bathroom, and before the bathroom door closed, I heard Two-Fingers say, "Looks like we're going to have to piss outside for a while, mind the wind."

Juanita locked the door behind us and started to slowly undress. She took off her blouse and revealed the most beautiful breasts I had ever seen. Of course, up until then, they were the only in person breasts I had ever seen. They were large, but not too big. Her nipples were pink on a brown canvas, they were works of art.

She slowly undressed me before turning off the light.

At approximately 6 a.m. the next morning, I was startled out of a deep, blissful sleep by Two-Fingers. He shook me by my shoulders and whispered, "Hey, White Guy, we've got to get out of here."

"Why? What the hell is going on?"

"Peaches went batshit crazy, I'll explain later," Two-Fingers said as he gingerly opened the bedroom door about an inch and peeked out. All the while, I was dressing as quickly as possible and trying not to wake Juanita.

Two-Fingers and I were quietly tiptoeing down the hallway when, all of a sudden, Peaches appeared from the shadows and started cussing Two-Fingers with such vigor that it caused both of us to temporarily freeze in place.

"Where are you going, you bastard? Do you think you can just screw me and then run off and leave me?" Peaches screamed at the top of her lungs.

She closed in on Two-Fingers, and before he was able to move, she reared back and hit him square on the chin. To this day, I have no idea how he remained standing, that's how hard she hit him.

We turned away and ended up jumping over several out-stretched, lifeless bodies as we ran out the front door as fast as we could.

After we cleared the porch, I peeked over my shoulder to see Peaches running after us and buttoning up her blouse at the same time. Talk about multitasking.

"You think you can use me and not think twice about it?" Peaches screamed as she picked up a rock and threw it at Two-Fingers. Luckily, it whizzed past his head and shattered a side window of one of the cars that had its doors left open. Glass flew everywhere.

That was when Peaches started to run after us in earnest, and before long, she stopped to pick up another rock.

"What do you think I am, a cheap piece of meat?" Peaches reared back and threw a strike, and that time, the rock hit Two-Fingers squarely between his shoulder blades.

"Ouch, that bitch has a better arm than Tom Seaver," Two-Fingers yelled as he found another gear.

I ran past him, sprinting for all I was worth. Not only was Peaches keeping pace, she was actually starting to gain on us. That's when Two-Fingers began to panic.

"Listen, she's faster than I am. We need to do something," Two-Fingers said as he kept sprinting.

"Why don't we split up?" I suggested.

"Split up? What good would that do? That bitch wants to kill me, she won't follow you," Two-Fingers said before a rock hit him in the back of his right leg, inches below the knee.

"Exactly right," I said, before turning and running off.

"Never screw with a chick from East Glacier; they all run like deer," Two-Fingers yelled as he ran down a crowded alley filled with sleepy winos and climbed over a fence.

I looked over my shoulder, and to my surprise, Peaches hurdled the fence without breaking stride. Two-Fingers was running out of gas, so he turned and ran toward his place. He ran all the way there before he was brave enough to stop and look behind him. Peaches remained in hot pursuit.

Finally, after dodging between cars and running around in circles, Two-Fingers pushed his parents' gate open and seemed surprised to see me sitting on the porch watching the whole thing.

Two-Fingers ignored me and ran to the basement door, quickly opened it, and shut it. Then he locked the door and braced his body against it, hoping it would be strong enough to keep her out. He has retold this story many times over the years, and I still laugh when I think his death would've been the ultimate price paid for getting laid.

Peaches stopped running when she saw me sitting on the porch. That's when she proceeded to unload on me by calling me everything but a white guy. She yelled, stomped the ground, and spit at me before suddenly stopping and looking around to see if anyone was watching her. At least that's what I thought she was doing, but to this day, I still don't know what Peaches thinks.

She did take time to adjust her hair and her partially buttoned blouse before starting her walk back to Moccasin Flats. Like a hurricane, she had finally blown herself out.

I remember skipping down the cement stairway to the basement and gently tapping on the door before saying, "It's safe to come out now, lover boy."

Two-Fingers cautiously opened the door and surveyed the

entryway before letting me in.

"Holy shit," Two-Fingers said as he leaned over and put seven fingers on his knees while trying to catch his breath. "What was that all about? Really, what the hell was that all about?" I asked as he slumped to the basement floor.

After regaining his strength, Two-Fingers stood up and walked over to an old GE refrigerator humming quietly on the mildewed cement floor. He opened the refrigerator, reached in, and pulled out two quarts of bottled Olympia beer.

He tipped one quart upside down and used its cap to pop the cap off the other quart. Mission accomplished, the cap popped off, and only a minimal amount of foam oozed out. He put the unopened quart back into the refrigerator before taking a long pull on the Oly. He wiped the saliva off the top of the bottle with his sleeve and handed it to me.

I watched him do this like he was in slow motion. After taking a long, satisfying drink of the beer, I handed it back to him, and once again I asked, "What was that all about?"

He was still shaken when he answered. "Well, while you were in there doing the horizontal bop with Juanita, I decided it was time for me and Peaches to get it on. So we went to Too Slim's bedroom and started making out, and I was getting nowhere fast. She let me do about anything I wanted except have sex with her. I was killing myself, getting hornier and hornier, and she didn't do anything but tease me."

"Finally, I wore down her resistance and made my move. Well, by that time, I'm so worked up that I'm only good for three, maybe four strokes before I shoot my load," Two-Fingers said as he finished off the quart.

"Well, that wasn't good enough for good old Peaches, oh no. She wanted more and said so in no uncertain terms. I told her I needed to rest a while and have a beer or two, and that's when she started calling me nasty, terrible names."

Two-Fingers stood and retrieved the other quart of Oly, and opened it with his teeth.

"I mistakenly thought I could get you and get out of there before she got dressed. That bitch is fast. Have you ever seen anybody run that fast? Fast runner, fast dresser, and a slow comer. I don't know how much more she could've stood. I gave her the best five strokes of my life," Two-Fingers said as he sat down next to me on the floor.

"I thought you said it was four strokes?" I asked, reaching for the quart.

"Four, five, who knows. Things were moving kind of fast, if you know what I mean."

"You should've left me; I could've used more sleep."

"Sleep? It didn't sound like you were getting any sleep. That bed creaked all night long," Two-Fingers said with admiration in his eyes. "Besides, if Charley had found your ass in bed with her, we wouldn't be having this conversation."

"Can you believe all the shit that's happened to us in the last twenty-four hours?" Two-Fingers asked as he stood up, stretched, and drank more Oly.

I reached for the bottle, and it slipped from my hand, crashing to the floor and sending glass and beer flying across the mildewed cement floor.

"Ah, hell with it, I'll clean it up later. Let's go for a walk and smoke some pot," Two-Fingers said as he turned and cautiously peeked out the basement window.

As we walked up the basement steps, I said, "Man, you're a young guy, and you let that old woman outrun you, that's sad."

Two-Fingers blankly stared at me for a while before saying, "She may be older than me, but she hasn't lost a step.   She should play for the Packers."

Chapter 10
Doing Good Has Consequences

We walked the half mile down Main Street to the theater before stopping to rest on the brick ledge near its entrance. That ledge is still a prime sitting spot, usually occupied by the town's winos. It's a little more than a foot wide, twenty feet long, made of red bricks, and not terribly uncomfortable. The best thing about that ledge is that it sits directly across the street from the Oasis Bar. If you sit on that ledge long enough, the entire population of Browning will pass you by, and so will your life.

It was early in the morning, somewhere around 7 a.m., when the winos began to emerge from the shadows. One by one, they stirred from their alcohol-induced sleep, seemingly ready to meet the challenges of the day. Two-Fingers immediately recognized the Governor and waved him over. Soon, the Governor, Maggie Stink Pits, and Rubber Joe were seated between Two-Fingers and me on the ledge. Other winos milled around, but only the five of us were sitting.

Two-Fingers lit a joint and handed it to the Governor, who was resting his head comfortably on his shoulder. After carefully inspecting the joint, the Governor took a small puff. "I haven't smoked any of this stuff since back in the '30s. I tried some hash when I was down in California, too," he said before passing the joint to Maggie.

"Thank you, cousin," she said, taking a big, record-setting hit. "My husband got me started on opium when I worked in Butte, smoked a lot of that stuff." She eventually passed the joint to Rubber Joe.

"I've never tried this shit before...what the hell, you only live once," Rubber Joe said before wrapping his sloppy, wet lips around the joint and inhaling for all he was worth. Smoke immediately started pouring out his nostrils and kept coming until he finally exhaled. "Shit, I've gotten higher on Bull Durham tobacco."

Rubber Joe handed the sloppy, disfigured joint to me. I must have taken a little too long inspecting the soggy, deformed thing, because when I looked up, the other members of the party were staring at me with anticipation written all over their faces. Not wanting to disappoint, I took a big hit and handed it back to Rubber Joe, who seemed much more receptive the second time around. We sat on that ledge on a beautiful summer morning smoking joints and telling stories, pretty much oblivious to everything happening around us.

"My full name is Joseph Many Guns," Rubber Joe suddenly announced, apparently having a moment of deep inner reflection. "I was raised on a ranch north of town." He pointed to something off in the distance. "Back then, things were different. We only went to town twice a year. We raised cattle and pigs. You can't grow crops in this godforsaken place, so we ate meat, occasionally some fish, but mostly meat. I married young and had two kids, a boy and a girl."

Rubber Joe took another hit, staring at a place only he could see. "One day, I took a truckload of cattle to Shelby to sell at the livestock auction. While I was gone, our house burned to the ground. I never found out how it happened. How could it happen? he asked rhetorically, shaking his head ever so slightly. "My wife tried to save our kids, but the place burned too fast. She was in the hospital for several weeks." He paused long enough to hand the joint to Maggie.

"She ran away after she healed up. I heard she went to live with relatives up in Canada. Shit, I never blamed her for leaving or for anything else. I always blamed myself, and I've never been able to shake the guilt. Not one day goes by without me reliving it all. I ran away too, into town and into the bottle, and I haven't been back. There are just too many ghosts, too many ghosts." Rubber Joe repeated himself a lot that day, and the pain in his voice never left. Pain was the one thing that never ran away from him. "Now I'm Rubber Joe. Rubber Joe with no place to go." Joseph Many Guns once again pointed to a place far, far away.

"That is a very sad, sad story, cousin." Maggie paused briefly while she summoned the strength to tell her sad story. "My full name is Margaret White Horse, and I am a Cree Indian from Canada. My people have lived for centuries near what is now known as Lethbridge, Alberta. I married an older white American when I was sixteen. He promised me a great life in the United States of America and, I naively believed him. I craved a new life, but I had never set foot in the States before moving to Butte."

Maggie passed the joint to the Governor. "My husband worked in the silver mines. Butte was prosperous and exciting in our early days. It was a good job, but he started drinking and wasting all of our money. He turned out to be a lazy, worthless bastard. He was drunk all the time, and when he got drunk, he beat me. He beat me so badly once, when I was pregnant, that I lost my baby. I could never get pregnant again."

She continued, "I never was any good after that, and he ended up getting killed over a poker game, good riddance. I was young and alone with nowhere to go. I never considered going back to my childhood home in Canada; my shame wouldn't let me. My pride is long gone, but my shame still hangs on me. So, I went to work at a whorehouse, where shame is welcome. My heavens, Butte had a whorehouse on every corner back then. There was lots of money in Butte."

"I saved my money, and after about a year, I quit whoring and got a good job cleaning rooms at one of the hotels in town. Rooms were rented in eight-hour shifts because Butte was so busy. I cleaned the rooms as soon as they emptied, time was everything. One day, I was cleaning a room on the top floor when a dirty, stinking miner came to the door. He was in a hurry for his room and wanted to know what was taking me so long. Before I could answer, he knocked me down and viciously raped me. When I reported him, nobody gave a shit. My word carried no weight. Like they say, once a whore, always a whore." Maggie stood, stretched her legs, and looked toward the Oasis Bar. "Drinking helps me to forget."

"I know why I drink. I drink to forget too... but I've been drinking so long I can't remember what it was I was trying to forget. I guess I've finally succeeded at something," the Governor said philosophically. "I do know this much, everybody can find an excuse to drink. Everybody has had bad things happen to them. Drinking is a weakness, and once you start down that road, it takes a lot of strength to turn back. I've never been that strong. Turning back never seemed like an option for me. The best thing to do is to avoid bad luck. What about you, my boy? Why do you drink?" the Governor asked Two-Fingers.

Two-Fingers sat in silence, pondering the question, when the front door of the Oasis swung open, and the day bartender placed a brick under it to keep it that way. Before Two-Fingers could answer, Maggie, Rubber Joe, and the Governor hastily made their way inside. After they disappeared, we looked at each other and shrugged.

"Wow, shit. That was pretty heavy. Why do we drink, Two-Fingers?"

"Hell, you got me. All I know is, I don't want to end up like them. Did you notice how quickly they got out of here once the Oasis opened?" We continued sitting on the ledge, lost in thought as Browning slowly came to life.

"I think I'm going to visit my dad." Two-Fingers said as he pointed in the direction of the Blackfeet Health Center.

"Yeah, I think I'll go see mine too," I said, pointing in the opposite direction.

Two-Fingers and I had been separated for approximately two years, yet when we reunited, it was as if we'd never been apart. The tragedies that struck our families further strengthened our friendship; true friendship is a rare and interesting phenomenon. We were affected by our encounter and conversation with the winos, not so profoundly that we joined a Bible class or converted to Hinduism, but enough to slow down on our partying and start taking care of business.

For an entire week following our time on the ledge, we were on our best behavior. Each day, after doing his chores, Two-Fingers sat with his dad at the Blackfeet Health Center. His family had pulled together, and Max got a little stronger with each passing day. I visited the hospital as often as I could, I was busy with family and work.

I was at Max's bedside when Two-Fingers and Max had the following conversation:

"The doctor said that as soon as the swelling goes down, I can get fitted for a prosthesis," Max said as he patted the side of the hospital bed.

"Really? Maybe I should call up Bandit Spotted Owl and find out where he buys his parts." Bandit had lost an arm in a car wreck years before and he had a prosthesis. Two-Fingers said with a smile.

"Well, if you talk to him, tell him I want a new leg, nothing used," Max said as he smiled and winked at his son.

"Seriously, I'm probably going to be in this place for quite a while. Then I'll need some extensive physical therapy and rehabilitation. I'll have to learn how to walk and drive with my new leg, so it's going to take some time," Max said. "I'm going to need your help, and I'm glad you decided to come home, son. Paula and Cindy Ann are needed at the apartments and the curios shop, so you're going to have to help out as much as you can." Max reached for a cup of water. "Man, these pills really mess me up."

Two-Fingers glanced at me before helping him with the water. "I'm feeling kind of sleepy, son. I think I'll get some sleep now. You think about what I said." Max leaned back against his pillow.

"Hell, Pop, sounds good to me. I never wanted to leave in the first place," Two-Fingers said as Max began to snore.

I remember standing at the door and looking back over my shoulder as Two-Fingers gently wiped sweat from Max's forehead. All was forgiven, and wounds continued to heal.

That happened to be the same day my parents told me they were planning to move back to Cherry Hill, N. J.

"What do you mean you want to move?" I asked Dad.

"Your mom and I have decided to sell and get out of here. She needs to get out of here, Tony."

"I thought you liked it here, Pop. You always wanted a gas station," I said, knowing full well I was going to lose the argument.

"One bad thing after another has happened since we moved here. Your mom hates the place, and I'm beginning to," Dad spoke emphatically.

"Yeah, but I like it here. Besides, I'll be a senior this year, and I don't want to move. What about Stan? He'll want to come back here."

"Listen, Tony," Dad said, holding my shoulders. "We have to accept the real possibility that Stan may not come back."

"I can't accept that, Pop. I won't accept that. He has to come home," I said as I slumped against the wall.

Dad leaned against the pop cooler and whispered, in a barely audible voice, "I hope, with all my heart, you're right. But your mother is having a nervous breakdown, and she needs to get the hell out of here. There's a greenhouse for sale in Cherry Hill, and I'm going to buy it for her if I can get this place sold."

"Well, you'll never get this place sold, Pop. No white family is going to move here now, not with all the militants running around. The reservation is changing so fast, I don't even recognize it," I said, staring out the front window.

"All the more reason for us to get the hell out of here," Dad said before walking outside to wait on a customer.

"I'm not leaving," I said as I followed him out.

"Look, Tony, business is off. Tourists are driving through town without stopping. We either sell now and get something, or wait and get nothing," Dad said as he washed the customer's windshield.

"Who is going to buy the place? Nobody in town has any money." I asked.

"I've been talking with Bobby Racine, and he's trying to get a loan through the tribe. Bobby is a good guy, at least he isn't drunk all the damn time," Dad said as he finished. "If I can't get this place sold, I'll board it up. Charley said he would loan me the money for the greenhouse and the move. I hate to do that, but I'm running out of options."

"Has Charley found Juanita?" I asked without making eye contact.

"Oh yeah, the funniest thing happened. I guess she went home a few days ago and was very remorseful about running away. Charley said she's stopped drinking and has been staying close to home lately. I don't know how long that will last, she's too damn young and wild. I feel sorry for Charley, he deserves better," Dad said as he handed change to the customer.

"Did he say where she ran off to?" I asked as I once again avoided making eye contact.

"He never said, and I doubt he knows where she went, exactly,"

Dad replied before walking back to the station.

I suspected Charley didn't want to know where Juanita had run off to; he was probably just glad she was home. I learned during our night together that Juanita had been diagnosed with endometriosis, an inflammation of the lining of the uterus. At the time of her diagnosis, she was told it was highly unlikely she would ever become pregnant. Charley was disappointed, but Juanita was devastated. Never very confident, she began to think of herself as a failure. Her insecurity overwhelmed her. To hide from the pain, she drank, and when she drank, she drank hard. The more she drank, the less self-esteem she had, and her downward spiral worsened.

It was always the same after Juanita returned home: she was remorseful for a while, then the fever would hit her and off she would go. Sometimes she'd be gone for a day, sometimes several days. But she always returned home.

I hadn't seen much of Jimmy B during our drying-out period, and he was only a few days away from going into the Army when we finally hooked up again. He had kept partying after the night we were all together at Too Slim's party. He looked like death warmed over when he finally showed up at our station.

"Fill it up, White Guy," Jimmy B said as he tumbled out of his Chevy.

"Where have you been, Jimmy B?" I asked as we shook hands.

"Been out breaking a few hearts before I go off to save the world. Man, I can't believe I go in next week. Time flies when you're having fun," Jimmy B said, waving a wad of cash in my face.

"Wow, where did you get all that money?" I asked.

"I sold the Chevy to AJ Hoyt for $2,000. He put down $500 and will give me the rest when I turn over the car," Jimmy B said leaning against the Chevy.

"AJ better hope you don't turn it over to him all busted up," I said as I began filling the tank.

"Shit, AJ would fix it better than new anyway. That reminds me, I'd better check the oil."

"So what have you and Two-Fingers been up to? I heard through the grapevine that you've been on the wagon,"

"Yeah, it's a long story. Basically, we decided it was time to dry out for a while and help out around home," I said, handing Jimmy B an oil rag.

"Well, Indian Days starts soon, and I say you boys fall off the wagon before then," Jimmy B said, inspecting the dipstick.

"I say you're probably right. Shit, I can't believe we've lasted this long."

"Well, since you're going to fall off anyway, why don't you jump in and we'll go find him?" Jimmy B asked, closing the hood.

"I don't know, the old man has been acting kind of weird lately. He's talking about selling out and moving back to New Jersey," I said.

"No shit. Have you told Two-Fingers?" Jimmy B asked.

"No, I found out this morning."

Jimmy B stared at me before saying. "You'd better ride with me and tell Two-Fingers yourself. You don't want him finding out from someone else."

"You're right. I'll go tell my dad I need some time off."

It didn't take long to find Two-Fingers; he was on guard outside their apartment house, smoking a cigarette and drinking a cup of coffee.

"Have you seen Peaches lately?" he asked as we approached.

"Not since the two of you were making out at Too Slim's. Why? You two thinking about running off and getting married?" Jimmy B asked before sitting down on the porch next to Two-Fingers.

"Well, she used me that night, and I haven't heard from her since. Not one phone call, not a word," Two-Fingers said, abruptly glancing over his shoulder.

"Whoa, you seem a little jumpy, partner. You don't think she's going to sneak up on you and start throwing rocks again, do you?" Jimmy B asked with a smile.

"You heard?" Two Fingers asked.

"Hell yes, I've heard. Half the town has probably heard by now," Jimmy B said, taking a drag off Two-Fingers' cigarette.

"That is so embarrassing," Two-Fingers said, hiding his face in his hand.

"Yeah, I know. The poor girl must be embarrassed to tears thinking that everybody in town knows she let you have sex with her, Two-Fingers," Jimmy B said, flicking the cigarette butt toward Main Street.

"Bone you, Jimmy B," Two-Fingers said, reaching into his Levi jacket for another cigarette.

Jimmy B laughed uncontrollably as Two-Fingers told him his version of the episode. To add effect, Two-Fingers stood and removed his T-shirt to reveal the welts on his back.

"Yeah, and the White Guy said we ought to split up so he's out of the line of fire." Two-Fingers smiled at me, and Jimmy B laughed so hard tears ran down his cheeks. He finally stopped laughing long enough to blurt out, "By the way, White Guy has something he wants to tell you."

I stared at him and cursed his name under my breath before telling Two-Fingers the news of our moving. Two-Fingers stared at me in silence.

"Now don't get pissed off, I only found out early this morning," I said.

"I'm not sure what I'm feeling. All I know is I haven't even finished my cup of coffee, and you're throwing a lot of shit at me. It'll take some time to digest it all," Two-Fingers said as he lit another cigarette.

"Man, what is it with you and these cigarettes?" I asked.

"I need to do something with my hand," Two-Fingers said.

"You ever try sitting on it?" I asked between coughs.

"Getting awful cocky since you got a piece of ass, White Guy," Two-Fingers said, blowing smoke in my direction.

"Hey, if you had given Peaches a little more cocky, she wouldn't have chased your sorry ass all over town."

"Crack you, White Guy, crack you." Two-Fingers stood up to face me.

"Bone you, Two-Fingers."

I couldn't tell if he was really mad or just messing around, so I left it at that.

"I see you boys have gotten a little feisty since you've been on the wagon. We'd better get some beer before there's bloodshed," Jimmy B said as he walked to his car.

Two-Fingers and I quickly followed, and before long, we were sitting in the parking lot of the Paradise Bar.

"I'll be right back, it's on me. You girls kiss and make up while I'm gone." Jimmy B jumped out of the Chevy and entered the Paradise like a man on a mission. He had a pronounced spring in his step now that he was at the watering hole.

"Girls? Who are you calling girls?" Two-Fingers yelled from the passenger seat before Jimmy B disappeared inside the Paradise.

"Always got to get the last word, Two-Fingers," I said.

"You want to get it on? We can step outside right now," Two-Fingers said as he reached for the door handle.

"You feeling froggy? Jump," I said as I started to get out of the back seat.

It was right around that time when Jimmy B came bouncing out of the Paradise headfirst. In the doorway stood Red Stabs-in-the-Back and two of his drinking buddies, looking like they were possessed by demons.

"Been looking for you guys," Red said as he and his friends approached the Chevy.

"Oh, shit," Two-Fingers said as he locked the passenger door and quickly slid down the bench seat and locked the driver's door too.

Red made his way to the driver's door and started yanking on the door handle and pounding on the window. Luckily, Jimmy B had left the car keys in the ignition, so Two-Fingers started the car while the other two thugs yanked on the passenger door handle. Red picked up a rock and began smashing it against the driver's side window with an intensity reserved for the truly insane.

Two-Fingers put the Chevy in reverse and gunned the engine. Dust and gravel flew everywhere as the Chevy traveled backward toward Main Street. Red and his friends returned their attention to Jimmy B. Two-Fingers slowed down slightly before shifting into first gear and flooring the accelerator. Gravel and dust temporarily blocked out the sun as Two-Fingers drove directly at Red. That move caused Red to momentarily freeze before he dove out of the way.

Jimmy B stood up, and when the Chevy slowed slightly, he threw himself onto the hood and grabbed the windshield wipers for support.

"Go, go, go," Jimmy B yelled as Red regained his footing and threw a rock that narrowly missed the rear window.

"AJ would be pleased about that," I said as we spun out of the parking lot and onto Main Street, narrowly missing a family in a pickup truck. I'm not sure of the nationality of the people in the truck, just saying.

"This is the rock-throwingest place I've ever seen," Two-Fingers said before shifting into second gear.

Jimmy B remained facedown on the hood while holding tight to the windshield wipers. As the Chevy roared down Main Street, he slowly lifted his head and made eye contact with Two-Fingers who continued to drive like a man possessed. Jimmy B used his head to motion toward the side of the road; his hands remained firmly attached to the windshield wipers.

"What do you think he wants?" Two-Fingers asked

"Looks like he wants you to pull over," I said as we swerved to avoid a pack of dogs.

Just then, Two-Fingers drove into the Junction's parking lot, slowed slightly, and slammed on the brakes. Jimmy B lost his grip on the windshield wipers and flew off the Chevy, bouncing across the parking lot before coming to rest at the feet of Vicki Eagle Feathers. He was flat on his back looking up at Vicki when he asked,

"What's it take to get a little service around here?"

"You're a funny guy, Jimmy B," Vicki said before stepping over him and going inside the Junction.

Two-Fingers and I were laughing as we helped Jimmy B to his feet. He was too shook up to get mad at us.

"Jimmy B, think of this as advanced training; you'll probably be doing a lot of this type of shit in the army," Two-Fingers said as he wiped his tear streaked cheeks.

"Can't come in here like a normal human being, can you, Two-Fingers? Always have to make an entrance," Vicki had reappeared.

"Just checking the brakes, I think she's pulling a little to the right," Two-Fingers said.

"Tony, why do you run around with this dip shit?" Vicki asked as she stared me down.

"Why are you always so angry, Vicki?" I asked.

"This place makes me angry, that's why. All I see is stupid shit all day long; it never changes around here. The reservation never changes, Tony."

I was scheduled to work that night, and before Jimmy B dropped Two-Fingers at the hospital and me at the station, we talked about what Vicki had said. Two-Fingers was convinced she was acting that way because she had a crush on me. Surprisingly, it turned out he was right. Back then, I was pretty much brain-dead when it came to girls or women in general. To this day, I can't truly say I've figured any of them out, and I've met a lot of them. They remain complete and total mysteries to me.

Things were quiet when I started my shift, but that all changed after the bars closed at 2 a.m. That's when the after-hours crowd descended on our gas station with a vengeance. Cars were gassed up and snacks sold at a feverish pace. Around 3:30 a.m., things had slowed to a crawl when, out of nowhere, Juanita showed up in a fancy new red half-ton Chevy pickup.

"What time do you get off?" she asked.

"Eight or nine in the morning, why?" I asked, as I cautiously approached her pickup.

"I'll pick you up, and we can go for a ride," she said.

"No, no rides." I shook my head vigorously.

"Why not? You scared to be seen with me?" Juanita asked.

"Look, we were both a little loaded the other night. Let's just forget it ever happened, okay?" I said.

"I wasn't loaded. You may have been, but I wasn't," Juanita said, taking a sip from a fifth of Southern Comfort. "I knew exactly what I was doing, and I don't regret it one bit. You got a conscience, Tony?" she asked, reaching out to touch my cheek.

"You're married to my dad's best friend. Yeah, I got a conscience," I said, taking a step back.

"That didn't seem to bother you the other night," Juanita said, turning off the engine. "Don't tell me you were too whacked. I know better. Maybe you didn't like making it with me?"

"I liked it. I liked it a lot," I mumbled, my head hanging down like a whipped, homeless pup.

"So what's the problem? You think it's easy for me to come to you like this? Shit, I'm an old married woman chasing after a younger man," Juanita said, raising the bottle of Southern Comfort to her full, moist, red lips.

"Yeah, so why are you doing it?" I asked.

"Because I can't stop thinking about that night. Can you?" Juanita asked, leaning her head back against the headrest and staring at me.

In reality, that was about all I thought about. I was consumed with guilt and overwhelmed with a desire to be with her. It was good versus evil, and evil was winning.

Before I could answer, a carload of partying Blackfeet pulled up and started demanding gas.

"I'm going to use your restroom. You'd better stick your gas hose into my pickup before people start getting the wrong idea," Juanita said as she slid out of her pickup.

After returning from the restroom, Juanita said, "So, what are we going to do about it, Tony?"

I was avoiding the question when I suddenly found myself asking, "Where's Charley?"

"He flew to Chicago on business, some kind of cattle convention or something. He'll be gone for a week or so," Juanita said, leaning back against her pickup.

"Look, Juanita, I,"

Before I could finish, Juanita interrupted me, asking, "What is that building over there?" She pointed to a building off to the side of the main station, where my dad fixed tires and drank beer.

"That's the tire repair shop," I said as Juanita walked in that direction.

I wasn't sure she heard me because she was walking fast. She stopped at the entrance and tried to open the door. It was locked.

"Do you have the key, Tony?"

After nervously checking around for witnesses, I unlocked the door and Juanita quickly stepped inside.

The shop was dark and smelled of musk, with a low humming sound coming from the vibrating air compressor. After taking a moment to adjust to the darkness, Juanita turned toward me, and before long, we were kissing and touching each other before I shut and locked the door behind us. Once again, desire and lust won out over guilt and conscience.

Chapter 11
Jimmy B and Stogie Man Go to the Vast Unknown

The annual North American Indian Days Powwow celebration began the next day. Two-Fingers and I had satisfied our family obligations and were ready to enjoy ourselves. "Yeah, Bobby Racine and Dad worked out a deal where Bobby will get some on-the-job training in case his loan comes through. He may change his mind after working a few graveyard shifts,"

"Well, my old man doesn't know I'm in the room half the time and Mom and my sisters are tired of me getting in their way. So, let's party," Two-Fingers said.

The annual parade was well underway, moving down Main Street in the opposite direction of the fairgrounds. On our way to the fairgrounds, Two-Fingers stuck his head inside the front door of Bob Scriver's Museum and yelled, "Bob, that bear really does look like he's taking a shit, good job." We quickly retreated before anyone inside could respond.

"Where do you come up with that stuff?" I asked.

"Right up here and there's plenty more where that came from." Two-Fingers said, pointing to his head.

We successfully crossed the highway without getting run over, and before long, we were at the entrance to the fairgrounds, where we found ourselves surrounded by tribal campaign booths and political posters.

"Damn, look at all that stuff. The tribal elections are still weeks away, and already they're polluting the place with their bullshit. The only thing missing is Huntley and Brinkley," Two-Fingers said.

The Blackfeet were, and continue to be, governed by a tribal council of seven duly elected tribal members. There are seven districts on the reservation, and each district gets representation. Once elected, the councilmen served two-year terms, and like American politics, the incumbents have an advantage in the electoral process. Everyone wants to be a councilman because they get a say in who gets the best housing, who gets a job, who gets assistance and who doesn't. Obviously, this governing technique was patterned after American politics where corruption and nepotism reign supreme. Being a councilman means you have money and power, which can be used to get re-elected. New candidates, since they don't have power, must show they have something else to offer. There has to be a groundswell of support over some galvanizing issue, and the election that year was more issue-focused than previous elections.

By 1970, voting-age younger Blackfeet had become politically active, and their awareness of the issues was at an all-time high. They began to distance themselves from the older generation that had allowed the status quo to continue for decades. Change was desperately needed in order to shake off the chains of government dependency and control; social unrest was the order of the day, and the change merchants were out in force on the reservation.

The formation of the American Indian Movement (AIM) had given younger Indians a platform from which they could advance their ideas. AIM was founded on the ideals of spiritual strength, complete control of reservation land, and the preservation of Indian traditions. They wanted to shake up the system as opposed to those within the system who wanted things to stay the same. The incumbents were feeling the heat and campaigned as if their livelihoods depended on it.

"I've never seen so many young guys running for office. Hell, even Johnny Kills-At-Night is running," Two-Fingers said. "I've never known him to be interested in anything but screwing. He should hand out a campaign button that simply says, 'Vote for me, and I won't sleep with your old lady.' Probably win in a landslide."

"Looks like there are a lot of different tribes here this year, more than usual." I said. Two-Fingers nodded in agreement as we watched the activity swirling around us; long-haired strangers wearing green army fatigue jackets and colorful bandanas dominated our space.

We leisurely walked around the encampment, taking in the various sights and sounds. It was a beautiful July day, and other than the activity surrounding the campaigners, things were pretty quiet. Most of the teepees and tents were already standing tall, and the late arrivals were working hard to get their lodging in place before the traditional festivities officially began. Outside the teepees, mothers put finishing touches on their children's attire, faces were painted, hair combed and styled, before eagle feathers were strategically placed. Tiny silver bells and colorful beads adorned buckskin, and the headdresses were worn with pride as the dancers strutted confidently into the dancing arena.

We stood watching in admiration before being startled back to reality by Jimmy B, who yelled out, "Hello, girls."

"Where the hell have you been, Jimmy B?" I asked.

"I dropped off the Chevy at AJ's and went to the bank to deposit the rest of the money he owed me. I should be a rich man by the time I get out."

"Did they offer you a toaster for opening the account?" Two-Fingers asked, suddenly interested in saving money.

"Naw, just a sweaty palm and a weak handshake."

"When do you report for duty?" I asked.

"Tomorrow morning at 8 a.m. at Government Square, and then I'm off to Helena on the Army bus, and after that, it won't be long before I'm on a slow boat to 'Nam'.

Jimmy B seemed to be suddenly struck by the magnitude of his decision.

"I still say we take your sorry ass up to Canada and get you married off to a Cree woman," I offered.

"Cree woman? I'd rather go to the jungle and take my chances fighting the entire Vietnamese army," Jimmy B said, steadfast in his resolve.

We were bullshitting about a number of mundane topics when Two-Fingers noticed his uncle Billy Spotted Eagle approaching. He exclaimed, "Oh shit, here comes Uncle Billy." Billy is Pam's older brother, and he was the spiritual leader of the Blackfeet Tribe long before I arrived on the reservation.

In the olden days, he would've been recognized as a holy man, and he would've been highly respected, even revered. But the unending and relentless assimilation process diminished the stature of the holy man. Only the very old Blackfeet remembered the old ways; several generations were lost to the white cultural experience, and with the passing of each generation, their heritage and culture eroded further. Things only began to change in the late 60s when younger Indians from all over the country yearned for a return to their roots, and the spiritual leaders of each tribe slowly began to regain their stature and influence. Billy sensed this change in attitude and wanted to strike while the iron was hot. He believed this particular Indian Days celebration would provide a forum in which he could spread the word; there was true spiritual and social unrest taking place, and the time to act was now.

I have always liked and respected Billy; he is one of the most honest and principled men I've ever met. Yet Billy knew he had a daunting task ahead of him. Even within his own family, there was a difference of opinion regarding tradition. Billy lived a traditional lifestyle as opposed to his sister Pam's modern lifestyle. Pam chose to accept white culture and embraced it as her own because she was influenced to do so. Billy, on the other hand, resisted losing his heritage because his mentors taught him the value of the traditional lifestyle, and he cherished it. This dichotomy existed in their family, and at the time, it existed throughout the entire reservation. Spiritually and socially, the reservation was a house divided, so to speak.

"Your mom said I'd find you here," Billy said as he approached.

"Hello, Uncle. What has brought you down from the mountain?" Two-Fingers asked.

"Well, it wasn't the cotton candy, my misguided nephew," Billy said before putting Two-Fingers into a bear hug. "It's good to see you, my boy."

Billy held Two-Fingers at arm's length and looked him over from head to toe without commenting on his appearance. "You've been gone too long." He hugged Two-Fingers again before adding, "I looked in on Max before coming here. What a shame."

"Yeah, I know." Two-Fingers said as he shook his head. "But, it's good to see you, Uncle. Do you know these two vagrants?"

"Of course, I know them. Hello, you two."

Jimmy B and I extended a warm greeting, and I got a distinct impression that Jimmy B wanted to go partying. Two-Fingers wanted to as well, but wasn't sure how to gracefully disengage from Billy.

"I'll come visit you sometime during Indian Days, and we'll have a nice visit. Jimmy B is going into the Army tomorrow, and we need to get him a shot of penicillin."

Billy laughed before saying, "You can get him a shot later. I'm setting up a sweat lodge down by the river, and I'm running behind schedule. There's a lot of interest in the sweat this year, and I'm going to need your help."

"How long will it take, Uncle?" Two-Fingers asked.

"If we hurry, we'll be done before sundown."

Jimmy B was visibly distressed by that development, but after a few minutes of coaxing, we finally persuaded him to help out.

Sweat lodges are associated with prayer and preparation. They are used to cleanse the body of toxins, thereby enhancing the religious experience. Sweats can last for several hours and are enriched by spiritual leaders who guide the prayers and storytelling. Billy had chosen the perfect spot for a sweat lodge, it was far enough away from the main encampment to give the participants privacy and close enough to get all the fry bread they could handle.

Two-Fingers, Jimmy B, and I quickly cleared a place for the lodge while Billy unloaded wood, rope, and bison hides from his pickup.

We dug a three-foot-deep pit in the sand next to the river, and it didn't take long. Next, a dome-shaped structure was assembled from the wood and rope Billy brought, then carefully placed over the pit. The bison hides were placed over the entire structure, and after several hours of work, Billy said, "Oki, looking good. Now I need you to gather up a bunch of rocks about the size of my head."

The rocks were to be heated in a separate, large fire pit outside the entrance of the sweat lodge, and when they were red hot, the rocks would be removed from the fire and placed in a circle inside the lodge where cold water would then be poured over them. The steam that was created would cause the temperature in the lodge to rise dramatically.

We had plenty of rocks to choose from, so collecting them didn't take long. After stacking them near the entrance, we stretched out in the cool sand and relaxed a little before Billy said, "Beginning tomorrow, I'm going to have a sweat every day of Indian Days. I want you two to come back and participate. Jimmy B, since you will be gone, I will include you in our prayers."

Two-Fingers and I reluctantly accepted his invitation, and the three of us returned to the main encampment. Billy stayed behind and began putting up his teepee.

"Let's move a little faster, boys, we're burning daylight," Jimmy B said as the sun began to set.

We ended up partying with Vicki and two of her coworkers, Veronica Comes-at-Night and Rhonda Dunham. Vicki's family had set up a teepee, and we spent the night there. It turned out to be a very mellow, quiet evening, and before long, Jimmy B was fast asleep.

When morning came, I was startled out of a deep sleep by Jimmy B yelling, "Holy shit! What time is it?" Without waiting for an answer, he grabbed his clothes and started running as fast as he could toward Government Square.

"Damn, I've never seen a guy in such a hurry to get his ass shot off," Two-Fingers said before he and I got dressed and went outside. The girls had fallen back asleep, and we both thought it would be a good time to get some coffee and stretch.

We ran across Stogie Man and a group of his friends while strolling around the encampment, sipping our coffee. As usual, they had been up all night drinking and raising hell. Stogie Man didn't have to worry about being drafted since he was married, crippled, and the sole support for his family. Of course, like most of the men in the group, he hadn't worked for months. They mentioned seeing Jimmy B running half-naked across the wide open prairie toward Government Square and rightly concluded he was no longer a free man.

We shared a bottle of wine with them before Stogie Man said, "Tough way to make a living, but at least Jimmy B has a job."

"Tough way to make a living? Hell, 'Nam isn't about living, it's about dying," Two Slim said as he passed the near-empty bottle of wine back to Two-Fingers.

Big Man Bear Claw was in the group, and he began telling stories about his Vietnam experiences. He had told the stories many times since returning from 'Nam, I suppose it helped him in some way. He spoke of the night patrols he and his unit went on and how Vietnamese snipers picked them off one by one, how the heat was so oppressive he thought he was going to die, and how the grunts hated their commanding officers and plotted their demise. He also talked about the destruction of villages filled with innocent civilians and the coverups that followed. Big Man had seen a lot, and Stogie Man and the rest of us listened in silence, only occasionally interrupting with a question. When the wine was finished, Stogie Man said goodbye and staggered off toward home.

Later that day, Two-Fingers and I heard what happened when Stogie Man finally made it home. The story was similar to others we'd heard or witnessed over the years. On the reservation, domestic abuse was all too common. Evidently, Cindy Ann woke early that morning to tend to her girls. They were growing fast and were a handful. She wasn't surprised when Stogie Man didn't come home the night before. He wasn't home much, and when he was, she wished he wasn't.

Cindy Ann, like far too many women on the reservation, was trapped in a bad marriage. The story was all too common: they married too young, had children too young, and grew old too fast. In between all that was the domestic violence brought on by drinking, and the drinking was brought on by a lack of self-worth, which was fostered by the lack of a good job. Everyone needs a purpose in life. Excuses were made for why this behavior existed, and Cindy Ann had made her share of excuses, even though she knew there was no excuse. Everybody knew there was no excuse, and this knowledge added to the lack of self-worth the abuser experienced. Once self-worth is stripped away, there are no boundaries left to restrain the abuser's actions. As far as Cindy Ann was concerned, Stogie Man destroyed all remaining boundaries on that day.

As the story goes, Stogie Man stumbled into their kitchen that morning and demanded a steak for breakfast. When Cindy Ann informed him that the only thing in the house to eat was some cold, leftover chicken, Stogie Man lost his shit and started yelling and intimidating her. This all took place in the presence of their young children, so she picked up the car keys from the kitchen counter and tried to leave, explaining to Stogie Man that she needed to go to her parents' place and help out. Upon hearing that, Stogie Man picked up the kitchen table and threw it against the wall. Cindy Ann gathered her two girls and ran out the front door in search of sanctuary. She said she cried all the way to her parents' apartment. She had remained silent over the years while the abuse escalated out of control. Now, she needed to talk to someone about it, and she decided to tell her mother and Paula.

After putting her girls down for their morning nap, Cindy Ann sat Pam and Paula down at the kitchen table and told them about the problems she faced at home.

"Has he ever hit you?" Pam asked.

"No, but he's constantly yelling at me and belittling me. I'm scared he'll fly off the handle and hurt me or one of the girls."

"Stogie Man needs to find a job and quit his drinking," Pam said.

"He doesn't even look for work anymore. He's been rejected so many times he feels useless," Cindy Ann said. "We live on commodities and federal assistance, and that makes him mad. He feels inadequate, and he has started to take it out on me."

"I know. But that's no excuse, and I think the best thing you can do is move back here. Your bedroom is big enough for the three of you," Pam said.

"What will Dad say?" Cindy Ann asked.

"Well, for now, we won't tell your dad. He'll get upset, and he doesn't need that right now. Besides, he won't be able to come home for a while, and maybe Stogie Man will come to his senses by then."

"Stogie Man doesn't have any sense left," Cindy Ann said.

While all this was going down, Two-Fingers and I had safely delivered the girls to the Junction for another day of work and were walking out the door when Paula drove up and honked.

"Get in, you two. We have something to do."

Two-Fingers and I climbed into the car and listened intently as Paula filled us in on the bloody details.

"I figured something was up. He's been partying like he isn't married. I don't know why we get married on the reservation, nobody stays at home," Two-Fingers said.

"Mom and Dad stay at home," Paula replied as she parked in their front yard, mere inches from the front door.

Paula entered their house and didn't wait for either one of us to catch up. We found Stogie Man sound asleep on the couch, and for a brief, shining moment, I thought Paula was going to take a pillow and smother him with it. That thought passed as she walked straight to their bedroom and began packing for Cindy Ann and her nieces. Two-Fingers and I remained in the living room and stood over Stogie Man as he slept. Unable to resist the temptation, Two-Fingers leaned down, grabbed Stogie Man by the shoulders, and shook him awake. Stogie Man slowly opened his rummy eyes and tried to focus. Soon, his entire world would become out of focus, and it would be years before he started to see straight again.

Two-Fingers held him down and said, "Just so you know, Cindy Ann is leaving your sorry ass, and we're helping her move out."

Stogie Man violently shook his head in an apparent attempt at making sense of it all.

Two-Fingers added, "Don't try to get tough with her either, Stogie Man, or I'll fix you good."

Stogie Man regained what little sense he had left and said, "She's moving out? I'm kicking her out! Good riddance to her and her whole damn family!"

Just then, Paula walked into the living room with two grocery sacks filled with clothing and other personal items and stared coldly at Stogie Man. She didn't say a word, she just stared at him. After she had her fill, she turned and walked out, letting the screen door without a screen slam behind her. Two-Fingers and I were exiting the premises when Stogie Man yelled, "She'll be back, Two-Fingers. The bitches always come back!"

Two-Fingers stopped dead in his tracks and started to walk back inside before I grabbed his arm and stopped him.

"It's not worth it, not now," I said. I knew Two-Fingers wanted to whip his bony ass, but that was not the time or the place. There would be no joy or glory in it. Two-Fingers beating a defenseless man would hurt him more than it would hurt Stogie Man. He may not have known that then, but I did. As we sat with Paula in the car, we could hear Stogie Man as he continued to yell, "She'll be back, Two-Fingers, she'll be back!"

Paula drove to the fairgrounds in complete silence. I believe it was the quietest she's ever been, at least since I've known her. She must have been thinking about how messed up life was when she finally said,

"I have to get away from here. I want to go to college so bad, and now Dad is hurt, and Mom needs my help, and I am going crazy."

"Shit, Sis, go. Just go. I can help out," Two-Fingers said.

"I have to decide soon; registration is in a couple of weeks. If I go, I'll go to the University of Montana over in Missoula. At least I won't be too far away, and I can come home on the weekends," Paula said as she drove up to the fairgrounds entrance.

"Just go," Two-Fingers said before getting out of the car.

Before I was able to get out of the backseat, Paula turned and put her hand on my arm.

"Any word about Stan?" she asked.

Upon hearing that, reality suddenly disturbed my relative tranquility. All I could do was look at her and shake my head no.

"Your folks must be going crazy."

I remember muttering to no one in particular as she drove off, "The whole world is going crazy."

Chapter 12
Farewell Juanita, Farewell

Two-Fingers and I stood beneath the fairground's entrance sign and watched as Paula drove away. When we turned and entered the campground, we noticed Kenny and Ronnie Joe Stabs-in-the-Back staggering our way. It was the first time Two-Fingers had seen the brothers since he'd left town and he was shocked by their appearance. They looked as if they had slept in their clothes for weeks on end. Kenny wore a greasy black patch over his left eye socket, and he looked like he had recently pissed himself. They were falling-down drunk and holding onto each other in an effort to stay upright. They stumbled toward us with their heads hanging down before Kenny noticed Two-Fingers. The blood seemed to drain slowly from his face as he looked around for a place to hide.

Two-Fingers walked over to them to take a closer look and immediately concluded that the last couple of years hadn't been kind to the Stabs-in-the-Backs. They appeared to be beaten down from their treachery and subsequent banishment. They had shrunk physically and in stature among the tribe. On the other hand, Two-Fingers and I were each a foot taller than they were and a lot more muscular. We also smelled better.

"You boys don't look so good," Two-Fingers said.

"Hey, Two-Fingers, how are you doing? Haven't seen you around for a while." Ronnie Joe said as he summoned enough strength to stand up straight. "How are you doing, Tony?"

"I'm doing a lot better than you two," I said. "How come you're not as smart-mouthed as you used to be?"

"Ayee, there's no sense fighting anymore," Kenny said as he leaned against Ronnie Joe.

"You guys sound like you've turned chicken shit to me. You scared we might kick your ass?" Two-Fingers asked. "I bet you'll try to get tough again when your gang shows up."

"Shit yeah, we got a gang," Ronnie Joe said as he glanced at Kenny. "You'd better leave us alone before our gang gets here."

"You don't have a gang. Nobody can stand being around you," I said. "Get your sorry asses out of here and stay out, and we won't kick them. Get going. If we see you around here again, we're going to give you exactly what you deserve. Are you listening?" Two-Fingers asked.

"Don't make us tell you again," I said as I stepped in front of Ronnie Joe.

Ronnie Joe mumbled incoherently and started walking toward the exit, with Kenny following close behind. They walked much better, scared straight, I suppose.

"Imagine, I used to have a little respect for those assholes," I said as they scurried off.

"Really? Respect? I never did. I always thought they were punks," Two-Fingers said as he started walking toward the center of the encampment.

"Well, I wouldn't exactly call it respect either." I began before Two-Fingers interrupted me.

"Hell, I know what you mean. You were scared shitless by those two," Two-Fingers said.

"Crack you, Two-Fingers,"

"Bone you, White Guy," Two-Fingers said as he shadow-boxed around me.

"There you are. I was hoping to find you two," Billy said after appearing out of nowhere. Billy has always found a way to sneak up on us. "I'm going to start the sweat in about an hour, and there's room for two more. Come along," he said as he walked toward the river.

"Oh boy, I get to take a sweat," Two-Fingers said as he rolled his eyes.

Billy walked fast, and it took a little time to catch up with him.

"Have you noticed all the long-haired Indians around here?" Billy asked.

"Yeah, we were talking about that yesterday, Uncle," Two-Fingers replied.

"A lot of these young guys are with the American Indian Movement (AIM). They have some good ideas," Billy said. "I'm having a meeting tomorrow with two of their leaders."

"What ideas do they have?" I asked.

"They're talking about Indian sovereignty and the re-examination of the broken treaties," Billy said. "They're also talking spiritualism and the preservation of our culture."

"You think all these different tribes are going to get along, Uncle?" Two-Fingers asked. "Shit, the Blackfeet have never had any allies."

"True. Our tribe will be the last to embrace unity. I think the other tribes already have, but we have a lot of traditional enemies," Billy said. "That's why there will only be Blackfeet at the sweat today."

We walked the rest of the way in silence, and as we approached the sweat lodge, I paused to take in the view. Billy's teepee was standing tall against the skyline, and a lone Appaloosa horse was tethered to a stake near the entry flap. In the distance, the Rocky Mountains rose high in the sky, providing a majestic backdrop to the entire scene. The sweat lodge sat next to a clear, blue stream that ran slowly between its banks. It was truly a magnificent setting.

Standing next to the sweat lodge were eight Blackfeet men of varying ages, anxiously awaiting the start of their spiritual and physical cleansing. Nearby, three young Blackfeet boys tended the fire and the glowing, red-hot rocks. Greetings were exchanged and everybody knew each other.

"Oki," Billy said to the assembled group. "Many of you have attended sweats before, and for those of you who have not, this is what happens." He looked directly at Two-Fingers and me. "After we undress, we will sit in a circle around the heated rocks. I will lead us in prayer, and you will be free to add your own personal thoughts and prayers. Water will be poured over the rocks, and the lodge will get very hot. That's why a sweat lodge is always set up next to water, you'll want to go for a swim and cool off later."

Billy raised the bison hide that covered the entrance to the sweat lodge, bent down low, and quickly entered. The rest of us followed, and soon we were naked and sitting in a circle while the young boys carried in the red-hot rocks on shovels and arranged them in a circle in front of us. Once they were in place, Billy poured cold water over the rocks. They sizzled and hissed as hot steam filled the air. It didn't take long for the lodge to become stiflingly hot, and the only light visible was the glow from the red-hot rocks.

Billy slowly and softly began chanting ancient Blackfeet songs and scattered dried sweetgrass over the rocks. When the sweetgrass caught fire, he waved the smoke in four directions with his hand. His chanting grew louder and intensified before reaching a crescendo. All the while, he continued pouring cold water on the rocks as steam filled the air. The young helpers maintained a steady supply of hot rocks, and at one point, I thought I was going to pass out.

Billy had surrounded himself with sacred medicine bundles that had been passed down from one generation to the next. He raised one of the bundles and continued his rhythmic chanting before lowering it and picking up another, all the while chanting in the mystical Blackfeet language of old. He said a prayer to the Sun, the principal deity of the Blackfeet, and the older Blackfeet joined in with chants and random hand signals. I sat quietly, entranced by the ritual, as sweat poured from my body in a seemingly endless stream, falling unceremoniously onto the sand floor before slowly disappearing. Soon, we were all chanting and saying prayers out loud.

I prayed hard for the safe return of my brother, and the other members chanted loudly. Two-Fingers prayed for his father, and the group responded with more chanting. Each member of the group said a prayer, and the chanting continued until Billy abruptly stood up and walked outside. The rest of us followed, and soon we were all swimming in the stream.

"This cold water feels good," Ivan Bear Medicine said.

"It's very refreshing," Sonny Mountain Chief said.

After cooling off, Billy stepped out of the water and returned to the sweat lodge, and the rest of the party once again followed dutifully.

Soon, more fresh, red-hot rocks were brought in, and the sweat began to pick up steam. The group sat quietly, lost in their thoughts, before they began talking in a nice, conversational tone about things they seldom discussed.

"I notice all these young Indians from different tribes are in town," Tommy No Runner said.

"Yeah, I noticed that too. Never seen this many Crow since we raided their camps and ran off with their women and horses," Joe Arrowtop said.

"Aye, and I never knew there were this many Flathead who could walk without limping," Big Gun Mad Plume said.

"You guys are exaggerating a little bit, don't you think?" Billy asked as he poured water on the hot rocks.

"Of course, we exaggerate. We haven't been at war with some of these tribes for over a hundred years, and we talk like we fought them yesterday," Ivan Bear Medicine said.

"Blackfeet never forget their victories and can never remember our defeats," Glenn Still Smoking said,

"These aren't our traditional enemies in town. These are Apache, Seminole, Choctaw, and a bunch of other tribes I've never heard of," Louie Heavy Runner said.

"They are with AIM. Things are changing rapidly in America and on all reservations," Billy stated.

"It's about time. We're always being told things are going to change for the better, but they never do. We are still living off government handouts like a bunch of refugees," Glenn Still Smoking added.

"I don't know, things seem to be different this time," Billy said as he poured the last of the water on the rocks.

"Well, I don't mind them being in town as long as they don't cause any trouble," Tommy No Runner said.

Two-Fingers and I sat patiently and listened to the elders discuss issue after issue. After a while, we realized no immediate changes in the social order were going to take place, so we excused ourselves and went outside for another swim.

"Man, I was sweating my nuts off in there long before they brought those last rocks in," Two-Fingers said.

"It was a good sweat. It felt good to pray," I said before submerging my body in the water and holding my breath. Hopes of drowning away my sorrow and troubles remained unfulfilled.

After the sweat, we returned to the encampment in search of Vicki and Veronica. They wanted to spend more time with us during Indian Days, so we went looking for their teepee to do just that. That proved easier said than done. Neither one of us was sure which teepee was Vicki's. Two-Fingers had pulled open the flap of a teepee we thought was hers and briefly stepped inside. Within seconds, he backed out and yelled, "Sorry about that, Mr. Boswell! Make sure you finish up before the evening show."

Two-Fingers grabbed my arm and quickly led me away from the scene of yet another crime.

"You won't believe who old man Boswell is screwing in there."

Without waiting for my response, Two-Fingers exclaimed, "Maggie Stink Pits!"

"No way! Man, don't tell me that," I said as shivers ran up and down my spine. "That makes my skin crawl."

"I know, I can't imagine anybody screwing old man Boswell," Two-Fingers said, relishing the last word.

We were standing there laughing when Vicki poked her head out of her teepee.

"There you are. Veronica and I have been looking all over the place for you two."

"Well, damn it, you found us. Get some clothes on, and we'll go down to the Club Cafe for lunch," Two-Fingers said, "I hope you got paid yesterday."

Two-Fingers and I waited patiently outside the teepee, and to pass the time, we played a game of stretch with Two-Fingers' pocketknife. I was closing in for the kill and about to throw it when Two-Fingers stopped me and said, 'Damn it, White Guy, be careful with that thing, I can't afford to lose any more parts.'

Before I threw, Veronica and Vicki stepped out of the teepee and into the bright sunlight.

"Wow, may I say you both look gorgeous."

I remember standing there staring at Vicki with my mouth open.

"Yeah, it was worth the wait," Two-Fingers said as he walked over and took Veronica by the hand.

I was in no hurry to move. I remained transfixed on how beautiful Vicki looked, it was as if I was seeing her for the first time. Her long black hair was tied behind her head, and her face was free of makeup. Her dark eyes sparkled in the light, and her lips were full and moist. Her tight body was wrapped in buckskin, and she wore knee-high, elk skin moccasins. I loved her in buckskin.

"Where have you been all my life?" Was the best I could come up with as I extended my hand.

Vicki giggled and replied, "I see you've already been smoking dope this morning."

We casually walked through the encampment on our way to the Club Cafe, stopping occasionally to visit with friends and family. The Club Cafe is situated on Main Street, across the street from the red, white, and blue fake teepee made of stucco. It is still owned and operated by the Bird family, and it's a popular meeting place with tolerable food, a jukebox, and an assortment of pinball machines. We were lucky to find a window booth that provided a full view of Main Street. Well, I thought we were lucky... until Juanita pulled up to the curb in front of the cafe in her fancy new red pickup.

She didn't get out; she just started honking her horn incessantly while motioning for me to come to her.

I excused myself and cautiously walked to the pickup.

"I was driving to the encampment when I saw you with that girl, Tony," Juanita said as she lit a cigarette. "My father has set up a teepee for me, and I would like you to stop by tonight."

"You always get to the point, don't you, Juanita?"

"You didn't seem to mind the other night, Tony," Juanita said as she flicked ashes out the window.

"That was the other night. I'm busy tonight."

I turned and walked back inside without looking back. Juanita gunned her engine and peeled out of her parking space, sending dirt and gravel flying everywhere.

"She want you to check her oil, Tony?" Vicki asked as she slid over and made room for me to sit back down.

"Something like that. Let's eat, I'm starving." I sat looking out the window, trying to pay attention to the conversation, when I noticed Juanita flip a U-turn and park in front of the Business Man's Club. As she entered, Johnny Kills-At-Night was trying to exit. As I mentioned earlier, Johnny was running for a seat on the tribal council, and it looked like he had been drinking and campaigning nonstop for days.

He finally staggered out of the Business Man's Club and fell up against the hood of Juanita's pickup. Juanita stopped, turned around, and helped him slide into the passenger seat of her fancy new red pickup. After getting Johnny seated, she walked inside, and within minutes, she returned carrying two brown paper bags. She was backing out of her parking spot when she noticed me staring at her. For full effect, she slowly rolled down her window, leaned out slightly, and flipped me the bird. By then, Vicki had finished her second cup of coffee and was clearly agitated over Juanita's appearance and my staring out the window.

"She must think her shit doesn't stink," Vicki said with conviction.

"I know it. She honked the damn horn, and Tony went running," Veronica said.

"What do you girls say to a game of pinball?" Two-Fingers asked, apparently trying to change the subject.

"Next time I see her, I'm going to ask her why she thinks she's better than the rest of us," Vicki said.

"I think pinball is a great idea, Two-Fingers," I said as I stood and walked over to a pinball machine.

Two-Fingers whispered in my ear, "Son, you have these women ready to go on the warpath."

"Naw, they'll get over it," I said as I placed a nickel into the slot.

"Guys get over it, girls never do," Two-Fingers said as he looked over his shoulder to see if anyone was listening. "Have you ever seen girls fight on the reservation, White Guy?"

"Yeah, a couple of times. It gets pretty wicked." I said, recalling incidents where Indian girls kicked the crap out of each other, hair pulling, scratching, and gouged-out eyes came to mind. "Vicki isn't the type."

"She's a female in love, and that makes her the type, trust me," Two-Fingers said before taking his turn on the pinball machine.

"Well, what do you want me to do about it?" I asked.

"There isn't anything you can do, really. I was thinking that maybe we should stay away from Indian Days for at least the rest of the day and night," Two-Fingers said. "You know, let them cool down a little."

Well, we tried talking them into doing just that, and they wouldn't hear of it. Then they insinuated that we were trying to hide something. They wanted to enjoy Indian Days, and no amount of coaxing would dissuade them. They had finally gotten a few days off from work, and they wanted to have some fun. It was at that very moment that I came to a stark realization; my mother never won an argument, and the other women in my life never lost one.

So, after lunch, we walked back to the Indian Days celebration and spent the day getting to know each other better. They performed in most of the traditional dance contests, and their inhibitions seemed to be swept away by the music, the dancing, and the crowds. People shouted their approval, and I forgot all about Juanita. In fact, later that night, Vicki invited me back to her teepee, and Veronica invited Two-Fingers back to hers.

Before leaving with Veronica, Two-Fingers said, "Don't wait up for me." Two-Fingers said. "I'm feeling lucky tonight."

The next morning, I was once again startled out of a sound, deep sleep by Two-Fingers, who was gently poking my head with the index finger of his left hand. I slowly sat up, and it took me a while to get my bearings. I had gotten a great sleep; there's something about sleeping in a teepee next to a beautiful woman.

After tiptoeing outside, I stretched my arms and asked, "So, how did it go with Veronica last night?"

"Well, let me put it this way, you don't see her chasing me down the street, throwing rocks at me, do you?" Two-Fingers said as he stood tall in the morning light. Finally, I thought, a sexual escapade of his that didn't end in bloodshed.

We went on our normal coffee run while the girls got ready for the day. After returning, Two-Fingers let Veronica hold his left hand, and Vicki and I smiled at them as we walked through the encampment. We were having a merry old time before Two-Fingers noticed Juanita and Johnny Kills-At-Night staggering toward us with their arms locked together.

I have to hand it to Two-Fingers; he tried to steer the girls away but was unable to do it in time. Juanita eventually noticed us and yelled, "Hey, Tony, what are you doing with that whore?"

Vicki turned around, and without saying a word, she walked right up to Juanita and slapped her in the face and started pulling her hair. Warpath redefined.

Juanita, initially stunned, shook free of Johnny and punched Vicki in the face. Vicki yanked on her hair as hard as she could, and they both tumbled to the ground, kicking and clawing at each other while they lay in the dirt. I rushed over and tried to break up the fight, but that only made them completely lose their minds and fight even harder.

Johnny staggered into the fray and took a swing at me before face-planting into the ground. It wasn't long before a large crowd gathered around us. Two-Fingers walked over to Johnny and helped him up before saying, "Johnny, there are a lot of voters looking at you. What do you think they're going to do come election day if they see you're involved in this?"

"I don't give a shit," Johnny said as he struggled to stay upright.

"Well, what about Charley? Do you think he will give a shit?" Two-Fingers asked as the chaos raged on and the size of the crowd continued to grow.

Johnny turned pale as the seriousness of it all finally seemed to sink in. He brushed himself off as he scurried away into the crowd. He made no effort to look back.

"Just like a politician to run away when the going gets rough!" Two-Fingers yelled to the crowd before walking over and helping me break up the fight.

I held Vicki in my arms, but she kept kicking and clawing at Juanita. Two-Fingers clamped both arms around Juanita, but she fought to break free. While Juanita was in Two-Fingers' arms, Veronica calmly walked over and slapped her as hard as humanly possible, blood flew everywhere.

Juanita became even more deranged and grabbed Two-Fingers' arm, biting down on it with what looked like all the force she could muster. Two-Fingers loosened his hold as blood gushed from the wound.

After breaking free, Juanita charged Veronica, and they both ended up on the ground fighting with an intensity I have seldom, if ever, witnessed.

"Who are you calling a whore, you bitch!" Veronica yelled as she straddled Juanita and pounded her with closed fists. When Veronica tried to pick up a rock, Two-Fingers dove on her and pulled her off Juanita. Juanita slowly stood up, glared at Veronica, then over at Vicki. She was breathing hard when she walked up to me and punched me square in the right eye.

Vicki tried to break loose, but I held her with all my strength, and she eventually settled down. Juanita looked dazed as she defiantly glared at the crowd around us. She stared at each and every one before spitting blood and walking away. Two-Fingers lay on the ground with Veronica in his arms, panting like a dog in heat, before finally saying, "Well, I'm really glad we let them cool down." The crowd, sensing the main event was over, slowly dispersed. Vicki and Veronica brushed each other off and fixed each other's hair. Vicki had a bloody nose and a few scratches on her neck. Other than that, she was fine. Veronica didn't have a scratch on her.

Shortly after that, Vicki and I decided to call it a day, and the two of us went to her teepee. Before we entered, I took her in my arms and hugged her. She slowly began to relax as she buried her face in my chest and sobbed.

"Are you hurt?" I asked, gently stroking her hair.

Vicki, still sobbing, shook her head and buried her face a little deeper.

"Well, what's wrong?"

Vicki lifted her tear-streaked face and asked, "What's between you and her, Tony?"

I turned and raised the flap of the teepee so we could enter, and after we were seated, I told her most of the story.

The very next morning, much to my surprise, I came face-to-face with Charley, who was frantically looking for Juanita. Vicki was with me, and he asked for our help finding her. We reluctantly agreed, and it didn't take long before we located her teepee, there was a trail of empty Southern Comfort bottles leading to it. Charley pulled the flap back and we entered, only to find Juanita passed out on the dirt floor. She was surrounded by half-empty bottles of Southern Comfort and was snoring loudly.

Charley leaned down and shook her awake, and Juanita bolted upright and started swinging. Charley held her firmly until she stopped. When she finally settled down, Charley let go and said, "Get your things, we're going home."

"I'm not going back to that place. Do you hear me?" Juanita said as she fell back to the ground.

"Juanita, I'm not arguing with you. Get your shit and let's get out of here," Charley said, picking up her purse.

"I hate your old man, and I'm not going back there," Juanita said before picking up a bottle of Southern Comfort and taking a long, record-setting drink.

Charley reached over and took the bottle from her as she slipped in and out of consciousness. Too heavy to carry, Charley began dragging her out before asking me to help lift her. I put Juanita's left arm over my shoulder and felt her go limp. Charley held onto her right arm and handed Juanita's purse to Vicki, asking, "Would you mind holding this for me?" We half-walked, half-dragged Juanita to Charley's car as tourists and locals watched.

Once we got to Charley's car, we put her in the passenger seat and locked the door.

"Tony, I need you to find Juanita's pickup and drive it up to your place. I'll have someone pick it up later." Charley eventually found the keys to her fancy new red pickup in Juanita's purse and handed them to me. I remember standing there, staring absentmindedly at her keys as Charley drove off.

"Well, that fancy new red pickup of hers shouldn't be too hard to find," Vicki said as she took me by the hand.

She was right, it was haphazardly parked behind Scriver's Museum. "Let me drive," Vicki said before grabbing the keys from me. After driving a few minutes, she turned off the paved highway and followed a small cattle trail that led to a stand of tall white birch trees where she parked. Vicki slowly began to remove her clothes, except for her panties and bra. Once undressed, she stripped me down to my underwear and lay on top of me, holding me tight as the sun rose high above the Rocky Mountains.

According to Juanita's parents, when Juanita finally sobered up, she and Charley had a very loud argument. Juanita demanded her pickup back, and Charley said if she ever acted like that again, he would divorce her. Juanita told him to go to hell and spent the night with her parents. The following day, Charley gave in and drove her to our place to retrieve her pickup. That was early Thursday morning.

That afternoon, the Montana Highway Patrol found Juanita's lifeless body inside her new red pickup at the bottom of the ravine east of East Glacier.

Witnesses to the wreck claimed Juanita was driving extremely fast as she approached the narrow, quarter-mile-long bridge that leads into East Glacier. Evidently, she had passed a number of vehicles, and her speed was estimated to be over one hundred miles per hour. She slammed into the cement pillars at the entrance of the bridge, flipped several times, and jumped the two-foot retaining wall before falling two hundred feet to the bottom of the ravine. No skid marks were found.

Later that day, Ivan, Charley, my dad, and I stood on that bridge watching in silence as workers from the railroad pulled her pickup out of the ravine with the help of a large excavator and a very long chain. After several hours of back-breaking and dangerous work, Juanita and her pickup were finally retrieved. Her beautiful body was covered with a non-descript torn, worn-out sheet and dutifully taken to Cut Bank in an ambulance. Her mangled pickup was loaded onto a flatbed truck and taken to AJ Hoyt's wrecked car graveyard.

Chapter 13
Betrayal Exposed

The Blackfeet community was shocked by Juanita's death. Car wrecks are all too frequent occurrences on the reservation, and after a while, news of another wreck is viewed as an inevitable part of everyday life. Unless, of course, it's a relative or close friend who is killed. Then, inevitability is swept away, leaving survivors with a loss that is painfully real and everlasting. Years of such tragedies have had a numbing effect on the Blackfeet community. However, Juanita's death was different, it seemed to shake nearly everyone to their core. Juanita wasn't born or raised on the reservation. Nonetheless, she was viewed as a Blackfeet Indian woman who had made it in the white world, and she was seen as someone who had achieved success. Her success gave them hope, and her behavior was excused; on the reservation, there's always an excuse.

Two-Fingers and I were at the sweat lodge, tending the fire and the rocks, when we heard of Juanita's death from two horseback riders passing by. After listening intently, we looked at each other and shook our heads in disbelief. I remember feeling like someone had kicked me squarely in the nuts, and as feelings of guilt and loss washed over me, I became weak-kneed and had to sit down. Two-Fingers remained standing, but was leaning heavily on his shovel when he asked, "What else is going to happen this summer?"

Billy was frantically trying to cover himself with a breechcloth as he ran out of the sweat lodge. "Did I hear right? Is Juanita dead?" Two-Fingers nodded before sitting down next to me. "She seemed lost. She lost her way, and that's what happens when you abandon your roots, your heritage," I was barely listening, Billy's voice was drowned out by my guilt. "We are losing our way." With that, he returned to the sweat lodge, and before entering, he untied his breech-cloth and threw it into the roaring fire.

Two-Fingers and I sat in silence as we watched the breechcloth turn to ashes. It was some time later that we stood and walked back to the encampment. We deliberately avoided walking past Juanita's teepee, and, following an all-too-familiar pattern, began talking about finding some alcohol and getting drunk. We initially resisted the temptation and decided to walk to the dancing area. On our way, we passed a couple of pretty Indian girls wearing their traditional garb. Two-Fingers and I stopped to discreetly watch them pass by. Suddenly, they stopped and looked at us.

"Oki, where are you girls from?" Two-Fingers asked.

"Lander, Wyoming, we are Arapahos," the taller one said.

Two-Fingers and I were staring back when the other girl asked, "Oh my, what happened to your hand?"

Two-Fingers lifted his left hand high in the air and said, "Garbage disposal."

The two girls looked at each other before turning and running away.

"Shit, I've never had that reaction before. Those Arapahos must have some serious mental problems, White Guy."

"I don't know, maybe they're a more intelligent breed of woman than you're used to," I said.

"You always have an answer, White Guy." Two-Fingers said as we turned around and found Vicki and Veronica glaring at us with their arms crossed.

"So, you two have been running with those girls all this time?" Veronica asked as they walked up to us.

Seeing Vicki suddenly brought back the feelings of guilt I had briefly suppressed. I sensed she, too was guilt-ridden over Juanita's death. News travels fast on the reservation. Veronica, on the other hand, displayed no such sentimentality.

"Damn girl, I didn't know you owned me," Two-Fingers said to Veronica. "Besides, you know I only have eyes for you."

"Bullshit, me and half the other females around here," Veronica said.

Just then, we noticed Billy walking our way. He was decked out in his dancing outfit, eagle feathers in his hair, a chest plate, a loincloth, and moccasins. He jingled as he walked; dozens of tiny silver bells were attached to his outfit.

"Damn, you've got knobby knees, Uncle. You shouldn't be going out in public dressed like that, you're going to embarrass the family," Two-Fingers said once Billy was within earshot.

"Oh, my wayward nephew, what will I do with you? Before you run off and start drowning your sorrow, I intend to tear down the sweat lodge in a few days with the help of a couple of AIM members, and I want you there. Stay in touch with me and don't make me come looking for you."

After getting a pop, Vicki, Two-Fingers, Veronica, and I went to Vicki's teepee to talk things over. Vicki was distressed and remorseful about her fight with Juanita. Veronica, on the other hand, continued to show absolutely no remorse. After an unbearable hour discussing the matter, I stood up and said, "Listen, for the last time, there isn't anything we can do about it. I feel bad, too. What if this, what if that? Shit, it's useless." Without another word, I abruptly left the teepee to seek solace elsewhere.

That's when I ended up in the company of my father, Charley, and Ivan as we watched in horror as Juanita's body was retrieved from the depths of that ravine. Her body was found, but solace never made an appearance. However, Two-Fingers did make an appearance later that day, and the two of us went searching for something neither of us was able to find.

A few days later, as usual, Billy was up early and waiting on us. He made a breakfast of dry meat and tea and then sat us down to talk about Lenny Iron Horse, an Oglala Sioux from the Pine Ridge Indian Reservation in South Dakota, and Jack Little Wolf, a Northern Cheyenne from the Northern Cheyenne Reservation in Montana. They had volunteered to help take down the sweat lodge as repayment for using it. As it turned out, Jack was the head of AIM in Montana, and Lenny was the head of AIM in South Dakota. They were both instrumental in the policymaking of AIM.

Jack and Lenny advocated revamping the American Indian policy that existed at the time, they sought change. They were both strong environmentalists who wanted to protect all land, not only reservation land. During their sweats, Billy listened to Lenny and Jack, and he was impressed with their spiritualism and social activism.

Billy sipped his tea and watched as Jack and Lenny approached. Lenny was tall, lean, and muscular, with long, thick black hair flowing freely over his shoulders. Jack, on the other hand, was short, plump, and wore his hair in braids kept in place by colorful rubber bands.

"Oki, Billy!" Lenny yelled as he approached. "Good day to get some work done."

"Glad you made it Lenny, Jack," Billy said, waving in their direction.

After introductions, Billy asked, "Can I get you a cup of tea or something to eat?" They both respectfully declined, and we got to work removing the bison hides before placing them in the back of Billy's pickup. We had worked for quite a while when Lenny stopped and said, "You have a good group of young men on this reservation, I believe they're going to help us rock the status quo."

"Yes, the old men running our reservations better start paying attention," Jack said.

Lenny and Jack went on at length about how the older tribal councilmen were only in it for themselves, saying what they thought their constituents wanted to hear, then doing nothing but lining their own pockets and those of their friends and relatives. The problem, as they saw it, wasn't tribe against tribe; it was young against old. Those with vested interests versus those with interests. Relevant social change versus being short-changed.

"What do you think?" Lenny asked Two-Fingers. "Are you going to become an AIM member and fight for your rights?"

Two-Fingers looked at me before answering. "What you say is true, but it's been true forever. How are you going to change it?"

"I'm not going to change it by myself," Lenny said. "We're going to change it together because it must be changed. The old men know it, and they're running scared. They've been good little apples for a long time, and when the BIA tells them to jump, they ask, How high? We need our independence. Indians, all Indians, must have more of a say in our destiny."

Jack said, "The federal government has never given a damn about us. We are American Indians from different tribes seeking individual tribal sovereignty, not the Native American bullshit they're forcing down our throats. They want to silence us by forcing us into one camp and forgetting about our unique cultures. They're trying to erase our individualism so we're easier to control. We come from individual tribes, and they seek to silence us while eradicating any mention of our tribal names. I am Cheyenne."

"But they give a lot to reservations, commodities, housing, lots of things," I said sheepishly.

"That's right, they give it," Lenny said. "It's not earned, and therefore it's never appreciated. Living on handouts instead of our own survival skills has weakened us all."

"There are no damn jobs on the reservation. How will we survive?" Two-Fingers asked.

"That's what AIM is all about. We say create our own jobs, take care of our own people and our land, and let the crazy white people screw up their own reservations," Lenny said. "We don't have much left, so we need to fight to keep what we have."

Billy nodded in agreement before adding, "The whites are greedy and destructive, and anybody who cares about the land is a 'tree hugger' to them. Their rivers are on fire, their air is polluted, and their minds are tormented. Everyone is chasing the almighty dollar and making excuses for why they do it. Jack and Lenny are right, we must embrace our old ways, our own culture, not the culture of the white man. We've become like them, everybody trying to get ahead of the other guy, and nobody caring how they get there. They have no honor. They're selling their souls for trinkets. If we don't change, how will they?"

With that, we returned to the task at hand, and soon the sweat lodge was completely dismantled and loaded onto the pickup's bed. Two-Fingers and I sat on the tailgate and listened when Billy started up again.

"You two need to understand that change is in the wind. You both go through life like the rest of the young, oblivious to all the problems in the world. You're old enough to start thinking about these things. Changes are coming, embrace them."

With that, Billy, Lenny, and Jack turned and walked back to the main encampment area, leaving the two of us alone with our thoughts.

The day after the North American Indian Days celebrations concludes is always hectic, and busy. The temporary structures, canvas gaming tents, teepees, and sleeping tents were taken down and removed. After that, the labor-intensive job of cleaning up the place began.

Two-Fingers and I were walking through the area looking for someone to help when we heard a voice behind us say, "Hey, you guys, you want to buy some peyote?"

Two-Fingers and I turned and watched as a skinny, long-haired American Indian wearing a red bandana approached.

"What the hell is peyote?" I asked.

"Man, it's a hallucinogenic, kind of like mescaline. Us Apaches use it all the time." The stranger then opened his clenched fist and revealed four red, hard-crusted buttons of peyote. "It comes from the cactus down in the desert where I come from."

Two-Fingers picked up one of the buttons and examined it thoroughly. It was round, hard, and had a disgusting, pungent smell.

"This is the shit you use for rituals, right?" Two-Fingers asked. "I remember my grandfather talking about this stuff."

"That's right. Take that, and you'll see the light, man," the stranger said, nervously looking over his shoulder.

Two-Fingers and I glanced at each other before I asked, "How much?"

"Five dollars a piece. They're worth more than that but I'm out of money and need to get back to Arizona."

"Shit, I can buy four cases of beer for that kind of money," Two-Fingers said, handing back the peyote.

"Yeah, but this shit will kick your ass like you drank a hundred cases of beer!" the stranger said before putting the peyote away.

Two-Fingers, always on the lookout for a bargain, quickly decided it was a hell of a deal and said, "Give us all four." Then he held out his hand to me, and I reluctantly gave him my hard earned $20. The stranger placed the peyote in Two-Fingers' hand, and, before scurrying off, said, "Take them at night, they work best at night."

"Tonight? Shit, I say we take them now," Two-Fingers said as we walked to a nearby hill that overlooked the encampment. When we reached the top, we sat down on a large boulder where we could see the vast horizon and all the activity unfolding before us.

Two-Fingers handed me two buttons, and after careful examination, I placed them in my mouth and slowly began to chew, trying not to gag. They were the most acidic, bitter, and disgusting things I had ever bitten into. I swallowed hard, and after a while, the taste became almost tolerable.

We sat there on that stone-cold, large rock in complete silence as the encampment slowly disappeared along with our senses. We drifted into a trance-like state of mind. At first, I was aware of what was going on around me, but it didn't take long before I began drifting further and further away from reality.

Two-Fingers looked possessed as he frantically searched his pockets for his knife. It took him a while to open it, and after he did, he leaned toward me and whispered, "Blood brothers."

With that, he cut a four-inch gash in his deformed left hand palm, and blood flowed freely from the wound before he offered me the knife. Without hesitating, I cut a similar-sized wound in my right hand, and immediately after, I took the knife and threw it at the clouds, watching it fall to the ground in front of us. Two-Fingers reached over, grasped my hand tightly, and our blood flowed together.

Minutes after cutting ourselves, the urge to puke overwhelmed us both. Vomit began to flow down the fronts of our shirts and pants like lava from a volcano. The vomiting pushed us into an even deeper trance, and the mixture of blood loss and the effects of the peyote caused a hallucinogenic reaction that washed over both of us. I vividly remember drifting toward the sky before swooping out of the clouds and crashing to earth. Our blood formed a river that washed over us and cleansed our minds and bodies, and time stood still. What seemed like minutes was actually hours as we sat on that boulder, oblivious to its cold, hard surface. I was taken to places I didn't know existed. We both experienced things in our own separate ways, yet somehow they were similar.

I saw Stan, but I couldn't get to him. Juanita suddenly appeared before turning her back on me and running away, never to return. Two-Fingers was young and then suddenly old, standing tall and proud, but old. Our minds escaped our bodies and we were unable to move; we were prisoners to the overwhelming impulses rushing over us. Suddenly, we were on a river together, rushing head-first down a series of steep rapids, and our blood continued to flow together, as did our thoughts. We became blood brothers, brothers. The peyote had strengthened the bonds of our friendship. We felt a kinship for each other stronger than anything we had ever experienced. A friendship that was strong became stronger, and our journey together continued.

By the time we emerged from the trance, the sun had disappeared behind the mountains, and it took us several minutes to get our bearings straight. When we finally did, we let go of each other's hands and inspected the damage. Through the dimmest light, we saw the blood and vomit surrounding us. After a while, we were sufficiently free of the effects of the peyote and able to walk home. It may be my imagination, but since that day, I've always thought Two-Fingers looked a little whiter.

When I arrived home, Dad was sitting alone in the kitchen drinking beer. After I walked in, he took one look at me and asked, "What the hell happened to you? Have you been fighting again?" I ignored him, went to the sink, and began to clean up and inspect the deep cut I had inflicted on my right hand. Thankfully, it had stopped bleeding, but I did wonder if I had any blood left. After drying my wound and wrapping my hand in a towel, I sat down at the table and asked, "Where's Mom?"

"She's in bed trying to get some sleep. You'd better go off to bed too. Juanita is being buried tomorrow in Cut Bank, and we'll be leaving early," Dad said before finishing off a can of Olympia beer and walking to the tire shop.

The line of cars going from Browning to Cut Bank stretched for miles. The graveyard is located on a rocky, steep hill that overlooks a windy stretch of Cut Bank Creek. I remember it being a cloudless day, and as the mourners made their way up the hill to Juanita's gravesite, a gust of wind swept upward from the creek, and it turned cold for a brief, unsettling moment.

Charley, dressed in black, stood over Juanita's coffin with a single, solitary red rose in his hand. Seated directly behind him were Ivan, Helen, and Bob. They stared straight ahead without acknowledging anyone as the mourners crowded around them. Father Ian Kelly stood majestically before us with his Bible in hand. The crowd was large, solemn and respectful, and Father Kelly performed his duty while Charley stood at attention. When the ceremony was over, and after Juanita's body was lowered into the ground, he threw that single, red rose onto her coffin and then turned and walked hastily to his Cadillac, not stopping to acknowledge or speak to anyone. The crowd remained standing as he drove off, and after paying their final respects, they too dispersed and carefully made their way down the steep hill to their cars.

It was so quiet on the ride home that I began to wonder if I had gone completely deaf. It took Dad a while before he said anything, and when he did, it was to express his concern for Charley. He was surprised Charley hadn't stopped to talk with him after the funeral. Evidently, they had spoken a couple of days earlier, and Charley had told Dad that Juanita's autopsy revealed only the slightest trace of alcohol in her system. The Highway Patrol officer investigating the crash was confused by the lack of skid marks. He told Charley that it might have meant the brakes had been tampered with, but there was no way of knowing because her pickup was totally destroyed.

So, the investigation ended unceremoniously when those in charge concluded there was no evidence of foul play. That wasn't good enough for Charley, who told Dad he was doing his own investigating. He had apparently heard through the reservation grapevine that Juanita had been running with other men and might have cheated on him. He had a mission, and that mission was to find the truth. Dad asked if I knew anything about that, and once again, I lied.

The morning following Juanita's funeral, I was startled out of a deep sleep by my dad yelling, "Wake up! Charley is in the kitchen, and he wants to talk to you." I remember walking into the kitchen to find Mom, Dad, and Charley sitting around the table staring at me. I sat down next to my mom and found myself asking, "Hi, Charley. You wanted to talk to me about something?"

Charley was looking down at his hands when he said, "I've spent the last few days in this godforsaken place asking questions. I needed to know if someone was sleeping with my wife." Charley raised his head and stared straight at me as he spoke, "I've heard from a number of people that someone is you, Tony."

I sat staring blankly at Charley as my world crumbled around me. I've never seen such hatred before or since. He stared at me with a mixture of hatred, anger, and disgust etched on his face. I actually hoped he would climb over the table and choke my lights out and end my misery, but I wasn't that lucky.

"Tony, is that true?" Dad asked.

Before I could say anything, Mom stood and walked to the kitchen sink for a drink of water. My silence must have told Charley all he needed to know.

"Well, it looks like you were man enough to screw my wife, but you aren't man enough to admit it," Charley said as he stood and walked to the front door. Before leaving, he turned to my dad and said, "You can forget about any loan from me. You can all forget that you know me." Charley slammed the door on his way out.

Before I was able to say anything, Dad said, "We are selling this place and leaving here as soon as possible." He stood and walked out the front door toward the tire shop. Mom stared at me for what seemed like an eternity before she turned her back on me and went to their bedroom, softly closing the door behind her. I sat at the kitchen table for a long time thinking about what I could've said. Charley already knew, and nothing I said would've changed that. I wasn't afraid of getting a beating. In fact, I preferred it to the unrelenting guilt I felt. The wounds from a beating would've eventually healed, but my feelings of guilt linger to this day. Perhaps that was why Charley showed such restraint that day, perhaps.

Events in the weeks following Juanita's funeral brought a number of changes to both of our families and Two-Fingers, and I rarely saw each other. I stayed close to home and spent my time working at the gas station. I desperately tried to repair the damage I had done to my parents, but nothing I did helped, I had really hurt them, and there was little I could do about it. It took them a long time to get over what they perceived to be the ultimate betrayal. So, when I insisted on staying in Browning and finishing my senior year, I received little to no resistance. Dad thought it was a good idea to stay and face the music, and Mom nodded her head in agreement. Max and Pam offered to give me a place to stay if and when we were able to sell the station. They liked having me around, and that has always meant a lot to me.

Speaking of Max, he was released from the hospital shortly after Juanita's funeral. He was cranky as hell, and he had a difficult time adjusting to life and his artificial leg. That was the good news. The bad news was that Max had started down the road of alcoholism. He began to drink with a fervor that surprised all who knew him. He was addicted to the pain pills the hospital handed out like candy, and once they were taken away, he turned to alcohol to ease his physical and mental pain. Max, prior to his accident, had never been known to be much of a drinker. Given the right circumstances, even social drinking can get out of control and that's what happened to Max. He suffered, and so did everyone around him.

During the time I lived with the Schwartzes, I did a lot of work for them, which allowed Paula, Cindy Ann, and her two girls to move to Missoula, Montana, where they attended the University of Montana. She had divorced Stogie Man by then and was awarded full custody of the girls. Stogie Man didn't take the divorce lightly, and after he was served with the divorce papers, he snuck into Cindy Ann's bedroom one night and tried to strangle her. Two-Fingers intervened and kicked the shit out of him. Shortly after that, Stogie Man was seen living on the streets and alleys of Browning with the winos aimlessly wandering around the reservation. None of us took any joy in his suffering, but suffer he did. Somehow, Pam was able to cope with the seemingly endless problems facing the family. In addition to the personal issues, business had dropped off at the curio shop, fewer tourists were stopping because of all the unrest, and all the businesses in town suffered. Pain on the reservation, there was always so much pain.

To the best of my knowledge, Charley never returned to Browning after Juanita died. Evidently, he and his father had a huge fight, and Bob eventually moved to Cut Bank to live by himself while Charley stayed at the ranch. Juanita's parents, Ivan and Helen, left the Owen

Ranch shortly after the funeral and now live in a cabin they built in the mountains near Heart Butte.

Summers on the reservation were usually a time of renewal for the Blackfeet. They helped to strengthen them against the inevitable ravages of winter. That summer, the hope of renewal fell considerably short of expectations. Hope was replaced with a large dose of heartache and despair. Close knit families were divided over the issues of the day; the young sought change and didn't understand why the older Blackfeet were so resistant to it. The tribal elections didn't help to soothe that division. Four of the seven council seats were won by younger, educated Blackfeet, and all hell broke loose as they gained control over the tribal council. Like it or not, change is inevitable, even on the reservation.

Chapter 14
Too Many Ghosts

Over that summer, the BIA finished building the tribe a new high school they had been working on for years. It turned out to be a large, round brick building without windows. The Blackfeet have always had a thing about breaking windows, and the BIA had finally figured that out. So, we attended high school in a building with no windows. I remember Two-Fingers and me checking it out on our first day of class, and Two-Fingers remarked, "Damn, I'm already feeling claustrophobic in this place. I feel like a mouse in a maze."

Two-Fingers and I were assigned the same homeroom. When we went looking for it, we were greeted by our friends and ignored by our enemies. We briefly made eye contact with Vicki and Veronica, and they quickly looked the other way. Up until then, we weren't sure if they were friend or foe. All doubt was erased when we learned they felt neglected over the last days of summer and were not in a forgiving mood. In other words, they were downright pissed off. I remember telling Two-Fingers not to worry about it because there were plenty of other fish in the sea. He nodded his head and said, "Yeah, but with our luck, they'll all turn out to be sharks."

That was the most interesting thing that happened to us on the first day of our senior year. As the year passed, Two-Fingers and I worked hard at getting good grades. Prior to that year, neither one of us worked very hard at school, and our grades showed it. Our senior year was different in that regard. We both decided to spend more time on our studies in case we decided to go off to college, and it paid off. In short, Two-Fingers and I had grown up over the summer and were no longer the carefree spirits we once were.

Our attitude toward education had changed, and so had our

attitude toward our appearance. We stopped wearing the collared white shirts and Levi's we had previously worn to school and replaced them with army fatigue jackets, T-shirts, and khaki pants. My short-cropped hair became a thing of the past and we occasionally wore bandanas on our heads and chains around our necks. We were both athletic, but neither of us participated in organized sports, we were too busy working. While the other school kids were busy with sports, Two-Fingers and I concentrated on our studies, jobs, and families. We avoided the petty arguments and fights that occurred daily and mainly kept to ourselves.

One bright spot for me personally was the addition of another white person in our class. His name was Michael C. Brown, and he was the only son of two employees of the Great Northern Railroad who had been transferred to Browning. The Great Northern is known for its symbol of a large white mountain goat emblazoned on their railcars and practically everything else they owned. His dad and mom worked together at the train depot east of town, and they had a house downtown near the Catholic church.

Mike, on his first day of school, was chased home by a group of rowdy Blackfeet who were on the hunt for fresh blood. He was eventually given the nickname, "Brownie." It was an appropriate nickname as far as nicknames go because Brownie loved his pastries, he practically lived at Greco's Bakery. Besides, the name "White Guy" had been taken.

Two-Fingers and I took pity on him and eventually took him under our wings. We constantly lectured him on what to do and what not to do on the reservation. I told him early on that the worst thing he could do was run when challenged; he needed to stand his ground, or his life was going to become a living hell. The usual bullies were merciless. They hurled racial slurs, attacked his manhood, and threatened his existence. One day, we pulled him aside, and I told him, "When they start that shit with you, go up to the biggest guy in the pack and bust him square in the face with a clenched fist."

Well, after school one day, he got his chance. A group of thugs jumped him, and they were making all kinds of threats and noise when, all of a sudden, Brownie walked over to the biggest guy in the crowd and punched him squarely on the chin. As it turned out, that proved to be a dumb thing to do. It only made the guy madder than hell, and he proceeded to beat the holy crap out of Brownie. When he was finished, I helped Brownie up from the hard, unforgiving ground, and he asked me, "What did I do wrong?" As I was brushing him off, Two-Fingers stepped up and said, "First of all, you listened to White Guy. I personally would've punched the littlest guy and then ran like hell." The three of us became good friends after that, and Two-Fingers and I protected him the best we could. Thankfully, after that ass-whipping, Brownie cut down on the pastries and discovered the newly built weight room at the high school, and he soon turned the fat into muscle. In short, he turned into one hell of a load.

I ended up spending a good part of the first half of my senior year trying to make amends with my folks. Mom continued to be despondent and spent most of her days in her bedroom, and Dad was quiet and reserved. I rationalized that he acted that way because he suffered from the absence of Stan and his best friend, Charley. From Mom and Dad's standpoint, the only good news during that period was that Bobby Racine had his loan approved, and they were able to finalize their plans to move.

Two-Fingers spent a lot of time with Max. Max was walking with the help of his prosthetic leg, but he was still unable to drive. That didn't sit too well with him, and he hated being cooped up all the time. So, Two-Fingers would drive him around the reservation searching for something neither one of them was able to find. As winter approached that year, the days grew shorter and the nights grew longer. The change in seasons didn't help Max's depression, and his constant drinking only made things worse. Despite Two-Fingers' best efforts at cheering him up, nothing seemed to help.

On the first Saturday in November, Two-Fingers and I, in yet another attempt at cheering Max up, suggested we go deer hunting. Max initially resisted the idea but was finally persuaded by Pam to go. So, Two-Fingers and I loaded their car with their .30/06 rifle, bullets, and a few bologna sandwiches. Two-Fingers drove, I was in the back seat, and Max was seated in the front passenger seat. Before we were able to leave town, Max insisted on stopping at the grocery store for a case of beer. Against his better judgment, Two-Fingers did as he was told.

We spent the rest of that day driving around the reservation looking for deer. It had snowed heavily the night before, and the roads were snow-packed and icy. As nightfall approached, we decided to drive out to Heart Butte for one last chance at success. We had convinced ourselves that the deer would be coming down from the higher elevations as darkness fell, and with any luck, we'd be able to shoot one from the road.

That day turned into one where we mostly watched Max drink beer and sip on a pint of Seagrams that he had stashed in his coat pocket. Max became very drunk, and he started to pour out his feelings of sorrow. He wouldn't stop complaining about his pain and how useless he felt, all the while clutching the whiskey like it was a life preserver. This went on for hours, and Two-Fingers' constant consoling only seemed to make things worse. Max was tired of living and said he wished he were dead. Not too long after we started our trip to Heart Butte, Max began crying hysterically and demanded that Two-Fingers pull the car over and shoot him, he wanted to be put out of his misery. Again, Two-Fingers tried to calm him down, and Max did, for a brief, shining moment.

When Heart Butte came into view, Max suddenly and completely lost it. He demanded that Two-Fingers pull over and put a bullet in his head. Two-Fingers pulled off the road and came to a complete stop on its icy shoulder. He reached over, pulled Max to him, and wrapped his arms around him until Max calmed down enough for us to continue. Only seconds passed before Max began to lose his composure again. He pleaded with Two-Fingers to kill him and was inconsolable. Two-Fingers abruptly stopped the car and spent several minutes trying to talk his father out of it. But Max refused to listen and insisted on being put out of his misery.

By that time, Two-Fingers was fed up with the whole damn mess, and he told Max to get out of the car and lie down in the snow-covered ditch next to the road. "If you want to end your rotten, miserable life… I'll help you do it!" Two-Fingers yelled before grabbing the rifle and jumping out of the car. Max seemed startled, but that didn't stop him from tumbling out and haltingly limping down the steep embankment before lying flat on his back in the ditch. I remember sitting in the back seat as this nightmare unfolded, thinking that somewhere along the line I must have been captured and placed into an episode of The Twilight Zone. Max lay in the snow covered, windswept ditch with his hands folded over his chest, eyes closed, quietly praying as he waited to be shot.

Two-Fingers stood at the rear of the car, steadying himself against the trunk. He slowly raised the rifle and adjusted the sights. When Max looked up to see what was taking so long, an explosive BANG rang out, and the smell of gunpowder permeated the cold air, lingering for an inordinately long time. I remember straining to see through a cloud of smoke and watching Max's prosthetic leg fly end over end before hooking onto a power line, where it hung precariously for a few seconds before falling into the snow-covered ditch only inches from Max. Max remained in a prone position as blood drained from his face. After a few moments, he propped himself up onto one elbow and looked around before yelling at Two-Fingers, "What the hell are you trying to do, kill me?!" He collapsed backward and lay there for about a minute before Two-Fingers walked down and helped him back to the car. Two-Fingers gently placed him inside, and before he closed the door, Max threw his remaining beer and whiskey into the ditch.

Two-Fingers took me straight home after we dropped Max off. I was shocked by what I had witnessed. "How did you know you weren't going to hurt him?" I asked. "I didn't," Two-Fingers said. "All I know is he isn't much good to himself or anyone else the way he is, and something needed to be done. You heard him, he swore he'd never drink again, and I believe him. He's never promised that before." "Well, I hope he quits. Man, that was the wildest thing I've ever seen." "Yeah, I cured him," Two-Fingers said proudly. "Alcoholics Anonymous uses a twelve-step program to help someone quit drinking. Personally, I prefer the one-legged approach."

Holidays are always painfully tough times for far too many residents of the reservation. Depression and feelings of despair peak during these times. The week leading up to Thanksgiving that year was no exception. Suicides had already reached epidemic proportions, and one death in particular had a deeply profound effect on Two-Fingers and me. Three days before Thanksgiving, Rubber Joe's body was found at the base of the city water tower. He had fallen over one hundred feet to his death; the cold, hard, unforgiving ground took what little life he had left.

According to the Governor, they had been drinking especially hard that day, trying to drown their sorrows, when Rubber Joe decided to take that fatal dive. They were lying beneath the water tower sharing a bottle of Muscatel and trying to keep warm when, all of a sudden, Rubber Joe stood up and started yelling, "There are too many ghosts, too many ghosts!" Before the Governor fully realized what was happening, Rubber Joe had already climbed halfway up the water tower's icy, slick steps.

The Governor watched helplessly as Rubber Joe ascended to the top of the tower. He slipped often, and each time he did, he was able to regain his footing and continue climbing. The Governor screamed for help, becoming hoarse before a small crowd finally gathered, just in time to witness Rubber Joe plunge to his death. Rubber Joe was finally at peace; death knows no pain.

Later that night, shortly after his body was taken away, a terrible blizzard descended upon the reservation. It snowed for thirty-eight hours straight before finally stopping. Schools, roads, and businesses shut down, and Browning became a virtual ghost town. Nobody went outside unless it was absolutely necessary.

On Thanksgiving Day, the weather situation was still very bad, so my parents and I dined alone at home. No need to worry about customers, there weren't any. We sat at our kitchen table and feasted on a traditional Thanksgiving dinner. Mom was more cheerful than usual, and Dad seemed to be getting back to normal. Maybe he realized the love of his son was more important than any friendship. At least I hoped that's what he thought.

Dad was helping himself to a piece of pumpkin pie when he said, "Your mother and I will be leaving for New Jersey before the end of the year. The new tribal council wants all the white merchants out of here. I guess it's a blessing in disguise."

"What about Stan? How will he know how to get in touch with you?" I asked.

"I will notify the War Department as soon as we know where we'll be living," Dad said.

We finished the rest of our meal in silence, and then I asked permission to go see Two-Fingers. Dad said, "Sure, be careful walking in this crap."

On my walk to Two-Fingers' place, I noticed there wasn't a car on the road. Off in the distance, I heard the buzzing sound of snowmobiles, but there weren't any cars driving around. There were plenty buried under the snow and abandoned, but none of them were moving.

I walked in knee-high snow the entire way, and by the time I arrived, I was worn out. Max greeted me at the front door with his new leg on. His attitude was upbeat, and I hadn't seen him that happy in months. True to his word, he hadn't had a drink since Two-Fingers shot his leg off. Pam rushed in from the kitchen and gave me a big, warm hug, and I have cherished that moment to this day. She wore an apron splattered with flour; she had been baking pies and fry bread for most of the day.

I took the opportunity to inform them that I would soon be taking up permanent residency at their place. They seemed pleased and invited me to sit and eat with them. I didn't want to appear rude, so I said yes. As Pam placed the turkey on the table, she said, "I wish our girls were here. This blizzard has closed most of the roads in Montana."

The Schwartzes said a prayer before we ate, and they were right, we had a lot to be thankful for. They were in a festive mood, and we talked about several events that had taken place on the reservation. We all agreed that Rubber Joe's death was a horrible tragedy, and Pam believed his soul was finally at rest and reunited with his long-departed family.

It wasn't long before the conversation turned to politics when Max said, "Looks like I'm going to have to run for council. These young bucks are going to ruin the place. They're scaring off the tourist trade, and we're going to be broke if they don't stop the militant crap."

"Pop, things have got to change around here," Two-Fingers said. "There's no way they can make it any worse than it already is."

"Yeah, but they're moving too damn fast," Max said.

"Too damn fast? Hell, if you ask me, they're a hundred years slow," Two-Fingers said. "I hope they burn the whole place down so we can start over from scratch."

Max and Two-Fingers went at it for a while before they resumed eating. I sat there soaking it all in, wondering if it wasn't too late to go to New Jersey. Before I could get too far into my thoughts, Two-Fingers nudged me and said, "Let's walk off some turkey."

The wind was blowing, and the snow was swirling in circles as we made our way to Government Square. As we approached the alley behind the theater, we were startled by vicious growling and barking before we found ourselves in the middle of a dogfight. Through the thick, swirling snow, we saw Old McGraw and a big German shepherd as they circled each other.

We approached cautiously and watched in silence as they launched their attacks. As the fight progressed, the younger German shepherd seemed to grow stronger, while Old McGraw grew slower and older. His tongue hung from his mouth, and foamy white slobber dripped to the ground, but he refused to give up or run away.

This went on for what seemed like an eternity before the German shepherd jumped on the faltering Old McGraw and bit him viciously on the neck. Old McGraw yelped loudly and violently shook his head in an attempt to fling the intruder off. The German shepherd clenched his teeth firmly and held on tight as Old McGraw fought bravely. They spun around and around in the snow as blood gushed from their wounds, but only Old McGraw's wounds proved fatal.

It was only a matter of time before Old McGraw stopped struggling, lay down, and slowly died. His death was very much like the deaths he had inflicted on countless other dogs, but it inexplicably saddened me. The snow in the immediate area turned bright red, it looked like one big cherry snow cone. We were again startled when the German shepherd let out one last bloodcurdling howl while standing over Old McGraw. He eventually tired of howling, and in one last act of defiance, he lifted his hind leg and pissed on the ground next to where Old McGraw lay before slowly sauntering off into the darkness.

Two-Fingers and I stood there, oblivious to everything except that moment in time. The attack was primal, and it resonated with us. Only the very strong survive, and even that is short-lived.

"No one and nothing lasts forever," Two-Fingers said before we turned and walked away.

Chapter 15
Wounds and Wounded Knee

True to their word, Mom and Dad left Browning shortly after Christmas. They left early in the morning on December 28, 1970, and I remember it like it was yesterday. There was a brief break in the weather, and that prompted them to get out while the getting was good. They hastily said their goodbyes, and as they slowly backed out of the driveway, a feeling of despair and loneliness suddenly swept over me.

I stood watching as they drove away before meekly waving back at them. That was when I heard myself saying, "You can't stay, and I can't go, you can't stay, and I can't go." Unexpected tears ran down my cheeks as I kept repeating that phrase over and over again. As they disappeared from view, I ran after them, all the while saying, "You can't stay, and I can't go." I ran about a mile or so down the road before I stopped. They had long since disappeared from view, and my running after them wasn't bringing them back, no matter how fast I ran. Before I reentered the city limits, I stopped to admire a new sign that read, "Welcome to Browning-Headquarters of the Blackfeet Indian Nation." It replaced the old sign that simply said, "Welcome to Browning Drive Carefully and Enjoy Your Stay."

After my parents moved away, I fought the loneliness by keeping busy with school, working at the Schwartzes, and at our old gas station for Bobby Racine. I had given up my paper route when Two-Fingers came home from South Dakota, but I still had plenty of other work to keep me occupied. Two-Fingers kept busy too, and our senior year of high school flew by. Vicky and Veronica had long since moved on from us, and Two-Fingers and I briefly dated girls from the Babb area, beautiful Blackfeet girls who were truly wild. Babb is on the reservation not far from the Canadian line, and it's so desolate and poor that it makes Browning look like Brentwood, California. Actually, I've never been to Brentwood, but I did follow the O. J. Simpson trial, just saying.

Anyway, on our graduation night, after partying into the wee hours of the morning in Browning, Two-Fingers, Brownie and I decided to continue partying in Glacier National Park, not far from Babb. Brownie had received a beautiful, used 1957 Ford Skyline convertible for his graduation present. That model is famous for being the first retractable hardtop convertible ever made. It was absolutely gorgeous. Why anybody would drive such a nice car on the reservation was beyond me.

The three of us were drinking and driving through the Park near the newly rebuilt Many Glacier Lodge on a warm, beautiful night. We never bothered a soul. All we did was drink and drive around; it was all very blissful. The next morning, after a decent amount of sleep, I was startled awake by a baby mountain goat. Evidently, mountain goats are plentiful in Glacier National Park, but it's the only one I've ever seen.

Anyway, this baby mountain goat was drunk as hell; he had discovered an open whiskey bottle we left lying open on the ground. I had passed out next to the Ford, where Two-Fingers and Brownie slept comfortably. I was trying to get the bottle from the baby goat, but despite my best efforts, it refused to relinquish it, and the whiskey spilled onto the ground, where the baby goat licked it up as quickly as possible.

When he finished, he began stumbling around the meadow where we parked. When Brownie woke and saw what was going on, he thought it would be a good idea to give the goat a beer chaser. So he opened the driver's door and waved a beer at the baby goat. Well, the goat quickly regained its balance, jumped into the car, and started drinking with Brownie. By then, Two-Fingers was fully awake. He rummaged around the car, found a pair of sunglasses and a baseball cap, and put them on the goat. The goat sat with them, real social-like, drinking beer. He seemed to have very good manners for a goat, but what the hell do I know?

We had a good laugh at the goat's expense, and when we decided it was time to go to town and leave the goat, he would have none of it and refused to exit the car. Two-Fingers eventually pulled it into the back seat, where it sat quietly next to him. Brownie seemed satisfied with the seating arrangements, so he drove off with me in the front passenger seat and Two-Fingers in the back seat with the baby goat wearing sunglasses and a baseball cap.

Before long, Brownie pulled off to the side of the road and stopped to lower the top of the convertible. It was a beautiful morning, and the heat from the sun felt good. As we neared the exit of Glacier National Park, a park ranger in his green government-issued pickup met and passed us, then suddenly made a radical U-turn. He must have noticed something was amiss. Who says you can fool a government employee?

After being chased for a while, we eventually stopped a few feet outside the Park entrance. The ranger jumped out and cautiously walked around the Ford before stopping and staring directly at the drunk baby goat wearing sunglasses and a baseball cap. That's when he started threatening us with every type of legal action imaginable for stealing a federally owned mountain goat. He was also going to charge us with underage drinking, we weren't sure if he meant the baby goat or us. When we asked him about that, he temporarily lost his mind and went ballistic. Thoughts of prison life ran through my head until Two-Fingers perked up and reminded the park ranger that we were no longer in the Park and he didn't have legal jurisdiction. Things settled down quickly once the ranger looked over his shoulder and noticed a very large, red-lettered "Welcome to Glacier National Park" sign behind him. Two-Fingers gently handed the baby mountain goat to the park ranger, after which the whiskey-soaked goat proceeded to vomit all over the ranger's nicely ironed lime-green shirt.

Out of booze and thirsty, we stopped at an old country store in St. Mary and bought a case of cold beer. Two-Fingers decided he wanted to ride shotgun, and I chose to sit in the back seat to get some much-needed fresh air. Once again, Brownie approved of the seating arrangements, so we blissfully started off on our journey back to Browning.

As we drove down a very, very steep hill, Brownie thought it would be funny and exciting to see how far down the switch-backed, windy mountain road we could go before he needed to apply the brakes. We quickly picked up speed, and before long, the trees began to fly by as the tires squealed into the turns. About a third of the way down the hill, I looked at Two-Fingers and noticed he was bracing himself by planting both feet firmly into the dashboard.

I was looking for something to hold onto when I noticed a red Park bus coming around the curve directly in front of us. At the last possible second, Brownie hit the brakes and swerved out of the way, and the convertible launched off the road, over a small stand of willow trees, and into a beautiful grassy meadow where a lone pine tree stood tall against the ravages of time. Brownie slowed down but was unable to avoid hitting that lone pine tree, and the front driver's side of the car caved in around him. The force of the collision caused the steering wheel to embed itself squarely into Brownie's chest; there were no airbags on a 1957 Ford. In fact, there were no seatbelts either. Two-Fingers didn't receive a scratch, but I suffered a whiplash that I occasionally feel to this day.

Brownie, as it turned out, was not as lucky. He died that day in the back of an ambulance while being transported to Cut Bank Municipal Hospital. His autopsy revealed the cause of death was multiple internal injuries. Brownie was buried in his parents' hometown in Nebraska.

Two-Fingers and I were unable to attend his funeral, but we did see him off. We helped load his coffin into a dark, musky Great Northern freight car that had a large white mountain goat prominently displayed on the side.

One good thing that happened that summer was the construction of the Blackfeet Pencil Factory. It was the Blackfeet's first major endeavor at creating jobs for the populace. They had received funding through various federal programs, and to improve their odds for long-term viability, the tribe received contracts from a number of federal agencies to supply them pencils. Everyone on the reservation was excited about the economic possibilities.

Two-Fingers and I were excited too. We decided to go in and apply for jobs, and after filling out a one page application form, we sat down and waited for our turn to be interviewed. We watched as a room filled with Blackfeet interviewed with Edward Bear Child, who didn't waste much time on the process. Basically, if you could walk and chew gum at the same time, you were hired. Two-Fingers was asked a couple of questions, and he was hired on the spot.

Two-Fingers sat next to me as I watched Edward briefly scan my application. After about 30 seconds, he looked up at me and said, "Sorry, White Guy, you're not qualified." I stared at him in disbelief before asking, "Not qualified? What do you mean, not qualified?" Edward seemed to be in a hurry to get out of there, but he did take the time to tell me one more time, "You're not qualified." With that, he stood up to leave. Two-Fingers grabbed his arm and asked, "What exactly do you mean, not qualified? How can anybody screw up a pencil?" Edward was clearly agitated, but instead of going ballistic, he leaned over and whispered into Two-Fingers' ear, "I decide who is hired, and I'm not hiring him." I don't have the best hearing in the world, but even I heard that.

I stood up and said, "So you're not an Equal Opportunity

Employer? Wow, so much for Affirmative Action. I always knew you were a racist, Eddie." Edward looked at me and said, "Tough shit, White Guy." With that, he rushed out of the room, leaving Two-Fingers and me to debate the merits of his decision. Two-Fingers knew I was pissed off, so all he said was, "That's what you get for stealing our land." Over the years, he has repeated that line so many times that I no longer resent it much.

Not being hired that day worked out for the best. I was able to find full-time work with Bobby Racine. The night shift nobody else wanted allowed me to go to the recently opened Blackfeet Junior College during the day. Two-Fingers and I had made the decision to eventually go off to a four-year college and make something of ourselves, and the junior college was a good place to start for both of us.

At that time, we weren't worried about being drafted. Not much demand for a one-handed soldier, and I was number three hundred and fourteen in the draft lottery. Back then, when Vietnam was winding down, the government went to a lottery system to decide who was going to be drafted. Number one had the highest probability, and number three hundred and sixty-five had the lowest. Like I said, I was number three hundred and fourteen, so there was no way I was getting drafted. I thought about enlisting, but I decided I couldn't do that to my parents. So, Two-Fingers and I worked our jobs and saved money the best we could. Two-Fingers has always had a hard time retaining money. Too many people on the reservation had bigger money problems than he did, and he has always been overly generous with his money, and mine.

Two-Fingers did well at the Blackfeet Junior College night school. He loved American History and American Indian Studies. He seemed to always have a history book of one kind or another in his hand. He had found a calling for himself; he wanted to teach history. I was a good student too, but I never had the same passion for studying as he did. We still partied, but Two-Fingers became increasingly obsessed with history, democracy, and capitalism. He was always studying something. He even studied the Constitution, who does such a thing?

During this period, the reservation continued its renaissance, out with the old and in with the new, and the Blackfeet were not too subtle about the "out with the old" part. There was a big push for self-governance and independence. Young Blackfeet wanted the chains of government control removed, and they were hell-bent on taking control of the tribal government. They were sick and tired of the BIA telling them what to do.

The Bureau of Indian Affairs (BIA) is a department within the Department of the Interior, which many of the younger Blackfeet referred to as the Department of the Inferior. In particular, they hated the local head of the BIA. His name is Trevor Kanowski, and he hadn't been in town long before everyone who came into contact with him despised the asshole. Nobody on the reservation liked him, nobody. Evidently, Kanowski was originally from Poland and ended up getting a cushy job with the BIA through marriage. As the story goes, after World War II, he ended up in Washington, DC, where he met the sister of a Department of the Interior bureaucrat.

They married, and as Trevor's brother-in-law rose in the food chain, so did Trevor. Isn't nepotism a wonderful thing? Trevor's wife, Roberta, lived with him on the reservation, but she was seldom seen. I saw her at the post office for the first time on a dark and cloudy day, and she was wearing a pair of poorly fitted sunglasses. She had dropped a handful of letters, and as I picked them up and handed them back to her, I noticed she was wearing heavy makeup in an attempt to conceal two black eyes.

Shortly after that, rumors spread around town branding Trevor as a wife-beater. It was also rumored that he had been a Nazi collaborator during World War II and that he only switched sides when the Russians invaded Poland. Personally, I don't think anyone knew for sure, but that never stops gossip from spreading, especially when the gossip is aimed at someone who is so intensely disliked. Nobody knew for sure, but everyone agreed on one thing: Trevor was a prick. The Blackfeet rumor mill had struck again.

All I know for certain is he turned out to be a petty bureaucrat who used his position of power to terrorize the Blackfeet at every opportunity. Trevor was a nickel living in a dime world, a small person who overvalued his value. He was one more reason why the Blackfeet sought change. Trevor was a living, breathing, in-person symbol of the oppressive federal government, and they both had to go.

In the early 1970s, social unrest was pervasive throughout the United States of America. It was during this period that AIM was at the pinnacle of its power. Their movement has been largely forgotten and placed in the trash bin of time, joining other movements that sought freedom from an oppressive government. It was also around this time that American Indians were no longer called by their tribal names. They were all categorized as "Native Americans." They were conveniently and effectively minimized and vanished, permanently banished by a society that wanted to purge them from its consciousness. That label persists to this day, and few understand how it has impacted tribal unity and the quest for freedom. Labels willingly accepted by tribes illustrate how easy it is for the government to control all of us. No longer were the Blackfeet called Blackfeet. Indian tribes were all the same in the eyes of those who labeled them "Native Americans." No respect was given to specific cultures; too lazy or too ignorant to know the difference between a Flathead and a Crow, a Comanche and a Sioux, an Apache and a Navajo. All of them are individual tribes with individual beliefs and customs. They were vanished; out of sight, out of mind. Do not, in any form, mention the names of individual tribes, or there will be hell to pay. Vanished is the order of the day.

It was also around this time that, Two-Fingers, along with a growing number of Blackfeet, began to actively resist the destruction of their heritage. They felt disrespected and believed strongly that it was an effort to hide and erode the individuality of all tribes. The power structure sought to have them disappear into the shadows of history. Like he always said, he was a Blackfeet, and he was always going to be a Blackfeet, and he took pride in that. He always said that once they start taking away pieces of you, it wouldn't be long before there wasn't anything left worth keeping. He had finally awakened.

From a "Native American" perspective, AIM elevated the fight against injustice to a higher, more intense, level when they invaded and occupied Wounded Knee in South Dakota in February of 1973. A number of Blackfeet AIM members on the reservation went to Wounded Knee to join the occupation, and as it turned out, 1973 was a pivotal year for the movement. By the way, the movement was called the American Indian Movement. It wasn't called the Native American Indian Movement, and there was a reason for that. The members knew which tribes they belonged to. That detail has been swept away and discarded into the history bin, too.

It was in the latter part of 1972 when Jimmy B was released from the Army. Two-Fingers and I heard about his discharge through the reservation grapevine but nobody had seen him. Not his family, his friends, the people down at the bank, nobody. Then, without warning, he mysteriously appeared in Browning and announced to anyone who would listen that he was going to Wounded Knee, South Dakota to fight alongside his brothers and sisters. Two-Fingers, with very little encouragement from anyone, decided to go along with him. I went along too because someone had to look after them, right? That's how the three of us ended up at Wounded Knee fighting for the cause. It's not an easy tale to tell, but I believe it needs to be told to fully understand Two-Fingers' plight.

For those of you who don't know, the City of Wounded Knee is the headquarters of the Lakota Pine Ridge Reservation in South Dakota. It was there, in February of 1973, that members of several different tribes from across America gathered and began their occupation. The Pine Ridge Reservation is home to the once gallant and brave Sioux Indians. The free and independent Sioux who lived in harmony with nature, who fought their enemies with valor, and provided for their families. The sick, the old, and the young were cared for. They were a proud and strong people who were led by Chiefs who cared for their people more than they cared for themselves. They put others before themselves. Chiefs who didn't eat until all of the people had eaten; Chiefs who were selected because of their courage, wisdom, strength, and honor.

The Sioux tribe is a combination of different bands of Sioux. Crazy Horse was the Chief of a band of Sioux, just as the great warrior Sitting Bull was the Chief of a band. Prior to the invasion of their lands, the Sioux lived free and honorably. By 1973, the Sioux lived on a reservation that had shrunk since it was established under the 1868 Treaty of Fort Laramie. That is the treaty that stated, "This land will be yours forevermore, as long as the grass grows and the sun shines." Or, as it turned out, until white settlers found gold in their sacred Black Hills. Once greed enters things, all bets are off.

Well, as history will tell you, on June 25, 1876, at the Battle of the Little Big Horn, Armstrong Custer and members of the 7th Cavalry paid for the sin of greed. In the battle that has become known as Custer's Last Stand, Indians from several western tribes won a major victory in a last-ditch effort to survive. Lies and broken treaties led to a battle that brought a small, short-lived victory. Along with it came an end to a way of life that's forever lost, a life of freedom and independence that was beautiful in its simplicity. A life built around the preservation of Mother Earth and family; a life of honor and pride. It was replaced with a life of government control, deprivation, dependence, and heartbreak.

On February 28, 1973, several AIM members went to Wounded Knee to right a number of wrongs. AIM was the American Indian version of the Black Civil Rights movement. AIM was officially formed in the late 1960s during a period when radicalism was first starting to sweep across America. Fueled by years of injustice and the events going on in Vietnam, a number of city-dwelling, college-educated American Indians began a movement to unite tribes in an effort to resist the government's unending efforts to silence and erase them.

In 1972, AIM and other activists called for a Trail of Broken Treaties march on Washington, DC, and a large number of American Indians from across the country descended on the capital. Their principal demands included the re-establishment of their sovereignty and the validation of treaties they had entered into back in the 1860s, particularly the 1868 Fort Laramie Treaty. That treaty was problematic for the federal government because it was favorable to the Indians. Chief Red Cloud, Chief of the Oglala Lakota Sioux, had waged a successful and protracted war against the United States Army, which forced the federal government to enter into the treaty to stop further bloodshed. From 1866 to 1868, against great odds, Red Cloud's band had fought the United States Army in an effort to maintain their Indian way of life. He fought to rid the Plains of the white man and his forts.

One battle in particular stands out. In December of 1866, the Oglala Lakota Sioux, along with their Cheyenne and Arapahoe allies, attacked a group of 81 men who were sent out from Fort Phil Kearny on a mission to gather wood. Fort Phil Kearny is located in the northeastern part of Wyoming near the present day town of Story,

Wyoming. The Indians had set a trap for them by using Crazy Horse as a decoy. Crazy Horse enticed the soldiers to chase him, and they did. Thinking Crazy Horse was alone, they chased after him and soon rode headlong into an estimated two thousand Indians. These Indians were under the leadership of Chief Red Cloud, and the ambush became known as the Fetterman Massacre. Captain William Fetterman was the commanding officer who disobeyed direct orders not to chase after Indians, and the 81 deaths resulted in the largest number of military casualties of any Indian battle to date.

For years, the federal government mistakenly believed that Indian tribes would never band together to fight them. Chief Red Cloud was instrumental in galvanizing individual tribes into a unified fighting force with the understanding that the federal government, the very people they had entered into treaties with, posed a greater threat to their way of life, their very existence, than their traditional Indian enemies. United, they posed a serious challenge to the federal government and its desire to expand westward. Divide and conquer was no longer seen as a viable strategy.

Not long after the Fetterman Massacre, a government peace commission was established and sent into Indian country to gather information in an attempt to find a resolution to the "Indian problem." The commission determined that white encroachment on Indian territory had provoked the war, and they decided that the best solution was to assign specific territories to the Plains Indians. A number of western tribes entered into negotiations with representatives of the federal government, and those negotiations produced the 1868 Fort Laramie Treaty. That treaty established the Great Sioux Reservation. That was its name, and it was a large reservation covering more than half of what is now South Dakota.

Over the years, through various changes in federal government policies, the reservation shrank by more than half of its original size.

This unilateral taking of Indian land was not unique to the Sioux, it happened to virtually every tribe in America. The repeated violation of treaties and the treatment of Indians as second-class fueled a growing interest in joining a movement, any movement, that might give a unified voice against these injustices. That desire for unity and justice was the driving force behind the creation of AIM.

AIM's decision to occupy Wounded Knee and use the occupation as a protest against past and present injustices was a direct response to those injustices. Since AIM's inception, their protests had been peaceful, but they had made little progress in advancing their ideals. By 1973, they were willing to do whatever was necessary to be taken seriously; they were tired of having their voices silenced.

Another factor that contributed to the eventual occupation of Wounded Knee was the killing of Raymond Yellow Thunder. He was beaten to death for being an Indian. He was an Oglala Lakota Sioux Indian with a serious drinking problem, go figure. He was 51 years old, and by all accounts, a good-natured and peaceful man. On the day he died, Raymond was stripped naked down to the waist and paraded around Gordon, Nebraska before being killed by two white brothers who were eventually convicted of manslaughter. The older brother received a six-year sentence, and the younger one received two years. Manslaughter, not first-degree murder sentences.

These lenient sentences infuriated many American Indians. Shortly after his death, AIM organized a two-hundred-car caravan and drove from Pine Ridge to Gordon to protest the light sentences. Their protests were ignored; once again, their voices were silenced. Tensions simmered throughout late 1972 and reached a boiling point when another racist attack occurred in January, 1973. A young Sioux Indian named Wesley Bad Heart was stabbed to death in Buffalo Gap, South Dakota. He was killed by the local town bully, who was heard that day saying, "I'm going to kill me an Indian." Once again, manslaughter charges were filed, not first-degree murder charges.

AIM members stormed the courthouse in Custer, South Dakota, where the trial was being held, and demanded justice. Police cars were overturned and burned, things turned physical. It was the first uprising and outbreak of violence since the Massacre at Wounded Knee in 1890. That massacre is another vivid example of the brutality inflicted on the Sioux Indians by the United States Army.

I mention it now because, in the years following the 1868 treaty, the federal government continued to seize Sioux land. Bison, the Sioux's primary food source, were hunted to near extinction. Broken government promises to protect reservation lands from settlers and from the hordes of gold miners invading their Black Hills created unrest on the reservation. Still, the Sioux remained calm until their great leader, Sitting Bull, was killed at his home on the Standing Rock Reservation.

Standing Rock was one of five reservations created unilaterally when the government decided to modify its original agreement and break up the Great Sioux Reservation into smaller pieces of land. On the day of his death, forty Sioux Indian policemen were sent to bring Sitting Bull to the Agency's headquarters for questioning because reservation officials believed he was behind the unrest that was sweeping across the Sioux and Cheyenne reservations. In reality, the Indians were starving. Promises of food and shelter had turned out to be lies. Dishonest reservation agents were stealing their food and selling it, and their crops had failed for two consecutive years. They were starving.

When the police arrived at Sitting Bull's home, his supporters tried to intervene on his behalf. When Sitting Bull resisted arrest, shots were fired, resulting in his death along with the deaths of eight of his supporters and six policemen. Fearing reprisals, two hundred members of Sitting Bull's band fled the Standing Rock Reservation to join Chief Spotted Eagle and his band on the Cheyenne River Reservation.

On December 23, 1890, Chief Spotted Eagle left the Cheyenne River Reservation and began a journey to the Pine Ridge Reservation and the protection of Chief Red Cloud. The group included more than three hundred members of Chief Spotted Eagle's band and thirty-eight members of Sitting Bull's band. On their way, they were intercepted and detained by the 7th Cavalry Regiment, Custer's old regiment.

In the early hours of December 29, 1890, this small group of Indians was peacefully camping beside Wounded Knee Creek. They were told to wait there until they were transported back to their reservations by train. Tensions ran high as five hundred troopers watched over them. The troopers were heavily armed and believed the Indians were armed as well. During a search for weapons, soldiers began to scuffle with a deaf Sioux Indian who didn't understand why they were taking his hunting rifle. During the struggle, a shot was accidentally fired into the air and the 7th Cavalry opened fire on the Sioux.

Panic and chaos erupted. Indians grabbed their hunting rifles and fought back. The so-called "battle" didn't last long, and when the killing stopped, more than one hundred ninety Indians lay dead, men, women, and children, indiscriminately slaughtered. Twenty-five members of the 7th Cavalry also died, though no one knows how many were killed by friendly fire. The Wounded Knee Massacre added yet another layer of symbolism to AIM's occupation as they fought against injustice. They fully understood that their occupation of Wounded Knee might very well end the same way the "battle" of 1890 did.

As news of the 1973 Occupation of Wounded Knee began to spread, hundreds of American Indians from across the country started their journey to that far-off place to show their solidarity. American Indians, who were once good little apples, were now militants willing to fight back against the atrocities of the past and present. This was where Two-Fingers, Jimmy B, and I found ourselves on March 8, 1973.

As it turned out, we took a more circuitous route than we originally planned, but we eventually ended up there. Better late than never, I suppose. As I briefly mentioned earlier, Jimmy B had been discharged, but none of us knew when, it turned out to be about six months before we arrived at Wounded Knee. After being discharged, instead of coming home to Browning, he went to Long Beach, California, with an Army buddy. Jimmy B found work in the shipyards painting and restoring older ships.

He spent a lot of time in the hull of those ships sanding and repainting them. He said the job sucked because he was always breathing in paint fumes; ventilation was terrible on the lower decks, and he was high on fumes all day long. That experience really messed him up. When he finally had enough, he came home to Browning, where it took him days to regain any semblance of normal. And with Jimmy B, "normal" had always been a stretch, but even Two-Fingers and I noticed he wasn't quite right in the head.

That didn't stop either one of them from hatching their plan to go to Wounded Knee and help their brothers in arms. Against my better judgment, as I mentioned earlier, I decided to go along. The night before we left, we got plastered, and I mean lit up like a torch. We were in an old, worn-out pickup Two-Fingers had recently bought from his uncle Billy, and as usual, we were drunk driving all over the reservation. The exact details of that night have been lost to me, let's chalk that up as being alcohol-related. I do remember us getting stuck in a huge snowbank near East Glacier and waking up the next morning wondering how the hell we were going to get out of that mess.

As it turned out, Jimmy B and Two-Fingers were wondering the same thing. After some careful consideration and heavy thinking, Two-Fingers decided Jimmy B and I needed to get out and push. He was in a hurry to get to Browning to pick up some money the BIA owed him. It was unusual for the BIA to hand out checks on a Saturday, but they were forced to. Apparently, there had been some newly discovered accounting irregularities, and the Blackfeet demanded immediate payment. Two-Fingers and Jimmy B planned on being the first in line to receive their $2,000 checks; each enrolled Blackfeet member was owed that amount. We needed to get to the BIA office at Government Square as quickly as possible. Two-Fingers had paid $300 for the pickup and promised to pay his uncle as soon as he cashed his check. Plus, we needed to get to Wounded Knee so we could save the world. Time was of the essence.

After several attempts, Two-Fingers finally got the pickup started, so Jimmy B and I moved as quickly as possible to the back of the pickup and started to push. We leaned down, got our hands under the bumper, and pushed with every fiber of our being. Nothing moved except a few discs in my lower back. It was freezing cold, but that didn't stop Jimmy B and me from sweating our asses off.

We were finally able to get the pickup rocking back and forth before it broke free from the frozen ground, the tires were literally frozen to the ground. When the pickup lurched forward, Two-Fingers gunned the engine, and the pickup escaped the snowbank and headed down an unplowed, icy path about thirty yards before Jimmy B and I were able to jump in. We sat there, sweating profusely and near the puke stage, when Jimmy B looked over at Two-Fingers and said, "Next time you get us stuck, I'm driving, and you're pushing." Jimmy B had brief moments of clarity.

About an hour later, we arrived at the BIA offices, and to our surprise, there wasn't much of a line. It was Saturday morning after a hard Friday night, and the Blackfeet were moving a little slow. After they received the checks, we high-tailed it to the Cowboy National Bank in Cut Bank. Special arrangements had been made for the bank to open on Saturday so all the federal checks could be cashed. They charged $10 per check to cash them, the Blackfeet are always paying to get their money. We were the first out of town, and Two-Fingers drove as fast as his old, worn-out pickup would go. After checking his rearview mirror, he yelled, "Oh shit, here they come." Car after car passed us by, Blackfeet like to drive fast and never give safety a second thought. Before long, a newer pickup overflowing with Blackfeet rushed past us, and one of the younger Blackfeet stood up in the bed and saluted us. He quickly sat back down after being handed a bottle of wine, and before long, they disappeared from view.

It took us about thirty minutes to reach Cut Bank. When we arrived, the bank parking lot was filled with vehicles of every make and model. Two-Fingers parked a couple of blocks away, and we walked to the bank with our heads held high. The place was already packed, standing room only. The tellers moved quickly, cashing checks at a frantic pace. Each person received $1,990 for their $2,000 federal check. The bank president paced the floor, puffing away on a ten cent cigar. Beads of sweat formed on his bald head and dripped onto the nicely tiled floor and over the etched logo of the bank. He didn't seem bothered by the sweat until he was forced to pull out a snot-stained handkerchief to stem the flow. He was having a hard time containing his joy, wearing a shit-eating grin as he mentally calculated his profits.

Jimmy B made short work of getting his check cashed and shoved the money into his coat pocket for safekeeping. That was not the case with Two-Fingers. He made the teller count his money out several times before he slowly and methodically gathered it up. With a handful of cash, he walked over to the bank president and said, "You always have to make money off of us Blackfeet. You steal our land, you steal our money, and you turn your backs on us when we need a loan.

You bankers are a bunch of thieves." The Blackfeet yelled their support as the bank president darted behind a large metal screen door and quickly locked it. He seemed stressed as he responded, "It's only business, it's only business."

Two-Fingers bent down and slid a ten-dollar bill under the bottom of the metal gate, and said, "Well, here's another ten dollars, buy yourself a personality. It'll be good for business." The crowd of Blackfeet cheered loudly as we walked out the front door.

After leaving the bank, we crossed the street to Western Union, where Two-Fingers wired his uncle Billy the $300 for the pickup. He attached a short note asking him to let his parents know where we were headed. Wounded Knee was the destination, and there was no way of knowing how long we would be gone.

As it turned out, Edward Still Smoking, the head of AIM on the Blackfeet reservation, was already at Wounded Knee along with several other Blackfeet who had traveled there before the actual occupation began. By the time we left Cut Bank, the occupation was already in full swing. American Indians from across the country were there to lend their support and more were arriving every day.

A lot of support came from American Indians who had survived Vietnam, and Jimmy B was one of them. Jimmy B was no longer the brainwashed Indian boy who willingly went off to war to fight our enemies. Long gone were his thoughts of heroism and a sense of duty to America. Duty was replaced with the reality that wars are run by a bunch of politicians who have no skin in the game, self-serving politicians who only advance their agenda and are okay sacrificing the lives of patriotic Americans called to battle. Jimmy B gladly and willingly went to war like thousands of other soldiers, only to be betrayed by the very government that had sent them into battle. The government had no answer other than to go to war, and when these brave soldiers returned, they couldn't walk down the streets they fought to defend without being spat on, called names, and vilified as warmongers. Vietnam cost America more than the lives of our soldiers; it damaged the very soul of America. Protests bordering on anarchy raged all across the country. Vietnam, at the risk of overstating the obvious, was a very unpopular war.

Jimmy B had let his crew cut grow out, and he braided his hair Blackfeet Indian style. He desperately needed to be Blackfeet again. He was healing from the horrible experiences he had in 'Nam, and he was beginning to sleep better after months of nightmares that woke him in the middle of the night. Jimmy B wore the look of a man much older than he actually was; the joy of life had been stomped out of him. Booze helped ease the pain, but it was the grass that helped him sleep at night. Jimmy B knew he was one of the lucky ones. So many of his comrades had come home in body bags. Too many were injured, horrific injuries that were unimaginable. Maimed and twisted bodies; limbs blown off, faces disfigured, souls destroyed, and Jimmy B had experienced a lot and suffered from it.

His closest friend in 'Nam was a white guy from Torrington, Wyoming, named Mike Edwards. Mike had been a platoon leader in 'Nam and took the safety of his men very seriously, and more times than not, he put his own personal safety at risk to save and protect them. His unit, which included Jimmy B, was deep in the country one day when they were ambushed by a sniper. One of his men got shot, and as Mike moved in to help him, he ended up getting shot in one of his elbows. According to Jimmy B, his whole arm was practically blown off, but Mike kept moving to help his fallen comrade. Jimmy B was able to find the sniper high up in a tree, and with one shot, he brought him down. It bears repeating: Blackfeet have very good aim.

Helicopters were summoned, and everyone was evacuated and returned to camp. To save Mike's arm, the field doctors opened up his stomach and placed his injured elbow inside it, then they grafted skin and stitched around the opening until the elbow was secured to the cavity of the stomach. Jimmy B visited him at the field hospital several times before Mike was shipped back home, and when Jimmy B was released, he contacted Mike and was told the procedure had helped with circulation, and his arm had been saved. He had limited mobility, but he still had his arm. Jimmy B considered himself lucky, with no missing parts or lasting physical injuries. His injuries were hidden deep inside of him. Nobody returns from war unscathed.

After wiring the money to his uncle Billy, we stopped and got a case of beer and a bag of chips before heading off to Wounded Knee. We planned on buying whatever we needed on the way, and as we left the city limits of Cut Bank, a car-load of Blackfeet going to Wounded Knee passed us and flipped us the finger. Two-Fingers shook his head and reached for a beer.

We drove slowly across the great expanse of Montana, only stopping for gas, supplies, and the occasional piss. As the sun set and darkness enveloped us, we drove on through the night. As we approached the South Dakota line, all conversation came to an end, and an uneasy silence filled the cab of the old, worn-out pickup.

Chapter 16
The Light Flickered Before Going Out

We arrived at the city limits of Wounded Knee on the morning of March 8, 1973. By the time we got there, the city had already been under siege for well over a week. The roads in and out of town were sealed off by the federal government, and hundreds of well-armed federal agents made entry into Wounded Knee virtually impossible. In addition to the federal agents, there were local tribal law-enforcement goons who were beholden to the older tribal council members who wanted AIM gone. The old leaders on the Sioux tribal council desperately wanted things to return to the way they were before the occupation began because they had a vested interest in maintaining the status quo. They provided little to no help to AIM. On the contrary, they were a major hindrance.

The situation worsened with each passing day as random shots rang out when least expected. Everyone was on edge. The occupiers had their hunting rifles, and the agents had automatic weapons, rocket launchers, helicopters, and armored vehicles at their disposal. The federal agents were initially ordered to show restraint while high-ranking government officials tried to negotiate a peaceful resolution to the problem. AIM leaders wanted action and were not interested in listening to any more lies; both sides were at an impasse, and patience was running out.

The power and water supplies had been cut off, and it was desperately cold. To add to the misery, the powers that be stopped food and medical supplies from coming in. Once again, American Indians were being starved into submission. On top of that, anyone trying to enter Wounded Knee risked arrest, and anyone leaving was stopped, searched, and questioned. Two-Fingers, Jimmy B, and I had been turned away at every roadblock surrounding the town. Unfamiliar with the terrain, we drove north until we came to the little reservation town of Anderson, South Dakota.

Anderson was, and remains, a typical reservation town: full of despair, desperation, and heartbreak. Like most reservation towns, there wasn't any urban or rural planning whatsoever, a dirt road for a main street, houses haphazardly scattered around decrepit businesses and more than their share of dogs running the streets. Cars were lined up in what appeared to be front yards, creating a buffer zone between the streets and the houses. The only viable business in town, other than the post office, was the Palomino Bar, Cafe and Motel. The Palomino had a freshly paved parking lot and a fresh coat of white paint. A large neon sign above the parking lot was on even though it was mid-morning; the Palomino was a welcome sight for three weary travelers who were lost and alone.

Jimmy B and I followed Two-Fingers into the bar, and upon entering, we were immediately overwhelmed by the pungent smell of decades old-cigarette smoke that all the air fresheners in the world wouldn't help. After adjusting to the dimly lit interior and regaining our sight, we stopped to admire the beauty of a large, hand-carved mahogany bar without taped-up mirrors behind it. The place even had barstools to sit on and booths with cushions; we were home at last. Down at the end of the bar, in a dimly lit spot, stood a brightly lit jukebox playing a mournful and somber country-and-western tune. It suited the place perfectly. Over the middle of the dance floor hung a bright light that shone down on a well-used pool table; it too was welcoming. The neon beer signs hanging on the walls were softly lit and in good working order. The place was clean and well taken care of, definitely not your typical reservation bar.

As we approached the counter, we were met with a warm "hello" from the owner of the Palomino, Faye Spotted Bear. As it turned out,

Faye had recently bought the place and spent a lot of money fixing it up, more money than she would probably ever make. We later learned that Faye was a widowed woman with a lot of money. She was around forty and had already lost three husbands. Each rich, white deceased husband had left her a sizable inheritance. Evidently, losing them had driven her back to the reservation where she was born. At the far end of the bar sat an old cowboy nursing a draft beer; he had the look of the town on his face, crusty, worn-out, and tired. We quickly bellied up to the bar and ordered beer. We were thirsty from the weed and the long drive, and we needed beer.

After a few beers, we began to feel almost human again. When the jukebox ran out of money and finally stopped playing, Faye walked to the end of the bar and struck up a conversation with the old cowboy.

"Yeah, I lost three good men," Faye said loud enough for everyone to hear. She slowly looked around to see if anyone would respond before the old cowboy finally asked, "What did they die from, Faye?"

With that, Faye stood up a little straighter and said, "Well, the first two died from eating bad mushrooms."

The place grew deathly quiet until the cowboy responded, "That's terrible Faye, just terrible. What did the third one die of?"

Faye looked over at Two-Fingers, Jimmy B, and me as we sat there staring at her with our beers raised to our lips,

"A crushed skull...he wouldn't eat his mushrooms!"

Jimmy B started to choke and gag before he finally spat beer all over the beautiful mahogany bar. Turns out, she was only joking. She had been asked so many times about her dead husbands that she came up with that story. Remember, fiction is always better than reality on all reservations. After Jimmy B got control of himself, Faye asked, "Do you fellas want anything to eat?"

Two-Fingers took a sip of beer before saying, "I'll take a steak with fries, hold the mushrooms."

After we ate, Faye sat down with us and struck up a conversation. Soon, we were telling her why we were in South Dakota, and she listened without voicing any objections or dousing the moment with reality. We told her about the roadblocks and our desire to get into Wounded Knee, and she told us there were a lot of American Indians picketing and demonstrating on the roads leading to Wounded Knee. To her knowledge, the only American Indians actually in Wounded Knee were those who arrived before the occupation officially began.

Evidently, most of the recent arrivals were staying in the town of Pine Ridge because there was more lodging there. A few American Indians had stayed in her motel the night before we arrived, but they had left before she opened the bar. Wounded Knee remained relatively quiet, but she didn't think that would last long. She was right, the area soon became a media mecca. News teams from the major networks eventually descended, and places to stay grew harder to find.

She served us one last beer and said, "Drink up and go get some rest. You look like you could use some. Ten dollars a night, and you can stay in my motel for as long as you like."

After the long drive with little sleep and way too much beer, she didn't have to twist our arms.

Later that night, I was roused from a deep sleep by the sound of chanting and the beating of drums. I remember crawling out of bed and taking a good, long piss before walking over to the motel window and looking outside. It was pitch black except for a very large bonfire burning in the middle of Faye's newly paved parking lot.

I ended up taking a soothing, hot shower that helped wash away most of my drowsiness, and after brushing the grime from my teeth, I splashed on some cologne, combed my hair, and put on my cleanest change of clothes. I couldn't find my coat, so I borrowed one of Jimmy

B's green Army fatigue jackets.

I recognized a surprisingly large number of faces as I approached the bonfire; it seemed like half the Blackfeet tribe had descended on the place. In the middle of the crowd stood Two-Fingers and Jimmy B, smoking joints and drinking beer. Faye was smiling and busily handing out sandwiches. Two-Fingers stepped closer to the fire and yelled, "About the time I think I've gotten rid of you sum bitches, you show up at my doorstep," Someone in the back yelled, "You were easy to track, we just followed the empty beer cans."

It didn't take the three of us long before we were standing next to Faye. We were seeking more wisdom from her, and I sensed Two-Fingers was on his way to becoming a very wise man when he apologized for the burning parking lot. Faye's response only enhanced his attraction to her.

"Ah, what the hell, it gives the place a lived-in look. Besides, you Blackfeet are a fun bunch. Consider it my contribution to the cause."

Faye turned and walked back to the Palomino while Jimmy B and Two-Fingers shared a joint. I patiently waited in vain for a hit that never came. I guessed it was more punishment for stealing their land.

"What the hell time is it, Jimmy B?" Two-Fingers asked as he peered up at the overcast, dark sky.

"I thought you didn't need a watch to tell the time?" Jimmy B said as he handed Two-Fingers the joint.

"I usually don't when the sun is out, but my guess is it's about midnight." Evidently, Two-Fingers had awakened shortly before I had.

"Well, I'm not really sure either. You and White Guy were snoring so loud that I couldn't sleep, so I decided to find us a way into Wounded Knee without getting shot. I eventually found a spot that may work, and as I was headed back this way, I ran into this group demonstrating at one of the checkpoints, and I talked them into coming back here and staying until we can get a plan of action figured out. Most of them want to go back home. They're pretty frustrated and tired. They got kicked out of a white-owned motel a few nights back and have been sleeping in their cars ever since. Too cold and miserable for that shit. When I explained the situation to Faye, she agreed to let them stay as long as they behaved. She said it was okay to build a small fire. It kind of got out of hand. Faye is a good woman. It's hard to beat a woman who owns a bar."

I stood next to them as they continued to pass the joint between themselves. I started to think I must've said something bad about them in my sleep.

Faye returned to the fire, and Two-Fingers couldn't stop staring at her. She was standing on the opposite side of the fire with a beer in her hand, staring intently into the flames as if she were in a trance. She had pulled her hair back from her face and held it there with a large, multicolored beaded barrette. This had the effect of accentuating her high cheekbones and coal-black eyes. She was free of makeup, but her lips glistened red as she sipped her beer. She wore an elk tooth adorned buckskin jacket over an aqua-blue blouse, and her Levi jeans were tight on her body yet fit loosely over her boots. She was a beautiful Sioux Indian woman who looked younger than she was, much younger.

She slowly raised her eyes and smiled sweetly when she noticed Two-Fingers staring at her. Then, she raised her right index finger and motioned for him to join her. As he approached, he started to say something, but she put her finger on his lips and said, "Do you dance? I feel like dancing." With that, she took his hand, and they walked to the Palomino Bar.

I was left standing alone next to the fire, the only white person in the crowd. Finally, having had enough of the cold shoulder, I decided to go to the bar and get a beer. As I turned to walk away, the crowd yelled, "Just messing with you, White Guy, come back." You know, it's a lot of fun being the only white person in a crowd of American Indians, you should try it sometime.

After entering the bar, I noticed the pool table had been moved off to the side of the dance floor, where couples slow danced to an old country-and-western tune. There, in the middle of the dance floor, were Faye and Two-Fingers moving rhythmically to the music as they slowly melted into each other's arms. They never moved far from that spot as they danced, drank beer, and laughed. Before closing time, Faye took Two-Fingers by the hand and led him away. I remember thinking it probably had been a long time since either one of them had sex, Faye by choice, Two-Fingers because he could never find anyone that hard up.

At closing time, drunk on free beer, I stumbled outside and partied until the wee hours of the morning with my Blackfeet brothers and sisters.

Later that morning, Jimmy B showed Two-Fingers and me the spot he had chosen for our entry into Wounded Knee.

"So, let me see if I have this straight, we're going to load up my pickup with provisions, and we're going to break into Wounded Knee?" Two-Fingers asked, trying to wrap his brain around the plan Jimmy B had come up with.

The three of us were sitting in Two-Fingers' old, worn-out pickup on top of a hill overlooking Wounded Knee. We had gotten there by carefully traversing a narrow cattle trail covered in knee-deep snow.

"That's right, you got it," Jimmy B said as he handed a fifth of Jim Beam whiskey to Two-Fingers. "We wait until three in the morning, then make a mad dash down the hill and onto the streets of Wounded Knee. I talked it over with some guys at the bonfire last night, and that's what we came up with."

Two-Fingers took a pull of whiskey, shook his head, and said, "The best you guys could come up with is we risk our lives, my pickup, and any future government payouts by crossing the wide-open range in the dark and breaking into Wounded Knee?"

"Oh yeah, it has to be at night and in darkness, or they'll see us. You'll have to turn your headlights off so it's pitch-black dark." Jimmy B reached across me to take the whiskey from Two-Fingers, but he wouldn't let go.

"That's the plan?" Two-Fingers asked before taking another swig of whiskey. "Where will our Blackfeet brothers and sisters in arms be while we're committing suicide?"

"They're going to be helping with a diversion," Jimmy B said as he wrenched the bottle from Two-Fingers' hand. "It's all worked out. There will be a commotion at that checkpoint down there at three in the morning. Jimmy B pointed down to the roadblock as Two-Fingers looked that way.

"While the feds are trying to figure out what's going on, we'll take off down this hill as fast as we can."

"Without any lights on?" Two-Fingers asked, then followed it up with, "What about the helicopters?"

Jimmy B was clearly getting agitated. "Hey look, if you want to go home, we can go home. I thought you wanted to help make a difference. Besides, you haven't heard my entire diversion idea." He lit a joint and handed it directly to Two-Fingers.

"Fair enough, what's your diversion plan?" Two-Fingers asked as he accepted the joint.

I sat there watching the two of them drink whiskey and smoke pot until I finally had enough and took the bottle and joint away from them. They both smiled and said, "Just messing with you, White Guy." Of course, neither of them asked me what I thought of the idiotic plan, so I quietly got stoned.

"Well, while you and Faye were dancing the night away, I was doing some investigating. At the bonfire, I ran into a Sioux by the name of Arthur Lone Elk, and it turns out Arthur works for the Sioux tribe as a wrangler of the tribal bison herd. It seems the Sioux have one of the largest bison herds in America, thousands of them. As he and I were talking, an idea popped into my head. What would happen if a few bison stampeded through the checkpoint? You know, like that checkpoint over there at the bottom of the hill." Jimmy B seemed very proud of himself as he reached in vain for the joint.

"As we spoke, it became obvious that Arthur wanted to do something for the cause, but he didn't want to quit his job and join the occupation. There are a lot of American Indian brothers and sisters thinking the same thing. So, after a few beers and a couple of joints, Arthur and I came up with the stampeding idea. Here's what's going to happen: Arthur and a couple of his Sioux wrangler buddies are going to round up a hundred head of bison, and at precisely three in the morning, they're going to stampede them through that checkpoint." Jimmy B once again pointed to the checkpoint at the bottom of the hill. "It should cause one hell of a ruckus, and that's when we make a mad dash into Wounded Knee."

Two-Fingers thought on it for a while before saying, "It would be easier if we snuck in on foot and left the pickup with Faye."

"Yeah, it would be, but the story on the street is that the occupants are running out of food, and we can be of great help bringing in some essentials," Jimmy B said, slowly nodding his head.

We sat there on top of that hill for a long time surveying the scene in silence. We smoked a couple more joints and pondered the situation before Two-Fingers finally said, "Well, what the hell, it's a good day to die."

"Well, technically, it wouldn't be today that we die, Two-Fingers. It would be more like 3:10 a.m. tomorrow morning."

"Crack you, Jimmy B." Two-Fingers said as he started his pickup and drove off in search of a grocery store.

We eventually found a small IGA grocery store thirty miles away in Hot Springs, South Dakota. Hot Springs isn't a reservation town, and that became obvious when we parked in the grocery store lot and noticed a group of white citizens staring and pointing at us. Turns out, the locals were tired of the commotion and publicity and wanted things to settle down and get back to normal.

We hastily entered the store each grabbing a large grocery cart and loading up essentials like sugar, flour, coffee, canned meat, and sacks of potatoes. We paused briefly at the beer cooler before deciding against it. Before we left the premises with our boxed-up supplies, I looked out the front window and noticed a mob forming around the pickup. White men and women of all ages were talking loudly and wildly waving their arms in the air.

As we loaded the provisions into the bed of the pickup, members of the crowd asked what we were going to do with the groceries. We didn't say a word. We finished loading everything, and as we started to get into the cab, a big cowboy stepped in front of Two-Fingers and asked, "You deaf, Indian? What are you doing with those groceries?"

It was then that Two-Fingers started yelling at the top of his lungs, "We are going on a picnic, do you want to come?" The cowboy seemed startled by that, and before he or anyone else could answer, Two-Fingers jumped in and started his pickup.

As he slowly backed up he yelled, "Watch your toes. You have to be careful around vehicles. I lost most of my hand when a drunk cowboy ran over the top of me." Two-Fingers waved his left hand high in the air as the crowd slowly backed away with looks of horror on their faces.

"Saved by the claw once again, Two-Fingers." Jimmy B said before rolling down his window and waving to the assembled crowd.

A little after 2 a.m. the next morning, we were strategically parked at the top of the hill trying not to doze off when we noticed the earth shaking. Even though it was very cold out, we rolled down the windows to see why the pickup was shaking uncontrollably. It was a dark, cloudy night, and we couldn't see five feet in front of us. As we tried to figure out what the hell was going on, we suddenly and simultaneously yelled, "Bison!"

Who says you can't fool three dumb asses sitting in an old, worn-out pickup on top of a hill while a bison stampede is taking place.

Two-Fingers tried to start the pickup several times, but he was shaking so badly that the keys kept falling to the floorboard. Finally, on his fifth attempt, the pickup started, and without any lights on, he drove down the cow path toward what appeared to be an open meadow. The roar from the stampeding bison was ridiculous and the visibility sucked, but at least we were moving.

Bison after bison ran past us, and the dust became so thick we couldn't see anything except bison. Hundreds of bison tore up the snow covered ground as they stampeded off into the night. We continued to drive onward with our lights off when, all of a sudden, a huge bison landed on top of the hood and stared at us through the windshield before falling off and running away. Two-Fingers accelerated hard and turned his lights on just as we went airborne. When we landed, we landed hard, and it took us a while to realize we were in American Indian-occupied, Wounded Knee.

American Indians in various stages of dress came running toward us, waving hunting rifles and screaming obscenities. Two very large American Indians flung the doors open and pulled Two-Fingers, Jimmy B, and me out of the pickup, throwing us to the ground. Soon, an even larger group of American Indians stood over us with their rifles aimed at our heads, and the only visible light was a faint glimmer from the pickup's headlights. We were lying flat on our backs on the cold, hard ground, looking up at them, when Two-Fingers, staring straight into the rifle barrels, said, "You Sioux have been aiming at us Blackfeet for centuries and still haven't killed any of us." He continued to smile as he slowly stood up and brushed the dust off his pants. As the crowd closed in on us, someone in the back yelled, "Is that you, Two-Fingers? It has to be you, no one else in this world is that mouthy." Eddie Still Smoking pushed his way through the crowd and said, "Don't shoot these three fools; it would be a waste of bullets."

Right about then, Arthur Lone Elk and three other horseback riders came racing down Main Street in our direction. He stopped, slowly dismounted, and said to Jimmy B, "Well, looks like I'm going to be joining the cause after all. We tried to cut out a hundred head of bison and ended up spooking the whole damn herd, and the next thing I knew, we had 3,000 head on the run with no way to turn them. Once bison decide to run, they run. They tore down fencing, the roadblock, and everything in between, and they're still on the run. I figure I'm either going to get fired, arrested, run out of town, tarred and feathered, or banished, so I'm staying in here where it's safe. By the way, I think the rest of your tribe survived the stampede, but I'm not sure."

"Well, I don't know how safe it is in here, but you're welcome, you're all welcome," Eddie Still Smoking said as he swept his arm in a wide arc. "Even you three." After he disappeared into the darkness, the crowd turned their backs on us and slowly dispersed, leaving the new recruits standing around looking at each other. Despite the initial cold shoulder, we became very popular once they realized we had brought provisions, supplies were more limited than expected, and they were grateful.

The first few days at Wounded Knee were not too bad, but that changed when the food ran out. We found ourselves under constant pressure from the authorities, never knowing when they might fire on us. They picked random times to keep us on edge and unnerved, and it worked. Luckily, nobody had been killed up to that point, but tensions were high, really high.

A full week passed, and I found myself freezing as my night watch ended. Another bitterly cold night in Wounded Knee had come and gone. In the distance, near one of the checkpoints, a reservation dog howled mournfully. Its sorrowful moaning was soon joined by howling from dogs all over town. It was a nightly ritual from dogs that were not fully domesticated, yet not truly wild and free. In that way, they were like the human occupants of the reservation. As the sun slowly rose above the distant hills and the last reservation dog stopped howling, the town of Wounded Knee slowly began to stir; the freezing cold weather made it hard to leave a warm, comforting bed.

Life on the Sioux Reservation hadn't been the same since AIM took over Wounded Knee, and many permanent residents deeply resented their presence. Their initial enthusiasm had noticeably waned. Two-Fingers, Jimmy B, and I had been assigned night patrol duties, and we took the assignment seriously. It was important, and we wanted to do the best we could. We were short on sleep, but our energy levels stayed high; it must've been the adrenaline rush every time shots rang out, and we ran for cover.

The longer the occupation lasted, the more determined the government was to end it. As I said earlier, they had cut off power and water along with our food supply, hoping to either freeze us into submission or starve us out. Still, AIM had galvanized the volunteers into a tight fighting unit. We were outgunned, but we were dedicated and committed to the cause.

Jimmy B was extremely vocal and active. When he wasn't on night patrol, he walked around the encampment with his assigned hunting rifle slung over his shoulder. He would aim it at anything that moved. Two-Fingers and I watched him do this again and again, and we worried he was reliving Vietnam. Just a few days into our stay, he had taken a shot at a helicopter, he was sick and tired of the bright light that beamed down from it and swore that if it held steady long enough, he would shoot it out.

Several days and nights had passed since that incident, and I was relatively relaxed as we walked the perimeter, trying to stay warm. It was quiet enough that Two-Fingers decided to head to the bonfire for coffee and heat. As we sat soaking up the warmth, a helicopter suddenly appeared and turned on its spotlight. We glanced over at Jimmy B just in time to see him raise his rifle and fire. Instantly, the light went out, and the helicopter flew off into the distance.

"Jimmy B better be careful or he's going to end up shooting down that helicopter," Two-Fingers said as he lit a joint and handed it to me. He exhaled, and a cloud of smoke drifted off into the cold night air. "He has gone full blown GI Joe over the last few days, and his nightmares are getting worse. I think he's beginning to lose it. He's constantly talking about 'Nam and killing gooks." I pondered the situation before answering, "I know. I think we should seriously consider getting him the hell out of here before he goes completely apeshit crazy."

Early the next morning, Jimmy B, Two-Fingers, and I were summoned to the AIM command center by Edward Still Smoking, who was still the head of the Blackfeet Nation AIM chapter. The town's Catholic church served as their temporary headquarters. I remember the three of us walking up its stone steps and opening the heavy door, inside it was dimly lit and smoky. A large cluster of candles burned next to the hand-carved altar, and leaders of AIM stood with their backs to us beneath a stained-glass window.

Next to Edward stood Jack Little Wolf and Lenny Iron Horse,

whom we knew from the sweat lodge at Billy's, it all seemed so long ago. They had gotten what they wished for, and they seemed overwhelmed by the changes they sought. Their noble ideals still persisted, and those ideals seemed to be the only things nourishing them. Nobility in the face of insurmountable forces made their efforts even more noble, and they clung to those ideals. They stood nicely dressed in their traditional tribal garb, their long black hair resting on their shoulders. Ideals, no matter how well clothed, come at a heavy price.

"We called you here this morning to have a good talk. It's been a while since we were together in Browning at your uncle Billy's sweat lodge," Jack said as he nodded his head toward Two-Fingers. "A lot has changed since that time. Change is what we want to talk to you about." Lenny, seemingly unable to contain himself any longer, butted in and said, "We are trying to draw attention to our plight as American Indians. We are here to fight against the injustices that have been perpetuated against us for over a hundred years. We are asking the United States government to live up to its own laws." Two-Fingers, Jimmy B, and I looked at each other, and realizing we'd be there for a while, sat down in the front row of pews and stretched our legs out.

"We are not trying to kill anybody, but we will die for the cause." Lenny looked over at Jimmy B, who stared back without blinking. "It's not a good idea to start shooting at helicopters. You must understand that the government can wipe us out at any time. The purpose of this occupation is to bring national attention to our treaty rights, the oppressive nature of federal and tribal governments, and our desire to be treated as human beings."

Lenny had stopped to take a deep breath when Edward interrupted, "Brothers, we appreciate your help. It's good to have a white guy fighting with us, but do you really know what you are fighting for? You need to understand why you are here. This isn't a game, we want to be recognized as a sovereign people. That's what was established by the Fort Laramie Treaty of 1868. This is our last chance at sovereignty. We are not asking for anything more than what the law states is ours."

"So, what you're saying is, I don't get to shoot anybody?" Jimmy B asked as Two-Fingers and I fidgeted in our seats. "Only if one of us is shot first," Lenny said as he stared at Jimmy B. "The federal government wants this to end peacefully, and they are sending a couple of senators for more peace talks. We need to chill out and hear what they have to say, and if they lie to us like in the past, I will be the first one to shoot."

Lenny sat down next to us and talked about the corrupt local Sioux tribal council and its leaders, and how they favored their friends and family for jobs and benefits. He spoke of the unbearable hardships the Sioux Nation had endured for decades. He spoke of Red Cloud, Black Elk, Sitting Bull, and Crazy Horse, and how they fought for the sovereignty of the Sioux. Lenny wanted to restore dignity and pride to his people by shaking off the chains of federal government control. His message was much broader than the mere occupation of a long-forgotten reservation town.

He envisioned support from other minorities in his quest for equality. That support hadn't materialized, but he still remained hopeful. He talked about the spirituality of their mission and the importance of traditionalists like Billy Spotted Eagle, Two-Fingers' uncle. He talked about the importance of being a human being, an American Indian. The threat of violence was important in getting the public's attention, but he didn't want to see his brothers and sisters sent home in body bags; he'd seen enough of that in 'Nam.

He spoke for over an hour, and before leaving, he extended his hand to each of us and quoted Red Cloud, saying, "I will fight no more forever." He turned slowly on the heels of his moccasins and walked down the row of pews and out into the morning sun, with Jack and Edward following close behind.

We found out later that the Sioux tribal council had grown increasingly frustrated with the occupation of Wounded Knee and with the members of AIM. They depicted them as troublemakers and requested a military solution to rid the area of the "rabble rousers." Their interests were being challenged, and they had no qualms about using firepower to rid themselves of the nuisance. They opposed any effort to bring a peaceful resolution to the problem; they wanted the federal marshals and the FBI to use force to take care of it. The power structure within Lenny's tribe had betrayed him.

Things had changed for the worse after Jimmy B shot out the helicopter's spotlight. Tensions in and around Wounded Knee rose exponentially after that, and we sensed something serious was about to happen. The long-awaited meeting between AIM and the senators did not result in a peaceful solution to the problem. AIM leaders were told that the Congressional Act of 1871 prohibited negotiations between Indians and the government, and when the AIM leaders pointed out that the Fort Laramie Treaty of 1868 predated the legislation by three years and should take precedence, the senators walked out of the negotiations. The US government had too much to lose if that treaty was fully recognized.

Once the government shut down negotiations, the random gunshots increased significantly. Public outcry for past injustices and support from other minorities were virtually nonexistent. The press labeled the occupiers as romantic primitives living in a dream world. They didn't appreciate the fact that American Indians were fighting in 'Nam only to come home in body bags or live as second-class citizens.

This irony hadn't escaped Jimmy B, and with each passing day, he grew more and more agitated and militant. He rarely slept: all he wanted to do was patrol and hold onto his rifle. He exchanged gunshots with people he couldn't see, and that became a nightly ritual. So after weighing our options, Two-Fingers and I decided to get him out of Wounded Knee and back to Browning. We had very little to pack, our biggest challenge was going to be persuading Jimmy B to leave, and that was not going to be easy. As I pointed out to Two-Fingers, "Jimmy B is a warrior, and we'll need to trick him to get him out of here. He will not go willingly. He hasn't let go of that rifle in days."

The sun was setting behind the distant hills when Two-Fingers said, "I know, and he's too big and strong to kidnap, and too smart to be fooled easily, even in his diminished state. I say we tell him we need to help the cause by getting more supplies, and that we can stay at the Palomino while we round them up. He liked that place; it was the last place he was semi-normal. At least it's worth a try."

Within minutes, a helicopter appeared out of nowhere and flew directly toward us. When it was directly above us, Jimmy B crouched down, took aim, and fired several times before anyone in the helicopter fired back. Jimmy B was firing as fast as possible when he suddenly stopped, dropped his rifle, and looked down at his chest as blood flowed from his green Army fatigue jacket. Then, he looked skyward, raised both arms into the air, and fell backward as life drained from him. Two-Fingers and I ran to him as all hell broke loose around us. American Indians had seemingly had enough, and many began returning fire with a vengeance.

The helicopter pilot must have been struck because the helicopter began to spin out of control before crashing into the Catholic church. As soon as that happened, the firing immediately stopped, and the place became deathly quiet. Two-Fingers ran to the burning helicopter, and was getting dangerously close when it exploded; his attempt to help went up in flames. The Catholic church quickly burned to the ground as a group of American Indians watched helplessly while it turned to ashes. There wasn't any water, it had been turned off weeks before.

Two-Fingers struggled to recover from getting knocked on his ass by the explosion, and he and I were stunned from losing Jimmy B. We gathered him up and carried his lifeless body to the bed of Two-Fingers' pickup, where we carefully lowered him into it. Two-Fingers went searching for blankets to wrap his body in, and I climbed up on the bed of the pickup and cradled Jimmy B's head in my lap. Two-Fingers returned with blankets and a canvas tarp, and we wrapped Jimmy B in the blankets before tying fencing wire around his body to keep them firmly in place. After making sure the blankets were secure, we placed the tarp over his body. Again, leaving nothing to chance, we used fencing wire to secure it around his body. When we finished, we sat down on the tailgate and surveyed the scene. While the Catholic church smoldered in the distance, American Indians from several tribes stopped to offer kind words and condolences. The leaders of AIM made a point of stopping by after providing aid to the living.

"Jimmy B was a great warrior, and he will be missed. He is now with the Great Spirit, and he is at peace," Edward Still Smoking said as he stared at distant stars with his arms held wide open. Two-Fingers listened to him for a while, then he abruptly jumped off the tailgate and said, "Ah, bullshit. He's dead, and I'm taking him home. Get in the pickup, White Guy, we're getting out of here."

I jumped off the tailgate and walked over to the driver's side and sat down as Two-Fingers once again checked to make sure the tarp was secure. After doing so, he joined me in the cab and handed me the keys. Edward was yelling at us to stop and think about what we were doing. He said it was a crime to remove a dead body from the scene of a shooting, and we would go to jail, but all of this fell on deaf ears. He continued yelling as I slowly drove across the barren prairie with the lights off, and as we approached a small hill, we could still hear Edward yelling, "It's illegal to take a dead body across state lines, you're going to get arrested!" His voice faded away as we reached the top of a hill surrounding Wounded Knee.

To my complete and utter amazement, we weren't shot at or stopped. It must have been the commotion back at Wounded Knee that spared us; both sides were probably wondering, now what? I drove the pickup onto an isolated dirt road before I turned the lights on. We drove westward, stopping occasionally to make sure Jimmy B was completely covered.

We drove along aimlessly and quietly, and before we realized it, we found ourselves passing through Anderson. It was early morning by then, and the Palomino was closed. The only light on in the entire town was the neon sign above the billboard advertising the Palomino Bar, Cafe, and Motel. As we passed by, the neon sign flickered a few times before going dark. That seemed like a fitting end to our crusade. As I drove onward, Two-Fingers stared straight ahead and never said a word. Soon, Anderson was in our rearview mirror, and our reservation was on our minds.

We continued to drive in silence, two people lost in thought. A noble cause had become anything but noble, and we both suffered from that realization. The miles passed slowly, and we were thankful when we reached Montana. A big, beautiful, blue sign welcomed us to, "Montana, The Big Sky Country." It was midday before we stopped for gas. We took turns using the bathroom, Jimmy B was never left unattended. Two-Fingers was meticulous in readjusting the tarp that covered him. It was bitterly cold, so we decided against getting ice for the body. Returning to Montana helped our attitudes, and it wasn't long before we opened up to each other and shared our guilt for not getting Jimmy B out of Wounded Knee sooner. Two-Fingers took it extremely hard and blamed himself for not saying no when Jimmy B wanted to go fight for the cause.

"Don't blame yourself. Jimmy B was going to go with or without you. He needed a cause, like Stan needed a cause. Some people need causes. They fight for all of us, and that's the way they are, thankfully. My dad fought too, but he never really talked about it. World War II veterans seldom do. Has Max ever talked about his war experience?"

"Pops? Hell no, he never spoke of it, at least not to me. You're right about that generation; they seldom talk about what they had to do. They suffer in silence. All of them are tough dudes. Makes me proud to be an American," Two-Fingers said as he pulled out his last joint from the front pocket of his Levi jacket. "At least they were treated like heroes when they came home. 'Nam vets are treated like shit and are no less the heroes. It's not their fault the war is unpopular; they did their duty."

Two-Fingers took a hit and passed the joint to me, and I took a long, satisfying hit before saying, "I hope Stan has been captured, even though it must be hell being in a P.O.W. camp in 'Nam. The stories about the way prisoners are treated make me sick to my stomach." Two-Fingers took the joint from me and said, "The thing I don't get about all these wars is, once they're over, the people we helped quickly forget about American sacrifices. Look at Russia, we saved them from speaking German, and they threaten us with nuclear war. I remember in grade school how they taught us to get down on the floor and hide under our desks in the event of a nuclear attack." Two-Fingers relit the joint before continuing, "I'm tired of hiding under desks. I'm tired of hiding."

Day turned into night as we traveled on; we drove at a pretty good clip considering we were in an old, worn-out pickup.

We stopped in Great Falls in the middle of the night and gassed up for the last time before getting to the reservation. Two-Fingers was driving, and I was curled up against the passenger door, trying to sleep as we passed through the town of Dupuyer. Within minutes, we were in Blackfeet Indian Country and not far from Jimmy B's parents' house on Badger Creek. When we turned off Highway 89 and traveled down the dirt road leading to Jimmy B's house, Two-Fingers was reminded of their childhood together and began to shake before gathering himself. By the time he had recovered, we were sitting in their front yard, looking up at their two-story house.

There was a dim light in the kitchen and smoke coming out of the chimney; it was March and still very cold in the Northern Rockies. I was wide awake by then and apprehensive about giving Jimmy B's parents the bad news. After Two-Fingers turned off the ignition, we looked at each other and nodded before walking up the front steps leading to their home.

We wiped our feet on a small brown mat that simply said "Welcome" before entering without knocking. Jimmy B's parents were awake but not yet dressed for the day; they sat in their robes at a round coffee table in the middle of their small, wood-stove-heated kitchen, drinking tea. They smiled and looked behind us, expecting to see Jimmy B, and when they didn't, blood slowly drained from their faces as they rose from their chairs.

They had lost loved ones all too often on the reservation, and they instinctively knew something was wrong. Two-Fingers and I were offered food, tea, and a place to sit before he explained what happened to Jimmy B. How can you possibly explain the death of someone's child? Jimmy B's mother was inconsolable, and his father remained hard-faced and stoic. They reached out and held each other while they tried to make sense of it all. Two-Fingers spoke of his desire to bring Jimmy B home for a proper Blackfeet burial, he couldn't bear the thought of Jimmy B being buried anywhere but in Blackfeet Country. After listening to all she could stand, Jimmy B's mother rushed outside to be with her only son while his father thanked us for bringing him home.

After thanking us and showing more gratitude than was necessary, he turned away and started his long walk to the pickup. Two-Fingers and I looked down from their front window and watched as he tentatively approached the pickup. He momentarily lost his balance and needed to grab onto the front bumper to steady himself; he needed to gather all the strength he could muster before he looked down at his dead son lying in the bed of an old, worn-out pickup.

Arrangements for Jimmy B's burial were made quickly. As I have stated on numerous occasions, death is an all-too-common feature of life on the reservation, and the tribe rallied together to offer assistance. Jimmy B was buried near where he grew up, at the cemetery in Heart Butte. That particular cemetery has been used by the Blackfeet for over a hundred years. In the olden days, the dead were laid to rest high above ground so that their spirit could easily soar to the sky. Laws were passed that no longer allowed them to do that. So, Jimmy B was buried in the cold, hard ground that is the Heart Butte cemetery.

Actually, as far as cemeteries go, it's a majestic one. It's in a large open meadow surrounded by pine trees, lying at the foot of the Rocky Mountains and enclosed by a barbed-wire fence with a cattle guard at the entrance to keep large animals out. There is an arched wrought-iron sign at the entrance that simply says, "Cemetery." Hundreds of white, wooden crosses dot the landscape, and occasionally, you'll find a granite headstone. Granite headstones are expensive, and most Blackfeet are poor. Every Memorial Day, the Blackfeet clean and repair the crosses at all reservation cemeteries. Plastic, store-bought flowers are then tied to the crosses in a vain attempt to keep them in place; the strong winds eventually blow them away, leaving behind the reality of death. The final resting place; cold, heartbreaking and forever.

Jimmy B's funeral was well attended. The small Catholic church was filled to capacity, and the overflow crowd stood outside in stone-cold silence. The Catholic priest, Father Ian Kelly, waxed poetic about

Jimmy B and his contributions to society, which seemed to comfort his parents. Billy performed a traditional ceremony that was appreciated by all. Over the previous year, the Blackfeet had once again embraced their old traditions, and their response was sincere; the ceremony was a mixture of old and new. Outside the church, the drummers and singers chanted a welcoming song as Jimmy B's casket was carried down the front steps. Two-Fingers and I were at the very front of the casket, holding it firmly on our shoulders with the help of four other pallbearers.

We carried the casket carefully across the parking lot, over the cattle guard, and onto the cemetery grounds, where we placed it on outstretched ropes laid on the ground next to his freshly dug grave. Then, in unison, we picked up the ropes and gently lowered Jimmy B's body into the rock-rich, dark hole. The Blackfeet crowded to the front of the procession as Billy spoke soothing words in Blackfeet and burned sage before blowing the smoke in four directions. When he finished, the crowd was startled by a twenty-one-gun salute performed by the local Veterans of Foreign Wars Committee. The pungent smell of gunpowder lingered in the air as Jimmy B's parents accepted an American flag from the head of the committee. Jimmy B's dad shook his hand vigorously and returned a sharp, crisp salute while his wife wept softly and the drummers and singers wailed and chanted loudly. When the ceremony was completed, the crowd slowly turned and walked to their cars and trucks.

The burial committee had started to shovel dirt onto Jimmy B's casket when Two-Fingers intervened. He insisted that the two of us should finish burying Jimmy B. The head of the committee strongly objected until Billy convinced him it was okay. Billy told him he would stay with us to make sure it was done right; there was no sense in everybody staying when two could do the job. Billy won the argument, and Two-Fingers and I removed our coats and ties and started shoveling dirt onto Jimmy B's casket. We shoveled fast and furious as

Billy looked on. We were drenched in sweat by the time we smoothed the last of the dirt over Jimmy B's grave. Afterward, we leaned on our shovels and admired our handiwork.

"That should be enough for today. It will be getting dark soon, and you can come back tomorrow and finish up. I made a special wooden cross for Jimmy B, and you can place it then," Billy said as he gathered his supplies.

"Nope, not yet, Uncle. We're not finished."

Two-Fingers and I ran to his old, worn-out pickup and carefully removed a granite headstone that we had purchased with the little money we had left. We had wrapped it in the same tarp that covered Jimmy B's body on his final trip home. It was a special rush order, and we had picked it up from Cut Bank that morning. Jimmy B was going to have a proper granite headstone, compliments of his two best friends.

Two-Fingers and I unloaded a bag of cement and a bucket that we had brought along for the occasion. From a nearby creek, we gathered icy water to mix with the cement, and when the texture was right, we carefully secured the headstone in place at the head of the grave, where it lay flat on the ground. Most granite headstones rise into the air, but not Jimmy B's, it would lie flat, out of the wind. Hopefully, it wouldn't erode as quickly as the upright ones do. When we finished placing the headstone in its new, permanent home, we stood back and took a look. Billy walked over to the headstone and nodded his head. The inscription on the stone read:

Here lies James Bailey No Runner

A Blackfeet Warrior

Who died fighting for his Country

"No dates or anything, Nephew?" Billy asked as he stared at the stone.

"Ran out of money. Besides, Jimmy B never knew what time it was, what day it was, and now it really doesn't matter." Two-Fingers said as he finished packing dirt around the headstone.

When we were finished, we both said words of remembrance, threw our gear into the back of the pickup, and looked straight ahead as we slowly drove out of the cemetery. Neither one of us looked back.

Chapter 17
Lost and Found

Within hours of burying Jimmy B, Two-Fingers and I went on a three-day, non-stop bender. We partied hard, and when we couldn't find anyone to party with, we partied alone. We drank and drank until we drank ourselves, and most of the bootleggers on the reservation, dry. Old habits die hard. When we sobered up, we found ourselves in the basement of Two-Fingers' parents' apartment house. After three days of hard drinking, we went looking for refuge, hoping we would find it there. Sleepy, hungover, and hungry, we dragged ourselves up the basement stairs to face the music.

"Well, look what the cat drug in. Nice to see you could come by and say hello to your family. Did you run out of money, or are you hiding from the cops?" Max asked smoking a Camel cigarette, ashes dropping to the floor next to his wheelchair. The smell of the smoke made my head spin and my stomach churn; his loud voice sounded like a bison stampede. I gently lowered my aching body down to their sofa as the living room began to spin out of control.

In a barely audible voice, Two-Fingers said, "I think we drank the whole reservation dry. We must have, I can't remember leaving any booze behind. I also can't remember where I left my pickup. Have you seen it?" He leaned back against the sofa and gripped the arm rests tightly.

"We haven't seen your pickup, Donny R," Pam said as she handed him a large glass of water. She gave me one too, but I was afraid I'd drop it, I was desperately trying not to fall off the sofa. With shaky, trembling hands, I took the glass and raised it to my lips, swallowing the cold, life-saving water down in one long, glorious gulp. Still unable to speak, I handed the glass to Pam, who refilled it without comment.

I nodded and leaned back against the sofa, praying for a quick and painless death. Pam returned with an even larger water container, and before she refilled our glasses, she said, "Maybe I should hook up the garden hose for you two."

"Now you know another reason why I quit drinking," Max said as he crushed his cigarette out in the ashtray that rested precariously on his artificial leg. "You're young, and you'll heal in a day or two. But at my age, hangovers last forever. The sickness eventually fades, but the damage caused by years of drinking never does. You hurt yourselves, your family, and your friends. The damage never goes away. How long are you boys planning on punishing yourselves with drink? When we are young, we drink to have fun, but eventually it turns into punishment. You see the winos around town? All of them are punishing themselves for something." The living room became deathly quiet as we contemplated his advice and hard-earned wisdom. Then, with slightly less trembling hands, we raised our glasses and savored the cold water like two weary travelers who had found an oasis. Eventually, the room stopped spinning, but it remained slightly tilted. To this day, that was the worst hangover I have ever experienced, mind-numbing, life-altering and wrapped in one imperfect package.

"Oh, I almost forgot. A letter from your father came a few weeks ago, Tony. I meant to give it to you at Jimmy B's funeral, but I forgot all about it." Max rose from his wheelchair with the help of his prosthetic leg and a cane, careful not to fall as he shuffled to a bookcase. He searched through stacks of papers before finding what he was looking for.

I stared at that letter, unsure whether I wanted to open it. My hands suddenly began to shake even more violently than before. Without saying a word, Two-Fingers took it from me and tore it open with the index finger of his left hand before handing it back to me. I struggled to focus on the writing; my eyes were having a tough time adjusting to the morning light streaming through the window behind me.

Dear Son,

I hope this letter finds you well. I have no way of contacting you in Wounded Knee, so I am sending this letter to Max and Pam. I wish I could talk to you in person about this, but that isn't possible.

Your mother and I found out the day after you left for Wounded Knee that your brother was killed in Vietnam. It's with the greatest sense of sorrow that I tell you this. That's something no brother or parent should ever be told, but it's a fact, a fact that I'm desperately trying to deal with.

An Army Captain from the Department of War came to our home and gave us the news. It seems the U.S. Air Force bombed the Vietnamese prisoner camp your brother was in; they claim they had no idea it was a prison camp. After the ground troops arrived to mop up, they found the remains of several Americans. However, they didn't find Stan's body. The only thing they found was his dog tags, which I hold in my hand as I write to you.

Your mother and I are holding up as well as possible. Please be safe and say a prayer for your brother. We miss you. Love, Dad

I read the letter twice before I stumbled into the kitchen and vomited into the sink, all the while anchoring myself to the counter so I wouldn't fall. It was there, against that counter, that I heard Two-Fingers reading the letter out loud to his parents, and it was there I heard Pam weeping quietly. It was there I heard Max say, "And they wonder why a man drinks." Drinking all the booze in the world wouldn't have eased the pain I felt at that moment, and it proved to be another mind-numbing, life-altering event that haunts me to this day.

For Two-Fingers and me, the spring of 1973 seemed particularly gloomy. In addition to the cold weather, cloudy skies, and late snowstorms, a cloud of death hung over us. Before then, neither of us gave much thought to death and its finality. Our mortality, and the ominous realization that we could go at any minute, began to weigh on us. The deaths of Jimmy B and Stan shook us out of our comfort zones, and the bad weather that lingered until late spring didn't help our moods. In addition to feeling on edge and uncomfortable, we both had severe cases of cabin fever and a strong desire to get on with our lives.

By then, we were both working at the Blackfeet Pencil Factory, and I'm still not exactly sure why they decided to hire me. Maybe they thought I was Indian enough after I participated in the Occupation of Wounded Knee. Or perhaps Max had helped me get on, he was always raising hell with management, and that was probably the main factor. In any event, I was happy to have a well-paying job, and the Pencil Factory provided that. The Blackfeet had secured additional contracts to supply pencils to all federal government agencies. It was the tribe's largest investment in its future economic survival, and everybody involved wanted to make it a success. Two-Fingers and I worked on the main production line, and even though the work was tedious, we believed we were accomplishing something that would benefit ourselves and the tribe. We had a purpose, and over time, we began to regain our footing.

Sunshine magically appeared the first week of May, 1973. The whole tribe seemed to brighten up as well; they were ready to shake the cold out of their bones and have some fun. It had been a hard winter and spring for everybody, especially the elder Blackfeet who worried about their sons and daughters returning home safely from Wounded Knee or 'Nam.

On May 10th, Two-Fingers and I were hard at work at the Pencil Factory when the overhead siren sounded, just like it did every workday to announce it was time for lunch. The workers grabbed their homemade lunches and walked down the hall to the lunchroom to eat.

All employees had a half-hour lunch break, so everyone moved quickly to find a seat at the long tables that occupied the center of the dining hall. Two-Fingers and I sat at our usual places next to the coffee pots and quickly devoured the peanut butter and jelly sandwiches Pam had made for us.

The foreman overseeing the workers was Eddie Racine. Eddie was Old Man Racine's youngest son, and he really liked his job. He was 45 years old at the time, and it was his first full-time position. Like the other workers, he was working and no longer totally dependent on the government payoffs that plagued the reservation. Eddie had a habit of standing at the entrance to the lunchroom and nervously checking his watch to make sure everybody got back to work in precisely half an hour. Eddie had taken ownership of the place, and he was serious about getting a full day's work for a day's pay. It was as if the money came out of Eddie's pocket, and he had a death grip on it. Every single day, Eddie said the same thing. "You work at a Pencil Factory, so let's get the lead out." It was sort of funny the first time we heard it, but eventually the workers turned a deaf ear to Eddie and tried to ignore him altogether. None of us knew why he stood in the doorway, because when the half hour was up, the siren annoyingly sounded and everybody went back to work right on schedule. To my knowledge, nobody ever attempted to escape or run off with a handful of pencils.

It usually took less than fifteen minutes to eat our lunches, and then it was smoke time for those who smoked. Cigarettes were bummed from those who had them, and once they were handed out, matches were struck in unison, and the smoke fest began. I usually grabbed a couple of pots of coffee and made my way around the room refilling coffee cups. After doing so, I would walk back to my seat to a chorus of, "Screw you, White Guy."

On that day, Two-Fingers, always on a quest to better himself, was reading the latest edition of the Big Sky Reporter published in Great

Falls. He leaned back in his chair, boot heels resting on the table, head cocked slightly to the side, with a cigarette he "borrowed" dangling from his mouth. When he got to page six, he stopped and read a tiny headline that announced, "Wounded Knee Occupation Ends." He fell forward, spread the paper out in front of us, and began reading the article out loud.

"On May 9, 1973, the Occupation of Wounded Knee came to a peaceful conclusion. After 101 days of unrest and occupation, representatives of the federal government and the leaders of AIM settled their differences and the occupation is officially over. As always, when more information becomes available, we will report it to you in a timely and thorough manner."

Two-Fingers continued to stare at the article before reading it out loud one more time. He looked up from the article, stared absentmindedly at me, and shook his head in disbelief before saying,

"Is that all they have to say? 'Thorough manner?' What the hell do they mean: 'in a thorough manner?' Nothing about a downed helicopter or a burned-out Catholic church or Jimmy B's death? What kind of reporting is this?"

I played along with him and said, "Well, in all fairness, we snuck Jimmy B out of there, and I doubt they know about it. The downed helicopter and the church...well, that's another matter. I'm not sure about that. It seems like they're trying to downplay the entire episode if you ask me. You know, the less people know about it, the better."

Two-Fingers stomped out his cigarette on the cement lunchroom floor and stood up to stretch. When the siren blared, signaling the end of lunch, the Blackfeet rose to their feet and walked single file back to their workstations. As always, Eddie Racine checked his watch before turning out the lunchroom lights and closing the door.

That weekend, it began to rain, sheets of rain poured down from every possible angle. The cold, hard ground thawed quickly as the rain kept coming. For three days and three nights, it rained nonstop. Everybody was ass-deep in mud by the third day, and the Blackfeet who had survived the flood of 1964 worried for their safety.

The flood of 1964 was the worst flood in Montana history. For several days back then, heavy rains poured down on the reservation and Glacier National Park. The endless rain melted the snowpack faster than anyone had seen before. In fact, it melted so quickly that people in several outlying communities were caught off guard and ill-prepared for what followed.

The dams on Birch Creek and the Two-Medicine River quickly overflowed and eventually burst open. These two events caused a twenty-foot wall of water to roar down the countryside, and flood everything in its path. Trees were up-rooted and carried sixty to seventy miles downstream before coming to rest in open pastures and meadows. Cars were literally swept off the roads and carried along the swollen rivers and streams as their occupants desperately tried to escape. Homes were pulled into the raging torrent, which gained speed and ferocity as streams and rivers merged together. Virtually everything in its path was destroyed. Debris was carried downstream, people drowned, homes were destroyed, and lives were ruined. Of the 31 deaths, 30 occurred on the reservation. About 8,700 people in the area were evacuated, and many Blackfeet families had no choice but to live in teepees and tents for the entire summer.

Fortunately for the residents of Browning, the three days of hard rain in 1973 didn't produce any major flooding. Unfortunately, many residents in the rural areas of the reservation weren't as lucky. As far as Browning proper was concerned, the only major downside was the loss of power. The antiquated power system the Blackfeet relied upon couldn't handle that much water, and transformers all around town blew up, causing the Pencil Factory to close indefinitely. It takes a lot of power to make pencils.

The Junction Drive-In had reopened for the summer mere days before the rains began. The owner, Clyde "River" Cross Guns, had invested in a generator shortly after the 1964 flood and was well prepared to do business when most businesses were not. The Junction was one of a handful of places that weren't left in the dark. It was there that Two-Fingers and I sat nursing our coffee when River gave us the evil eye and threatened to throw us out if we didn't order some food. The place was getting busy and he needed to sell something. So, we ordered cheeseburger deluxes and milkshakes.

Shortly after we were served, Edward Still Smoking and Johnny Skunk Cap came storming in and muscled up next to us. The Junction has hardwood bench seating so, Two-Fingers and I "skinnied" up to make room for them, they insisted on sitting next to us. Two-Fingers was smashed up against the wall and I was smashed up against him. That left plenty of room for Edward and Johnny, one of the perks of being elders, I suppose.

Not wasting time saying hello, they immediately started talking about Wounded Knee. They had returned home the previous night from South Dakota and apparently needed to tell everyone who would listen about their fateful adventure. According to them, they had spent a couple of nights in jail after the occupation ended or they would've been home sooner. Johnny had started a fight with a couple of white ranchers at the Palomino Bar, and after Edward stepped in to break it up, they both ended up in jail. Johnny has a bad temper and was one of the more militant Blackfeet at Wounded Knee. However, to my knowledge, he wasn't militant enough to shoot a helicopter. He never served in the Army or anything like that, his war was waged against white people. Anyway, they both cooled their heels in the jail at Pine Ridge for a few days before being released.

"What the hell happened after we left?" Two-Fingers asked as he dipped a French fry into his ketchup. "I read in the newspaper that there was some sort of peaceful conclusion and that you had settled your differences. What's up with that?"

"Yeah, like we could settle our differences. You might say that we were left high and dry. As you both know, AIM hoped the occupation would raise awareness of our plight. With the civil unrest surrounding the Civil Rights and 'Nam movements, we mistakenly believed we could bring attention to the injustices we suffer and everybody around the country protesting would rally around our cause." Edward proceeded to take a bite out of my cheeseburger before continuing. "That never happened, and the federal government won the war of attrition, beat us down, and starved us out. They always starve us out."

I glanced at Johnny, who was staring out the window at a couple of white tourists on bicycles. Without warning, he jumped up and said, "Follow me." He proceeded to kick open the screen door before running after the two bicyclists, who were laboring to get up the steep hill leading out of town. We followed him out, and by the time we caught up, he was shaking their handlebars and cussing like a madman. He literally shook with anger, his face bright red as he yelled, "How long are you two going to be squatting on my reservation?" Johnny shook both bicycles violently, and the bicyclists fell to the ground as he yelled, "I asked you how long are you going to be squatting on my reservation?"

A small crowd had formed and watched as the bicyclists struggled to their feet before one of them spoke, "We're passing through, and we're headed to the Park!" For some reason, that really seemed to piss Johnny off. He grabbed the fronts of their jerseys and yelled, "If you don't get off my reservation in ten minutes you'll never see the Park!" He shook them one last time for effect before releasing them. They mounted their bikes and effortlessly raced up the hill and out of town, it must have been the adrenaline.

Johnny turned to face the crowd and yelled, "That's what I'm going to do every time I find a white squatter on my reservation!" He walked back to the Junction to a chorus of chants. The younger Blackfeet slapped him on the back as the older Blackfeet shook their heads in disgust.

"Times are changing, but they're not changing fast enough to suit the young bucks. They blame me for not being militant enough at Wounded Knee, maybe they're right. There are just too many of them and not enough of us," Edward said before crossing the road and re-entering the Junction.

Two-Fingers looked at me and asked, "How long are you going to be squatting on my reservation?"

"Bone you, Two-Fingers. I'll squat here as long as I want. But, as a sign of respect, I will pay for your cheeseburger."

To which he replied, "Damn white people, always buying us off with cheese."

We were walking back to the Junction, when a tribal work truck stopped directly in front of us, and two older Blackfeet jumped out and started pounding a political campaign sign into the ground next to the highway. After they drove off, we read the sign out loud in unison: "Vote for Robert 'Stubby' Grant for Tribal Chairman." In smaller print, at the very bottom, it read, "A vote for Stubby is a vote for the future."

Two-Fingers laughed and said, "Future? Stubby doesn't know what day it is, and if Stubby is the future, we're all royally screwed."

When I was younger, racism on the reservation never really bothered me. I was the only white kid in my class for years, and I was teased and had more than my share of fights, but it never really bothered me, and as time passed, the teasing and fighting slowed after I fortified myself against it. But in the early 70s, people like Johnny were angry. The younger Blackfeet were desperate for change, and they began to strike out at those they perceived to be their oppressors.

Racism, as I've learned from Two-Fingers, is a manifestation of hate. All races are susceptible to hate as well as greed, lust, gluttony, and all the other sins. Sins and emotions can't be eradicated by laws, and it's the folly of the government to think they can change something that is deep inside someone. There are many downsides to this foolish thinking. The most harmful result is government becomes more powerful by taking advantage of the division. Even well-intentioned citizens lose freedoms and control over their lives. Two-Fingers knew this to be true, and he spoke of it often. His life has been filled with insults, slights, and irrational hatred. The difference between him and so many others is that he never cried about it. He used those slights to strengthen himself, and it helped to build and strengthen his character. Do you know anybody worth a damn that hasn't overcome adversity? Adversity molds a person, and you either conquer it or it conquers you. An overbearing, divisive government does not conquer adversity, it creates it.

Hate was on the reservation, and there was no denying it. Fortunately for me, I was liked by the entire Schwartz family. In fact, they liked me so much, they invited me to Paula and Cindy Ann's graduation ceremony that took place in Missoula. They had finished college early by taking extra classes and going to summer school; they seldom came home during their college years. Once they decided to do something, it got done. By then, Cindy Ann was divorced from Stogie Man, and she put her energy into raising her girls and getting a college degree. During their time in Missoula, Paula, Cindy Ann, and her two little girls lived together in a large house they rented near the campus. It was during her college years that Stogie Man fell further into the depths of alcoholism. He was rarely seen, and rumor had it he was living up north near the Canadian border with a Chippewa Cree from Alberta, Canada.

Anyway, on the day before graduation, Pam and Max drove to Missoula in their Buick, and Two-Fingers and I followed in his old, worn-out pickup. We hoped that by the time we got back, the Pencil Factory would be up and running, and we could get back to work. Until then, it was time for a road trip, and we were eager to get out of town.

After driving five hours on a mountainous, windy two-lane highway, Two-Fingers and I were relieved when we finally arrived in Missoula. It was well worth the trip. Missoula is a beautiful place, with lots of trees and a river running through the center of town. The campus of the University of Montana is spectacular; it's filled with well-maintained buildings and beautifully manicured lawns. It looked like paradise to me. There's a huge white M high up on a hill that was built out of large rocks painted white. I don't want to sound racist or anything, but I really admired that big, beautiful, white M.

Two-Fingers and I decided to hike the steep, slippery path to the base of the M, where we smoked a joint and lost ourselves in the moment. We ended up talking and day-dreaming about someday going to college there. We eventually returned to reality and decided to walk the short distance to Cindy Ann and Paula's house, leaving Two-Fingers' pickup in a large parking lot at the foot of the hill.

When we arrived at their place, the kids were happy to see their uncle and even seemed pleased to see me. The backyard was filled with tables and chairs, and there was a fire pit with elk venison roasting on a grill. Max was in charge, and he seemed happy about that. We drank pop, played with the kids, and told stories about each other. It was a great day, and we were happy to be together. I spoke briefly to Paula about Stan, and that temporarily cast a pall over the festivities, but it faded quickly. She had moved on from Stan and seemed more interested in comforting and consoling me.

The following day was graduation day, and after the ceremony, caps were thrown in the air and hugs were exchanged, a typical ceremony, I guessed. Two-Fingers and I were impressed with virtually everything that happened that day. In fact, we were so impressed, that we decided right then that we were going to college there. Cindy Ann had already made plans to move back to Browning after graduating and run for a seat on the tribal council. Paula would stay on in Missoula to continue her education at the University of Montana School of Law, she had decided to become an attorney. Paula would soon have plenty of room in her rented house and suggested we could stay with her as long as we behaved.

That is how we ended up going to the University of Montana. Before moving in the fall of that year, we stayed on the reservation and did everything in our power to help Cindy Ann get elected to the tribal council position she sought. She won handily and became the first woman to serve on the tribal council. She wanted to help the tribe and serve her people, and she understood the need to shake off the chains of dependency that were created by a bureaucracy that didn't care about providing a brighter future for the Blackfeet. Freedom is good; dependency is an affront to freedom, and it is bad.

Two-Fingers, over the course of many years, ended up feeling the same way about the dependency issue, but it wasn't easy for him, it required personal sacrifice. He had been offered Affirmative Action help, tribal help, and he qualified for enough grants to choke a mule. So, at that time, he thought changing the system right then was a bit hasty. After a lot of discussion and persuasion, Paula talked him into only taking the loan the tribe offered, and I'm not sure he has ever forgiven her for that. He worked as a part-time custodian on campus for his spending money, and every night after work, he would come home and quietly cuss her name.

College was a lot less expensive to attend back then. I don't think either of us could have afforded it at today's prices. Education offers freedom once you are freed from the debt you are burdened with while chasing knowledge. I ended up working nights in order to afford the place. Every time my personal plight came up in casual conversation, Two-Fingers would always say the same thing: "That's what you get for stealing our land." After which, he would proceed to laugh hysterically and clap like a trained seal. Personally, I never found any humor in that, especially not at three a.m. in the dead of winter when I was loading packages into the back of a UPS truck.

Chapter 18
Swallowed by the Whale

Under the advice of counsel, I won't get into much detail regarding Paula and me falling in love or the events surrounding our courtship, I've been sworn to secrecy. Besides, this is the Two-Fingers story. It's a story about how he became the most beloved and revered Blackfeet leader of all time.

As you can plainly see, up until Two-Fingers went off to college, there was little to no evidence that he was special. Far from it, he was a young Indian boy raised on an Indian reservation, and the odds of success were never in his favor. He was socialized in a very unique way, but he refused to be a victim of circumstance. To this day, he remains the most concerned and honorable person I have ever known. He has lived by a code of ethics that is more important to him than personal glorification. Meaning, if he had to lie or cheat to gain something, he did without. He believed in doing the right thing because it's the right thing to do.

In all the years I have known him, he has never used his race to define who he is. He refused to allow his people to use race as an excuse for failure, or for success. He has more pride than that, and he refused to play the race card. Once the race card is played, personal accountability goes out the window, along with self-respect. He grew up surrounded by people who blamed being Indian for their failures. He never blamed white people for his plight. He had too much honor and dignity to do that. He rose above the indignities he experienced and gained the respect of his people; respect and honor outweigh thirty pieces of silver.

He succeeded in that quest, and he is a stronger person because he never allowed himself to be preyed upon by those who wanted to use race as the rationale for turning their lives over to government control. He grew to despise the federal government and fought against its harmful effects his entire adult life. He witnessed the deprivation brought on by government control, and he also witnessed what happens when you are no longer dependent, when you are truly free. Government control is like a cloud hanging over your head. It doesn't provide rain, it only serves to darken the sky and take away the drive needed to succeed; it kills independence and freedom.

He learned the hard way. He learned that people must take personal responsibility for their actions, or they will become prey, easy prey. Big government provides excuses for failure instead of holding people accountable. Government enables people to shirk their responsibility; a big, controlling, and out-of-control government is never a good idea. Especially, when unelected bureaucrats have absolutely no accountability. The administrative state has sucked the life out of our Constitutional Republic. The administrative state isn't government. We the People are the government, and we are being silenced and replaced.

He honed his philosophy over many years by combining large amounts of book learning with practical experience. Two-Fingers has common sense and an encyclopedic knowledge of American history, specifically American Indian history. He studied these subjects as an undergraduate and as a student of the law. To this day, he continues to study the Constitution and the case law derived from its interpretation. Our Constitution is the genesis of our entire legal system, and strict adherence to it must be maintained at all times. Without it, America is just another landmass filled with rudderless people. It provides Americans a track to run on.

Two-Fingers believes the Constitution is the principal reason America is the greatest country on earth. He has spent his entire adult life defending it against those who use it for their evil purposes.

Communists hate our Constitution and are always looking for "workarounds" to destroy its meaning and essence. Over the years, he's dealt with too many politicians who violate it and too many criminals who hide behind it. The Constitution, in the hands of the immoral or criminal among us, becomes the antithesis of We the People.

So, if you ask me to point to the things that made Two-Fingers exceptional, I would point to his patriotism and his love for the United States of America and our constitutional republic. He believes, now more than ever, that it's time to put away the past and look to the future. When was the last time the government did that? To that very point, I believe it's meaningful to tell you that Two-Fingers knew Indians were fully aware of the realities of the right of conquest. American Indians, more than any other tribe of people, knew what you honorably fought for was yours. He would often talk about how the Blackfeet ended up with Crow territory, how the Blackfeet originated in what is now Canada. American Indians fully embraced the idea of the right of conquest; they thrived on that principle. Tribes battled other tribes for land, horses, women, food, etc. He also knew that the Spanish were conquerors of Mexico and had inhabited that land for over three hundred years, and that they had the right of conquest.

Over the years, virtually all lands have changed hands and who can say who was really there first? First doesn't matter to an American Indian; the power to fight and conquer does. In the olden days, Indians didn't cry about being conquered; they understood it. What they didn't understand was why the white man lied and broke treaties. Lying and dishonorable conduct were foreign to them. In their world, anyone who lied or cheated was banished from the tribe. If you were a coward and brought shame upon yourself and your family, you were banished. Honesty, courage, and sacrifice were the qualities that were revered and honored. America once lived and flourished by these ideals, but they have long since disappeared, and he knows that.

Politicians and unelected bureaucrats, above everyone else in society, must be honest and trustworthy. Their dishonest acts are killing America, and they must be held accountable. "We the People" must become more than a slogan, and he knows that, too. It was a hard-fought lesson that has shaped his life and legacy, but as you can probably tell, he wasn't gifted with these ideals; he had to earn them, as we all must.

Even though Paula has sworn me to secrecy regarding our personal lives, I can tell you this much; Paula and I ended up getting married after she graduated from law school. She was offered a full-time position at a local law office in Missoula, and she accepted. By then, Two-Fingers had given up on the idea of being a history teacher and decided he and I should go to law school. So, Two-Fingers and I went to law school after graduating from college, and Paula and I are happily married. Paula may not agree with my assessment, but it remains my firm belief.

For those of you who have never been to law school, here is the crib-note version of what it's like. The first year of law school is when they try to scare you to death. They put enormous pressure on you to see if you are cut out for law school and the practice of law, because pressure is the underlying theme of an attorney's life. They try to weed out the weaklings, and they do that by making the students study torts, contracts, constitutional law, evidence, criminal law, and civil procedure. Then, in class, you are called on to discuss the subject matter. If you think my writing is boring, crack open and read a copy of the Federal Rules of Civil Procedure, you'll end up wanting to cap yourself.

Here's the really weird thing about Two-Fingers: he liked that stuff, but he especially liked constitutional law. He was the wunderkind when it came to constitutional law. In class, he would challenge the constitutional law professor over some mundane issue, and they would debate it ad nauseam. The other students loved him for doing that because it took the pressure off them. The last thing a first-year law student wants is to be called on to recite some case that interprets a constitutional amendment. Every time I was called on, my ass puckered up, and my mouth ceased to work. As soon as I started to struggle, Two-Fingers would come to my rescue, and off to the races he and the professor would go.

The second year of law school is where they try to work you to death. They pile on twice the workload of the first year. The light at the end of the tunnel comes into view during your third and final year. The brain continues to be stretched and pulled in all directions, but the light is there, and the hope of graduating becomes a reality for those who continue to persevere. I persevered; Two-Fingers flourished. And when he graduated, he was eager to take on the world with his new wife. That's right, Two-Fingers got married the day after graduation. I've been sworn to secrecy by my wife regarding our personal life, but as far as I'm concerned, Two-Fingers' personal life is fair game. That's what he gets for letting me steal his land.

It was sometime during our first year in law school that Two-Fingers met a fellow student by the name of Linda Johnson. She was known to everybody as "Lindy." Lindy was a little hippie girl who was going to change the world. She was hellbent on fighting every injustice known to mankind, real or imagined. Lindy, in addition to being an advocate for justice, was a drop-dead, gorgeous blonde with an ass that would stop traffic. Probably a little more information than you needed to know, but I'm all about transparency.

Anyway, Lindy's dad was the Governor of the great State of Montana at the time. In fact, Franklin T. Johnson was in his second term when Two-Fingers and Lindy started dating. Franklin, Frank to his friends, loved being Governor. Before taking office, he was a rancher from the Butte area. According to reports, he was a humble guy when he was first elected. He appeared to be dedicated to public service and promised to serve only two terms. Well, like most politicians, he began to enjoy the power that came with his office, and he ended up breaking that promise as well as many others. Over the years, he employed a number of devious tactics to remain in power. In short, he is no longer a public servant, he's a professional politician. Frank has blown so much smoke up people's asses you'd think he was a chimney.

Paula and I were busy romancing the stone during their courtship and were casual observers to Lindy and Two-Fingers' romance and their falling in love. I seldom saw either one of them outside of school. I know this much; they fell hard for each other and ended up moving in together at the end of our first year of law school.

Frank proved to be a real racist when it came to Two-Fingers. In one of our rare conversations involving Lindy, he told me Frank went ballistic when his daughter, his only child, wanted him to move in with her. I suspect he feared it might not look good politically. With Frank, it was always about politics. Despite his wrath, they moved in together.

Two-Fingers and Lindy eloped the day after graduating, and as soon as they crossed the Idaho line and back into Montana, the Montana Highway Patrol met them and "escorted" them to the state capital in Helena. Immediately upon their arrival at the Governor's mansion, Frank proceeded to lecture Two-Fingers on a variety of topics. When he started to belittle his ancestry and heritage, Two-Fingers kept his cool and adeptly pointed out that Montana was home to seven reservations filled with American Indian voters, and that it might not be such a bad thing to have an American Indian for a son-in-law.

According to Two-Fingers, it took Frank a while to figure out the obvious importance of such a thing. Of course, Frank was a professional politician by then, so he must be excused for being dimwitted and slow. Why is it that, as soon as politicians are elected, they lose what little sense they had in the first place? I've always surmised they sniff the glue that holds their campaign signs together, but I could be wrong.

Frank, after digesting the idea that their marriage might get him extra votes, put down his whiskey glass and cigar and proceeded to slap Two-Fingers on the back. The number one priority for politicians is getting re-elected. They will sell their souls and the souls of their constituents to get re-elected. His daughter's happiness was irrelevant. Frank had warmed to the idea, but he didn't take any chances. He appointed the newly graduated Two-Fingers to a high-paying job as the head of the newly created "Montana International Trade Organization." The primary duty of the head of this organization was to travel the globe promoting Montana trade opportunities. Two-Fingers spent four years traveling virtually nonstop, promoting the sale of Montana products to foreign countries. He traveled to Africa, Russia, Europe, the Far East, Canada, and Mexico. The program was so successful that Montana's exports to these countries skyrocketed. Of course, Frank took the credit and was easily re-elected to another term.

Lindy, the sensitive, loving, and caring wife who was going to change the world, became despondent over the fact that Two-Fingers was seldom home. She occupied a good portion of her day drinking. The occasional martini with dinner became a nightly ritual that spilled into the wee hours of the morning. She suffered from sleep deprivation and soon fell into an unrelenting state of depression. Booze followed her throughout her bout with depression, and before long, she descended into the depths of alcoholism. They tried to have children, and every time she became pregnant, she miscarried. Every time she miscarried, she increased her drinking to ease the depression and the pain. With each loss, she fell deeper and deeper into the vicious pit of alcoholism, and it eventually destroyed her. Two-Fingers threatened several times to quit his job, but Frank wouldn't hear of it. It was a phase, Frank said; Lindy would get over it. Besides, Two-Fingers didn't know if he could afford to quit. He had been bitten by the snake of consumerism, and the fangs went in deep. He felt trapped. He had car payments, a house payment, and enough credit card bills to choke a maggot. He was indebted and no longer free.

Then, one cold winter morning, while he was away promoting trade, their housemaid found Lindy hanging from the center beam of their horse stable. Her lifeless body dangled from the end of a long rope with a well-fashioned noose around her neck. She was no longer depressed. Two-Fingers, wracked with guilt, turned his back on his career and everything else, and he literally vanished. Nobody, I mean nobody, knew where he went. He stayed lost, not only to himself but to his family and friends, for over two years. The passage of time helped him sort things out and begin to heal from his devastating loss. When he resurfaced, he was a changed man.

To this day, he has never talked about that time in his life, and I respect him too much to pry. All I know is a man spends a little time living and a lot of time sorting things out. For our part, Paula and I seldom saw Two-Fingers and Lindy during their marriage. Schedules never worked out; everybody was busy with their careers, which came at a heavy price. In retrospect, we should have found the time. Paula and I were living in Missoula, busily working for a law firm that specialized in contract and corporate law, and we both should have found the time. It's an age-old story that is never relevant until it hits home, and it hit home for us. We should have found the time.

While living in Missoula, Paula developed an interest in gaming law. She had personally witnessed how tribes across the country were improving their lives through gambling revenues. Casinos were being built in Indian country, and reservations that suffered unspeakable poverty were becoming prosperous. Indian reservations were able to enter into gambling accords with the state in which they resided. The way it works is, if a state allows a particular kind of gambling, reservations can't be precluded from establishing that same type of gambling operation. White entrepreneurs immediately began flooding into reservations to set up partnerships with different tribes, hoping to provide the know-how and capital for a large share of the action in return.

Paula wanted the Blackfeet to be the first tribe in Montana to have large-scale gaming, and she worked hard to make it happen. When she approached the tribal council with her idea, she was initially met with a lot of resistance. She was finally able to get their full approval when she pointed out that the recently abandoned Pencil Factory could be converted into a casino that would employ a lot of Blackfeet. The Pencil Factory had sat vacant for a couple of years; pencils had gone the way of the dinosaur. When was the last time you bought a pencil? In any event, when it shut down, it put hundreds of people out of work, and the tribe was hurting financially.

Eventually, the tribe agreed to put money into the venture on one condition: Paula had to come back to the reservation and run it. That was all she needed to hear, but she still went through the exercise of weighing the pros and cons of us moving back to the reservation together. Before she finished with me, I half believed it was my idea in the first place. I remember sitting at our kitchen table when the final decision was made and Paula saying, "The white man's greed has taken our land away, and the white man's greed is going to give it back." I piped up and replied, "Are you sure you want it back? Be careful what you wish for."

Two-Fingers was back living on the reservation when we wrapped things up in Missoula and moved to Browning. He was living a very solitary life. He had lost his way in the wilderness of life and was healing. He hand-built a small log cabin four miles from town on

Willow Creek. He was trying to find his footing. When I first went to visit him there, I immediately noticed he was a changed man. His zest for life was replaced by introspection. He questioned his every move and thought; he was filled with self-doubt, guilt, and confusion. The things he thought were right in life had turned out to be wrong. His attempt at being a good little apple, red on the outside and white on the inside, failed miserably. His pursuit of trinkets, money, and acceptance turned out to be an unmitigated disaster for him.

He couldn't escape his guilt, and he refused to drink it away. He was sober for the first time in a long time, and he began to have clarity of thought. He told me he had visions, and I jokingly asked if any of the visions featured snakes. He stared at me for the longest time before he finally smiled. That was when I knew things were really serious. Two-Fingers had lost his sense of humor along with his sense of being. He was consumed by the proverbial whale, swallowed whole, and every moment of his day was spent trying to swim out of the bowels of the whale to freedom, at least that's what I was told. Not knowing exactly what he meant by that, I asked, "Why don't you just let it shit you out so you can get on with your life?" That was when he politely asked me to leave his cabin. If you haven't been inside the whale, you will never understand the question or the response.

Paula and I visited him as often as possible, hoping to shake him out of his malaise. We repeatedly suggested that he needed to go back to work and find a purpose in life. We never succeeded, but that didn't stop us from trying.

It was shortly after one of those visits that Billy moved in with Two-Fingers to help him find his way back. Billy rightfully believed that Two-Fingers had lost himself just as Juanita had; they both abandoned their roots and their heritage. Billy helped him through spiritualism, Indian spiritualism. Billy was right. Our attempts at helping him were founded in the modern, materialistic "chase the trinket theory," and it hadn't worked. That theory was largely responsible for his pain. Billy's approach worked best, and neither of them disclosed the exact details. It worked, and I find it ironic that the man Two-Fingers made fun of in his youth for his beliefs became an integral part of his healing and salvation.

Unannounced, and out of the blue one day, Two-Fingers came to see us and told us he was going to run for the tribal council. Somehow, it had become his calling. He hated politicians in general and thought the only way to beat them was to beat them. He was going to be a leader for his people, no matter the cost. He would help them rise above the abject poverty that haunted the reservation by ridding it of the corruption and dishonesty that had reached plague-like levels. He wanted to be a Blackfeet Indian leader like his forefathers.

He had specific, concrete plans for what he wanted to achieve, and when he finished telling us about them, I asked, "Do you have any room for me in your master plan? I'm tired of working for the old lady and could use a job." In reality, I worried about him and wanted to help him in any way I could. That's when I became his campaign manager. Paula, not surprisingly, didn't miss working with me. It hurts a little to admit this, but she actually seemed relieved. She had become obsessed with getting the gaming operations up and running. She liked and wanted complete autonomy, and that is exactly what she received. In my opinion, to be successful, every venture must have a leader with a vision. Tireless, endless dedication to the cause is necessary for success. When there are too many people injecting their ideas and wishes into something, nothing gets done. The vision becomes blurred, and eventually everything grinds to a halt. Paula lives by one principle in that regard: lead, follow, or get the hell out of my way. I got the hell out of her way.

That is another difference between a successful business and government. Governments are bogged down by bureaucracies that seldom get things right. Eventually, things get done, but they are seldom done efficiently or correctly. Too many chiefs and not enough Indians is never a good thing. That may sound racist, but after all, I am a white guy. Paula relentlessly pursued her vision, and soon money poured into the tribal coffers. She had complete autonomy, so she hired outside consultants who were paid a salary. Then she hired capable Blackfeet to learn from the consultants, and as soon as they had the knowledge necessary to run their departments, she got rid of the consultants. Soon, gambling on the reservation was under the complete and total control of the Blackfeet tribe.

The tribal elections were less than a year away when Two-Fingers announced he was running. At the outset, he was apprehensive about how to mount an effective campaign and worried he might lose. I told him his fears were unwarranted, and to ease his mind, I immediately started working on a campaign strategy to get his message out to the citizenry. Luckily, the reservation isn't that large and consists of only a few populated areas, and if you win Browning, you will be elected to one of the seven seats.

By then, Cindy Ann was a force on the council, and that proved to be extremely helpful. She desperately wanted him to have a purpose in life, and getting him elected consumed her. She brought us up to date on the most pressing issues facing the tribe. Two-Fingers and I had been gone a long time, and we needed her advice. Turns out, they were the same issues that always plagued the reservation. Cindy Ann explained that even though there were two other young members on the council, the majority of the members were the same old guys who had always found a way to get control. After a brief time in the majority, two of the young council members were voted out of office and replaced by the old guard. Of the seven seats, four were occupied by the old professional politicians, and the other three seats were occupied by younger councilmen. The majority rules on the reservation, and the four older members always voted in lockstep with each other. Nothing changed. Allegations of graft, cronyism, distrust, and greed ruled the day. The older members were in bed with the BIA and Trevor Kanowski, the bureaucrat from hell, and they bled the reservation dry. The reservation's dependency on the federal government was at an all-time high, and the tribe was kept on a very short leash.

After meeting with Cindy Ann, Two-Fingers decided the federal government and its chains of dependency had to go, once and for all. He committed to making that happen, and that became the theme of his campaign. After one hundred and fifty years of federal government control, Indians were worse off than ever. They were still dependent on handouts, and the effect of that policy was evident in the destruction of the human spirit, which continued to manifest itself in the alcoholism, deprivation, and short life expectancy that were prevalent on the reservation. Most importantly, it was an affront to individual growth and freedom.

The chains had to be removed, but how is that done when several generations were addicted to dependency? That was the challenge. Two-Fingers had never met anybody who willingly turned down commodity cheese. Come to think of it, neither had I. Two-Fingers campaigned on the notion of liberty, freedom, and self-respect, those long-forgotten ideals that were buried under the minutiae of government control. He vowed to bring those virtues back. In clear and precise terms, he went straight-up American Indian on them. Not the "Native Americans" they had become. He wanted to raise the Blackfeet up and bring them back to their glory days, when they were free, noble, and proud.

Chapter 19
Victory, Tragedy and Redemption

I don't believe the Blackfeet had ever witnessed a campaign like his first, it was legendary. He met with virtually every voter on the reservation and when he talked, they listened. He spoke of honor, self-respect, and pride. He wanted to return to the ideals that were key to the Blackfeet way of life centuries before, not the twisted ideals foisted upon them by previous administrations. The denigration of tribal sovereignty was an act of betrayal to his people, and he repeatedly pointed that out to all who would listen. He promised to be a leader of change and that the tribe would come first, always. He spoke of sacrifice and how change was necessary, how it wouldn't be easy and wouldn't come overnight. He spoke about the failures of the current political system and the harm being inflicted on the entire tribe. The young and old alike witnessed their leaders doing and saying dishonest things, which created an atmosphere of dishonesty and mis-trust throughout the entire tribe. It's a disgrace to lie, cheat, and steal, but somehow, politicians are excused for their bad behavior and never held accountable by the tribe. What kind of system is that? Politicians have to be held to the very highest standards. If they are dishonest and their deception is accepted, the entire tribe suffers.

He often quoted Chief Joseph, the great chief of the Nez Perce whose Indian name was, "Thunder Rolling From the Mountains." Chief Joseph is a great example of what a leader is and he lived his words: "It's a disgrace to lie. A real leader is always honest." He's also known for saying, "Never be the first to break a bargain." In short, Two-Fingers preached ethics, and it worked. He won his seat in a landslide, and the good guys regained a majority of the seats on the tribal council.

The first thing he did as a council member was help create a position for a tribal lawyer who had the interests of the tribe in mind. Up until that point, the tribe was at the mercy of the BIA counsel and dependent on their legal advice. That was like having the fox guard the henhouse. Two-Fingers wanted to change that. He was convinced the harmful effects of the BIA had to be minimized. So, in a 4-3 decision, I was hired as legal counsel for the tribe. My duties included sitting in on council meetings and coming up with a plan to get the federal government out of their hair and off their backs. The majority of the council members saw the wisdom in tribal autonomy and were happy I was hired. When I thanked Two-Fingers for getting me hired he said, "Don't thank me, you were the only one who applied."

The tribal council and the tribe became his life, and he gained strength from them, and they benefited from his strength. He became known as a man of his word, and that was important to him. As he grew older, he would refer to the residents on the reservation as "my children." He believed that once you become a parent, life is no longer about you, it's about your children. Once he got involved with tribal politics, life was no longer about him; it was about his people. He made personal sacrifices and provided the type of leadership that was desperately needed, and when the elections rolled around two years later, he won handily and ended up getting more votes than any other council member, which meant he became the new Chairman of the Blackfeet Nation.

As Chairman, he had immense power, but that power was never abused. He focused his energy on changing the attitude of the tribe. For decades, the tribe had been told they were inferior and irrelevant, and that was evident by the government programs forced upon them. He set out to change everybody's view of who they were. He helped create a positive mental attitude by constantly speaking of the great virtues of Indians. He continued talking about the virtues of honesty, integrity, and self-respect, and the need for these virtues was drilled into the minds of everyone who listened. They were exceptional, and he believed that. If a tribe doesn't believe they are exceptional, their enemies won't either. He gave them a prolonged course in attitude adjustment, and it worked. It was time to rise up after decades of being beaten down. Believing you are exceptional leads to exceptional results, and if you think you are inferior, you probably are. He also preached unity, hard work, and dedication to the task, and that worked too. Attitudes changed, and people began to look at things in a positive light, not in the dim light that ominously flickered from Washington, DC.

As I said earlier, being Chairman gave him enormous power to effect change on the reservation. Two-Fingers presided over the council fairly and adeptly. He willingly listened to opposing views and encouraged everyone to speak freely and honestly. The older council members opposed change, but that never deterred Two-Fingers from listening to what they had to say.

As Chairman, Two-Fingers and the majority were able to implement a number of good programs. It helped being flush with cash from the gaming operations. Capitalism at its finest, Two-Fingers knew that wealth fuels democracy and hope. Gaming provided much-needed jobs; everybody who wanted a job was able to find one. The tribe invested in all types of new businesses under Two-Fingers' leadership, and most of them proved to be money makers.

One of the projects near and dear to Two-Fingers' heart was establishing a tribal bison herd on the reservation. He worked out a deal with the Sioux tribe in South Dakota to buy a hundred head of their bison, and on the day they arrived, Two-Fingers and I watched as they were unloaded from several large, semi-trailers. After the last bison was unloaded, he moved closer to me and said, "I think I recognize a couple of them." It was nice to see that his sense of humor had finally returned. He was no longer grief-stricken and desolate. He had found what he sought, a purpose in life. He no longer drank, and we both quit smoking weed when we started law school. He was dedicated to building a better life for his people and believed he needed to keep a clear head to do that. When we were young, we did childish things.

One of the things that always impressed me was the fact that Two-Fingers got things done; he was Paula without the pantsuit. We all know people who have great ideas and then never get off the couch long enough to do anything about them. All the good thoughts and ideas in the world are useless without action. Two-Fingers was all about action. By the way, not everything he tried worked, but that never stopped him from trying.

Another thing that impresses me about Two-Fingers is the depth of his humanity and his caring for others. He doesn't have a narcissistic bone in his body, and when he's spoken to, he actually listens. There are numerous stories that speak to his humanity, but one in particular is worth mentioning. It relates to the life of Levi Bird Rattler, who lost his entire family in the most horrific, unbearable, and unspeakable way. Levi was able to rise from the depths of hell, turn his life around, and bring glory to his people. Even on the reservation, where failure, heartbreak and hopelessness often reign supreme, there are stories of redemption, hope, and the indomitable human spirit. This is one of them.

Leon Bird Rattler, Levi's father, had been a Bird Rattler his entire life by the time he and Two-Fingers met. He was born into that position, into a family of Bird Rattlers who came from the Bird Rattler clan of the Blackfeet Indian tribe. Some things are unavoidable, and for Leon, being a Bird Rattler was one of them. Given the situation he found himself in, Leon ended up marrying another Blackfeet Indian by the name of Mary Spotted Eagle. Leon and Mary attempted to raise their eight children on the reservation near the town of Heart Butte,

Montana. Reservation life, it bears repeating, is a hard life no matter where you live, and the town of Heart Butte is another example of that hardness; it's cold and immovable, like most of the residents.

Leon decided early in his marriage to raise his family as far away from Browning as possible while still remaining on the reservation. Given his limited options, he chose Heart Butte. Heart Butte remains the second-largest town on the reservation. It has a small grocery/clothing store, three bars, a gas station, a school, a small Catholic church, and the large cemetery where Jimmy B and many other Blackfeet are buried. It has all the essentials required for living and dying. The Bird Rattler ranch is located approximately five miles west of Heart Butte at the end of a long, narrow dirt road, and it was there their fifth son, Levi, was born.

Leon and Mary always considered themselves fortunate. Fortunate to be far enough away from the chaos of Browning and fortunate to live on a ranch that had grown in size over the years. They were indeed fortunate. Unlike many ranches on the reservation that suffered from a lack of abundant water, they were blessed to have the beautiful and enchanting Birch Creek at their doorstep.

The abundance of a ready supply of water helped them grow their hay operation into a thriving enterprise. Their meadows were filled with grass, trees, and wildlife. The fishing was good, but Blackfeet were, and still are, meat eaters, and the Bird Rattler family was no exception. They butchered their homegrown beef, raised their own vegetables, and milked their way to a healthy life. They lived a rich, solitary life on a ranch near the Rocky Mountains, on a creek that flowed year-round.

Levi took to that way of life more so than his older siblings. Going to town was never something he looked forward to, but he did allow himself to be formally educated in a small, one-room school near Heart Butte, within walking distance of their ranch. He didn't like going, but he went to appease his loving parents, and he promised to graduate from the eighth grade, and graduate he did.

Back then, those who wanted a high school education had to make the trip to Browning because that was the only place on the reservation that offered such a thing. When given the chance to go to high school, Levi rejected it out of hand. His four older siblings, on the other hand, were curious about the outside world and readily agreed to attend high school and stay with friends living in Browning.

Levi stayed on the ranch and found happiness in his world of cattle, horses, and ranching. Levi was a loner, and a loner he would remain for most of his life. He was alone even when he was in a crowd. After completing their high school educations, it came as no surprise to anyone that his older siblings would stay in Browning permanently and leave Levi, the three younger siblings, and their parents at the ranch. Times were good back then, dreams were being fulfilled, and the future looked bright.

That changed in the spring of 1989, when severe flooding once again hit the rural areas of the reservation with a ferocity not seen since the great flood of 1964. The tranquility surrounding the Bird Rattler way of life came to an end when the poorly rebuilt dams on Birch Creek and Two-Medicine burst open and released a torrent of water that eventually swept away the Bird Rattler cabin on the bank of Birch Creek. Night had fallen, and in the darkness, Levi found himself fighting for his life and the lives of his younger siblings and parents. Levi survived, but his family members were swept away. Their bodies were recovered several days later. Tragedy has always been a staple of reservation life, and a tragedy it was.

The Bird Rattler family funeral was well attended. The small Catholic church in Heart Butte was filled to capacity. The Catholic priest, Father Ian Kelly, was sixteen years older than he was the last time Two-Fingers and I attended a funeral there. Once again, he waxed poetic, this time about the Bird Rattlers and their contributions to society, and that seemed to comfort Levi and his older siblings. However, it was Two-Fingers' uncle, Billy Spotted Eagle, who provided the spiritual message that was desperately needed on that sad, solemn occasion. Over the years, Billy's prominence as the dominant spiritual force for the Blackfeet tribe had grown, and his message was both strong and comforting.

It was on that burial day, inside the little Catholic church, that the remaining Bird Rattlers decided Levi would take sole possession of the ranch. The older siblings had made lives for themselves elsewhere and wanted nothing to do with the ranch. The memories and pain surrounding the loss of their younger siblings and parents would only be exacerbated if they returned. The very thought of returning was more than they could handle. They didn't want the ranch, and Levi had no intention of leaving it. In fact, on that day, Levi refused their offer of a ride home. He walked the five miles of muddy, rutted, and washed-out road alone. Levi thrived on being alone, and alone he was on that loneliest of days.

The extent of the destruction on the ranch was overwhelmingly severe. The log cabin that once sat on the bank of Birch Creek no longer existed. In its place were remnants of a life gone forever, swept away in the blink of an eye, like time itself. It took several days for Birch Creek to recede, and when it did, it revealed the full extent of the damage, including uprooted trees, old cars, a large semitruck container, and a massive "Welcome to Glacier National Park" sign. After surveying the scene, Levi began to better understand the force of nature and the massive flood he had managed to survive. He was grateful to be alive, and he faced the daunting tasks ahead with a vigor reserved for those who have been given a second chance, a second chance at life.

On that day, shortly after the funeral, Levi began working on salvaging what he could. Miraculously, the large barn and corrals had remained intact in a large meadow far enough away from Birch Creek that no lasting damage was done. Inside that barn sat another old, worn-out pickup. It had quit running a couple of weeks before the flood, Levi vowed to get it running.

When light turned to darkness, Levi built a roaring fire using a small piece of flint and some dried kindling, just as his father used to do. He was a Bird Rattler, and that was something nobody, or nothing, could take away from him, and he rejoiced in that realization. He was a survivor, and he survived that night alone and unafraid, though it was a night filled with constant reminders of his profound loss.

It wasn't until the next day that Levi learned of another tragedy that would forever change his life and his perception of life itself: his older siblings were killed on their way home from the funeral in a head-on collision with a large motorhome. They died on impact, and the four of them were burned beyond recognition in the flames that engulfed their small car. Their instantaneous deaths left Levi with a lifetime of loss and sorrow.

Levi learned of this tragedy from Two-Fingers, who had taken it upon himself to deliver the news. It was an unenviable task, but Two-Fingers instinctively knew that he, and he alone, had to do it. How do you tell someone that their entire family is gone, gone forever? Two-Fingers told me he struggled mightily with that question as he drove out to see Levi.

In the olden days, the Chief of the tribe performed these types of duties. Since the shakeup of their civilization and the implementation of the new corporate business model, the Chairmen of the Indian tribes had taken the place of the Chief, and the duty fell to them. However, that wasn't the only reason Two-Fingers called on Levi. He felt a personal and immediate attachment to Levi the moment he heard about the accident. That particular tragedy hit him hard; it was a reminder of his own loss, and it became his mission to mitigate the damage that a loss of that magnitude foretold.

After parking in what appeared to be Levi's front yard, he exited his pickup and began his search. Two-Fingers told me he found Levi in his barn, under the hood of his old, worn-out pickup. He was hard at work and oblivious to Two-Fingers until he made his presence known. Levi immediately recognized the look on Two-Fingers' face. It was the unmistakable look of tragedy and death, a look Levi had become all too familiar with, and for a brief moment, he felt sorry for Two-Fingers.

That feeling disappeared as the harshness of the news sent never-ending waves of agony pulsating through his body. Hearing the gory details of their deaths forced Levi to the ground, where he wept and moaned; the grief was overwhelming. Two-Fingers knelt beside him and held him as tightly as humanly possible. He made no effort to silence Levi because he knew Levi would be crying for the rest of his life, and in all likelihood, his crying would be the only true comfort he would ever receive. Spoken words, comforting thoughts, and rationalizing would never take the place of that initial weeping. Uncontrolled and desperate weeping provided Levi temporary relief from his permanent pain, and the Chairman of the tribe let him weep.

On that spring day, in that barn, time stood still for both of them. When Levi finally found the strength to stand, Two-Fingers gathered him up and led him to his pickup. He had decided that Levi was going to live with him, and Levi had neither the strength nor the desire to argue with him. Besides, once Two-Fingers made a decision, there was no sense in arguing with him. You don't become Chairman of the tribe by being weak and pliable.

Levi was grateful to Two-Fingers for taking him in at a time when he desperately needed something and someone to cling to. He stayed with him, but the emptiness he felt was constant, and he searched in vain for something, anything that might fill that void. According to Two-Fingers, the memories of his family and their deaths haunted him. The depth and intensity of his pain were unrelenting, and he had no choice but to separate himself from his loss by any means possible. The excruciating pain could only be dampened by his ability to find peace in a fantasy world where thoughts of the past were suppressed; it was his only hope for survival.

He was told that time healed all wounds, and Levi tested that theory to its fullest. He found that the passage of time, coupled with an alternative reality, helped, but those things, in and of themselves, were insufficient for a complete recovery. The deaths of his parents and his three younger siblings weakened him, but the loss of his four older siblings not only destroyed his hope but also destroyed his will to live. The cumulative effect of all those deaths left a hole inside him that no amount of time, help, or encouragement would ever change.

Outwardly, he appeared to be getting better over time. He interacted well with Two-Fingers, his family, and me. We gave him all the love and support we had to give. Levi tried to reciprocate, and on the surface, it looked like he was healing when, in fact, he wasn't. He needed something more, something to help silence the voices of the ghosts, and that was when he sought and found solace in the bottle. Booze. Lot's of booze. It was the only thing that helped him with the pain and the nightmares. Booze provided him with the alternative reality he desperately sought. His occasional drinking, like so many alcoholics, quickly turned into a full-time job, and soon he was roaming the streets and alleys of Browning with the winos who drank their lives away in pursuit of their own alternative realities. That went on for the entire winter following the deaths and deep into the spring; Levi didn't draw a sober breath that entire time.

That all came to an abrupt end when the Chairman of the tribe decided enough was enough. It goes without saying that Two-Fingers had witnessed enough alcohol-related carnage to last a lifetime, but I'll say it anyway. He knew Levi would have to drink himself dry before realizing he had something to live for. Levi, Two-Fingers reasoned, needed a purpose in life or the drying-out process would last forever, and Levi had already lost enough of his life to drink. It was personal for Two-Fingers. Levi, like Two-Fingers, had fallen away from himself and still hadn't found his way back. Two-Fingers took it upon himself to show him the road to recovery.

So, Two-Fingers and I went searching for him, and Levi didn't see either of us coming. Two-Fingers always had a way of sneaking up on people, you don't become Chairman of any tribe without being able to sneak up on people. As for me, I'm just naturally sneaky. We found Levi passed out in an alley littered with empty Muscatel wine bottles and drenched in days-old piss. Two-Fingers literally dragged him out of the alley, and I helped throw him into the bed of his pickup. Levi didn't raise so much as an eyebrow the entire trip to his ranch. Piss-limber and passed out had become an all-too-familiar condition for Levi, and piss-limber and passed out he was when Two-Fingers parked in what appeared to be the front yard of his ranch.

Billy sat patiently on the bank of Birch Creek watching as Two-Fingers and I tried to figure out how best to unload Levi. In his capacity as Chairman, he had tasked Billy with helping Levi dry out. Billy eagerly took up the task and had spent the previous four days building a sweat lodge to aid in his efforts. Billy was always good at selecting the perfect place for a sweat lodge, and this time was no exception. He built it on the sacred ground where the Bird Rattler cabin had once stood. It was so close to Birch Creek that digging the four-foot pit proved relatively easy, there were very few rocks and plenty of sand.

After taking one look at Levi passed out cold in the back of Two-Fingers' pickup, Billy decided that, for everyone's sake, Levi needed a bath before being put in the sweat lodge. To make that happen as seamlessly as possible, Two-Fingers slowly backed his pickup to the rapidly flowing creek and lowered the tailgate. Levi, oblivious to all things natural, soon had an immediate and unexpected spiritual renewal. Two-Fingers, with Billy's help, slowly lifted him from the bed of the pickup and tossed him into the deep, cold, spring-fed creek. Not surprisingly, it took Levi about a minute to resurface. He was about a quarter of a mile downstream before he finally came up for air, and he was a better man for doing so. Two-Fingers, Billy, and I sat comfortably on the bank and watched as Levi thrashed around in the water before finally reaching high ground. It was harsh treatment, but at least he didn't get his leg shot off.

That was step one of his recovery. Step two came when he was stripped naked and forced into the hot, steam-filled sweat lodge. He sat there surrounded by the three of us, quietly cussing our names and our very existence. It wasn't long before he'd had enough of the suffocating heat. Without warning, Levi bolted to the creek, willingly jumped in, and was completely submerged when the three of us joined him. After cooling off, we returned to the sweat lodge, where we sat in silence as the red-hot rocks glowed in the darkness.

It was there, in that sweat lodge, that Two-Fingers announced step three on Levi's path to recovery. He took his time and was very deliberate and direct as he presented Levi with a way forward, and he didn't care whether Levi liked it or not. Levi was tasked with using his skills as an experienced cowboy to round up fifty head of wild, tribally owned horses and cull them from the tribal herd. Ranchers had complained that the herd was too large and was cutting into their profits. They argued there wasn't enough grassland to feed them all, and certain tribal councilmen were swayed to give the ranchers their support. Profits were given priority over the freedom of the herd. Two-Fingers initially fought their decision, but you don't become Chairman without compromise, and compromise he did.

On this particular issue, Two-Fingers was surprisingly outvoted; only Cindy Ann was on his side. So, being the leader he had become, he came up with a solution that he believed would benefit everyone. Levi needed direction and a task, and when he proposed the idea of Levi helping care for the tribal herd, with Billy's help, the tribal council gave their unanimous support.

Billy and Levi would be given complete autonomy with only one condition; instead of merely culling horses that would normally be taken to the cannery or sold as working stock, they would round up the rankest, wildest, and strongest members of the herd and sell them to a local rodeo outfitter named Larry NoRunner, a Blackfeet tribal member and friend of Two-Fingers. Larry made a very good living raising and selling his personal stock of wild horses to rodeo promoters, but he never had enough supply to meet the demand. Two-Fingers' plan would create a new industry on the reservation by utilizing the tribe's wild herd, and the ranchers would receive the additional grazing land they had petitioned for. It was a win-win situation for everyone, including Levi. When asked to participate, Billy enthusiastically accepted the challenge for both spiritual and practical reasons.

After spending a week in and around the sweat lodge, Levi eventually began to feel human again, almost. Although he was less than enthusiastic about spending the summer trying to gather and corral wild, mean, and vengeful horses, he accepted the task with as much vigor as he could muster. It was during that summer that Levi and Billy began their careers as wild horse wranglers, and they were better men for having done so. Billy didn't need much emotional improvement, but getting bucked off wild, mangy horses did help keep him grounded.

Dried out and cried out, Levi began the journey of finding his way back and took great comfort in knowing that he was not alone on his journey. So, with a small advance from the tribe, he and Billy purchased a couple of well-mannered horses and enough provisions to see them through the ordeal ahead. To his surprise and undying gratitude, Billy had repaired the old, worn-out pickup that had been abandoned in the barn. The tires were inflated, and it had enough gas in the tank to make it to Browning, where he and Billy picked up the provisions they would need for the grueling summer. The well-mannered horses they'd purchased were delivered to a predetermined location at a campsite in the shadow of the Rocky Mountains that Two-Fingers and I had chosen for them.

That experience, living Indian style in the most rugged terrain imaginable, proved to be the elixir Levi desperately needed. Like most Blackfeet, he learned to ride horses before he could walk, and that experience served him well. He soon became a cowboy's cowboy, and there wasn't a horse he couldn't ride. He spent the entire summer riding, roping, and sleeping on the hard ground that is the reservation, and he grew strong.

Levi and Billy both cherished freedom, and they worked extremely hard without complaint. By the end of summer, they had gathered more bucking stock than the rodeo outfitter could handle. They were some of the rankest, meanest, nastiest animals ever created, and Levi rode each and every one of them to prove to himself, and to them, that he was equally mean, nasty, and rank. He never wanted to break their spirits because that would diminish their value and usefulness, but he desperately needed to prove that he could ride them and that life was worth living, no matter how tough the ride.

With his share of the cold, hard cash from the sale of the horses firmly in hand, he returned to his ranch and began fixing the place up. The barn leaked, so he fixed the roof. The corrals needed repairs, so he fixed them. His livestock had either drowned or run off during his absence, so he pledged to slowly replace them. With Billy's help, he erected a large teepee that would provide shelter for the cold winter days and nights ahead. Those hard times helped him focus on what he wanted to do with the rest of his life. It was during that time that he decided to compete on the rodeo circuit and prove to himself that he was as skilled as he believed he was. His dream of competing and the glory that came with winning pushed him through that winter. When spring returned, he put his plan into action. He became a rodeo cowboy.

Levi started his new career at the local level. On the reservation, there were rodeos; not far from the reservation, there were rodeos; rodeos were everywhere, and so was Levi. Hardcore, experienced cowboys were constantly trying to prove their manhood. They were competitive, and they needed plenty of rodeos to showcase their skills. Levi proved to be the most competitive and the hungriest. He won every saddle bronc and bareback event he entered; riding bucking horses was his specialty, and nobody did it better. Prize money came, and so did the notoriety associated with winning. Everyone with an interest in rodeo whispered his name and marveled at the achievements of the young Indian boy from the Blackfeet Indian Reservation.

Before long, he was traveling by himself to larger rodeos, bigger purses, and tougher competition in his old, worn-out pickup. It never mattered where he went or who he competed against, he dominated the circuit. Calgary, Pendleton, and the Cheyenne Frontier Days rodeos were the largest and most prestigious rodeos in the West, and he won them all. The mystique surrounding him grew with every successful ride, and the price of victory eventually began to take a toll on him.

The pressure came to a head shortly after he qualified for the World Championships of rodeo, held annually at New York City's Madison Square Garden. The Big Apple, the cream of the crop, that rodeo was the most prestigious and largest event of the year, and it awaited his arrival. Making it to the Garden was a big deal and the dream of all serious cowboys. Levi never gave it much thought until he began to overthink things. Instead of concentrating on his next ride, he began thinking about winning a world championship, and the enormity of that task began to wear on him. For the first time, he started thinking about failure, and that thought overwhelmed him. So much so that he failed to finish in the money in the final three regular-season events he entered. Even after those failures, he was still ahead in points, but his lead was precarious at best.

With his success and the notoriety of qualifying for the finals came money, sponsorships, pressure, and an insatiable need to release his tensions. That was when, once again, he looked for an escape and found it deep inside a bottle. He initially resisted the temptation, but the desire became increasingly hard to ignore. On the train from Browning to New York City, somewhere in North Dakota, he made his way to the club car and didn't leave until he was forcibly removed. Drunk, rowdy, and strong, it took half the train crew to get him to his sleeping car.

Somehow, some way, he found the will and mental fortitude to rouse himself from his self-induced coma the next day as the train pulled into the station in Pittsburgh. Disoriented, depressed, and ashamed of his relapse, Levi vowed never to drink again as he stumbled back to the scene of the crime, the club car, in search of sustenance and anything that might help his hangover. After arriving in New York City, he departed the train at Grand Central Station and took a cab to a hotel close to the Garden. The rodeo was set to start in two days, and he was still disoriented, depressed, and not entirely sure whether he was on foot or horseback.

On the day of the first go-around, Levi was feeling much better and completely focused on the task at hand. He had met up with cowboys he'd competed against all summer, and they busied themselves with the business of rodeoing. Levi had taken time to familiarize himself with his surroundings, but nothing prepared him for the size of the crowds. They were massive, noisy, and demanding. He scored an 87 in the first of his two events, the bareback competition. With each jaw-breaking leap, his confidence grew to the point of distraction. No matter the obstacle, when rodeo time came, he was always able to answer the bell. When he was on the back of a bronc, he was completely focused.

Next up was the saddle bronc event, which had become his specialty, and he was lucky enough to draw the only horse on the entire rodeo circuit that had never been ridden; the famous, undefeated, and defending champion of the world, Twister. Twister was a dark gray roan gelding feared by every cowboy on the circuit. Even the spectators feared him. He was nearing his prime and Levi knew that if he was able to ride him, his place in the finals would be assured and, in all likelihood, the all-around championship would be his.

As Levi stared down at Twister from the safety of the top rail of the chute, he couldn't help thinking that Twister didn't look that tough. So he slowly and confidently eased down onto Twister's back, adjusted his grip on the rope, pulled his hat down over his ears, and nodded for the gate to be opened. Twister, true to his name, jumped out of the chute and immediately went into a frenzy, twisting around and around, jumping higher with each turn. Levi was ready for him, and he knew he had him even before he removed his hat and began whipping Twister squarely between the ears with it. Twister went berserk, his twisting intensified as Levi continued to showboat in an arrogant act of defiance.

When the buzzer sounded and the ride was officially over, Levi continued his assault as the crowd rose to their feet and roared their approval. Time seemed to stand still as Twister, equally arrogant and defiant, reared up and slowly fell backward, driving Levi into the hard, unforgiving ground of the arena. The entire right side of his body was buried under Twister's weight. Levi desperately tried to escape the suicide move, but to no avail. Buried he was, and buried he remained until pulled from the hole created by the force that had driven him into the ground. Two days later, Levi woke up confused, disoriented, and in a cold sweat in a hospital bed. Wires and tubes ran in and out of him, and his right leg was hoisted high in the air by a mechanical arm. Levi was bandaged from head to toe, but he was alive, a survivor of another tragedy, a tragedy of his own making.

It was several days later when Billy and I showed up to take home the only cowboy to ever ride Twister. Before leaving the hospital, the orthopedic surgeon who had worked on Levi's shattered right leg sat down with us to discuss the seriousness of his injury. In short, the only man to have ever ridden Twister would be lucky if he ever walked again without the assistance of crutches or a cane. He surmised that rodeoing was out of the question; one more injury to his leg would cripple him for life. To add insult to injury, Levi was told he missed winning the Cowboy of the Year honors by two points. His failure to make the final round cost him more than his career, it cost him a shot at immortality. On that happy note, Levi was gathered up and taken to a waiting ambulance that delivered the three of us to Grand Central Station, where we boarded the train to Browning.

It began as a relatively quiet trip. There was plenty of activity and noise around us, but few words passed between us. Levi was deep in thought contemplating what never riding again would mean to him. We let him stew in his solitude and only offered encouragement when we thought it appropriate. After spending half the trip staring out the train window, he began to unburden himself about what had happened that season. He went into great detail in an effort to free his mind, and we listened, and responded. He began to heal mentally once again.

When the train arrived in Browning, it seemed like the entire tribe was there to greet the only cowboy ever to have ridden Twister. Levi was slightly amused by the fact that he would forever be linked to the horse that had destroyed his life. Twister was famous before Levi rode him, and his legend grew even larger after winning another Bucking Horse of the Year award. For Levi's part, he took little comfort in knowing he was the only cowboy who had ever ridden Twister. Twister's popularity soared, and Levi crashed to the ground, both literally and figuratively, and it took him a long time to fully recover from the injuries and the fatigue, the never-ending fatigue.

Levi spent an entire month at the Blackfeet Health Center rehabbing his broken body. His main focus was his right leg, but he had a number of torn muscles, scrapes, and bruises that needed to mend. The staff worked with him, and he worked hard at recovering. At the end of the month, Levi walked out of the center without the aid of crutches and only needed a cane when going up and down stairs.

Billy was with him the entire time, and Two-Fingers and I checked in on him every chance we could. It was Billy who was there to take him home in his old, worn-out pickup. Billy had convinced Two-Fingers that he should be placed in charge of helping Levi heal. Levi was broken, but his bones were mending. It was his mind and spirit that Billy was concerned about. It didn't take much persuading for Two-Fingers to agree that was the best course of action for both Levi and Billy. Billy, found another purpose in life and took great pride in helping the only cowboy who had ever ridden Twister.

Winter came early that year, and somewhere along the way, it decided to never end. For survival reasons, they abandoned Levi's teepee and moved into the barn, calling it home. The money Levi earned that summer rodeoing was enough to sustain them through that harsh winter. Levi never had much money growing up, and had a natural distrust of banks, so he figured the prudent thing to do with his money was to put it in a coffee can and bury it in the middle of the barn.

Billy would drive to town only when absolutely necessary in the old, worn-out pickup to spend that money on provisions. They sustained themselves on the provisions they purchased, the deer they shot, and the commodities they received. The more primitive the conditions, the more Billy liked it. I sensed Levi initially hated the arrangement, but he grew to embrace it, too.

Every day that winter, regardless of the weather, Levi worked his leg until he couldn't work it anymore. He devised different types of leg exercises, like walking up and down the ladder that ran from the barn floor to the hayloft. He would go all the way to the top and then walk back down to the bottom, and his legs grew strong. He did this for days on end when the weather was too harsh to go outside. It wasn't long before he no longer needed the cane or Billy's help, so he got rid of the cane and kept Billy around for company and spiritual healing. They spent endless hours talking about the challenges that lay ahead, the impact of the tragedies Levi faced, and how best to handle them. Being a loner has its benefits, but Levi learned that company, the right kind of company, has its rewards too.

By late winter, Levi had decided he would start rounding up wild horses again. Instead of selling the horses to Larry NoRunner, he decided he would keep them and become a direct supplier to rodeos. Bucking horses sold for good money, but the real money was in leasing them out and retaining ownership. A supplier who owned the horses and leased them out had a better opportunity to make serious money. The better the stock, the more the supplier made.

The owner of Twister, for example, had gotten rich off Twister. For being the top draw at a rodeo, Twister's owner received top money. On top of that, bucking horses had their own championships and prize money. The winner was determined at the end of the season based on how many contests they were in and how few times they were ridden. It was a points system, and Twister always had the most points at the end of the year. Twister's owner had banked a bonus of $50,000 the previous year, and Levi wanted in on the action. He always smiled a little at the fact that the cowboy who rode Twister made less than Twister, a lot less.

Levi couldn't ride competitively anymore, but he needed to continue rodeoing, and that was his solution. When the idea was presented to the tribal council, Two-Fingers' eyes lit up, and he pounded the large wooden conference desk with more force than necessary. He thought it was a great opportunity for Levi and for the tribe. Levi had the connections in the rodeo world, and the tribe seemed to have more wild horses than they knew what to do with. Plus, as luck would have it, the Blackfeet rodeo stock buyer, Larry NoRunner, wanted to retire and needed to sell his equipment and gear. At the ripe old age of seventy-eight, he had finally had enough. When the tribal council meeting ended, Two-Fingers personally contacted Larry and worked the deal to the benefit of all concerned.

Levi became the principal partner in the joint venture, and was given complete autonomy in getting things up and running. That venture has proven to be another success story for the tribe under the leadership of Two-Fingers. The Blackfeet herd is renowned for producing multiple Bucking Horses of the Year. Wild horses from the Blackfeet herd are the most sought-after rodeo stock in all of America, and it started with a tragedy so severe it would have permanently crippled a weaker man.

Levi Bird Rattler is not a weak man, and his strength helped him find profound happiness and love when he met and married a woman from the Lone Wolf clan, who blessed him with a large family that they raise on their ranch in a new, large cabin built on solid, high ground. Roberta Lone Wolf became a Bird Rattler, and like Levi, she will remain one for the rest of her life.

Chapter 20
Blackfeet Justice

During a particularly tedious and long-winded tribal council meeting, Stubby Grant complained about how racist America was and suggested selling the reservation to the Russians. Stubby, like most of the tribe, had no idea what an average Russian's life was like. He hated America and figured Russia was the best alternative. Stubby had actually served as Chairman of the tribe before Two-Fingers unseated him, and he was still on the council, having secured enough votes to remain there. He was constantly bringing up nonsense like that, and Two-Fingers and the other council members would sit and patiently listen to his whining. Of course, his complaints were recorded in the minutes of the meetings. The stenographer would often stop typing and ask Stubby to repeat himself, he talked so fast she couldn't get it all down the first time. Loud and fast, that's Stubby. So, we'd sit there and listen to him repeat the nonsense over and over again.

At this particular meeting, Two-Fingers had enough of his rambling and asked, "Stubby, have you ever been to Russia?" Stubby looked more perplexed than usual before replying, "Of course not, the farthest I've been from the reservation is Great Falls." "Well, I've been to Russia, and the place sucks. By the way, how do you think the Russians would treat us Blackfeet?" Two-Fingers asked as Stubby reached for another donut. "Well, I bet it would be better than the way this racist country has treated us." That's when Two-Fingers completely lost it. He stood up and gave a detailed explanation about communism and how the people of Russia were treated. He explained what a totalitarian government is, how little freedom the citizens of Russia have, and how they mistreat their women and minorities.

"Stubby, have you ever heard of any Russian women holding a position of power in Russia? Have you ever seen a black person in Russia? How many blacks and women serve on the Politburo?" Stubby chewed on his donut for a while before asking, "What's your point?" "The point, Stubby, is this isn't a perfect country, but it's a country of opportunity. Every time you start with your racist bullshit, it takes me weeks to get the young bloods to stop feeling sorry for themselves. You're an enabler, Stubby, you enable the weakest among us to find an excuse for failure. You're always crying about something that happened a hundred and fifty years ago while I'm trying to govern for today. You weaken us with your constant complaining. I'm trying to teach our people the meaning of personal responsibility, and you give them an excuse to fail."

I remember looking over at the stenographer, she was typing like crazy. No way in hell was she going to stop and interrupt Two-Fingers. Two-Fingers finally sat down and calmly added, "Besides, you do our relatives who fought against communism a terrible disservice when you speak like that. If the Russians were in control of our country, do you think they would be as altruistic toward us as the whites among us have been? I'm not talking about the whites of a hundred and fifty years ago, I'm talking about the whites of today. It's hard enough dealing with today's issues; you don't make it any easier by always talking about the past. Finish your donut and let's get on with the business of today." Cindy Ann was the first to stand and start cheering, and before long, everybody was on their feet clapping, everybody except Stubby, that is. That's Two-Fingers, an American patriot to the bone.

Once the economic situation stabilized on the reservation, he improving the tribe's social services. He hired the best alcohol counselors money could buy, hired the best doctors, and made sure the hospital had state-of-the-art equipment. He introduced a mentoring program that paired young people on the reservation with responsible adults, which then led to apprenticeship programs where the young learned different trades. Soon, the tribe had all the plumbers, electricians, machinists, painters, and carpenters they needed. Apprenticeships are the best way to learn the skills necessary for these jobs. Plus, you get paid while you learn, no student loans.

Two-Fingers's favorite social program was caring for the elderly Blackfeet. Unlike most of society, the Blackfeet care for their elderly in their homes. They don't stick them in old folks' homes where they suffer and die. That is not the Indian way. Two-Fingers provided in-home care, and there was never a shortage of nursing and assistance. The old stayed with their loved ones and were cared for until the day they died. His plans took care of the young, the old, and everyone in between.

The work programs he created are legendary. As I mentioned earlier, anyone who wanted to work had a job. He assigned the task of creating a program where young Blackfeet men and women went into the tribal forests and cleaned them up to Two Shoes Cross Guns. Two Shoes turned out to be a taskmaster who didn't tolerate laziness, and the young thrived under his leadership. It's amazing the degree of success one can achieve once the chains are off. Blackfeet forests were cleaned up, and the trees were selectively harvested and then replanted to ensure future growth. Camps were set up for the young workers, and they lived in them all summer long doing the work. In the fall, the workers went to trade schools, apprenticeships, or the Blackfeet Junior College. The program proved so successful that the United States Forest Service hired them to clean up the forests in Glacier National Park. Sawmills were built on the reservation, and soon we were shipping lumber all across the country. Nations are only as strong as their forests, and for far too long our forests have been neglected.

By the way, after helping Levi, Billy took a part-time job as an instructor at Blackfeet Junior College where he teaches American

Indian History classes. He is very good at it, and has finally received the honor and respect he rightfully deserves.

During the early years of his chairmanship, Browning was cleaned up, and tourism flourished. The Blackfeet were proud once again, and it showed in their work ethic and drive. The Blackfeet soon became the envy of Indian tribes across America, and their leaders frequently consulted Two-Fingers, who was happy to help. More importantly, the tribe was happy for the first time in decades, and they had Two-Fingers to thank for that. Success should be measured by the degree of happiness experienced by every tribe. I know far too many people who are "successful" but remain bitter, sad, skeletons of themselves.

A quick side note: Stogie Man and Liquid Louie were two of the first people enrolled in the new alcohol treatment program Two-Fingers was instrumental in establishing it on the reservation. Two-Fingers had personally gone to Canada and dragged Stogie Man back to Browning screaming and kicking. Liquid Louie was easier to find, he was at his designated drinking spot behind the Paradise. That was nearly thirty years ago, and they have been clean and sober since. After they cleaned up, Stogie Man and Liquid Louie went off to the University of Chicago, where they both received doctorates in Applied Science. Their stories are truly inspirational examples of what can happen when you are given good guidance and leadership. Two-Fingers never gave up on anybody, no matter how hard they made it on him.

At yet another one of our tribal council meetings, we were approached by representatives of the Cable TV Company. They wanted to capitalize on the success of the tribe, greed always follows the money. At the time, we only had one TV channel. It was transmitted from a TV station located in Lethbridge, Alberta. It provided limited programming that included such exciting things as curling, hockey, and the occasional coronation of British royalty. That was fine because the tribe didn't watch much TV. I remember well the day the suits from the Cable TV Company sat down across from Two-Fingers and the other council members. They laid out their plan to wire the city of Browning in order to "enlighten the Blackfeet." They pitched how wonderful it would be to have forty-plus channels to choose from, and all they needed to make that happen was exclusive rights to distribution for fifty years. They sought exclusivity.

Two-Fingers listened politely to what they had to say, only occasionally stopping them to ask a question. The suits would perk up and elaborate on their plans to bring the world to the doorsteps of the Blackfeet. Well, after listening to their horse shit for about an hour, Two-Fingers stood up, stretched, and said, "So, you want us to become enlightened. You want us to sit on our asses watching other people live their lives. You want us to watch reality shows that aren't real. You want us to watch games and not play them. You want us to give up our ability to think and reason for ourselves? You want us to ignore one another until there's a commercial break. Is that what you are proposing?"

The suits looked at each other, then wisely picked up their briefcases and exited stage left without saying another word. After they vacated the building, I went up to Two-Fingers and said, "I think you were a bit hasty there, I really would've liked watching some Monday Night Football." "Crack you, White Guy. I finally have everybody up off their asses, and I'm not about to have them sit back down and watch their lives pass them by." That was that.

The Blackfeet lived in a time of harmony and happiness. They worked hard and played hard. Money from gambling and other ventures continued to flow in, and the tribe became less and less dependent on the federal government. When the federal reservation system was first established, tribes were given the right to occupy their lands; members weren't title-holders. This communal occupancy concept changed in 1887 with the passage of the General Allotment Act, which divided American Indian treaty lands into individually owned allotments held in trust and overseen by the Bureau of Indian Affairs (BIA). The BIA was established in 1824 and was originally part of the United States War Department. The BIA has a fiduciary responsibility to oversee the collection of fees for Indian lands and then distribute the money to the tribes or the individual allotment owners. Over the years, some reservation lands were sold to individuals who were non-tribal members, and Two-Fingers wanted to purchase that land to further expand and strengthen tribal sovereignty.

To that end, Two-Fingers established the Blackfeet Land Company, Inc. and bought back the land on the reservation owned by whites and other non-Blackfeet. By doing this, that land was no longer subject to the rules the BIA had established decades before, and this singular act helped reduce the BIA's power on the reservation. It also reduced the power of the bureaucrat from hell, the aforementioned Trevor Kanowski. Trevor Kanowski had reigned terror down on the tribe since his arrival, and he hated Two-Fingers because Two-Fingers represented change. He liked the status quo of skimming what he could from the tribe and making them beg for what was rightfully theirs. Trevor was the modern-day Indian agent of old, crooked and self-serving. Bureaucrats always like the status quo.

At the end of each month, Two-Fingers and I had to go to the BIA office down the street from tribal headquarters and listen to Kanowski boast about what a great job he was doing for the tribe. Then, Two-Fingers was required to sign off on the payments the tribe received from the government, never knowing if the accounting was accurate or not. Everyone knew Kanowski was living large, but nobody could prove he was stealing from the tribe. After each meeting, Two-Fingers swore he was going to get rid of the parasite. He wrote letters to the Department of the Interior requesting Kanowski's removal. These requests were largely ignored because Kanowski's father-in-law was the head of the department. Two-Fingers was convinced nobody in Washington, DC wanted the bastard back.

One day, out of the blue, Two-Fingers received a call from the principal of the middle school regarding Kanowski. Evidently, Kanowski had been spending a lot of time parked in front of the playground. His big, fancy Cadillac was seen there during recess the prior two weeks, and the principal was concerned that something nefarious was going on. Two-Fingers seized on the moment and summoned me to drive him to the school so he could get a firsthand account of what was happening. We snuck up on Kanowski, and sure enough, there he sat watching the young children on the playground until recess ended. After he left the playground, we went to see the principal, and after getting a full briefing, Two-Fingers was convinced Kanowski had evil intentions in mind.

As soon as we returned to tribal headquarters, Two-Fingers called Smiley Heavy Runner and had him drop whatever he was doing so he could meet with him. Smiley, at that time, was the acting Chief of Police and was always on the lookout for crime. There wasn't much crime on the reservation, but that didn't stop Smiley from looking. After Two-Fingers explained the situation to him, he was all too eager to set up surveillance on Kanowski. He quickly assigned a team of his crack investigators to keep an eye on Kanowski. His team consisted of Buzzy Still Smoking and Chubby Skunk Cap. Buzzy and Chubby had recently completed a two-day seminar on surveillance and were eager to put their newfound skills to work.

Chubby and Buzzy staked out the playground, hoping to catch Kanowski in the act. After about a week of surveillance, Kanowski abruptly stopped going to the playground. Chubby and Buzzy figured he was onto them and reported this development back to Smiley. When Smiley heard the news, he decided to call off all formal surveillance until further notice. Smiley knew better than to call Two-

Fingers about his decision, so he drove over to meet with him in person. I watched as Smiley knocked on Two-Fingers' office door before entering, and before long, Smiley was waving his arms and frantically pacing the floor.

All the while, Two-Fingers remained seated as he patiently listened to him tell his story. When he finished, Smiley marched out of Two-Fingers' office and almost tripped over Roberta Kanowski, Trevor's wife. Roberta had shown up unannounced and wanted to talk to Two-Fingers. She wore heavy makeup and sunglasses, and when she saw Smiley, she started crying hysterically. I jumped up from my seat and helped escort her into Two-Fingers' office, where the three of us waited patiently for Roberta to gather herself. She was crying her eyes out, and the more we soothed her, the more hysterical she became. About halfway through a box of tissues, she stopped crying long enough to remove her sunglasses, revealing bruised, swollen cheeks and black eyes. She had been viciously beaten.

After settling down enough to speak, she slowly and methodically began to tell us her story. She had decided to come and talk to Two-Fingers in private; she didn't want the entire reservation to know about her pain and shame. She asked us to keep what she said between us, and we quickly agreed.

Actually, some of what she told was already common knowledge. For example, we knew her father had helped Kanowski get his job, and we all knew he was a weasel and a thief. We suspected he was a child abuser and a wife-beater. Plus, we knew he was a little man, a nickel living in a dime world. Worst of all, we knew he was a lifetime bureaucrat. But what we didn't know was that he really, really loved his sheep, which surprised us.

Roberta told us how she had discovered him being affectionate with one of their sheep, a lamb named Mary. They lived on a small ranch north of town where they raised sheep, horses, and cattle. She loved animals, and taking care of them kept her sane. Evidently, she didn't love them as much as her husband, Trevor. When she caught him in the act, he vehemently denied any wrongdoing. Typical bureaucrat, always lying and making up stories when caught with their pants down.

According to Roberta, they were in the barn yelling and screaming at each other when Mary came to and ran off. Roberta told Kanowski she would no longer tolerate him or his abusive, sick behavior, and when she tried to leave the barn, he beat the holy hell out of her. She had lived in shame for years and never admitted her mistake to her family, so she suffered in silence, until that day. Kanowski's recent behavior sickened her, and she knew she had to do something about it. Instinctively she knew Two-Fingers was someone she could talk to. He was her last, best hope.

We sat there with our mouths open in total, absolute disbelief. Two-Fingers was pale as mayonnaise and visibly shaking when he picked up the phone and called his sister, Cindy Ann. Roberta would stay with her until he could figure out what to do next. After Cindy Ann took Roberta away, the three of us remained in Two-Finger's office and pondered the situation. Legally, Kanowski had broken enough laws to choke a maggot. I couldn't add them all up without a calculator. Smiley wanted to go and arrest him right then and there and throw him in jail, and Two-Fingers sat and listened while the two of us went on and on about what we should do.

Jurisdictional issues came into the discussion. We weren't sure if sheep abuse was a federal or state crime. Kanowski was a federal employee with powerful federal friends who notoriously circled the wagons when one of their own was challenged. Plus, he was sure to deny everything; it would be her word against his, and this horrible thing could drag on for months without resolution. Two-Fingers finally spoke up and said, "Well, I don't know what's worse, being a bureaucrat or being a sheep molester, but when you're both, it's time for a hanging."

One thing was certain: the issue wouldn't stay a secret long, no matter how hard we tried to keep it that way. Remember, you can't fart on the reservation without everybody knowing how it smelled. Knowing that, Two-Fingers figured he would let nature run its course. One thing the tribe would not tolerate is the molesting of an animal. So, the three of us decided to go to the Club Cafe for lunch and let the chips fall where they may.

The Club was extra busy that day, and there wasn't an empty seat in the entire place. So, we stood in the middle of the room waiting for a table to open up. Smiley started a conversation by nonchalantly asking Two-Fingers and me if we had any knowledge of Kanowski's interest in sheep. Smiley wasn't all that quiet or subtle in his asking, and after he finished speaking, a deafening silence fell over the lunch crowd, you could literally hear a pin drop. Two-Fingers and I acted shocked when Smiley laid out the entire story. We were awestruck and had no idea that such a thing was happening. It turns out neither did the lunch crowd, and the patrons began to raise their concerns in a not-so-quiet, subtle manner. It got loud quickly, and it stayed loud. Johnny Skunk Cap happened to be in the crowd that day and yelled out, "That son of a bitch should be tarred and feathered and ran out of town!" Upon hearing that, Two-Finger's eyes lit up and we immediately knew that an equitable solution to the problem had been found. The beauty of the reservation's legal system is that if a crime is committed, there are no appeals. Justice is swift, and the punishment fits the crime. Criminals are either banished from the tribe, sent to jail, or, as in this case, tarred and feathered.

It was around midnight that night when Kanowski was dragged out of his barn and unceremoniously tarred and feathered. After that was expertly done, he was placed in the back of a pickup with his hands securely tied behind his back and forced to stand as the pickup was slowly driven around Government Square for all to see. Two-Fingers and I stood at the front door of tribal headquarters and watched the whole thing, another late-night tending to tribal business.

Luckily, by the time this happened, I had a smartphone and filmed the whole thing. Shortly after the second lap around Government Square, one of the concerned citizens jumped onto the bed of the pickup and draped a placard around Kanowski's neck that simply said, "So many sheep, so little time." After a few more laps, the driver took him to the reservation's eastern border near Cut Bank and released Kanowski into the vast expanse of Montana.

Several months later, we received word that Kanowski was back living in Washington, DC. However, he was no longer working for the BIA, and, as most bureaucrats do, he had failed upward. He was given a high-paying and powerful position in one of the many healthcare agencies that plague America. Bureaucrats never really go away, picture recycling used toilet paper. In any event, the Blackfeet were satisfied with the outcome, and they really didn't care where he was as long as the tribe didn't have to deal with him. Good riddance to the bum is all I have to say. By the way, Roberta still lives on the reservation, and she's happily married to a Blackfeet rancher. They only raise cattle.

Chapter 21
Two-Fingers to the Rescue

During his early years as Chairman, Two-Fingers grew into his role as protector and benefactor of the Blackfeet Tribe, and as he grew, so did the vitality and strength of the tribe. The progress made on the reservation under his leadership was, and continues to be, remarkable. Success is measured in terms of happiness, and the Blackfeet, for the most part, are happy.

Unfortunately, by 2015, most of the nation at large was unhappy. The predictable economic collapse began to take a devastating toll on the rest of America. The politicians were in denial and wouldn't admit that their irrational spending had created more debt than the citizens could ever repay. Their quantitative easing programs were finally coming home to roost. That fiscally irresponsible program was promoted as temporary but remained in place. Bloodsucking government policies and bureaucracies are never temporary; they build on each other like mold on manure. As a direct result of the Federal Reserve's unsound monetary policy, inflation skyrocketed, and the value of the dollar plummeted. The citizens of America were feeling the pain, and to put it mildly, they were unhappy.

Think about that: America in 2015 was $19 trillion in debt with no viable way to pay it off. Paying it off would mean cutting back on exorbitant spending, and no government agency was willing to do that. The bureaucrats would lose power, and that was unacceptable to these unelected decision makers. On the contrary, they let the debt grow exponentially, and the leaders of our great nation didn't have a clue how to pay it off. They were clueless in DC. Washington, DC, the Babylon on the Potomac, was ass deep in debt, fraud, and foreign interests.

Two-Fingers, in 2015, watched as our nation began to fall apart at the seams. America had become morally and financially bankrupt, and he knew it was only a matter of time before the entire monetary system collapsed. For far too long, the leaders of our great nation denied us the ability to produce. We had become a nation of consumers with very little production, the good jobs were shipped overseas and elsewhere. The North American Free Trade Agreement (NAFTA) led to the loss of hundreds of thousands of good-paying factory jobs. Those jobs had been shipped to foreign countries and our workers suffered. American workers were betrayed.

In 2015, it was so bad that 94 million working-age Americans were out of work, and our government tried to convince us that things were great. If things were so great, why were we $19 trillion in debt? The gullible and the ignorant actually believed that nonsense. Not Two-Fingers, he saw the writing on the wall regarding our federal government's fiscal irresponsibility and debt. He knew those things were going to doom us if the policies weren't changed.

Two-Fingers waited for the powers that be to do something and hoped things would improve after the 2014 midterms. The Republicans won majorities in the House and the Senate, surely they would hold the line on runaway spending. Nope, that never happened. The Republicans caved and approved the irrational spending plans of the Democrat President at the time without so much as a whimper, We the People had been betrayed once again.

So, by early 2015, Two-Fingers had seen and heard enough and decided to do something about it. That was the motivating factor behind his decision to run for the United States Senate from the great state of Montana. He ran as an independent because, in his opinion, both parties had betrayed us. He decided he would attack his opponents' individual policies and the policies of the Democrat and Republican collectives.

Senator Frank Johnson was his main competition. That's right, by then Frank had become a senator and had been since 1986. Three terms as governor of Montana hadn't satisfied Frank's lust for power and prestige. He had become the leader, the elder statesman, of the Democrat Party in Montana, and what he said went. So, when he announced his run for a sixth term as US senator, no one was surprised. Two-Fingers was actually happy because, for the first time in Frank's political career, he was vulnerable. His policies over the years were abject failures, and he voted right down the party line and obstructed any meaningful legislation that didn't fit the liberal agenda. In 2015, these reckless policies were imploding, and the financial juggling act was coming to an end.

Two-Fingers' Republican opposition, Pete Reynolds, was an eighty-year-old lifetime politician who had been in the House of Representatives so long he no longer called it the House; he called it home. Pete was stepping up in class and seriously believed he could beat Frank. Little did he know his real competition would turn out to be Two-Fingers. Two-Fingers didn't sweat either one of them; he had faith in the Montana electorate.

Soon after announcing his intentions, early polls showed Two-Fingers running well behind the Democrat and Republican candidates and was given little chance of winning. As I stated earlier, Frank was firmly in control of the Democrat Party in Montana, and he used his enormous power to try to defeat Two-Fingers. He leaked information to the liberal Big Sky Reporter about Two-Fingers smoking pot and falsely accused him of being a drug addict and therefore unworthy of serving in the United States Senate. The press carried his water and attacked Two-Fingers with a vigor never before seen in Montana politics.

As his campaign progressed, polling continued to indicate that Two-Fingers was the candidate of choice for less than twenty percent of Montanans. He was caught off guard by the negativity because dirty politics had no place on the reservation; personal attacks are frowned upon here. As his campaign manager, I developed a strategy to fight back against Frank.

I had recently discovered the power of the internet and started using the new technology to get his message across. I suggested we go on the attack against the Democrat policies of the last seven years because Frank was a pathetic lapdog of the current President and had supported every ill-conceived plan he came up with. We had to take the gloves off or we would lose. At first, Two-Fingers resisted the idea, but after experiencing attack after attack from Frank and the dependent liberal press, he finally had enough and went on the offensive.

Shortly after announcing his intention to run, I was contacted by a young female reporter/editor from American Indian Sovereignty Magazine. It's a publication out of Flagstaff, Arizona run by the Navajo. The Navajo Indian woman who wanted to interview Two-Fingers was named Mary Little Feather. She was curious about an American Indian running for the Senate and convinced me that American Indians across America would also be interested. It made sense to me, but Two-Fingers was hesitant; he didn't want to make a big deal out of the fact that he was Indian. He wanted to run on his record and his record alone. It took a while, but I finally convinced him that the more attention he received, the better it would be for him. Positive publicity is a good thing. He finally agreed when Mary said she would come to Browning for the interview and not take up much of his time. It proved to be a pivotal point in his campaign.

I had reserved the Blackfeet Recreational Center's bingo hall, and the three of us sat down for the interview. I had a newly purchased tape recorder and recorded the interview for posterity and evidentiary purposes. By then, Frank had started to threaten Two-Fingers with legal action on a number of bogus issues, so I thought it best to record and preserve every word he spoke so it couldn't be misconstrued or used against him later. In any event, here is what I have from that interview dated 7-5-2015:

Mary: "I understand your given name is Donny R. Schwartz. Would you prefer that I call you Donny R?"

TF: "I would prefer you call me Mr. Schwartz and then bow down and kiss my ring. After all, I am a politician."

Mary: "Are you serious?"

TF: "Of course not. You appear to be a little uptight, and I'm trying to loosen you up. That's the name that will appear on the ballot, but my friends call me Two-Fingers. So, please call me Two-Fingers. Should I address you as Mary, or do you prefer Ms. Little Feather?"

Mary: "Mary is fine. I would like to know your reaction to Senator Johnson's allegation that you smoked pot in your youth. Is it true, and if it is, do you think it should disqualify you from running for the Senate?"

TF: "You get right to the point, don't you? I like that, obviously, you're not a politician. I'm not sure why Frank is so curious about my past drug use. Obviously, they don't make you take a piss test to be in the United States Senate. Those people must be smoking something, no one in their right mind would do what they have done to this country."

"To answer your question, it's 100% true. As a young person, and during a brief time in college, I did partake of the bud. I never abused it, but I did enjoy smoking it. By the way, I quit years ago, but I'm not against people smoking it. If you smoke, I believe you should do so in moderation; don't let it become a crutch. You see, I grew up in a culture of alcohol and alcoholism. The streets of Browning were drenched in alcohol, and alcohol caused more carnage than pot ever did. I no longer drink because I had a front-row seat to the damage that alcohol causes. And since we are on the subject of bad choices, you may want to ask Frank if he still consumes a quart of vodka a day. Personally, I don't care. But, if you throw stones, you probably shouldn't live in a glass house. I have always been honest about my imperfections. I don't know anybody who has lived a pure life, one free of sin or bad choices. Honesty is my virtue, and unlike Frank, I have always been honest and truthful."

"By the way, what is dishonest and phony is when a politician says he smoked pot but didn't inhale. That should raise a red flag. A politician who lies about not inhaling pot will lie about anything. No, smoking pot should not disqualify me or anyone else. Lying about not inhaling pot should result in a hanging, figuratively speaking."

Mary: "I see. Why have you decided to run for the Senate?"

TF: "Quite frankly, the country is going to hell in a handbasket. I'm concerned about the very survival of our great nation. I have never seen us more divided. Republicans hate Democrats and Democrats hate Republicans. The United States of America isn't united."

Mary: "Is that why you decided to run as an independent?"

TF: "I'm running as an independent because the entire political system is broken, and the two party system has failed us. Washington, DC is dysfunctional because we have two parties that are choking democracy to death, and we are morally and financially bankrupt. Besides, I have always been independent. We don't have a party system in tribal politics; you run on who you are, not what some party says you are."

Mary: "You have made government control and socialism a major platform issue. Would you like to elaborate?"

TF: "Socialism is the manifestation of envy; socialists are envious of individual, personal success. Success requires freedom, hard work, and dedication to the task, and that's something socialists adamantly oppose. Success makes them uncomfortable because if you and I are successful, they have to take a good, long, hard look at themselves, and that makes them squirm. That's why they want everyone to become comfortable with being common, they advocate commonality. They don't advocate, nor do they want, exceptionalism. In short, socialism was spawned from a depraved, corrupt, and immoral ideology. It's a system founded on hate, and you are right, I do speak out against it and big government. Before voters get into bed with the liberal Democrat/socialism concept, they should go live on an Indian reservation and see what 150 years of government dependence and control have done to American Indians. Big government is never a good idea, and there is no such thing as a free lunch. Big government is bad for the economy and for the human spirit. Remember, you don't get to choose your 'Easter egg' house; under socialism, it is assigned to you."

"But, if you do decide to become socialists, the reservation would like to have your business. Once the liberal Democrat/socialists run out of other people's money to spend, you will want affordable housing, and I highly recommend one of our handmade teepees. They are made from the finest buckskin, and they are the best money can buy, and for a limited time, we are offering very attractive financing plans. Of course, you will have to buy on the fly. We don't want you to live on the reservation because anyone stupid enough to get rid of democracy and capitalism has no place with us. We have enough problems."

Mary: "In the past, you have mentioned the executive order regarding immigration. What is your position on such a complex issue?"

TF: "Well, it's really not that complex. Either we are a nation of laws or we aren't. Why is the United States not allowed to have secure borders? "When did America become the ass wipe for the world, the floor mat where invaders can come in and wipe their feet without consequences?"

"What is equally troubling to me is the sanctuary city concept. Sanctuary cities defy federal law by not enforcing the immigration laws that are on the books. They are doing this, and the federal government isn't doing anything to stop them, and I think that establishes a very dangerous precedent. Our leaders, by letting this happen, are saying to Americans that it's okay to break federal laws. Once Americans lose faith in their government institutions, all hell will break loose. That's a slippery slope that ends with unintended consequences."

"What if a city decided, for whatever reason, not to enforce civil rights laws? Those laws are no more potent than the immigration laws; they are both federal laws that trace their viability and legitimacy back to the 14th Amendment, and neither of them should be violated. Our elected officials violate the Constitution, and the criminals hide behind it. Don't these people take an oath of office to defend the Constitution? The politicians and the bureaucrats currently in charge attack the Constitution: they no longer defend it. Congress makes the laws, and the President is duty-bound to uphold them, not to change them because he doesn't like them. Should foreigners be allowed to cross our borders and take up residency in the United States illegally? Well, let me tell you a story I heard years ago. It goes something like this:

When Indian lands were being invaded by white settlers, several Chiefs got together to decide what to do about the invaders. At a powwow, inside a teepee next to a roaring fire, one Chief said to the others, "I'm worried about the strangers coming to our land. They have a strange religion and smell about them, and they refuse to speak our language." In unison, the Chiefs nodded and continued to smoke their pipe, and before long, another Chief spoke up and said, "I think you're being heartless and insensitive. Let them in, what harm can they do?" Well, that pretty much sums up my feelings on the matter. I hope the United States of America has better luck with this than we American Indians. I'll tell you this much: if our current leaders continue to allow this invasion, I'm going to build a wall around the reservation to keep the politicians out."

Mary: "Aren't you afraid you're going to offend the politically correct crowd?"

TF: "That's what's wrong with our politicians, they are concerned about being politically correct. I prefer being correct. A leader has to do what's right, not what's politically expedient. Political correctness isn't the Indian way."

Mary: "I see. What's your stance on another hot topic this political season, gun control?"

TF: "I defend every word of the Constitution. Once the Constitution is destroyed, what is left for us? America is great because of our Constitution and our rule of law. It's not a matter of banning assault rifles; the issue is, once the anti-Constitution crowd starts taking away our constitutional rights, where will it end? There's all this terrorist activity in our country and around the world and if we take guns away from law-abiding, patriotic Americans we will play right into the hands of the criminals and terrorists. We have gun-free zones now, and where is the first place the criminals and murderers go to start shooting? That's right, the gun-free zones. Americans should be armed with the knowledge they need to protect our land from foreign and domestic threats. On the reservation, we are armed to the teeth, and we have safety lessons and classes on how to fight and shoot."

"Here is another American Indian lesson: When we peacefully handed over our weapons after signing all those peace treaties, we were summarily massacred throughout this land. Today, we remember what giving up our weapons meant, it meant near extinction. We value our 2nd Amendment rights because we know firsthand what happens when the government takes away your weapons. We must defend the Constitution at all costs. Their political answer to these terrorists who are killing us is to take away the rights of law-abiding citizens. It's not only illogical, but it's also dangerous. We need to maintain a well-regulated militia. Besides, it's not the right of current politicians to take away any of our constitutional rights. These rights are God-given and enshrined in the greatest legal document ever created, the Constitution. If it's to be changed, there is a built-in mechanism to do so, called amendments. The problem with far too many citizens and politicians is that they are ignorant of what the Constitution says or means. It only takes one generation of ignorant citizens to lose our hard-fought freedoms and liberties."

"Having said that, solutions can be found, but we need our elected officials to work together to find them. We need a strong leader who has the interests of the majority of Americans in mind. Currently, we have no such leader. Our military must have the best weapons, and the peacekeepers must have the very finest equipment to keep us safe."

Mary: "Since you brought up the military and peacekeepers, and I assume when you say peacekeepers, you're talking about police officers, what do you think of all the anti-military and anti-police behavior? It seems to be getting worse every day."

TF: "Well, it's certainly not the Indian way. We respect warriors because we know they are the ones who fight to keep us safe. They are the ones who put their lives on the line every single day for the American people, all Americans. Can you imagine the violence and terror they see and deal with on a daily basis? I'm not talking about Iraq or Afghanistan; I'm talking about Chicago, Detroit, Baltimore, and practically every major city in America that is run by Frank's party. There are bad people in every profession, but to indict an entire profession for the actions of a few is not right. American Indians respect warriors."

Mary: "You brought up a good point about violence in our major cities. How would you, as a senator, solve the problems facing the Black and Hispanic youth in the inner cities? After all, they are the ones most affected by these senseless murders and shootings?"

TF: "Wow, that's not an easy question to answer. People have puzzled over that issue for over fifty years. All I can say is that Democrats must really hate blacks and Hispanics because their policies of government dependence are largely responsible for their situation. Democrats are in charge of most of the major cities experiencing this nightmare and have been for decades. They should approach the situation much like the way we handled our dependency on the reservation. They must get rid of their federal government control reflex and provide jobs and hope to their citizens. There is too much idle time and not enough effort being focused on achievement."

"Federal Indian policy was the policy on the reservation for eighty years before the 1964 Civil Rights government-dependency programs went into effect. These Civil Rights laws, as implemented, have been harmful to the very important concepts of freedom, liberty, and the pursuit of happiness. Dependency of any kind is harmful to the spirit, and it never helps to be dependent. On the reservation, after all these years, we are still shaking dependency off our backs. Progress has been made, and it can be changed, but it won't change overnight because there are too many politicians and others who have vested interests in the current harmful system. The socialists like to maintain control over We the People, and we can't allow that to continue. Again, socialism is a doctrine of evil, and socialists fear successful people because it's harder to control them."

"Quite frankly, if we peel back another layer of the onion, it's also a way to buy votes. Every presidential election since 1964 has resulted in blacks voting overwhelmingly in favor of Democrats and what have the Democrats done for them? If they really cared about the black youth of America, like I do, they would get rid of the harmful programs they have instituted and put them to work. I can't overemphasize the freedom and liberty a person receives from working."

"Here is what I have learned as a Blackfeet Indian: being constantly dependent on the federal government made my tribe slaves to their policies, and we had very little freedom. This resulted in us drinking ourselves to death, shooting ourselves in the head, or jumping off water towers to our death. We lost our pride, self-respect, and honor. That's no different from what's happening in America today."

"But here is the real problem: getting the dependent to admit the dependency. No one dependent on something sees it as harmful, and that's what the government counts on. Consider this: when a person chooses freedom, meaning taking personal responsibility for their actions, that person needs to understand that decision is going to be met with distain by others in the dependency class. You will be called names, you may be injured, and you certainly will be cast out and shunned. What the dependency crowd must understand, and trust me, it's not only blacks and Hispanics who are encumbered this way, the hand of dependency reaches up from the ground and drags all of us down, ethnicity be damned. Let's not get bogged down in any racist crap because it affects all of us one way or another. Those who have fallen into dependency are slaves to the system, and their freedom has been taken away. Nothing is free; there's a price for everything."

"Government control is evil; it saps character and strength by encouraging greed and weakness. On the reservation, we recognized this and developed programs where our people worked and took pride in working. We, as a people, have taken responsibility for our actions, and we no longer seek the trap of how bad we had it based on events that happened over 150 years ago."

"Remember this: American Indians had their lands stolen, treaties were broken, we were massacred, scalped, subjected to slavery, and then hidden on reservations where we were left to die. But the worst thing the government ever did to us was to make us dependent on them. It took us years to wake up and begin the task of shaking off the chains of dependency. How long before those dependent do the same is a question only they can answer."

"Believe me, it wasn't easy for us because change never is. It requires hard work, sacrifice, and a strong desire to be free. But here is the good news: in America, freedom and liberty are still possible, for now. That's not the way it is in Russia, China, Canada, Iran, and the other totalitarian governments in the world. The first step is to take personal responsibility for your actions. Don't listen to the enablers who are constantly telling you how rough you have it, they want to keep you down because they believe it raises them up. There's big money in despair; ask any rap music mogul."

Mary: "But what about finding them jobs?"

TF: "First of all, they, like the rest of us, have to look for and find their own jobs. We created jobs on the reservation by cleaning up our forests. Every summer, we have crews thinning the trees so the entire forest is healthier. It's labor-intensive and not very glamorous work, but it's necessary for a healthy forest. Our national forests burn every summer, and no one in government is doing anything about their health. A nation is only as healthy as its forests."

"By extension, the federal government isn't doing anything for the health of Americans or the economy. Instead of paying people not to work, why doesn't the federal government pay people who are on public assistance to clean up our forests, our lakes, our streams, and our streets? The work is there, don't tell me there isn't any work. But if you don't want to get your hands dirty, there really isn't any hope for you."

"One other point: for Americans who rely on the federal government for help, the federal government is bankrupt, and when their credit is cut off, what programs do you think will disappear first? But look on the bright side, that will solve the illegal immigration issue because once the money is cut off they will leave this country so fast it will make your head spin. So much for wanting to be an American."

Mary: "Well, I don't have any further questions for you at this time. Would you like to add anything?"

TF: "Only this: Frank, the Democrat Party and their principal propaganda machine, the Big Sky Reporter have attacked me since the day I announced my candidacy. That's fine, I'm a big boy, and I understand it. However, if you no longer understand them and think they are harming our great nation, remember this: when we are stoned, we are all Democrats. It's time to put the pipe down, clear our heads, and start doing what is right for America. By the way, I want to wish everybody a belated Happy 4th of July. Thank you."

It was a Sunday night, and that meant bingo time. When the hour-long interview ended, and the hall began to fill with eager participants, there was a $1,000 blackout, and everybody was excited. Before the games began, we sat around talking, and I noticed Two-Fingers staring at Mary as she gathered up her things. I told him she was single and it was time for him to get over being the grieving widower, he had punished himself long enough.

When Mary finished packing up her things, she came over and thanked us, saying, "I like what you have to say. So, if you don't mind, I would like to come back for another interview when your schedule allows."

Two-Fingers mulled this over for a few seconds and then said, "If you think your readers can handle the truth, I'm all in." Mary smiled at him before walking out of the hall.

"I like her, I really do. You don't find many young people interested in politics these days," Two-Fingers said as he watched the door close behind her.

"Talking about liking something, I really liked your speech. Wow, all that without any notes! That was simply amazing. In fact, I was getting a warm feeling up my pant leg just listening to you."

Two-Fingers slowly turned to face me before saying, "Crack you, White Guy."

Chapter 22
The Reservation is the Only Safe Place to Live

We doubled our efforts after that interview and took our message directly to the people. We worked hard, and so did the Democrat propaganda machine, they poured money into smearing Two-Fingers in an unprecedented way. This bears repeating: never in the history of Montana politics had there been such a vicious attack on an opponent. I couldn't turn on the radio without hearing a negative ad about Two-Fingers, and the liberal newspapers in Montana ran front-page editorials calling Two-Fingers everything but a white man, they were brutal. How can we have a free press when 95% of the main-stream media is shackled to the Democrat Party?

Fortunately, Two-Fingers was running in Montana, where the citizens took offense to such bullshit. Montanans had heard of his record, and many actually took the time to drive through the reservation to marvel at the changes that had taken place under Two-Fingers' leadership. It helped that a number of voters knew him from his time as head of the Montana International Trade Organization, and his popularity began to grow as his message spread. As his following grew, so did the Democrats' anxiety, and they became even more desperate when the polls showed that Two-Fingers was gaining support. Their panic was reflected in their increased spending. They spent hundreds of thousands of dollars on ads, mailers, and posters. Two-Fingers' entire campaign cost less than $40,000 because that's all we had. Two-Fingers has never had any real money; he gives it away to the less fortunate faster than he earns it. I wasn't much help financially either; I had recently finished paying off my student loans from law school, so money was tight.

After weeks of listening to all the negativity coming out of Frank's camp, Two-Fingers decided to show him what he was all about. He had been well received at the town meetings that I arranged, but the crowds were still small. We needed greater exposure if we were going to have a chance. Trust me when I tell you this; money goes a long way when it comes to buying elections.

As it turned out, we had the best candidate, and luck was on our side. The article Mary had written about Two-Fingers in the American Indian Sovereignty Magazine was published and well-received. It turned out to be an extremely popular American Indian source of information with subscribers in all 50 states. Soon after it was published, Two-Fingers began to receive hundreds of small contributions from American Indians across the country. The money was greatly appreciated, but what really helped Two-Fingers' confidence was the outpouring of support. He was energized and convinced he could help Montanans and Americans across our great country. I decided to take some of the money he received and pay our local Blackfeet Printing Company to make bumper stickers that simply said, "It's not the Indian way." Holy shit, we had a slogan and nearly $22,000 in the bank! It wasn't long before we had the Democrats on the run.

After several weeks of intense campaigning across the state, we needed to return to the reservation to take care of some urgent tribal matters. Shortly after our return, I received a call from Mary Little Feather. She asked if she could come to the reservation the following Sunday for another interview. That was a question best answered by Two-Fingers, who I believed needed to decompress from the political stuff and talk to a pretty woman for a while instead of worrying about everyone else. So, I made an executive decision and transferred her call to his office, and they ended up talking for over two hours.

The following Sunday, the three of us were back at the bingo hall for another interview. I had my trusty recorder with me, and after everybody settled in, the interview began.

Mary: "It's been almost a year since you announced your candidacy. What are your impressions so far?"

TF: "Well, I always knew that politics wasn't for the weak of heart, but I have been surprised by the level of bloodlust. The personal attacks are brutal and self-serving, and the negativity further illustrates how the two-party system has failed us. The established parties have the money and the power, and they abuse both, they try to drown out all opposition. What are they afraid of?"

Mary: "Even with that, your poll numbers have risen dramatically. What do you attribute that to?"

TF: "Well, I credit most of the rise to our first interview. I wasn't very well known, and neither were my policies. I spoke with you about a few things that seemed to resonate with the voters, and I have received a lot of support from people in Montana as well as from people all across the nation. I want to personally thank you for that."

Mary: "That's very nice of you to say. American Indians have always been the nation's first environmentalists. What are your thoughts on climate change?"

TF: "The environment has always been a priority for Blackfeet too. As their Chairman, I say leave it to a politician to think they can change the weather. I have no such thoughts. The climate has changed ever since it was created. It's a natural occurrence, and it will continue to change."

"But I do marvel at the rich environmentalists who want you and me to give up our cars, electricity, and running water while they fly around in their private jets. They have multiple homes and leave a much larger carbon footprint on the climate than you and I do. Democrats act like they are the only ones interested in a clean environment, and all they end up doing is desecrating our sacred lands with gas-turbine windmills and solar panels that don't generate enough power to light a popcorn fart. Hideous, ineffective windmills and solar panels clutter our beautiful hills, valleys, and oceans."

"They tell us electric cars are the answer. Bullshit. First of all, there's no such thing as an 'all-electric' car. They are battery-driven cars that have to be plugged into an electric grid. The electric grid is fueled by fuels. The lithium batteries they use require the destruction of our environment. The mining process required to dig up rare earth minerals destroys our planet."

"If the liberals/Democrats/socialists cared about the environment, they would insist that every vehicle be converted to natural gas, which emits 60% less carbon than gas cars. However, carbon isn't the problem, man needs carbon to live. Carbon helps our crops grow, and, last time I checked, food is essential to human life. Natural gas is so plentiful that we will never run out of it. It's clean, it's cheap, and it's environmentally sound. Natural gas is a solution. Using solar and wind as our energy source is a mental orgasm. What we need to know is: who is blowing smoke up our asses when it comes to converting to battery cars?"

"I suggest to you that they don't care about the environment, they only care about controlling We the People. By controlling our energy, they control us. You are right; American Indians care about our environment, and I hate the fact that it's being polluted and destroyed by these moronic policies. They take away our energy, so we are perpetually in the dark. They want us to go back to prehistoric times. What's next, candlestick making?"

"Democrats' policies are always based on events that may happen 150 years in the future or events that happened 150 years ago. They never have solutions for today's problems, never. As a member of Congress, I will work on the problems of today."

Mary: "In light of the recent events regarding race relations in our country, do you believe you will be given a fair chance, given the fact that you are an American Indian?"

TF: "As I have said many times, racism is a manifestation of hate. Hate is a human emotion like greed, conceit, envy, and lust, and none of these emotions can be eradicated by passing a law or by labeling people as racists. There are certain things you can't legislate away, and the folly of big government is thinking they can. Human emotions cannot be eradicated by passing a law."

"Personally, I believe Republicans and Democrats use race as a rallying point for their own interests and not for the interests of minorities in our country. They have always exploited minorities for their political gain, another reason the Democrats get 93% of the black vote. They like the whole race-war thing, and they like the whole sexist thing. They want us at each other's throats so we will vote for them based on these wedge issues. They want us distracted so we don't challenge them on the real issues of the day, like, for example, the destruction of our constitutional rights and the huge federal debt. Remember, the best way to destroy a democracy is to bankrupt it. Prosperity fuels democracy."

"Our country has come a long way over the last 150 years. I'm proud to live in a country that elected a black president. How many black presidents have there been in France? England? Germany? Canada? Mexico? Italy? Russia? China? I hope you get my point. We have a long way to go to fully heal from the past sins of our great nation, but we can never give up on each other and let special-interest groups tear us apart. United we stand, divided we fall. If we don't get it together and become one nation again, we will all pay the price. Our enemies are betting against our ability to reconcile. If you think America is racist or sexiest, check out how the Russians treat women, gays, and blacks. If you believe that race and identity politics are the main issues facing us, you lose credibility, and I will never play that card. I'm not weak, and it's not the Indian way."

Mary: "As you know, I'm from Arizona, and the recent Executive Order related to immigration has really stirred things up for us. If elected, you'll have to deal with this issue. Would you like to comment on it now?"

TF: "Only this: if the current President felt so strongly about the issue, why didn't he change the law through the legislative process? He had control of the House and Senate. Instead, the Democrats gave us the Affordable Care Act and didn't do a thing regarding immigration reform."

"Executive Orders are an affront to the Constitution of the United States, and he has set a very dangerous precedent. If a President can change or delete a law because he doesn't like it, we no longer have separation of powers. If he can get rid of Congress, or make it ineffectual, how long will democracy last? It's a dangerous precedent. Once Congress is gone, how long will the Supreme Court survive? Conversely, if the Supreme Court is packed, how long will Congress survive?"

"Executive Orders have limits in terms of scope. We currently have three branches of government that are supposed to be coequal. When there is only one branch, the head of that branch is known as the king or queen. Is that what you want? No, if he really cared about immigration, he would've had the laws changed constitutionally."

"It shows a lack of character when you believe in something, and you don't follow through with your convictions because you fear it will cost you an election. Same thing with the war on terrorism and gun control. He could have passed any law he wanted to, and yet he abandoned his principles for the hope of getting four more years. They always want four more years."

"I will do the right thing because it's the right thing to do. I will not make excuses, blame my race, blame the fact that I only have one hand, or blame the fact that I'm ugly... I will stand by my convictions because that's the Indian way."

Mary: "You're not that ugly. What about the terrorism issue and the response to it?"

TF: "That horse has been beaten pretty hard lately. Let me ask you, do you feel safe? Personally, I don't think it's a good idea to release terrorists who have killed Americans. As far as overall safety, I feel safe, but I don't live in Chicago. How long are Americans going to tolerate the violence in our major cities? It goes to show you how screwed up we have become when we lecture other countries on how to behave, and we can't walk down our streets without fearing for our lives. The Democrats claim that terrorists are using the internet as a recruitment tool. If so, I say to combat terrorism, we should put out a video that says: 'Anyone who commits a terrorist act will be caught, disarmed, and sent to the South Side of Chicago to spend an entire weekend.' They wouldn't last ten minutes there, and they call American Indians savages."

Mary: "Speaking of savages, what do you think about the recent Federal Circuit opinion regarding the Washington Redskin copyright issue?"

TF: "Another example of the politically correct crowd exploiting American Indians. It's another example of them wanting to vanish us. We have been suffering for decades under their abusive federal government policies, and this is the issue they make a fuss about? Really? We were stuck on reservations and left to die, and the best they can do for us is get rid of a name? The only Indian I know who is actually offended by the name is Stubby Grant. Of course, Stubby hates everything and everyone. I guess it's nice that we are finally getting some publicity, even if it's phony publicity."

"Personally, I'm not offended by the name Redskin. However, I am deeply offended when they violate the word Chief. In the olden days, the Chief was revered and was a person of honor and integrity. The word Chief reflects honor. What offends me is when they use the words Commander-in-Chief. In that context, it's no longer a meaningless word on a football jersey, it's a symbol of leadership. A Chief in the olden days would never abandon his warriors, he would not eat until the other members of the tribe had eaten, he would never blame the previous Chief for the difficulties he faced, and he would never lie to the tribe. A Chief was courageous and strong and the first one to go to battle; he was a warrior. Chiefs in the olden days would sit in council and listen to advice. They would never be vindictive towards another member of the tribe who had an opposing idea. The Chiefs brought everybody together for the common good; they didn't divide the tribe into factions. A Chief admits his mistakes, and a Chief never rewards cowardice. But, most importantly, a Chief never thinks of his legacy, he thinks of his people. So, in my opinion, until these so called 'Chiefs' begin to display these qualities, they should not be allowed to use the word Chief in any context. Call them commanders, kings, queens, or what have you, but don't dishonor the word Chief."

Mary: "Well, you're running for a national office, and you will be asked to vote on a number of national issues. Would you vote to close Guantanamo?"

TF: "Of all the campaign promises that were made, that's the one the President is interested in fulfilling? What about the debt? All I can say is, can you imagine what would've happened to us Indians if, instead of killing Custer, we had captured him and then released him? There wouldn't be an American Indian alive today. He would have killed us all. Never release people who have killed Americans, it's not the Indian way, and I would vote against closing it."

Mary: "I'm curious, have you gotten any negative blowback from our previous interview?"

TF: "Actually, everything I've heard has been pretty positive. There have been a few complaints about breaking the chains of government control, but that was expected. As I said at the time, those on the government tit never see the harm that is being done to them. Government control is an abomination. I will add this: American Indians were forced onto reservations. Today, the folks dependent on the government have created their own reservations and succumbed to them without a fight. Break the chains and strive for freedom and liberty while you still can. Commodity cheese is never free."

Mary: "I don't have any further questions for you, and I see that people are starting to file in to play some bingo. Is there anything else you would like to say?"

TF: "Only this: I will be a leader for every Montanan like the Chiefs in the olden days. I will bring honesty and integrity to politics. Both political parties have betrayed our trust; they have pitted us against each other in an attempt to better themselves. Nothing is getting done in Washington, DC, and our so-called leaders act like children. They are vindictive and greedy. That is why I'm running as an independent. The two-party system has failed us. With your help and the help of all Americans, we can begin to take our country back, and we need leadership to do that. Thank you."

It wasn't long after that interview that the economic bubble finally burst; the ill-conceived policies of the previous seven years started to show their disastrous effects in concrete, meaningful ways. The shell game came to an end. Interest rates began to race even higher, inflation skyrocketed, world markets collapsed, and our stock market began to show the strains of the 19 trillion debt. Our government was officially bankrupt; it didn't have enough money to buy a popsicle without charging it. It was an unprecedented collapse, and the geniuses in government were clueless. America is the tail that wags the dog in terms of worldwide solvency, and we are bankrupt. Foreign governments pleaded with us to fix our financial nightmare. Nationwide, things got so bad that people had to give up their cable TV subscriptions and actually have conversations with their family members. It was absolutely terrifying.

Then, as Two-Fingers predicted, things got really, really ugly. The government couldn't find anyone stupid enough to loan it money. When they did find someone, it was at very high, usurious interest rates. The money the Federal Reserve lent out at less than one percent the previous seven years was now being borrowed back at sixteen percent, and the only institutions that had any money were the banks we bailed out back in 2008.

Government checks continued to be printed and sent out, but they had little to no value. The government's solution was to print more money, and the dollar's devaluation accelerated. Inflation continued to skyrocket, and the stock market eventually collapsed. Shortages began to take their toll, and riots swept across the country.

Our financial collapse was much worse than the Depression of the 1930s. Back then, the economy was terrible, but the government wasn't 19 trillion in debt. Socialism had failed, and the only way out of the mess was to get private investment involved. The government had to get out of the way and let capitalism get back to work; the government's stifling economic policies had ruined the financial health of America. Like Two-Fingers always said, the best way to kill democracy is to bankrupt it. Private investors had to be given a reason to invest in America again, and that meant all the onerous regulations and high taxes had to go. Prior to the collapse, the government received record revenues and still ran up 19 trillion in debt. Big government does not create jobs, it stops economic development. Of course, the politicians were busy pointing fingers and blaming the other guy as America suffered.

The Montanans who had listened to Two-Fingers's message,

believed he was right, and the collapse proved it. His popularity soared, and his numbers in the polls reached unprecedented heights. He was the only candidate who warned of the economic collapse, and more importantly, he was the only one with solutions to the problem.

Two-Fingers had very little money to run his campaign, and the financial collapse didn't help matters. The little bit of money he had raised from individual donors didn't go far, and those donors eventually quit sending money. He didn't blame them, he knew they needed the money more than he did. Besides, I had come up with a solution. I focused on the power of the internet and decided to make a political movie starring Two-Fingers and put it on YouTube. Social media is the future, and I used it to the fullest of my capabilities. The Democrat-controlled liberal press had lied to the people for years, and Two-Fingers, on the other hand, had told them exactly what would happen, and his message needed to be heard by a larger audience. Reality had to replace the fiction perpetuated by the liberal press. The internet and social media provided a format to circumvent the stranglehold main-stream media had on messaging. How can we have a free press when it's controlled by one party?

I was actually getting pretty good with the camera, I had filmed Kanowski's tar and feathering, and I was well aware of the importance of good lighting. Two-Fingers isn't the most handsome person in the world, and there is no good way to light him, but I tried my best. I set up the camera in Two-Fingers's office one night, and the two of us got down to business. I served as the off-camera moderator, and he either answered my questions or went off on tangents, mainly, he went off on tangents. I titled the movie, "The World According to Two-Fingers." Pretty catchy, huh? It turned out to be one of the most-viewed videos of 2015. Here is the unedited transcript of what was said that night:

TF: "My name is Donny R. Schwartz, and my friends call me Two-

Fingers. I am a Blackfeet Indian from Browning, Montana, and I am running for Senator. For nearly thirty years, I have been the Chairman of the Blackfeet tribe. Don't hold this against me, but I am an attorney. I am legally trained, and I have spent most of my adult life studying the Constitution of the United States of America and the Supreme Court cases that serve as precedent. As a Blackfeet Indian who was raised on a reservation, I know firsthand the terrible effects our government's dependency and control programs have on people. These programs suck the life out of every American who has the misfortune of living under their spell. Today, we suffer because of these failed government policies. We are all in the same boat, and that boat is sinking fast."

"Our Constitution is about freedom and liberty. The Founding Fathers tried to protect us from an abusive, totalitarian government. They knew that freedom and liberty would lift the human condition in a way that no amount of money in the world could. Over the years, the Constitution has been violated by our elected officials, and our liberties and freedoms have been slowly taken away from us. Every time they pass a regulation or law that inhibits our freedom and liberties, they violate the principles on which this great nation was founded. That nation is now drowning in regulations and debt."

"Big corporations don't mind the regulations because they have legal staff and accountants that help them navigate the treacherous waters of regulation. They pass on the costs of dealing with all these regulations to the consumer, to all of us. Small businesses can't afford to deal with the regulations and collapse under the weight. This leaves the big corporations in charge, and that's the way they like it. Big corporations don't have to worry about competition because the burdensome federal government has buried the small entrepreneurs under a pile of regulations and government control. These corporations control where the manufacturing of their products takes place. America no longer manufactures anything of importance; we have become a consumer-only country, and that's the main reason for the financial collapse. We live under the weight of corporate socialism."

"Our government is controlled by lobbyists and special interest groups that don't have the interests of We the People in mind. Big corporations are just as harmful to us as our big government is. The irony is, we need corporations now because they have the money to spur economic growth, our federal government is broke. Corporations will soon realize they will no longer exist if We the People no longer exist. Who will buy their trinkets?"

"The easy money of the last seven years hasn't evaporated; it's in the hands of the monied class. It has always been that way in every country since the beginning of time. The monied class survives while We the People suffer. Knowing this, we have to make a pact with the devil; we must lower the corporate tax rate so the corporations invest in America."

"Unlike big government, they do provide jobs and economic growth. They have taken that growth offshore, and Americans have suffered. The government policies have enabled them to do that. The government, in an attempt to fool us, says it is going to raise taxes on the wealthy and corporations to help finance the government. That's probably the stupidest thing they've ever told us. Do they think we are naive enough to believe the rich are going to willingly give their wealth to the government? No, the pain and the tax burden will ultimately be placed on the shoulders of the middle class. We currently have the highest corporate tax rates in the world and that has caused the loss of American jobs as corporations go offshore to produce their products."

"Corporate profits will suffer tremendously during the current financial collapse. Nobody has money for the latest cell phone or even their bare essentials. Hopefully, the corporations will realize that when the American middle class is destroyed, so are they. We need them to invest in America again and we need to motivate them into doing so.

We the People need to get rid of the government regulations that impede our economic freedoms and growth."

I turned off the camera and walked over to Two-Fingers and said, "Look, you're doing good, but you're getting a little far out there, way too heavy. You're getting too windy. Speak slowly and loosen up. Say something funny; this will not play well in California."

Two-Fingers stared at me before saying, "California? I'm running in Montana, I don't care about California. By the way, how do I look? They say the camera adds ten pounds, and I want to look my best."

"You are the ugliest human being I know. Don't worry about how you look; we already have too many shallow politicians who only care about their looks. Snap out of it; we need a leader, not someone obsessed with their looks," I said before adding. "To be safe, I'll turn down the lights and try to hide your face. On second thought, maybe you should wear one of those witness protection masks government informers wear when they're doing television interviews. Your viewers would probably appreciate that."

"Crack you, White Guy," was all he said before we resumed filming.

TF: "We the People have been violated by our elected officials, and we need to take the blame. We elected them, re-elected them and now we are morally and financially bankrupt. We must demand honesty from our elected officials or all the changes and sacrifices we make to correct things will be ineffectual. We can change things, but We the People must unite and the politicians must stop lying to us. If we continue to hate each other, we will lose. If we don't pay attention to the politicians and hold them accountable, they will continue to destroy our country. Voter apathy is an affront to our constitutional right to vote, and we need to pay closer attention to the issues and the candidates."

"My opponents' policies have created the nightmare the country currently faces. Frank's party stands for the profound policy of, 'Vote for me and I will give you free tuition. Or vote for me, and I will give you free healthcare. Or vote for me, and I will give you free food, housing, and a monthly stipend.' Pete's party didn't do a thing to stop the nonsense, and he voted to pass budget after budget without fighting for fiscal responsibility."

"Now, after the financial collapse, you never see either one of them. Have any of you seen your elected representatives since the financial collapse? They are hiding because they don't have answers on how to fix things. Come to think of it, I did run into Frank the other day in Helena. He was in town looking for space for his library. He wanted a big place to showcase his achievements and I told him his achievements could be housed in a small broom closet in Havre. That's when he got in his chauffeur-driven limousine and drove to the airport. By the way, Frank refuses to debate me. Pete told me he wouldn't debate me unless Frank shows up. Another example of how the two-party system works is that they always blame the other guy. We are $19 trillion in debt and they keep telling us the United States of America is in good shape. All I can tell you is this: the government is so broke the Treasury Department called me the other day and wanted the tribe to lend them money. I told them no way in hell were we going to pay for their insanity. I hung up on them before they started crying. It was the very next day that we started building a wall around the reservation in an attempt to keep the stupid out."

I shut off the camera until I stopped laughing. Two-Fingers wasn't laughing, he took the destruction of America very seriously. Not I. I always figured I would stay on the reservation because the reservation is the only safe place to live. Business was still pretty good on the reservation; I'm constantly amazed by the fact that broke tourists can find money to gamble and buy booze. The worse the economy, the more they gamble and drink. The reservation was flourishing because it was debt-free and the entire tribe was working. Things had changed in the nick of time, and we had Two-Fingers to thank.

After I quit laughing, I asked Two-Fingers if he wanted to add anything, and he sat there staring at me. I imagined he was pondering my question, but I wasn't sure. Finally, he said, "Do you think any of this matters? I doubt I'll be able to change a thing. There are too many crooks with vested interests in maintaining the status quo. The deception permeates every department of the government at every level; there's more honesty in a fistfight than there is in all of politics. I would gladly fight any one of the thieves, and I'm not sure an honest person can survive in Washington, DC."

"Two-Fingers, that is a fact, and we have talked about this before. You decided to get into the race because you needed to fight for change. Besides, it's too late now."

Two-Fingers paced around his office seemingly digesting this before he sat back down and told me to roll the camera.

TF: "The world is literally blowing up around us. Frank and Pete both supported the failed policies and We the People suffer. Our domestic policy and our foreign policy are total disasters. Thanks to Pete and Frank, the Iranians, Russians and the North Koreans are threatening us with nuclear war. America is worse off now than it was during the Cold War. Their parties have ushered in a period of unrest that is unprecedented in our country's history. We don't have competent leadership in Washington, DC, and We the People are paying the price. I believe in a clean environment, but I understand the environment will disappear along with all humans if we get into a nuclear war. When one bomb explodes, the countries with nukes will start firing them off, and we will all die. Mother Earth may regenerate itself after a few billion years, but we will all be gone. Our borders are not secure, and the President hands out executive orders like they are candy. Pete and Frank have allowed this to happen."

"The President's recent executive action on immigration is overly broad and I believe it will be struck down by the Supreme Court. Having said that, I believe the inaction regarding our immigration laws by Congress is totally unacceptable. Congress and the Supreme Court need to clarify who is and who isn't a citizen when they are born on our soil. This inaction and lack of clarity has created all kinds of stupid."

"Right now, the way the 14th Amendment is being interpreted, a foreigner can come here, give birth to a child, and that child is automatically a citizen, regardless of the citizenship of the foreigner. That, in my opinion, is an incorrect interpretation of the 14th Amendment. The present interpretation of the birthright citizenship clause is incorrect. It was not intended to mean that, as soon as a baby is born here, it has a vested right in citizenship. Using that stupid, lazy interpretation, an alien from Mars could come here, give birth to an alien baby, and that baby would automatically be a citizen even, though the parents and the baby immediately fly back to their alien home. If you don't believe this old country attorney, ask one of the Harvard-educated attorneys back in Washington, DC if I'm wrong."

"That's how stupid things have become. Of course, most people don't believe there is life outside our planetary system. I personally don't discount the possibility. What other explanation is there for Stubby Grant? That dude must have come from outer space. There's no way he's from Earth. ET, phone home. Our Constitution is being violated, and once it's destroyed, all the money in the world isn't going to help us. Once Americans lose faith in their institutions, all hell is going to break loose. Things will get a lot worse for everyone."

I stopped the camera and walked over to Two-Fingers and said, "You're getting too complicated. I don't even know what the hell you're talking about." Two-Fingers rarely got pissed at me, but I could tell I pissed him off.

He calmly counted to ten before standing and retrieving his copy of the Constitution. He carefully laid out the pages that he had enlarged, and I could see there were notes in the columns, and the entire document had been heavily highlighted. There were copies of case law in his stack as well. Once he had his papers arranged to his liking, he looked up at me and said, "Did you spend any time studying law in law school, or were you only there to chase after my sister?" I always knew he was mad when he qualified his remarks with, "my sister." I thought, Oh shit, here comes the lecture, so I sat down across from him and braced for the inevitable.

"People are furious about the current state of our immigration laws, and I'm trying to highlight the stupidity and the inaction of our elected officials like Frank and Pete. Am I the only person on the reservation who reads a newspaper? Americans are mad as hell, and it's getting worse everyday. The main point of contention is the idiocy of bestowing citizenship to babies that have no connection to the United States other than the fact they were born here. Citizens have a right to be concerned because the 14th Amendment is being misconstrued and violated."

He placed his enlarged copy of the 14th Amendment in front of me and asked me to read the first sentence in Section 1 out loud. I nodded my head, cleared my throat, and said, "All persons born or naturalized in the United States, and subject to the jurisdiction thereof, are citizens of the United States and of the State wherein they reside." I read it a couple of times to myself and then said, "Well, it seems pretty straightforward. However, I'm not sure what 'subject to the jurisdiction thereof means." Two-Fingers nodded his head and said, "Exactly, that's the key part of the 14th that is conveniently overlooked. So, let's focus on the born in the United States aspect of this, naturalization is a completely different issue."

Two-Fingers took a drink of water and leaned back in his chair. I wanted to take a piss but wasn't about to endure his wrath by mentioning it. When the professor talked about constitutional law, nobody moved. I sat, hoping he didn't go through every frigging amendment.

"As you know from law school, you shouldn't look at the Constitution in a vacuum. You must educate yourself on the intent of the lawmakers at the time and the circumstances that existed when the amendment was passed. That is called legislative intent, and it's very important. An amendment may only consist of a paragraph or two when adopted, while legislative intent writings can be hundreds of pages long before they are reduced to those short paragraphs of an amendment." Two-Fingers took another long drink of water before continuing. "The 14th Amendment was passed in 1868 in an attempt to strengthen the Civil Rights Act of 1866. You do know that an amendment to the Constitution carries more weight than an act, don't you?" He didn't wait for my answer, he just kept going. "Both of these measures were designed to help blacks. They were enacted after the Civil War, and our lawmakers' intent was to give blacks more rights. Think about it, back then, there were mostly whites, blacks, and Indians populating America. These laws went a long way in helping the plight of the blacks."

He shuffled through his papers, pulled out a copy of the Civil Rights Act of 1866, laid it out in front of me, and said, "You know the drill." I briefly glanced at him before shifting uncomfortably in my chair and reading the Act out loud. "That all persons born in the United States and not subject to any foreign power, excluding Indians not taxed, are hereby declared to be citizens of the United States." Once again, I had to read this section a couple of times to myself, and when I finished, Two-Fingers asked if I noticed any difference. "Well, other than the obvious, that Indians were not granted citizenship if they were not taxed, I don't see any difference."

That's when Two-Fingers came completely unglued. He stood up and yelled, "How in the hell did you ever graduate from law school? I swear, White Guy, you drive me nuts. Did you sleep through our constitutional law class?" I sat there rather sheepishly before saying, "Yeah, I was awake, and I would've spoken up in class more, but you were always talking." That didn't sit well with him, and he immediately started counting to fifty, "Concentrate on the words, 'and not subject to any foreign power.' How do you interpret that? Remember, it all comes down to interpretation and legislative intent."

I read it again before replying, "Well, it seems to me the passage is intended for the parents of the child, and if the parents are citizens of another country, they owe their allegiance to that country and that country's power. So, unless the parents are in the United States legally and have given up their previous citizenship, any baby born here isn't automatically a citizen."

"Bingo!" Two-Fingers exclaimed, slapping his desk with a ferocity that was clearly overdone. He was overjoyed. Suddenly, I was his star pupil. "There must be more of a connection to the United States than coming over here and having a baby. The parents must have surrendered their previous citizenship and loyalty to that foreign country."

Two-Fingers was really enjoying himself, and my kidneys were about to explode, but I didn't interrupt him. "Did you know that American Indians were not granted birthright citizenship automatically even after the 14th Amendment was passed? American Indians who were born here, who lived their whole lives on American soil, and whose children were born here, were still not granted citizenship at birth. That's additional proof that lawmakers required stricter guidelines for gaining birth citizenship than simply being born here. Illegals and foreigners can't automatically be granted citizenship for their child. It's illogical."

"Remember back to who occupied America in 1868, white adults and their children, black adults and their children, and American Indians and their children. White and black babies were granted citizenship at birth because the whites and blacks had a connection to the United States: they were born here, lived here, were domiciled here, and were subject to the laws of the United States of America and the state where they lived. Indians were viewed as having allegiances to their tribes, not to the United States, and therefore Congress excluded newly born American Indian babies from citizenship, even though they were born here."

"This was true all the way up until 1924, when Congress passed the Indian Citizenship Act. So, if American Indians who lived on, died on, and were born on American soil were denied birthright citizenship because Congress, judges, and other lawmakers determined that we, when born, owed our allegiance to our tribes and not the United States of America, how can anyone rightfully claim that foreigners who are citizens of another country don't owe that country their allegiance?"

"Their babies, born here, have the same allegiance as the parents. Both passages in the Civil Rights Act and the 14th Amendment must be read in the present tense; future allegiance isn't the issue. Allegiance at the time of the birth is. No infant has allegiance to anything other than its mommy's teat. So the question becomes: what is the allegiance of the parents? That's what was said about American Indians, and it must apply to the situation at hand. If there isn't more of a connection to the United States of America, the Mars analogy is right on point. Earth is such a mess I'm not sure any right-thinking Martian would want to live here, but if they did, under the current interpretation of the 14th Amendment, their babies would automatically become citizens when born on American soil. Think about it, if a Martian gave birth to a baby in the United States of America, under the interpretation, that Martian baby would automatically become a citizen and someday return from Mars and be eligible to run for President of the United

States of America."

"By the way, the 14th Amendment is more restrictive regarding who can become a citizen by birth than the Civil Rights Act of 1866, as evidenced by the omission of the part that says, 'excluding Indians not taxed.' They made it more restrictive because they weren't going to grant birth citizenship to Indians, even if we paid taxes. They were concerned about our allegiance to the United States. I know you don't give a shit, but here's the kicker: the 14th Amendment that speaks to birthright citizenship was patterned after the 1866 Civil Rights Act, and the legislative intent language behind that Act must be thoroughly examined. So much for the 'plain meaning' argument that has eroded our legal reasoning."

Two-Fingers finally took a breath, and I sprinted to the john.

After returning from the restroom, I engaged Two-Fingers in more conversation about the Constitution. I figured he had worn himself out, and I could take advantage. "So, do you lie awake at night and count constitutional amendments before you can fall asleep?" Two-Fingers smiled at me and said, "Actually, I do. America is 19 trillion dollars in debt and foreigners are pouring into this country and taking advantage of our social services. Billions of dollars are being spent on people who have no allegiance to this country. That is only one example of the idiocy that is prevalent in Washington, DC. The Supreme Court has the power to clarify the law so it's not misinterpreted. Somebody needs to bring a case and get the issue before them. Something has to be done for the citizens of America. Remember, the Supreme Court does not give advisory opinions. There must be a case and controversy in order for them to exercise their Article III powers."

"Clearly, the 14th Amendment and the 1866 Civil Rights Act were intended to help blacks, and American Indians were an afterthought. My people have always been an afterthought. I get that and I don't blame anybody for it. But if American Indians were held to such high standards regarding birth citizenship, how can illegals be held to a less stringent test? No, the legislative intent seems clear to me. There must be more to gaining birth citizenship than merely flying or swimming here and having a baby. I know I'm belaboring the point, but if we continue down this road of stupid, I'm going to have an even taller wall built around the reservation."

"By the way, you need to look into getting a dome built over us as well. Have Liquid Louie and Stogie Man get on that."

I sat there looking at my watch, thinking it was late and he'd probably want to go home and get some sleep, I was wrong. "Start up your camera, I want to get something off my chest." Two-Fingers said as he stood and started doing jumping jacks, I was worn out and the guy started doing jumping jacks. "What's bothering you?" I asked from behind the camera. "As you know, I'm concerned about the minorities in this country, and I have a message for them that needs to be said. It may not be politically correct, but it's my hard-won opinion. Now start the camera and get comfortable, this could take a while." I started the camera before going over to his cowhide-covered sofa and lying down.

TF: "Well, we have a presidential election coming soon, and the Democrats and Republicans are out pandering for your votes. They're telling us minorities how bad we have it in America. They want us to know that everybody is out to get us and they're here to protect us. They stress how much they care about us and how important our vote is. Of course, after the elections are over, we won't see them again until the next one."

"As an American Indian whose ancestors were slaves, whose ancestors were scalped and massacred, whose ancestors were raped and maimed, whose ancestors had their land stolen from them when the treaties we entered into were violated, I say this: nobody can turn back time and change what has happened in the past, nobody. Many of us have been given free education, free housing, free food, free money, and now the country we live in is broke. It's time we start acting like Americans. We need to quit rocking the boat and start rowing together, or we're going to drown. We need to ignore the professional politicians who only care about getting re-elected."

"That's the message I've delivered to my tribe, and it's a message I think needs to be heard by all Americans. Everyone must start taking personal responsibility for their actions and quit blaming the other guy for their failures. If you think your pain is anywhere near the pain of an American Indian, think again. I say this to help you, and it needs to be said, you're being played by the politicians, and you're willingly letting them do it to you."

"Welfare is an abomination, and it has ruined more lives than it has ever helped. Poverty levels are higher now than when they passed those idiotic laws. The politicians use us as pawns in their evil game; all they care about is getting elected and re-elected. The leaders in this country should invest the welfare money into job creation. Be a plumber, an electrician, or a machinist. Pursue a trade because that's where the money is, and there is little to no competition for those jobs. Nobody wants to get their hands dirty anymore."

"Every time I need an electrician, it costs me a minimum of $200, and the woman spends less than an hour at my cabin. She does great work and all, but as the Chairman of the tribe, I only make $20 an hour. Other than not asking you to take personal responsibility for your actions, what are our leaders doing for you? If you want to work, the deck is stacked in your favor."

"I've heard a lot of complaining about the lack of civil rights. Where were the civil rights activists when American Indians occupied Wounded Knee back in 1973? American Indians were bringing attention to their plight, and I never saw another minority there. No other minority had our backs. I didn't see one black person or Hispanic come to our aid. I guess civil rights are only important when they're your civil rights you're concerned about. As I said, I didn't see one minority other than American Indians at the occupation, but I did see a white guy. Come over here, White Guy, let the folks see what a real warrior looks like."

I was half asleep when he startled me awake, and I wasn't given enough time to comb my hair before I found myself standing in front of the camera. I stood next to him at his desk and stared sheepishly into the lens while Two-Fingers went on the attack, "You talk about a minority? Here is a minority. For a long time, this dude didn't have anybody other than me to hang out with on the reservation. He was surrounded by a bunch of Indians. He had his ass whipped, he was teased, he was chased, and ridiculed from the day he moved to the reservation until now, and I have never heard him cry about it once. Think about this: we are all minorities at one time or another. The difference is that he didn't get free college, job preference, or welfare of any kind. He does get to sleep with my sister, that's an entirely different issue."

"On the reservation, it took us a long, long time to change. Too long. Change is never easy, and it requires hard work and sacrifice. If you don't want to work, then there's no hope for you. But when you don't work, don't blame anybody else for your failure. Here on the reservation, we don't lock our doors, and our children can now walk safely to school because we all share the same values and we respect each other. If you don't know right from wrong, no one can help you. Color isn't the issue, being an asshole is the issue. Quit blaming others. It's not the Indian way."

I turned off the camera before lying back down on his sofa. I broke the silence by saying, "$20 an hour? I can't believe we pay you that much money." Two-Fingers choked on his apple while I continued,

"You know Washington, DC has some of the highest crime rates in the country, right?" Two-Fingers thought on that a second before saying, "Screw it, I'm going to get bodyguards like the rest of our public servants." I laughed at that and said, "What's the first thing you're going to do when you get to Washington?" Two-Fingers quickly replied, "I'm going to find the Black and Hispanic caucuses and ask every member this simple question: 'Why do you hate your constituents so much?'

Two-Fingers finally went home, and I posted the film on the internet. It was unedited because I didn't know how to edit anything. I was lucky to get it posted. I have a confession to make; I'm not a technical person.

Early the next morning, as usual, Two-Fingers and I met at the Club Cafe for breakfast. He was seated with a copy of the liberal Big Sky Reporter spread out in front of him. He was engrossed in an article and didn't immediately acknowledge my presence, so I ordered a cup of coffee while I looked over the one-page menu. Minutes passed before he looked up and said, "This article says that a state supreme court judge down in Alabama is refusing to enforce the gay marriage thing. I knew something like this was going to happen. Has it come down to only obeying the laws you agree with?"

I looked up from my menu and asked, "Is that a rhetorical question or do you want my opinion?"

"I'm opening up the floor for discussion knowing full well you'd rather discuss the comic section," Two-Fingers said as he closed the paper.

"Personally, I think the world is so screwed up there's no saving it. That's why I'm staying on the reservation while you go off to Washington, DC."

"Bullshit, you're going with me. I'm going to make you my chief of staff." Two-Fingers motioned for more coffee before continuing, "I'm not paying you anything, but you'll have a nice title." I thought about that for a moment before moving on to a different issue.

"I have a question for you, if women have it so bad in the United States of America, how come Bruce Jenner wants to become one?" That probably wasn't the best question to ask while he had a mouthful of coffee, he spewed it all over my freshly ironed $10 shirt.

It turned out to be an EF Hutton moment at the Club; the breakfast crowd suddenly seemed energized as they directed their attention to our table. Liquid Louie piped up with his opinion that Bruce should be forced to return his gold medal from the 1976 Olympics.

"Well, hell, if the dude is really a woman, then he should be forced to return the medal," Louie said as he hovered over us.

Soon, a large group of Blackfeet stood around our table voicing their opinions. I sat there thinking we had finally discovered an issue that galvanized the electorate.

"Think about it," Louie continued, "If he really is a woman and was competing in a men's event, he should be forced to give the medal back."

It was quickly pointed out that being a woman and winning a men's event was an extraordinary accomplishment and it made no sense to return the gold medal. This seemed to catch the highly educated and intelligent Liquid Louie off guard. His mind always seemed to work in incomprehensible ways. His best response to that astute observation was,

"Well, all I know is that if a man won a woman's event, they would make him give the medal back, and if he doesn't have to, it's sexist."

I sat there thinking the world had truly come to an end. Liquid Louie had actually used the word, "sexist." I actually blacked out, and my entire life flashed in front of me. After regaining consciousness, I realized there was no place to hide from the insanity sweeping across our country. The reservation, my little cocoon, had been swept up by the tornado of political correctness swirling across the land, bringing chaos and destruction to everything in its path.

Two-Fingers, showing little concern over my passing out, launched another attack.

"Well, since you're talking about sexism, I've been catching up on the Democrat Party's demands that taxpayers pay for abortions. I know that's a touchy subject, but you've got me thinking." Two-Fingers said as the room slowly stopped spinning around me.

"Hey, don't start up with me. I had a vasectomy, and I've paid the ultimate price for birth control. Leave me out of it." That was all I was willing to say on the subject.

Then, from way over in the corner somewhere, someone yelled, "So, you got your nuts cut off, White Guy?" It was as if we were on a speaker system or something, you can't say a word in the Club without everybody knowing what you're talking about, and I really resented that.

Two-Fingers ordered a stack of pancakes before collecting his thoughts.

"Push, push, push and take, take, take, and they wonder why the United States is about to implode. They start attacking our gun rights, freedom of the press, freedom of religion, and freedom of speech, and they slowly take it all away. Our leaders are always telling us their policies don't have any harmful effect on our rights, bullshit."

I remember looking at the door and seriously considering running away and hiding. Please, no more Constitution talk.

Two-Fingers was tiring, but that didn't stop him from talking.

"The Democrat Party died in Dallas in 1963. Remember JFK? He was the last, and perhaps the only, great leader of the Democrat Party. At his inauguration in 1961, he said, "Ask not what your country can do for you; rather, ask what you can do for your country," Fifty-four years later, the answer seems to be, 'We are going to suck the lifeblood out of the American taxpayer and piss on the Constitution.' That's no way to govern, and it's not the Indian way."

That was the moment I called for my check.

Later that day, after returning to my office, I noticed that Two-Fingers' movie had already gotten over a million views. Since there were only 800,000 Montanans, I figured his message had gone mainstream. That fact reaffirmed my belief that if you have the right message, you don't have to buy elections.

Chapter 23
The Disappearance of Two-Fingers

In the days immediately following the release of the video, Two-Fingers began receiving a lot of attention across the state and the entire nation. He rose to the top of the polls and suddenly dominated the race. That's when his anxiety hit an all-time high. The reality of being elected started to sink in, along with his uncertainty. He was concerned that no one would listen to him once he got to the Senate; he'd be walking among snakes, and he knew it. I worried about many things, but I never questioned or doubted his ability. Two-Fingers feared his noble and pure motives for serving would be drowned out by the hypocrisy of Washington, DC.

With each passing day, the economy worsened as interest rates climbed, inflation soared, and unemployment skyrocketed.

Then, out of the blue, he was summoned to appear before a Senate subcommittee to testify in a long-standing lawsuit we filed over the government's misuse of tribal funds. I had filed the lawsuit early in my career as the tribal attorney. The tribe was seeking billions in damages, and the tribal Chairman was suddenly asked to testify and possibly reach a settlement. Normally, as their tribal attorney, I would have gone with him. But he didn't want both of us to go, and since he had to go, I was to stay behind. In hindsight, the timing of the meeting raises more questions than answers. We had been working towards a satisfactory resolution for years, so why did they suddenly need to see Two-Fingers?

A few days before leaving for Washington, DC, Two-Fingers received a call from one of Frank Johnson's aides. Frank wanted to meet with him to see if they could bury the hatchet. Two-Fingers agreed, knowing full well the only place Frank wanted to bury the hatchet was between his shoulder blades. He had one condition: Frank had to come to the reservation for the sit-down. Frank accepted, and the meeting was scheduled.

I clearly remember the day Frank came to town in his chauffeur-driven limousine with its darkened windows and wet bar. It was Frank's first visit to the reservation, he never associated with the Blackfeet because he never needed them to win an election. When he arrived at the tribal complex, his fancy hat-wearing, impeccably dressed chauffeur opened the rear door, and Frank exited the limo like a king, careful not to step in the puddles scattered across the parking lot. He looked like a man who lived in the lap of luxury, bloated by fat and power. He shuffled about like he was inconvenienced, as if he'd come down from the mountain to meet mortal man.

His wife Ann had died several years earlier, and she, according to Two-Fingers, was the only human being in the marriage. She must have been his anchor, because after she died Frank totally lost whatever morals and ethics he once had. He may have been human once, but political life had stripped him of all that was real. He was a complete phony, and Two-Fingers hated phonies. He tolerated a lot of things, but he wouldn't tolerate a phony.

After a decidedly cold and clumsy greeting, Two-Fingers, Frank, and I sat down in the tribal conference room. Frank's oversized chauffeur stood guard in the hallway. After I closed the door and sat down, the meeting began.

The first thing out of Frank's mouth was a demand to meet with Two-Fingers in private. Evidently, what he had to say was for Two-Fingers' ears only. Two-Fingers thought about that for a couple of seconds before he said, "White Guy is here for protection."

"Protection? You don't need protection. I've brought all the protection you'll need," Frank said, gasping for air.

"I'm not talking about my protection, Frank. I'm talking about yours. I'm not sure I'll be able to control myself once you start spouting your bullshit, and White Guy is the only person I will listen to. All the security in the world won't prevent the ass-kicking you deserve, and the only person who can stop me is White Guy. So I suggest you agree to his staying."

I'm always amazed by Two-Fingers' brass. He was 62 years old at the time and could hardly beat an egg, but that never stopped him from talking shit.

Anyway, Frank needed to talk to Two-Fingers more than Two-Fingers needed to talk to him, so Frank moved on to why he was there. "Listen, I came to make you an offer. I know you're leading in the polls right now, and things are looking pretty good for you. But if the economy hadn't collapsed, you wouldn't have had a chance," Frank said, painstakingly trying to catch his breath. "I would like to propose that you drop out of the race, and if you do, I will personally see to it that you will be my party's nominee in six years. You'll be a shoo-in. I have a lot of unfinished business and need to get re-elected to get things done. You have my word that my party will support you 100% in 2022."

Two-Fingers sat listening patiently as Frank pleaded with him to step down. He made promise after promise and was on the verge of tears when Two-Fingers finally interrupted him. "You want six more years? This country can't take six more weeks of your bullshit. We are ass-deep in debt, and you have no answers on how to get us out. You and your crew are the ones who got us into this mess. It wasn't White Guy or me. You've shipped our jobs overseas and increased government spending and control, and you want six more years? Why is it that you career politicians always want six more years? We are a divided nation, and you have Americans at each other's throats, and you want six more years? Americans are not safe to move around their own country, and you want six more years?"

I glanced over at Frank, who appeared to be physically shrinking, like a balloon losing air, as Two-Fingers continued his verbal assault.

"You have offended and abandoned our foreign allies, and you want six more years?"

At that point, Frank looked shocked by the news. Obviously, he had only been reading the liberal press and was unaware of the damage he'd done to the country. Reality suddenly took hold, and he abruptly stood up and said, "I'm finished here. I'll see you next week when you're on my turf. You'll no longer have the safety of your reservation to hide behind."

With that, he stood and shuffled out of the tribal complex with the help of his chauffeur. Two-Fingers and I sat quietly in the conference room for several minutes before I said, "You know, I thought that went pretty well. What do you think?"

Two-Fingers laughed before saying, "I think I'd better win the election, or there won't be a wall high enough to help any of us."

The days leading up to his trip to Washington, DC were extremely busy; there were a lot of last-minute details to attend to. Before he left, he had amassed a double-digit lead in the polls, and his Senate victory appeared inevitable. The drive to Great Falls to catch his plane was relatively stress-free. We reminisced about our youth and the changes we had seen. He was settled in his belief that he could help the country become united again, and he was willing to make the sacrifices required to make that happen. He was going to leave his ego in Montana and go to work for the entire country. In short, he was feeling optimistic about the future and eager to get started correcting wrongs.

While sitting at the curb near the airport entrance, he gave me last-minute instructions on what he wanted done while he was away. It was the third time I'd been told but I acted like each instruction was a new revelation. When he finished, he slapped me on the back, grabbed his small bag from the back seat, disappeared into the airport lobby, and didn't look back.

Two-Fingers had promised to call me as soon as he arrived at his hotel in Washington, DC, but that call never came. Due to the time difference and his late arrival, I wasn't overly concerned. However, when I hadn't heard from him by noon the next day, I began to worry. I called the Ambassador Hotel, hoping to reach him there. He always stayed at the Ambassador, and he had a reservation there. The problem was, he never checked in, and no one had seen him. That was when an uneasy feeling overwhelmed me.

I called the airline to make sure the flight had arrived, and I was told it arrived on schedule, but they couldn't say whether or not he had gotten off in Washington, DC. They confirmed he had checked in at Great Falls without checking a bag, which made sense because he hadn't taken anything other than his small carry-on bag. After digesting that information, I called airline security at the Washington, DC airport, and they couldn't help me either. Next, I called the Washington, DC Police Department, and they were less than helpful. Finally, in desperation, I called the FBI and reported Two-Fingers missing. After a lengthy discussion with the agent assigned to me, John Dixon, it became clear I needed to get to Washington, DC, as soon as possible. So, we arranged a meeting for the next day.

After making travel arrangements, I weighed the pros and cons of telling Two-Fingers' parents and his sisters that he was missing. I decided against it. That is a decision I regret to this very day. The rationale I used was based on my fear that it would cause panic on the reservation, and I thought it prudent to wait until I had concrete evidence of his whereabouts. Instead of telling the truth, I told everyone concerned that I was needed in Washington, DC, because the settlement of the lawsuit was imminent. It was my version of "fiction is better than reality."

On the redeye flight to Washington, DC, I pieced together all the events that had taken place over the last few months. After doing so, I became even more anxious. Two-Fingers always stayed in contact with me when he traveled, always. Invariably, he would have something for me to do. He never shut down; he was always thinking about tribal business. As Washington, DC, came into view, a feeling of loss and helplessness swept over me. Where is Two-Fingers?

John Dixon had an office in one of those large, white granite buildings the government is so proud of. It was located on the fifth floor, and when the elevator doors opened, I was overwhelmed by the activity swirling around me. Agents were running back and forth, telephones rang incessantly, and the male agents had their ties loosened and hanging haphazardly around their necks. They were fighting hard not to lose ground to the upsurge in criminal activity sweeping the nation. Agent Dixon had suggested meeting there, and I concluded he did so because he feared losing more ground to the onslaught.

John Dixon turned out to be a very intense agent. He'd been on the job for over five years, and looked like a guy who needed a vacation. He was in his early thirties and already had dark rings under his eyes and wrinkles on his forehead. His office was in the middle of the room and looked like a kiosk you'd see at a mall.

When we sat down to talk, I noticed the absence of pictures or any other personal memorabilia. There wasn't a picture of a dog, a cat, or a family member anywhere in sight. However, there was a plaque commemorating his fifth year of service to the cause sitting next to his computer. He seemed to me like a guy stranded on a deserted island without a lifeline. Finally, someone dedicated to national security, Two-Fingers would've liked him. As soon as we were seated, Agent Dixon got down to business. He asked to see the pictures I had brought of Two-Fingers, and as he carefully examined them, he told me he had called the Washington, DC Metro Police Department and informed them that the FBI was taking over the case on jurisdictional grounds. They would work together, but he was in charge. Personally, I really didn't give a damn who was in charge, I wanted Two-Fingers found.

My interview lasted quite a while as I laid out exactly what had happened over the last several days. I told him about dropping Two-Fingers off at the Great Falls airport and then not hearing from him. He held Two-Fingers' photograph in his hand while taking notes. He repeatedly asked, "So, you were the last person to see him?" I kept saying, "I hope I'm not the last person to see him." After finishing his questions, he stood up and stretched for an inordinate length of time. I sat patiently as he popped his knuckles and did deep knee-bends before recommending that I shouldn't leave the country or DC and that I should contact him immediately if I learned anything regarding Two-Fingers' disappearance. What did he think I was going to do, run off to Bermuda or something? Before I left, he said again, "So, you were the last person to see him."

I had also reserved a room at the Ambassador, and that is where I went after my meeting with Agent Dixon. I started asking questions of virtually every employee I encountered and, even though he hadn't checked in, I insisted on being shown to the room he had reserved. The bed was made, and it was clear no one had slept there recently. I spoke with the lady who cleaned rooms, and she confirmed that. Nobody I talked to had seen him, though several remembered him from earlier visits. It became clear he never arrived at the hotel.

After a late lunch, I decided to go to the airport and look around. To be honest, I really wasn't sure what to do. I had read about things like this happening to people, but I never thought in a million years I would be faced with such a nightmare. I spent that evening at the airport asking questions and making a fool of myself. The next morning, after a restless night, I decided to rent a car and visit my folks in Cherry Hill, NJ, the hell with John Dixon.

At that time, my folks were doing pretty well considering their age. They were both in their eighties and lived in their own home. Over the years, Paula and I had flown out to visit them several times. In fact, we flew them out to visit us on a number of occasions, and every time they came to the reservation, they paced around and seemed overly eager to return home. Paula and I asked them to move in with us, and they always came up with an excuse not to. Maybe if we had children, they would've stayed longer, who knows.

As I drove the 150 miles from Washington, DC, to Cherry Hill, I couldn't help thinking about how I was going to tell Paula that her brother was missing. I knew I had to tell her, but I couldn't bear the thought of doing it. It was a Friday, and I decided to give it the weekend before I let her know.

My folks had sold their greenhouse and nursery business years before my visit. They lived in a small house in a nice neighborhood not far from Mom's favorite church. When I entered their home unannounced, they were very happy to see me, and we sat and talked late into the night. Early the next morning, I took Dad for breakfast at his favorite diner to not only feed him, but to seek his advice.

After we were seated, I immediately came clean about why I was in the area. He listened intently, sipping his piping-hot black coffee as I described the events leading up to Two-Fingers' disappearance. He was still as sharp as a tack and seemed both saddened and excited at the same time. He liked reading Sherlock Holmes novels, and now he had a chance to aid in solving a mystery. So, he grilled me hard about every little detail.

Finally, he sat back and said definitively, "Frank Johnson had him killed, no doubt about it. Who else had the motive to do him in?" He leaned forward and sat on the edge of his seat, eagerly awaiting my response. Actually, I thought he might be on to something. Frank was livid with Two-Fingers at their recent meeting, and he had the most to gain if something bad happened to him. I, on the other hand, couldn't wrap my head around the possibility of a sitting United States Senator getting involved in Two-Fingers' disappearance; the implications were mindboggling. True, he had a lot to gain, but he also had a lot to lose, right? Two-Fingers was winning the Senate race in what appeared to be a blowout. Pete Reynolds, the old, worn-out Republican, was so far back in the polling that he thought he was ahead. No, the winner would either be Two-Fingers or Frank, no doubt about it.

My Dad made a convincing case and concluded by asking, "Who else would do it? Two-Fingers didn't have any enemies, did he?" Good questions. I can honestly say he was loved by the entire tribe, and I couldn't think of anyone who thought badly of him, not even Stubby Grant. Of course, there was always the possibility of an accident or amnesia, something not as sinister. Murder? I wasn't convinced. I decided to spend Saturday night there and leave for Washington, DC, the next morning. Before I left, Dad suggested I call Paula as soon as possible and let her know what was going on.

On the drive back to Washington, DC, I decided to take the old man's advice and call her as soon as I got to my room at the Ambassador. As it turned out, I was too late. Paula had already received a call from John Dixon. She was sobbing when I called and was in no mood to talk to me. When she gets mad, she gets mad all over. After a few minutes of her lighting me up, she suddenly hung up, and I found myself staring at the phone, thinking I must be the dumbest son of a bitch in the world. Of course, the FBI would be calling the reservation as part of their investigation. Damn, just my luck, a federal agency actually doing its job on a weekend.

I was lying flat on my back staring at the ceiling when the phone rang. It was Paula. I quickly tried to get a few words out in case she decided to hang up on me again. She alternated between being angry, sad, fearful, and really, really pissed off. She told me to come home; obviously, I wasn't doing any good there. After she got done talking to me, I hung up and called Agent Dixon's office. The phone rang several times before he answered. "Hello, Agent Dixon here." I explained to him that I had to leave immediately and go home, and all he said was, "So, you were the last one to see Two-Fingers alive... let me know when you get home and don't leave the country."

I caught the redeye back to Great Falls, and it was midday when I arrived at tribal headquarters. I shouldn't have been surprised to see the crowd of people formed there, but I was. There was a line of people that stretched from the tribal headquarters lobby all the way out to the parking lot, and the whole place buzzed with activity, chaos reigned supreme.

As I squeezed my way through the front door, I was confronted by what appeared to be the entire tribe yelling, "What did you do with him, White Guy?" The tribe was anxious, and they were striking out at "the last person to see Two-Fingers alive." That was what the headline of the latest edition of the liberal Big Sky Reporter stated in bold, black letters. As I slowly made my way through the lobby, people shook the paper in my face and yelled at me. The power of the mainstream media had struck again.

I eventually made it to my office, where I locked the door behind me. There, spread out on my desk, was another copy of the paper. Someone had taken the time to highlight the entire article. I tried to focus on the article while members of the tribe stared at me and paced back and forth in front of my office windows. Their glares and menacing looks reminded me of my first day of school on the reservation. The only difference was that my best friend was unable to come to my rescue.

My head swirled as I tried to concentrate on the article and the headline that read: "Here Is the Last Person to See Two-Fingers Alive." An unflattering picture of me was prominently displayed, and the story was filled with rumors and conjecture. It kept referring to unnamed sources and an ongoing investigation. Anyone who read it would conclude that I was guilty of first-degree murder. Of course, at the end of the article, they wrapped it up with, "As always, when more information becomes available, we will report it to you in a timely and thorough manner."

After reading the article a second time, I stood up as straight as possible and unlocked the door to face the music. I was temporarily pinned against my office door as tribal members peppered me with question after question. Nobody seemed interested in anything I had to say. They listened, but I could tell by the look in their eyes and their loud voices that they weren't buying it.

Thankfully, the sea of humanity parted as Max, Pam, Cindy Ann, and Paula made their way down the hallway and into my office before shutting the door behind them. Max and Pam looked like they had aged ten years since I last saw them. I could tell they were hurting, but they still comforted me as they listened to my side of the story. Finally, Max picked up the newspaper from my desk and said, "I've read this article several times, and my conclusion is it's a hit piece. If what you say is true about Frank, and I believe it is, they're covering for him. They've protected him for years. Unnamed sources, my ass." We nodded in agreement as he continued, "The liberal press has had their collective noses up Frank's ass for so long, he will never be held accountable because it would make the paper look bad."

"You know, I'm not sure we'll find Two-Fingers unless we hire a private detective," I said. After pondering my suggestion for a few seconds, Cindy Ann, Paula, and Max agreed. Pam continued to have a hard time believing the government couldn't be trusted, but she did agree that something had to be done. "Two-Fingers' disappearance will be a big story for a day or two before it's relegated to the back pages. I'm sure the powers that be aren't going to break their backs finding out what happened to him." I listened quietly as they expressed their opinions and ideas, and I agreed when Cindy Ann said, "I think you're right about getting a private detective. Someone will have to go back to Washington, DC, and that someone is going to be me. Besides, I need to find out where we are on our lawsuit, and while I'm there, I'll hire a private detective." Paula looked directly at me and said, "You need to stay here and take care of tribal business. There are a lot of angry Blackfeet, and you need to stay and answer their questions. There are so many who aren't thinking rationally right now."

Early the next morning, I went to the Club Cafe for breakfast, and as soon as I entered, I was immediately bombarded with questions and insinuations. The place was packed, and everyone seemed on edge and extremely grumpy. I remember standing in the middle of the one-room cafe answering questions to the best of my ability when Johnny Skunk Cap pushed his way through the crowd and yelled, "What did you do to him, White Guy?" That was the moment all hell broke loose in the Club. Johnny and I went at it like we were teenagers. I finally got the better of him and was beating the hell out of him when I was dragged off his prone, motionless body. I stood over him as I glared at every individual in the room before turning and walking out the door.

Several weeks passed before any of us heard from Cindy Ann. I knew her well, and I knew she would only call if she had something important to say. I've always found that to be an admirable trait. She was a very unique politician. She didn't run off at the mouth spouting nonsense like so many of them do. Her nonexistent communication was the least of my concerns. I was overwhelmed with questions and demands regarding Two-Fingers from every member, and nonmember, of the tribe who lived on the reservation. They were anxious, and they would stop me on the street, come to my office, or follow me home and wait outside my door for answers. They all wanted to know what was going on in Washington, DC. Their anxiety increased with each passing day, and so did their calls for action.

Of course, the Big Sky Reporter provided no help. To the contrary, every edition of the liberal rag carried stories aimed at damaging Two-Fingers' reputation. They had the unmitigated gall to suggest that Two-Fingers had skipped the country due to his alleged embezzlement of tribal funds, and one article even claimed he was drunk in Moscow, Russia, doing drugs with hookers. However, the most outrageous and egregious lie they passed off as news claimed he was in Moscow colluding with the Russians to sell the reservation so they could set up a military base here. They seldom wrote a story that didn't mention Russia.

No story was too preposterous for their moronic liberal followers; they ate them up with spoons. On the other hand, everyone who knew him recognized it as bullshit. The level of dishonesty and corruption took a while to be fully known. How can there be freedom of the press when the media is enslaved to one specific party? This question deserves an answer. Of course, the attacks and constant propaganda ended after the elections were over. With Two-Fingers effectively taken out of the race, Frank won a surprisingly close race against the old, worn-out Republican candidate, Pete Reynolds.

When Two-Fingers disappeared, I wasn't convinced that sinister elements within our government and press were to blame. Two-Fingers always had a more skeptical view of the ruling elites and their propaganda machine. He had an unwavering belief that rich folks, unelected bureaucrats, and corrupt politicians had sold us out years ago. He, as I have mentioned on numerous occasions, believed in our Bill of Rights and our constitutional republic. He told me more than once that elites violated the Constitution and the criminals hide behind it. What good are laws if they are not enforced equally? What good are elections when the will of the people is disregarded? We the People are rapidly becoming a historical footnote.

Initially, I wasn't able to wrap my head around how evil people would have to be to destroy our individual rights and freedoms in an attempt to destroy the United States of America. What could they gain by destroying all things holy? I've had plenty of time to think about this, and now I wonder if my initial reluctance was based on my fear of the truth. What if it's true and not a conspiracy theory?

At the risk of overstating the obvious, Two-Fingers is much wiser than I am. He spent his life on the reservation and had a front-row seat to the negative impact and devastating effects of our federal government's failed Indian policy; he lived beneath it. It's a policy he fought against his entire adult life. It's a corrupt and flawed system created by the government. Two-Fingers has always believed that federally controlled programs are an abomination, and when you believe in something that strongly, you're going to make enemies. Here's a reality check for all of us: there are a lot of people who profit from other people's dependencies. Dependencies make people weak and easy to control. Drug dependency, alcohol dependency, and government dependency limit our freedoms. We the People become weak and spineless. We blame other people for our frailties and failures. We become prey. Promoting dependency is an integral part of an evil plan, and the only way we get our freedom back is to shake off the chains of the dependencies that choke the life out of us.

Two-Fingers took personal responsibility for his actions, and he despised anyone who wouldn't, especially politicians. Nobody takes responsibility at the highest level of our federal government, nobody. The cowards all blame the other guy. Two-Fingers has too much honor and dignity to blame anyone for his failures. It bears repeating: when the politicians go to the slum areas that they helped create, they shed a few tears, make a speech, have a photo op, and then get out of the area as fast as possible. Once they are back in the safety of their womb, Washington, DC, they throw more money at the problem they created, and nobody in the slums sees them again until the next election cycle. Two-Fingers knew that the chains of dependency had to be broken on the reservation and across all of America.

Two-Fingers also knew with absolute certainty that it wasn't easy for his people to break the chains of alcoholism, drug abuse, domestic violence, and poverty, abject poverty that decimates a person's pride and self-worth. It wasn't easy on the reservation, and it sure as hell wasn't going to be easy for the rest of America. Two-Fingers knew that every man, woman, and child needed a purpose in life. The reliance on an all powerful federal government blinds those among us who are dependent. Two-Fingers preached this for years and was making significant progress right up until the day he disappeared.

Personally, I didn't handle my anguish and pain over his disappearance very well. I cut back on doing tribal business and practically banished myself from the tribe. I made this decision shortly after the incident at the Club Cafe involving Johnny Skunk Cap. That incident wasn't the only event that led me to that decision; it was the culmination of several things. I needed to step back from the day-to-day chaos that was prevalent and focus on finding Two-Fingers, a task far more monumental than even I could imagine. At the very peak of his powers, he was taken from us. I tried to figure out why. The only thing Two-Fingers was guilty of was his insistence on liberty and freedom for all. The government's overreach and the nectar of dependence were his enemies.

His efforts endeared him to his people, and they love him for it. In the olden days, Blackfeet women would maim themselves when one of their loved ones was killed. They would cut off their fingers, disfigure themselves in the most grotesque ways, or literally slash their wrists and wail their lives away. During his absence, I was surrounded by endless wailing and moaning.

Chapter 24
The Chains are Broken

Any skepticism I may have initially had regarding the evils of the rich, ruling class completely vanished after I received a call from Cindy Ann. I was seated in my office with little more than my thoughts to keep me company when my phone rang. She didn't waste time with pleasantries and got right down to business. My initial concern that Washington, DC, would turn her into a babbling, incoherent politician was unwarranted; I guess she hadn't been there long enough to learn how to waste her mind and time.

She informed me that she had received a call from FBI Agent John Dixon, and Two-Fingers had been found. According to Agent Dixon, a staff member at the Ambassador Hotel, found him lying face down in the alley behind the hotel. He was naked in a pool of blood. How he got there was anyone's guess. In any event, after being notified, Agent Dixon dropped everything he was doing and hurried to the Ambassador, where he found Two-Fingers in a comatose state. He wasn't dead, but he was a long way from being alive. Two-Fingers was taken to a local hospital where Agent Dixon and Cindy Ann agreed to meet. After consulting with the medical professionals and Agent Dixon, she decided Two-Fingers needed to get the hell out of Washington, DC. as soon as he was stable enough to travel. She didn't trust anyone, but she did allow Agent Dixon to make travel arrangements for her and Two-Fingers to fly back to the reservation. Cindy Ann relayed this information as soon as she had all the details and ended the conversation as abruptly as she had started it. She asked that I contact the rest of the family and let them know what was going on, which I did the second she hung up.

Agent Dixon was able to secure passage on a large military cargo plane heading to Malmstrom Air Force Base in Great Falls, no frills, but it beat walking. I arranged for a tribal ambulance and one of our best nurses, Rosa Many Guns, to help transport him home. Billy and Levi Bird Rattler insisted on going with me. The four of us sat near the runway anxiously awaiting their arrival. After the plane landed, we went to work getting Two-Fingers comfortably and safely secured for the ride back to Browning. Cindy Ann and Rosa rode in the back of the ambulance with Two-Fingers, while Billy, Levi, and I rode in the front with the driver.

Our conversation on the ride back to the reservation centered on how bad Two-Fingers looked and what we needed to do to help him. Billy prayed and chanted while Levi and I said our personal prayers. Two-Fingers looked and acted like death warmed over. When the praying and chanting stopped, and silence filled the cab of the ambulance, Levi laid out a plan to help him. Billy and I listened as Levi described his willingness to sacrifice his time and money to help the man who had helped him get his life back. No sacrifice was too great, and no effort would be spared.

It seemed like the entire staff of the Blackfeet Health Center was waiting for Two-Fingers's arrival. The temperature outside was a balmy ten degrees, and most of the staff were coatless and seemingly unconcerned about the unrelenting wind. They stood patiently as we approached and then went into a controlled frenzy when we parked in the emergency room parking area. The rear door of the ambulance was flung open, and Rosa and Cindy Ann were helped out, and every move after that was focused on getting Two-Fingers into the main examination area.

Paula, Max and Pam were there and insisted on going in with him. In fact, we all wanted to go in, but we were summarily rejected. They, along with Levi, Billy, Cindy Ann, and I, waited patiently in the waiting room while the professionals did their work. Over the years, we spent more time in that waiting room than any of us wanted to, but we waited. It was in that room, after hours of pacing and handholding, that we learned the extent of the injuries Two-Fingers had suffered and their severity. He was on the verge of starvation, badly dehydrated, and suffering from drug withdrawals. The attending physician stated that Two-Fingers was covered with needle marks from head to toe and drifting in and out of consciousness. He advised that it would be several days, perhaps weeks, before Two-Fingers could be released. He eventually let us go into his room, where a large number of staff continued to attend to his needs. IVs and monitors filled the space, and we watched from a distance. That was when Pam fainted and had to be given a sedative to calm her hysteria. All of us could've used sedatives, but I'm not sure they would've had enough to satisfy the need.

Over the days that followed, Levi, Billy, and I formulated and solidified a plan of action. Billy rightfully surmised that no modern medicine treatment would cure the damage done to Two-Finger's psyche. His mental health could only be restored with spiritual treatment, and that was Billy's area of expertise. The plan we developed was simple in design but proved complex in application. It required twenty-four-hour, around-the-clock care, and the three of us were dedicated to making that a reality. Two-Fingers was eventually released into our care, and no one objected.

While Two-Fingers lay in the hospital recovering from his physical injuries, Billy and Levi re-erected the teepee they had used for Levi's recovery. In addition, the sweat lodge was prepared for a long winter of sweating and healing. Levi had long since moved his family away from Birch Creek into a modern log cabin built on high, solid ground where he and his wife raised their family. At the time of Two-Fingers' disappearance, Levi was well established as the premier bucking stock outfitter in Montana. His success hadn't gone to his head, and he took it upon himself to help Billy build the type of Blackfeet structure used in the olden days. Billy went full-on native in his design and treatment methods. They worked through January, one of the coldest months on record. They refused help and insisted it be done the Indian way. Billy, in particular, was steadfast and unwavering when I suggested warmer accommodations.

When Two-Fingers was strong enough to travel, I helped Levi and Billy transport him to their makeshift care unit out on Birch Creek, where the water was frozen solid, where the sweat lodge was cold, and the teepee shook from the wind. That was where Two-Fingers was taken and where he stayed until late spring. Billy would not allow visitors, phones, or other modern distractions, and he kept a close eye on Levi and me while we coexisted that winter. It proved to be the right thing to do for Two-Fingers, but it also proved beneficial for the three of us. Two-Fingers's mind had been noticeably damaged, and the untreated mental health issues the three of us suffered from may have been more subtle, but they existed nonetheless. I have never met anyone who has escaped life unscathed, and I recommend periodic cleansing of the mind and soul. We all need to be rebooted from time to time.

So, we helped Two-Fingers reboot, and he eventually recovered, but he was a changed man. It was his quiet period when he seldom spoke. He was more pensive than usual, and he fought to survive, but survive he did. It was only after he was completely free of addictions and physically fit that he started talking about what had happened to him while he was in DC. Many details of his disappearance were lost to him.

He did remember landing in DC and being picked up in front of the airport by a driver holding a sign with his name on it. He didn't give it much thought at the time, chalking it up as one of the perks allowed to Senate candidates. He was helped into the back of a waiting limousine and offered a bottle of water. He drank it down to quench his thirst, and the next thing he remembered was waking up in a dimly lit room attached to intravenous tubes. He was in a semi-conscious state the entire time he was in that room. People came and went, tending to him as if he were hospitalized. The figures hovering over him were mere shadows who seldom spoke. On the rare occasion he heard a voice clearly, he was certain it was one he knew, but he always drifted off into a deep sleep before making a definitive connection. Later, he wasn't sure how much later, he revisited that moment in his mind and swore the voice belonged to Trevor Kanowski, the bureaucrat from hell who had been tarred, feathered, and run out of Browning.

Rumors regarding Trevor had circulated like wildfire after his unceremonious and humiliating departure. One of the rumors was confirmed when it was verified that he had, in fact, landed on his feet back in DC. He was appointed head of one of the many alphabet health agencies that control our existence. Over time, Two-Fingers convinced himself that Trevor was involved in his disappearance and the subsequent smear campaign waged against him. It wasn't a stretch to think that Frank was involved as well. Who would gain the most if Two-Fingers lost the election and was destroyed politically? The four of us discussed this event extensively and collectively came to the conclusion that nothing could be done about the past, but there was a lot that could be done in the future.

Two-Fingers had always been wary of the all-powerful federal government that had wreaked havoc on his people and on the citizens of America. The debt crisis continued to escalate and grew exponentially despite the best efforts of the newly elected Republican president. He was interfered with from the outset of his administration and soon found himself embroiled in one phony controversy after another. Bureaucrats resisted his best efforts, and the nation suffered. After the elections, the fiscally irresponsible and corrupt politicians who benefited from this calamity were still in charge, or so they thought. Unelected, unaccountable bureaucrats love the status quo, and We the People suffer from their treasonous behavior. The national debt soon reached 25 trillion dollars, and Two-Fingers' resolve to eradicate the federal government from the reservation intensified. After his kidnapping, every move he made was aimed at preserving tribal solvency and regaining its sovereignty.

When he had fully recovered, Billy went back to teaching, Levi returned to being a rodeo promoter full-time, and I resumed my duties as the tribal attorney. Two-Fingers no longer needed to campaign to get elected, so he and I focused solely on tribal business. The entire tribe was solidly behind him and grateful to him, and the women no longer wailed and maimed themselves. Their tears remained, but they were tears of joy.

2017 proved to be another pivotal year for the tribe under Two-Fingers' leadership. He went after the federal government with renewed vigor, and before long, his negotiating skills were used to obtain a three-billion-dollar settlement from the Department of the Interior. They capitulated in an effort to make the issue of their malfeasance go away. The government was sued by a number of people and organizations for past sins, and the new administration wanted a clean slate so they could focus on the major issues of the day, issues that were created by the incompetence of previous administrations and the bureaucrats who ran the government.

To add insult to injury, the new Republican president was swept up in one phony investigation after another. Everything he tried to do was opposed, to the point of him being impeached on trumped-up charges with no merit. The bureaucracy was entrenched, and they were going to teach him who was boss, national security and prosperity be damned. Treachery was the order of the day, and Two-Fingers took advantage of their division and weaknesses by implementing policies that renewed and strengthened the sovereignty of the tribe.

The chains of dependency were broken and replaced with liberty and freedom for all. The federal government had abandoned those principles, as well as the constitutional republic for which it once stood. Two-Fingers embraced these principles and every word of the Constitution, to secure our future. The Constitution is bulletproof if it isn't violated. It gave the tribe a track to run on, and run they did. The remaining properties that weren't under the ownership and control of the tribe soon were.

The government education system was replaced and made to function for the benefit of the community. The Blackfeet Health Center was expanded, and the best physicians in the country were recruited to come to the reservation, where they could make a difference and not be under the thumb of totalitarian hospital administrators with their endless red tape, the greatest threat to our health. Two-Fingers sought freedom from DC, the Babylon on the Potomac. The life-altering, blood-sucking, and dehumanizing chains of government control were finally broken, and the tribe rejoiced.

It soon became clear to everyone that less government is better for citizens. The tribe quickly became self-sufficient and self-reliant. Commodities were phased out and replaced with bison hunts, not slaughters. Only the bison necessary to feed the tribe were taken, and the herd and the tribe grew strong. So too did the wild horse herd: Levi made sure of that. Any new lodging built by the tribe conformed to the needs of a Blackfeet, not to the needs of a city-dwelling aristocrat. Two-Fingers commissioned a large fence to be built along the boundaries of the reservation, ostensibly for keeping the bison in. The real reason was that he wanted to keep the stupid out. He knew the benefits of nationalism and pursued it for physical health and sanity reasons. One hundred fifty years of failed Indian policy and forced integration were proof that coexisting is no existence at all. Both parties to the arrangement suffer, and few prosper.

Indian leaders from across America consulted with Two-Fingers because their tribes suffered too. The same chains bound them and tied them to the government, and they were fed up with the arrangement, especially when it became undeniably apparent that the government was bankrupt and the end of commodities was close at hand. Not all leaders wanted change, because in every tribe, there are people like Stubby Grant, narrow-minded, greedy, scared, and worthless people. The tribes that accepted the new challenges and the new opportunities prospered, and the ones that continued to be controlled suffered. Survival of the fittest is nature's way, and it's the Indian way.

It was a glorious, uplifting time for tribes and for hard-working citizens of America in general. The new Republican administration provided four years of peace and prosperity. No new wars, a new car in the driveway, and a chicken in every lunchbox. That's when something really strange happened. It was almost like mass hypnosis. The popularity of the new president and his policies triggered something in the power elite that influenced them to do the unthinkable. They conspired to distort, defame, and attack the greatness achieved by the new administration with propaganda that would have made Joseph Goebbels blush. Up became down, down was suddenly up, right was wrong, and wrong was right. The entire world was turned upside down, and the brainwashing was nonstop. Elite-owned mainstream media, elite-owned social media, and elite-owned newspapers devoted their time and energy to destroying the president's agenda and, as a consequence, America itself. There was no price too high to pay to protect the status quo. You don't get to be an elite if you aren't able to control things, and they had lost control, and they were angry. Cut-off-your-nose-to-spite-your-face angry. As the 2020 presidential election approached, their efforts to destroy intensified.

Chapter 25
Finally, a Solution

Out of the blue and suddenly, as is the case with blights, America became blighted when a Democrat president was elected. Evil won out over good, and their ill-gotten gains blighted the entire country. No good comes from evil acts and deception. We the People suffered through one disaster after another. Foreign and domestic policies were sabotaged against our best interests and We the People suffered. The presidential election of 2020 blighted our great nation.

That wasn't the case on the reservation. Two-Fingers' honesty and integrity helped shield us from the ravages of the new Democrat administration's policies. Before long, rumors began to spread across the nation of tribes that their new found prosperity was in jeopardy. The elite class needed money to fund their philosophies, and America was broke. Tribes that had followed Two-Fingers' lead were relatively wealthy. At least they were self-sufficient and debt-free. They had utilized their natural resources, and they hadn't destroyed their lands with windmills and solar panels. The Blackfeet had built new dams that they could trust to prevent flooding and provide hydroelectric power that fueled our development. We were energy-independent and we protected the environment and the animals that lived on the reservation. Tribal sovereignty and prosperity didn't sit well with the elites and their efforts to regain control over us came in the form of a newly discovered plague, an epidemic so monumentally devastating that it threatened the existence of human life.

It was mid-June of 2021 when Two-Fingers called an emergency meeting of the tribal council. Stogie Man and Liquid Louie had been tasked with finding out all they could about the plague and the implications it might have on the tribe. Once they had completed their studies, the meeting was called.

"We seem to be in the midst of a global plague, and I am getting a lot of heat from the new administration regarding what we must do to save the nation and ourselves." Two-Fingers was seated at the head of the conference table when he made his announcement. "They view my resistance to shutting down our lives as selfish and self-serving. I am trying to wrap my head around their explanation as to what has caused this plague, and it doesn't make sense to me. I am being told a new virus suddenly appeared, and civilization itself is in danger of becoming extinct. Since Stogie Man and Liquid Louie are experts in Earth science, I have asked them to sit in on this meeting and answer our questions to the best of their ability."

Two-Fingers then opened the floor to questions, and I asked, "Where did this virus come from, Stogie Man?"

"They say it came from a bat," Stogie Man replied with the utmost sincerity.

"A bat? What kind of bat, and where did the bat come from?" They seemed to be logical questions, so I asked.

"Well, health officials are saying it came from a bat from a cave in China." Stogie Man busied himself with a stack of papers that lay in front of him while I pondered my next question.

"How did the bat get the virus? Was the virus buried deep inside the cave, and the bat found it?" I'm not a health expert like so many people in government, but it seemed to be reasonable questions to ask.

"Well, exact details continue to be sketchy, but the health professionals are absolutely certain that we need to shut down the reservation and start wearing masks."

That's when Stubby Grant perked up and asked, "Masks? Why do I need to wear a mask?"

He's so ugly I thought he should've been wearing a mask since birth, but I bit my tongue and didn't comment. However, Liquid Louie felt compelled to answer his question. "The health professionals are saying the masks will help prevent the spread of the virus. They also recommend that we stand six feet away from each other."

Two-Fingers could no longer contain himself, so he asked, "Six feet? Why not five feet or seven feet?"

Liquid Louie had the look of a guy astounded that anyone would challenge such a profound scientific determination, but instead of challenging Two-Fingers, he added, "They are also recommending we place plexiglass barriers around us when we eat."

That was when Two-Fingers adjourned the meeting.

Two-Fingers had spent a lot of time by himself after his abduction. As I stated earlier, he became pensive, thoughtful, and determined in a way I had never witnessed before. He continued his commitment to sovereignty, and that commitment ruled his every action. The process of unwinding the horrific Indian policy, the real plague that haunted the tribe, was daunting, and it took all of his skills to make it happen. From the time of his abduction until the summer of 2021, he was consumed with his plan, and when it came time to execute it, he was prepared. One plague at a time.

Over that period, Two-Fingers seldom came into the Club Cafe to socialize, so I was surprised to see him there one day with a copy of the Big Sky Reporter spread out in front of him.

"It says here that inflation is skyrocketing and the national debt is exploding. Frank is quoted as saying the gang he represents needs trillions of taxpayers' dollars to solve the problem."

I sat down across from him and prepared myself for the inevitable sermon. "Frank has always thought spending and printing money we don't have will solve the problems we face as a nation."

Two-Fingers eventually put the paper down and turned his attention to me.

"White Guy, the Centers for Disease Control (CDC) contacted me bright and early this morning, and they have requested a meeting with me sometime this week. I wanted to consult with you before setting anything up. Since you are addicted to fry bread, I figured I'd have you testify as an expert on addiction." Two-Fingers took a sip of coffee from a green, fluorescent coffee cup that was popular back in 1960. "You need to eat up. I want you to have a full stomach before I tell you who they are planning to send." Two-Fingers smiled as he placed the coffee cup on a napkin. The Bird family frowned on rings on their tables.

"I can order later. Who are they sending, and why?" I figured it wasn't to see me because no health professional in the world could save me from my fry bread addiction.

"It's regarding the plague that's sweeping the world. That's not the news, the news is they are sending the new head of the CDC to see us. That person is an old friend of ours, Trevor Kanowski." Two-Fingers seemed more interested in my reaction than in the essence of Trevor's visit.

"Trevor Kanowski? You mean to tell me that the bureaucrat from hell, the nickel living in a dime world, the violator of all things sacred, is the new head of the CDC?" My reaction seemed to satisfy him, so he advanced the conversation by saying, "That's right, another example of failing upwards. Merit is seldom considered in our elitist government. You need to be a failure or someone with pronouns to get a promotion in their world. As long as you extol the party line, you're getting promoted. Another reason we are 30 trillion in debt and counting. Remember what I've always said, the best way to destroy democracy is to bankrupt it, and we are morally and financially bankrupt. Luckily, we've insulated ourselves from the stupid the best we can. I've been working on a plan that will benefit the tribe, and Kanowski will unwittingly help us achieve that. Whatever he tells us, we will do the exact opposite." Two-Fingers seemed pleased with himself and I trusted his instincts. You don't get to be Chairman if you don't have good instincts.

Trevor Kanowski's arrival on the reservation occurred in the middle of the night, just like his expulsion. He was trying to hide from his obscurity. He snuck into town in a large motorhome that had the name of the agency he represented emblazoned on the side: "Centers for Disease Control." Below that, in big black letters, were the words, "WE SPARE NO COST IN PRESERVING YOUR HEALTH." Evidently, that was true because they flew that humongous motorhome to Montana, and it must have cost a fortune to do that. Kanowski appeared to have gained a tremendous amount of weight when he stumbled out of the monstrosity at 10:30 a.m. for our 10:00 a.m. meeting. Luckily for all concerned, his team had parked it in the middle of our tribal parking lot, and they only had a short distance to walk. Otherwise, he might not have shown up until noon.

Two-Fingers had arranged to meet in our conference room, and he had invited the entire council, Stogie Man, Liquid Louie, me, and a recent hire, Dr. Alfred Martinez. Dr. Martinez was a renowned oncologist, Harvard-educated and had been practicing medicine for over twenty years. He loved the freedom he had found on the reservation. He took a large pay cut to be free.

We sat patiently waiting for Kanowski to show up, and when he did, there was just enough room for him, so his ten-member entourage waited in the hall. Most of us knew the parasite, but Two-Fingers still took the time to introduce Kanowski to Dr. Martinez who, after shaking his hand, reached across the table, grabbed one of the disinfectant bottles scattered around the conference room and the rest of society, and took his time rubbing the soap over his hands, arms, and neck before taking his seat. The disinfectant had been sent to us by the CDC, which spared no cost in preserving our health.

Once everyone was seated, Two-Fingers immediately turned the meeting over to Kanowski. The nickel cleared his throat, sprayed some kind of green disinfectant into his mouth, and proceeded to tell us the purpose of his visit. "You and your tribe are isolated from the rest of society, and you may or may not know what is happening in the rest of the world. There is a serious, life-threatening plague sweeping across the globe. The CDC is working diligently to find a 'solution' to this massive problem, and we have established guidelines for you to follow to help mitigate the damage until we find an effective cure. We are very close to doing that, and we are testing the 'solution' on mice. Once it's ready, we will begin to distribute the 'solution' to the citizens of the world. In the meantime, it's imperative, for your safety, and for the safety of the citizens of the world, that you conform to these guidelines. These are not suggestions; these are federal mandates. My agency, as well as the Occupational Safety and Health Organization, have been granted the authority by the current administration to enforce these mandates."

With that, he handed out a very nice, colorful brochure with a person on the cover wearing a mask. Despite his profound belief that we lived in the dark ages, most of us knew more about the issue than the nickel. We stayed quiet when Dr. Martinez asked questions.

"Is it the CDC's position that we must wear masks? If so, are you aware that your predecessor wrote extensively about the inadequacies of masks used during the Spanish Flu epidemic that occurred last century? The masks your agencies are handing out like candy do not work. Yet they are scattered around our sacred land and filling our landfills at an alarming rate. They don't biodegrade, and they don't stop the spread of the thing you're trying to stop. People don't wear them properly, and they don't change them out in a timely fashion, and they are getting sick from the germs that attach themselves to these cloth masks. Knowledgeable doctors know what kinds of masks to use, and we know how to use them. The average citizen is doing more harm than good every time they use one of your masks. They simply do not work."

The nickel took a few moments before he responded, "In this administration, they work. Any further questions?"

"On page 9 it states that we should maintain a distance of six feet from one another at all times. What is the scientific reason for that?" Stogie Man and Liquid Louie were leaning forward, ready to pounce, but they remained quiet.

"The CDC is not to be questioned. If we say it's so, it's so. Any other questions?"

After hearing his curt response, Liquid Louie could no longer contain himself. "I was down in Great Falls last week when I went to K-Mart to get some Vaseline, and I noticed there were footprints painted on the floor to help guide people around the place. I followed the footprints until they stopped, and I was uncertain what to do next. It sounds like you people at the CDC are experiencing the same type of problem." I never really appreciated Liquid Louie until that moment.

Stogie Man also seemed emboldened when he asked, "Yeah, I was over in Missoula a while back, and I went into Applebee's for some lunch, and every table was enclosed in plexiglass, and the waitress was wearing a helmet. I decided on getting an order to go."

The nickel stood in front of us, looking exactly like he did the night he was tarred and feathered.

Dr. Martinez sat patiently listening before he asked, "When is your 'solution' going to be ready, and has it been tested on humans?"

"Once the 'solution' is authorized to be injected into the public, we don't have time to test it on humans," Kanowski stated with as much gusto as he could muster. Bureaucrats are always in a hurry to implement the 'solution.'

I sensed Cindy Ann had enough of the nickel's bullshit when she asked, "We already know most of what you've told us. What I want to know is why you and your fancy, taxpayer-financed motorhome are polluting our reservation?" Trevor was used to talking down to women, so Cindy Ann's assertiveness seemed to catch him off guard. It took him a while before he finally sputtered out the words he came to say: "I am traveling in that motorhome to the seven reservations in Montana to spread the word that you will be expected to comply with the mandates when issued. I came here first because Two-Fingers is very influential with the other tribes, and they will follow his lead. I am here to ask him, and all of you, for your help in preserving the health of your communities and the health of the nation. As you are well aware, over the last few years, we have lost a great deal of control over you and the other tribes. Your sovereignty has been strengthened, and our control over you has diminished substantially. I am here to extend an olive branch to you and ask for your help."

The nickel's capitulation and weakness were like blood in the water, and the shark reacted decisively. It suddenly became a feeding frenzy. "You came here to seek my help and the help of our tribe? You came late to the meeting, and you want to extend an olive branch? You disrespect us and demean us, and you want our help? I think being tarred and feathered and run out of town enlarged your balls but completely destroyed whatever brain power you had left. You are right about one thing. You have no control over us because we don't take your money anymore. We build and pay for our own lodging. We staff our schools, our hospitals, our fire department, and our police department. The only thing the federal government ever gave us was dependency, and we are no longer dependent. We have money, and more is coming in every day. Your government is broke, and ours is thriving. You have abandoned the Constitution, and we have embraced it. We don't need you, you need us. You mandate us at your own peril."

Like they always say, sunshine is the greatest disinfectant, and the sun shone brightly that day. The only cloud in the sky appeared when Stubby Grant blurted out, "You mean to tell me you are giving up our commodity cheese?" Over the years, I would ask Two-Fingers why he kept Stubby around, and he eventually told me that he kept him as a visual aid on what not to be.

The nickel got the hint to leave when Two-Fingers told him, "Get in your phony-ass motor home and get off our reservation. It's a long way between reservations, so you'd better use your 'We Are Broke' credit card to fill up as soon as possible. Don't do it here, we already spend too much time going after deadbeats."

The nickel's reception at the other reservations proved to be equally painful for him. Two-Fingers had contacted the chairmen of each tribe well in advance of Trevor's visit to Browning. They were in agreement regarding the chains of government control, enough was enough. They had fought long and hard for their freedom and sovereignty and had no intention of backsliding. Two-Fingers' actions proved to be a model of governance that they all embraced. Finally, the tribes in Montana were united, working together to strengthen their rights. Two-Fingers convinced them that the power the government had over them was the power of its money, and that dependence came at a heavy price, a price they were no longer willing to pay. It also helped that the federal government was bankrupt and running on fumes, printing money just to stay afloat.

When the mandates were enacted, they were sold to the public as the "Safe and Effective Solution Act of 2021." It proved to be a designation as fraudulent as the "Inflation Reduction Act of 2021." That act had the direct opposite effect of reducing inflation.

Unchecked spending and money printing caused inflation to skyrocket, and everyone became poorer. Everyone but the elites, that is. In the olden days, American Indians were made fun of for eating dogs in order to survive. Americans were now faced with that real possibility, and suddenly they no longer saw the humor in it.

No good comes from ill-gotten gains, whether it's an individual or a government behind the deception. Eventually, a price will be extracted from the perpetrator. Our government's ill-gotten gains cost the perpetrators a great deal, but the brunt of the damage was borne by the citizens. The nation at large was blighted. Natural disasters reached unprecedented levels. Debt and deprivation wrecked family life. People stopped having children because they feared they couldn't support them. A nation that turned away from God was now grasping at straws. The blight continued with no end in sight.

The 'solution' delivered the predictable results. It was neither safe nor effective, and the carnage created by its implementation threatened the existence of everyone on earth. The 'solution' was never tested on humans before it was released to the public. The unsuspecting citizens were the guinea pigs, and they suffered the consequences of the 'solution.'

I lost both of my parents the day after they received the 'solution.' They were elderly, and they had been convinced that, because of their age, they needed to get the 'solution.' That was the case for untold millions across the globe. The 'solution' was worse than the disease. News of the debacle was sporadic and inconsistent. Two-Fingers consulted with other tribes across America who were witnessing unprecedented death to get the real truth. What he found was shocking: American Indians weren't dying off; it was the white and brown people who had taken the 'solution' who were dying off. Members of the tribes who had been coerced into taking the 'solution' were surprisingly unaffected. There wasn't a single reported American

Indian death related to the 'solution' or the disease. Two-Fingers was puzzled as to why that was, so he called another meeting with Stogie Man, Liquid Louie, Doctor Martinez, Cindy Ann, and me. It was a very serious meeting and there was no need to have Stubby Grant and the other members of the council in the room until decisions were formalized.

Doctor Martinez started the meeting with a prayer before launching into his findings regarding the disease and the 'solution.' He had tested every tribal member, and none of them was infected with the disease. Even more surprising, several had taken the 'solution' against his advice, and they weren't showing any adverse effects from taking it. He had consulted with doctors across the nation whose patients were non-Indian, and they all reported the same thing: the 'solution' was killing or severely injuring people, but it was limited to non-Indians. His recommendation at that meeting was not to take the 'solution' and to make that the policy for the entire tribe.

Two-Fingers listened intently to everything he said before speaking. "Are you saying that somehow American Indians are immune to the effects of the 'solution' or the disease? How can that be? Is it possible that, after all the years of speculating, our DNA is uniquely different from other races? American Indians have been told for over a century that we can't handle alcohol because we are wired differently and that's a historical fact. American Indians have a propensity to alcoholism because we have something in our blood that is different from other humans. Maybe there is a difference in our DNA?" His last question seemed to be more rhetorical than the others, and it was fitting.

Nobody had any definitive, concrete answers to the problem, and everyone seemed to be grasping at straws. The only certainty we knew was the fact that the people who were still alive were striking out at the authorities. They got vocal, and the authorities took draconian measures to silence them. Freedom of speech, freedom of expression, freedom to re-dress government, and virtually every other freedom were taken from them. In America at large, the Constitution was shredded when the mandates were enacted. In addition to the aforementioned freedoms being taken, people were being fired for not taking the 'solution.' The military was decimated because many of our finest warriors refused to take the untested 'solution.' They were fired, and the military suffered.

Social unrest was the order of the day, and concentration camps were built to house noncompliant citizens. Warrantless searches and seizures were used against the people under the guise of national security. People were ordered to get the 'solution' and to stay in their homes. Old folks in nursing homes were not allowed to have visitors. Children were jabbed, masked, and denied entry into schools. Society was collapsing outside the reservation but we remained strong and vigilant. So too were the other tribes. They seemed to be blessed and unaffected as the blight raged on. The 'solution' proved to be the final solution for far too many non-Indians, and the death toll mounted.

Two-Fingers and I always seemed to do our best thinking at the Club Cafe; it must have been the day-old coffee that we consumed by the bucket. That was where we found ourselves the morning after Doctor Martinez's report. Two-Fingers started the conversation off by saying, "I find it rather ironic that the rest of society is being treated like our ancestors were when they threw them onto reservations and isolated them. Today, we are freer than we have ever been, and the rest of the nation is on their very own reservations, chained to mandates. I wonder if they are getting commodity cheese?"

After giving the topic as much thought as I could muster, I responded, "I don't think so. I've heard they have killed their cows because they farted, and Trevor won't let them milk the sheep, that's his job." I was unable to get the image of Trevor and Mary out of my mind.

After Two-Fingers stopped laughing, he said, "It's interesting that Doctor Martinez believes there is something in our blood that makes us immune to this plague and the 'solution'. He's the expert, so I'll take his word on it. It's gotten me to thinking though, aren't you glad I made you my blood brother? If I hadn't poured my blood into you, you would've been in the same boat as the other white people."

Two-Fingers seemed overly pleased with himself, so I had to interject, "True enough, but the price I've paid for knowing you is unjust compensation. Since you brought up the blood issue, don't you think we should help out by donating blood? What if American Indians got together and donated their blood? Think of the lives that can be saved."

Two-Fingers sipped his coffee as he stared out the window and watched a large group of Blackfeet gather in the parking lot directly across from the Club Cafe to watch as the very large, tall, red, white, and blue stucco teepee with the fake totem poles was demolished. Over the years, it had been rebranded several times. The original enterprise was the Standard Oil gas station. Its last rebranding was as an espresso stand. It had also been a beauty salon that specialized in braids. A video rental outlet until eight-track tapes became obsolete. It had served as a smoke shop until it mysteriously caught on fire. It was always on the cutting edge of the ever-changing demands of modern society. The current demands of the Blackfeet centered on it being demolished, and demolished it was. If only the allure of trinkets could be taken care of that easily. The crowd cheered wildly as it crumbled to the ground, ashes to ashes, dust to dust. It no longer dominates Browning or the Blackfeet Nation.

Two-Fingers smiled broadly while he watched the crowd slowly disperse. After finishing his coffee, he put down his empty cup, looked me squarely in the eyes, and answered my question: "Let's not be too hasty."

Over the years, Two-Fingers and I talked about who was more evil, a person with no conscience or one with a guilty conscience. Two-Fingers always maintained that it was the person with no conscience who was the most evil. At least, he reasoned, the person with a guilty conscience knew they had done wrong. I was surprised that, on that day, in that cafe, Two-Fingers struggled to find his conscience.

The End

9 798902 351474